D0233085

THE PICTURE
SHE TOOK

Also by Fiona Shaw

Out of Me (*memoir*)

The Sweetest Thing

THE PICTURE
SHE TOOK

Fiona Shaw

Virago

VIRAGO

First published in Great Britain in June 2005 by Virago Press

Copyright © Fiona Shaw 2005

Lines by T.S. Eliot from 'Little Gidding' (Four Quartets) in the *Collected Poems 1909–1962* reproduced by kind permission of Faber and Faber Ltd.

A CIP catalogue record for this book
is available from the British Library.

ISBN 1 84408 000 5

Typeset in Centaur by M Rules
Printed and bound in Great Britain
by Clays Ltd, St Ives plc

Virago Press
An imprint of
Time Warner Book Group UK
Brettenham House
Lancaster Place
London WC2E 7EN

www.virago.co.uk

For Hugh

And the end of all our exploring
Will be to arrive where we started
And know the place for the first time

T. S. Eliot

MISTER ICARUS

CHAPTER ONE

The day being bright made a difference. Having paid the tuppenny entrance, virtue was rewarded if the sun also shone, and so the visitors doffed their hats in tribute and allowed themselves the leisure of sitting a moment on the benches between the columns.

The girl at the desk, her head ducked to her knitting, would look up as if surprised at each new person, then find her smile, tear a ticket off and make change.

'There's nothing too . . . ?' a lady might say, and the girl would shake her head, reassuring.

'No, nothing like that. I'd even bring my grandmother. And besides, you can sit down in between, if you want. The benches are quite comfortable.'

So they paid their 6d, 3d for ex-servicemen and children, and walked in, their step apprehensive despite the aspidistras.

It was the lunch hour and the room was quite full. Although the ceiling was high and the windows open, the air was warm and people were caught at the door for a moment by the smell. It was nothing more than the fading perfumes and colognes and the half-day's sweat of so many bodies, but it checked them until they found that the girl was right; there was nothing to fear, and their noses became accustomed.

'Our Brave Men who Battle On', the poster said outside.

The first photographs showed soldiers just out of battle. Torn and dirty uniforms, bloody bandages. Some were on stretchers, some on the ground, others in ambulances and lorries and tents.

Their eyes were wide and dull with injury, their bodies looked heavy. The visitors stood before the blood and mayhem, and quickly understood the crueller tones of blacks and greys. If they could, searched out the smaller details: the laces on a boot undone, the stretcher handles which reminded them of the rake left in the garden, that the man wore a wedding ring.

The next set were easier, everyone ordered once again. Lines of white beds, nurses in white uniforms, smiles, everything tidy and covered over. Even in the makeshift places, which looked little more than a cellar or a rough tent, the blanket corners were neat and the men held out cigarettes or mugs of tea.

The visitors stepped in closer, sometimes peering right up. It would be all right to recognise a face now. Women exchanged smiles and could wonder safely about the injuries beneath. Conversations started up, and they thought they felt again something of that spirit so remarked upon at the time.

The men stood more alone, and they didn't dawdle or catch each other's eye. They moved round the little knots of women with abrupt, careless steps, affecting not to notice the images pinned to the wall, and they glimpsed up through the windows at the blue sky, tugging at their collars as if more air were needed.

In the last photographs, young men seated on chairs outdoors in smart, double-breasted suits, arms across one another's shoulders, faced the camera with serious, intent expressions. They were like members of a sporting team, a proud nurse to one side instead of a coach. And where their legs should have been there was only air, their tucked trousers the trophy of their sport. A young man held a life mask up close to where his face used to be, his hair slicked back and shiny, his eye socket puckered tight. And men with pinned sleeves were painting signs, one foot crossed beneath them, the other extended, toes pointed like a dancer's, the paintbrush just visible between. A poster on the wall behind read 'Men Made Here', and showed men with calliper hands sat at a table of metal parts.

'What they can do now,' a young woman whispered.

'Marvellous,' her companion said.

It seemed to be understood among the visitors that one must behave dispassionately; that it was all to the good, what one was seeing, the men leading useful lives. The lunch hour pressed on and the air remained warm. Sandwiches could be eaten in the park, if one was quick, and anyway it wasn't the thing, to linger.

The exhibition was still busy when the young man with the limp bought his ticket from the girl at the desk. She didn't need to say that a limp wasn't unusual in here, and besides, beggars couldn't be choosers.

'I could come round to a bit of arm or leg gone,' she told her friend on her lunch break. 'It's funny what you get used to.'

He was a nice height, not too thin like lots were. Plenty of hair, ordinary colour, somewhere between brown and fair. And well-dressed. Bespoke suit, not a thirty shilling number. He didn't smile.

'They often look fierce,' she'd added to her friend. 'It's these pictures. Takes them back.'

The girl sold the man his ticket with a smile, 3d rate like she'd guessed, and watched him go in.

Daniel Brown hadn't meant to come here. He'd thought he could get back to the office, but it was too far.

'Bloody vanity,' he said to himself. 'Bloody fool.'

He sat down on a bench and stretched his right leg out before him. He didn't know why it should be so sore today, but the pain cut up through his body, hard into his skull. He closed his eyes and waited for the pulse to ease. He sat with his fists on his thighs, thumbs tucked in, back straight, his eyes closed. Once the pain relented, he'd leave. But for now, he must just sit still.

He knew people would be looking. There were plenty like him and worse around, and most people didn't give you the time of day any more. But there'd be the women his mother's age who'd want to ask him was he all right, bending and putting their faces to one side, which only made him want to shout at them. And the girls who'd think he was a hero, always standing off a way and looking him up and down to see whether he was all there. And the men with tired eyes who didn't want reminding.

The colours behind his eyes were sharp, jagged. Lines of orange and black firing off, figures running off and beyond his sight. And when finally the colours had died down and he opened his eyes, the room had emptied and he was almost on his own.

'Going to be late back?' the girl said.

She must have been watching him. He picked up his hat, then got to his feet. He walked up close to the frames of wounded men. This one wasn't his war. He'd never been in a trench, never got shelled. He didn't want to look at them, but he was damned if he'd hurry in front of the girl. He walked slowly, listening to his awkward step on the marble floor, letting the images brush over the top of his mind. He set his thoughts on the afternoon, the tasks that waited back in the office. She was still watching him. Why didn't she pick up her knitting again? He went on looking, more closely than he wanted, but only half-seeing the pictures before him.

What a joke, he thought, him ending up looking at these.

'What a joke,' he said out loud, and with a final glance at the men, all bloody with arms round one another's shoulders, he left.

The wounded men. They didn't know how lucky they were, bloody innocents. It was enough for him to go about his life now. The pavement felt very hard as he walked towards the office. He measured his steps. It used to be a stride and a half to cover these city slabs, but now it took him over two, first his left foot and then his right, catching the bears between the cracks, which he had never done as a child. Head down, he watched his feet, his shoulders hunched with the habit of it.

Daniel had been at his desk no more than a few minutes before his father walked in. Mr Brown was taller than his son. His suit was impeccable and his shoes never grew dusty. His natural movements were precise, clipped, and he crossed the office floor in less than two strides. He set some papers down on Daniel's blotter.

'Your signature's as good as mine,' he said.

Daniel uncapped his pen.

'Good lunch?'

Daniel nodded. 'Lamb chop.'

The tickety-tick from the secretaries' desks in the room next door ebbed and flowed. Right now they were quiet and Daniel could hear his father's breathing.

'And you've just got back in?'

'I stopped in the park. Forgot the time, watching the boys and boats.'

'Home as usual?'

'I expect so.'

'Good,' his father said. 'I'll see you downstairs at five-thirty-five.'

He left the room, shutting the door with such care you might have thought he was visiting an invalid in hospital. Daniel got up and stood at the window. The sash was open at the top and he could tell, from the spill of cool air down the glass, that there was quite a strong breeze. Two pigeons were necking on his window sill, Renaissance ruffs of feathers round their necks, their toes shuffling in the dirt. City pigeons, running the gauntlet of motor cars and trolley buses, they were used to his body behind the glass and didn't pause or fly when he appeared, just carried on with their wistful song. He stared out beyond them at the walls and windows opposite. You couldn't see anybody from here. No people. Only stone and brick and these resolute birds.

Doesn't stop the pigeons, a duff leg, he thought. He should be getting down to his work, reports to write, invoices to send, but something was nagging at him and he stood on at the window, hoping it would surface where he could see it.

Daniel took the lift down to meet his father. His leg was easier after the hours at his desk, and he opened the lift door with force, relishing that snap of metal closing on metal. His mother had always been sure he would trap his hand in one of these doors when he was a child, concertina'd between the bands of steel. He still didn't like to touch the criss-cross of metal, but in defiance of his mother, he traced his finger along the shiny, polished tracery of leaves that decorated the doorway.

He thought he had the lift to himself, but several girls from the secretarial division arrived as he was about to press the button for the ground floor.

'If you don't mind, sir,' one of them said.

He inclined his head and made a show with the folding metal door, opening it gently this time so there was barely a click. Waiting for them to chivvy in with all their clutter, then sliding it shut again. They smiled and chirruped thanks to him, but he kept his face stern. They saw his limp. Even before they saw him as the boss's son, they saw his limp, he knew they did.

Four storeys down they stood closed-in together, and as the lift descended Daniel watched the metal leaves and vines rise up from below, the top of each leaf curve soft with thick, white dust.

'Your leg is worse tonight,' Mr Brown said as they walked across the river.

With the warming weather, Daniel could smell the water. Something ached at the base of his skull, like the beginning of a headache, like the weight of something forgotten and nearly remembered.

'It's worse,' Mr Brown said again.

The water shone in the late sun. It shone and it smelt.

'Just tired,' Daniel replied.

He'd been proud the day his legs were long enough for him to match his father's pace. For years he'd marked his stride when they were out walking the dog along the river or in the park, his two quick steps to his father's one, the skip he'd put in to come up level again. His father's irritation if Daniel, his attention straying, fell too far behind. And then one day he didn't need to try and he wondered that he'd ever had to.

Mr Brown checked his watch.

'We'll catch the slow train,' he said, his irritation hobbled.

The carriage was warm and Daniel reached up for the window cord. Mr Brown opened the evening paper. The train moved slowly out of the station into the evening light and Daniel fought with his reflection to see out, the sun lighting the streaks of soot into patterns on the glass, raddling the air. Out through the sidings, black bricks and grubby weeds. Buddleia bloomed, purples, whites. He remembered Johnnie telling him it would grow anywhere, on a coal tip even. Butterflies, tortoiseshells, orange tips, fritillaries, went about their business in the flowers. He watched their wing flicker, their jerky elegance. Two painted ladies, flirting in the air, kept pace with the train a few seconds, then dropped away.

Daniel turned back into the carriage. His father wore his newspaper like a shield. Another man slept and a woman read a book in the corner. He shook his head. Still watching butterflies, fiddling, and Rome already burnt.

The sidings widened and the train made its slow way out and through the city. Sounds came in like memories of themselves: a blackbird's song, motor cars, a horse's bray, another train's whistle. There were high tenements outside, washing hung like bunting, open windows making holes to their insides. In the winter the darkness let you in for a glimpse, a peep show. And tonight, when the summer light kept him at bay, people still held things out of the windows for him to see. A boy with a puppy; a woman stretched forward, her mouth wide in a yell; an arm flung out several floors up, the fingers fisted round a cigarette.

Then there was a high street crossed over, motor cars, carts, advertising hoardings, beaming faces eating mustard, drinking ginger wine, the bric-a-brac of small shops, two cats on a wall, a boy running round a corner, an old woman with a basket on wheels, stumbling at the kerb. A smell too, something frying. He leaned back in his seat. There it was again, the pressure at the back of his skull, as if someone were pressing their fingers in. The smell reminded him of the breakfasts they'd had in Ireland. They were different from England, the bacon tasted different, and the tea. There was something in the day he needed to remember, if it would only rise higher. He took out his novel, refuge for a short while.

There were boys at cricket on the green, over at the far side near the theatre, where the grass was longer and they wouldn't be yelled at. Walking down Duke Street, Daniel could already hear them, the nippy shouts, the keen dull sound of a bat striking a ball. And he saw Mr Brown forget him and lengthen his stride, eager to round the corner and see the lads at play. Daniel stopped and leaned against the railings outside the Baptist chapel. It was Johnnie who'd played. He'd been good.

A man was rolling barrels onto a wagon. His horse, a heavy, white dray with dirty fetlocks, had his head in a bag of feed. Each time, at the top of the ramp there was a moment of suspense, the man's strength, arms crooked to take the barrel's weight, the lines of muscle picked clear, braced against the curved wood, each perfectly weighted as if they could hang there together for good, before the man gained the edge and tumbled it in. Daniel watched with narrowed eyes, the man's grace, his economy of gesture, as if he could gather in the secret, recover it for himself again.

Daniel could still have sat on a cart and pulled on the reins. It wasn't *that* that he envied. It was the man's ease, his physical competency, known and unquestioned. Daniel had been a better horseman than his brother, a better horseman than most people. It had been as natural to him as breathing and now all that was gone.

The light was flattening, as if the end of the day sucked out perspective. The cricket game had slowed. The boys couldn't trust their eyes quite any more, the ball lost in the air until it was upon them. Mr Brown still watched, a hand raised as if shielding his sight though the sun had long dropped away. Lights had gone on in houses, but too much of the day remained as yet, and they kept themselves to themselves, threw out no glowing pools.

Those people still returning home felt excluded, left outside things, and hurried now. Even the men standing outside the pub drank their pints down quickly and excused themselves, or slouched back inside to find some light and human jostle again.

Mr Brown checked his watch. 'She'll be worrying,' he said.

'It was only a bit of cricket,' Daniel said. 'She won't mind a few minutes.'

They walked down Old Palace Lane and on to the towpath. Fishermen were setting up, the glow of their cigarettes, the dull glint of a thermos, their lines tipping the water, invisible in the dusk. A mallard trailed her brood towards the bank. Daniel counted more than half a dozen ducklings, a long, straggly line.

The last duckling had become distracted by some river plant, tugging at it with its beak.

'They've no eye for detail,' he said.

'What?'

'Look. The mother hasn't noticed. She's just paddling on.'

'Come on, Daniel,' Mr Brown said.

'Win some, lose some.'

Daniel squatted down to see the duckling better, his trouser cuffs lost in the river weeds. The mother was almost out of sight, her flotilla zig-zagging behind her.

'We used to watch for hours when we were boys,' he said. 'Coots and moorhens are careful, they count them up. One's missing, they send out a scouting party. But not the mallards.'

'Your mother will be waiting at the window,' Mr Brown said.

'We saw a rat take a duckling once.'

'She can't see us from the window this time of year, but she'll still be standing there,' Mr Brown said.

'We'd been crouched for ages, watching something, but I can't remember what. I do remember that Johnnie had a nettle stroking his leg and didn't dare move, and you could still see the white bumps the next day. And we saw a rat, sleek, pretty, slip into the water, just its head visible. It swam without a ripple straight to a stray duckling – the mother mallard was way ahead – and carried it gently by the neck back to the shore.'

'I'll wave from the bridge, anyhow,' Mr Brown said.

It was the time beyond their return that Daniel dreaded. Once the bustling was done – the shedding of coats and baggage, the washing of faces and hands, the enquiries over the journey, his leg, the office, the traffic, the pouring of sherry – then his mother would take off her apron and allow his father to sit her down before the fire with her drink. Daniel knew she couldn't help the look on her face. It was as if she hoped, despite herself, that he would somehow be more than he was.

When he was younger, he told jokes for her. To distract her, especially when she was fed up, or there was an argument.

'Come here my little fellow,' she'd say, before he was even finished, and he'd let her put her arms around him, or place her hands, flat, on either side of his head and she'd stare at him so that he'd be too abashed to finish.

It was a private game of theirs, hers and Daniel's, a conspiracy. But when Johnnie was killed, their game was over.

'We stopped to look at the cricket,' Mr Brown said.

Mrs Brown nodded. She'd been watching the road for them and now she held the front door to her like a lover, as they walked up the path. Mr Brown took her hand and kissed her on the cheek.

'The green was nice with the sun going down,' he said. 'People outside in shirtsleeves, you know. Pigeons.'

Mrs Brown laughed, an abrupt, uncertain laugh, new to Daniel since his return.

'You needn't have worried,' Mr Brown said and she shook her head and looked at Daniel coyly, and at the ground.

'Just you dawdling,' and she tapped the back of her hand as if in rebuke. 'I know.'

'Sherry,' he said, leading her back indoors.

'Dinner will be ready soon,' she said.

Daniel followed his parents into the house and went to wash his hands in the cloakroom. He could hear his mother asking after him, her voice lowered so he couldn't hear.

'He's very pale,' she said. 'Is it hurting?'

'It's the end of the day. We're all tired.'

'Is that why you stopped on the green? So he could rest?'

The house was muggy with old air and the smell of cooking. Daniel dipped his face into the basin, held it there. The cold water made the skin on his neck tighten. He'd have liked to sink his ears into the water, but the basin was too shallow. He loved it, in the sea, to lie back and float, let the water fill his ears so that all he could hear was the shift and crunch of the pebbles at the edge of the tide as they were lifted and turned. He'd float until his head ached with the cold.

'Is it hurting?' Mrs Brown asked him as they sat down to dinner.

12

Daniel shook his head. 'It's all right.'

And she nodded, and gestured to the maid to bring in the soup.

Mr Brown began to talk about his day, meetings, sales figures, northern contractors. Daniel ate his soup and watched his mother. She appeared to be listening, but she wasn't really there. They both knew it, he and his father.

Although it looked out onto the garden, the room was airless, the windows closed tight. Too late to see any birds now, but there were bats through the glass, little more than dancing shades in the twilight. Usually he didn't ask, just waited till the meal was over and then slipped outside. But tonight something was pressing on his mind and his patience, even with his mother, was wearing thin.

'Could I open a window?'

Without waiting for an answer, he pushed back his chair and got to his feet.

Mrs Brown put down her soup spoon.

'It might let in a draught,' she said.

Daniel pushed the sash upwards. The garden air was like balm, cool now, and fresh. Leaning out, he breathed deep, the stale behind and the sweet before him, and reeled, putting a hand out for balance.

'Daniel?' His mother's voice was pitched high, and he turned back to the table to reassure her.

'Needed some air,' he said.

He couldn't bear his mother's face, her soup spoon gripped like a talisman.

'Don't, Mother,' he said. 'I just wanted some air.'

'Charlotte,' Mr Brown said, his voice stern.

They had slipped into old roles, Daniel and his parents, since his return, as if to make for themselves a cocoon against the recent years. The very things that should have changed his birthright – his brother's death, his own heroic wounding – had left them now in thrall within an earlier kingdom. And just as his mother couldn't help herself but feed him milksop and warm his bed with a hot jar at night, so Daniel found a certain old childish incontinence returned. He knew, because his mother had told him, that when

13

she looked at him, she saw Johnnie, and now he spoke quickly, the first thought, to distract her.

'I went to an exhibition at lunchtime,' he said.

He hadn't meant to speak of this, and immediately he regretted it.

'You didn't tell me that,' Mr Brown said. 'You just said something about boys and boats.'

'I only went in because I needed to sit down,' Daniel said. 'The walk back from the pond was harder than I'd expected.'

He took a mouthful of soup. It was tepid, coating the back of the spoon like some viscous medicine. He was tired. The shake began in his hand and he set down the spoon quickly.

'You've been biting your nails again,' Mrs Brown said.

Daniel looked across at her. 'The soup's good.'

'So what was it about? The exhibition?' Mr Brown said.

'Just some photographs.' He shouldn't have let it slip. 'Anyway, tell Mother what you were telling me. About the bearings, and northern sales.'

'But we'd like to hear about the exhibition that left you so late back to work, wouldn't we?' Mr Brown said, turning to his wife, who was still looking at her son as if his face held something she had lost. So, feeling caught out by himself just as he used to as a child, Daniel was forced to tell them. He said as little as he could, but it was enough for Mrs Brown.

'Injured soldiers?' she said.

'Yes.'

'On the front line?'

'Some, yes.'

'Did you look closely?'

'Mother, please,' Daniel said.

'Did you?' she said again, her voice fierce.

'He wasn't there. Just strangers.'

'Tell me about them then, the strangers,' she said, and she carried on eating her soup, her knuckles still white around the spoon.

'I didn't mean to go, and I wasn't going to tell you,' Daniel said.

Mrs Brown continued with her soup. It wasn't her fault, he

knew that, but her grief was like a diviner's rod. It drew a fury from him, dragged his rage up through his body till it seeped out of his skin.

'All right,' Daniel said. 'One of the soldiers, you can see the bone coming out through his thigh. His head is slumped down and two others are dragging him through the mud. There's a dead horse behind him. Another picture, a lad is on a stretcher, bloody bandage round his head. They've put a blanket over him, but he still looks so cold, pinched. And another, it's a soldier sitting on the ground, one leg out before him, boot off. His mouth is wide open and you can see he's got a tooth missing at the side. He's being given a drink, tea, in a mug, and they're doing something with bandages to the foot. But it's his face – that blank look they get.'

Daniel would have gone on, he was finding his stride now, his recollection of the photographs collapsing in with other memories. Mrs Brown sat perfectly still, her hands on her lap, her face bleached in the growing dark and pared down to elements: cheekbones, nose, chin, brow.

But Mr Brown pushed back his chair and spoke to his wife now, and his voice was so gentle, the thought crossed Daniel's mind that this must be how he'd made love to her when they'd first met, with these soft tones.

'I think we've heard enough, Charlotte, don't you.' He took her hands and drew her to her feet. Then he turned to Daniel. 'For God's sake.'

Daniel watched his father lead his mother from the room and the maid come in and clear the soup bowls. He nodded his head when she asked, would she put the meat and vegetables in the warming oven. And he sat on at the table.

Except for the windows to the garden, he'd never liked this room. They ate their meals in here every day, and yet it still felt unlived in, with its heavy furniture, its smell of polish, the dark-leafed plants in the cold grate. When they were little, it was the place Johnnie went, playing hide and seek, if he didn't want to be found, because Daniel wouldn't go in there.

15

'Cowardy custard,' Daniel sang under his breath. 'Cowardy custard.'

Johnnie had set the rules in their games. He was older, and it went without saying. But Daniel nearly always won them. Hide and seek or grandmother's footsteps. He was shrewder about how not to be noticed, more furtive. Daniel had demanded that the dining room be off limits, threatened not to play otherwise, so it was only when Johnnie broke the rules that he won.

Johnnie had broken the rules to enlist, upping his age by a year. The last photograph they had of him was from the day he went to war. He stood on the doorstep, his haversack beside him. Daniel had watched his brother in the bathroom with his new shaving tackle, teased him over his smooth chin. And in the photograph he could see the chafing on his brother's skin, darker patches in the black and white.

Of course he'd looked for his brother in the exhibition photographs. You always did that, couldn't help it. But it wasn't to do with Johnnie, whatever it was that hung, like a tiny lead weight, at the back of his mind. It was to do with somebody else. And the lead weight had been there for years. It was just that he'd forgotten it for a while till today.

The girl was there with the same bit of knitting. She greeted him like a friend, wouldn't take his threepenny payment.

'Forget something?' she said.

'Something like that,' he said.

'Well, we're all still here,' she said.

'Yes. Thank you,' and he turned to go in.

'Nobody's got any worse since yesterday,' she said with a little laugh. 'No new casualties.'

As soon as he saw the photograph, the lead weight dropped, a plumb line into his past. It had been taken in what looked like a cellar – a low-ceilinged room with a small stove and some rough shelves visible on rusty gallows brackets holding boxes and bottles. One of the boxes said OXO. Trestles supported a stretcher and on the stretcher lay a wounded man, an officer. Beside him stood another officer who was feeding the wounded man a cigarette. Daniel could see that his tunic was torn and his boots were thick with mud. A nurse dressed in breeches, boots and a man's overcoat stood to one side. They were all smiling for the camera.

'Colonel Whittam,' Daniel said.

Colonel Whittam was dead now. He'd walked away from the path near the White Lodge in Richmond Park three years ago and been found face down in the bracken two days later by a woman walking her dog. When Daniel first read about it, it was the two days that he wondered about. He imagined a spider starting its web across the colonel's ear lobe, stretching its silk between the cold velvet skin and a blade of grass. He wondered whether the deer had been frightened shy by the smell of the body, and whether the crows had been lured down to peck.

Daniel had admired Colonel Whittam. He respected him and knew that he'd done his best by his men and that the ambush hadn't been his fault. He'd been wounded himself, hadn't he? A shoulder wound, Daniel remembered. But he hadn't been surprised to hear the news. The obituary had said that he'd served with distinction at the Western Front during the Great War and in Ireland, that he'd had a fatal accident while out shooting rabbits and that he would be sadly mourned by his wife, family and regiment. But Daniel knew differently. He knew Whittam had never recovered, never forgiven himself, though there was nothing he could have done. He'd heard that Whittam's wife had stopped him once before when she'd found him with a pistol, so this time Whittam had made sure he was safely alone.

Daniel stood in front of the photograph for a long time. It showed the other officer, smiling, holding a cigarette delicately between thumb and forefinger for the wounded man to smoke. They were clearly friends. It was something about the way the officer's other hand rested behind Whittam's head, as if he were cradling or shielding it. Daniel had brought his notebook with him this time, and flicking over the bird drawings, he found a blank page and sketched out what he could. He did it quickly, only taking his time over the faces. Then he stood looking again. The other man had the kind of face you might think you knew, but that would be too much of a coincidence. He looked a little while longer, until the ticket girl gave a little cough.

'You all right? Only there's a couple of ladies would like to look at that picture,' she said. 'Really I think they're curious to see what you've been stood staring at for so long.'

'Fine, thank you,' he said.

'Daydreaming,' the girl said with the wisdom of weeks in this job. 'You're not the first. Lots do it, get lost like that. Though maybe dreaming's not the right word, because I don't suppose it was very nice, was it?'

'Thought I recognised somebody,' Daniel said, and then regretted it when her face opened with curiosity. 'Thank you, anyway,' and he left.

It was over two years since he'd left the hospital. When he arrived, the nurses were glad of him with so many other men going. The early weeks he was too ill to notice much. It was his leg that was hurt, as he observed in those first, lucid hours after it happened. But once he stopped pretending that he could keep himself separate from the pain, then it occupied the whole of him. He lay in a bed, his body braced, and when it rode him, he bared his teeth and clenched his fists, bit his lips, his cheeks to bleeding not to let it out beyond. He knew that if he gave it voice, it would take over everything, and then nothing – not the bed or the nurses, or the window above him or the strip of sky, which seemed to have a colour for each day of the week, or the tree he could sometimes see, upside down, its roots blossoming – nothing would be outside it. Sometimes, despite his efforts, it escaped him and then he roared and moaned, the sweat breaking out on his forehead.

The nurses gave him little rubber balls to squeeze, a gag to bite on. They gave him tea in a cup with a lid and a spout, coloured blue for a boy. They washed him and changed his bed and by the time he was getting better, he'd have married any of them.

'You wouldn't, would you though,' he said to one nurse. 'Marry a man who wasn't whole, a broken doll,' and he sang the last phrase, like the song.

18

'Course I would if they were my chap,' she said. 'But I've already got mine and so it won't be you, sweet young Mr Brown.' But she didn't take her arm away and he continued stroking it. 'Anyway, haven't you got a girl?' she asked.

'No,' Daniel said. 'Just as well, probably,' and she rolled her eyes at this.

'I've seen plenty a lot worse off than you,' she said. 'And their girl by their side, often as not.'

But Daniel hadn't meant it for self-pity. More that since Johnnie's death something had drawn itself in inside him. Something that was turned away from people, rolled up on itself. Like a woodlouse. Curled up, every soft part tucked away.

'I did, before the army,' he said, 'have a girlfriend, but it didn't work out. She's married, got a baby now, my mother said.'

'You'll find yourself another, when you're out of here,' she said, 'handsome chap like you.' Daniel didn't reply. He couldn't bear much curiosity, even from himself.

Something was still bothering Daniel about the photograph. He'd find himself standing stock-still, in his bedroom or the kitchen, even on the street, as if stopping all movement might clarify something. Once they went camping on Dartmoor, he and Johnnie, and when he dipped his mug into a stream, it filled with icy brown water that smelt of the rocks and the peaty ground. He watched the water swirl, then grow still and clear itself, so that after a couple of minutes he could see down through it to the sediment covering the white tin. Now he felt that something similar should happen to his mind, that if he stopped his bustle, something would clear and he'd be able to see straight down into the back of his own memory.

Mr Brown read things out of the newspaper. He read them slowly, steadily, and without any inflection so that to his listeners the price of eggs sounded as grave as news of the Bolshevik Revolution. There had been a time when this drove Daniel nearly to distraction, but by now he had learned to block out the sound. He heard the words but they didn't go in. His soldiering had helped, the noise of the mess hall. And now his father's steady drone was like a filter for Daniel's thoughts and his mind kicked free of the dining room and the breakfast things, of his mother's blank face and his father's voice.

Instead he could hear a different man's voice, his own at first, hard and angry. Then it was someone else's shouted over him, words and half-words dropping, making sense and no sense. And the smell of the cigarette. The cigarette. It looked like it was cut into his lip from below, then in his fingers and the ash dropping down to Daniel, on Daniel, the man not noticing because why would he?

Mr Brown liked to finish on something cheerful. Then he could leave for work feeling he had given his wife something uplifting to take into her day about the house. He began with the new Noël Coward play, then moved on to the Egyptian excavations.

Daniel could feel the pain in his leg and across his shoulders, could feel it rising to his lungs and up his throat into his mouth, and then, through the pain, the man's voice again and a gun being fired, sharp, efficient, and somehow Daniel kept the pain in, gave it no voice. Lay doggo. He didn't want to remember, but the memory wouldn't leave, and always there was something there that he couldn't name and that he didn't understand.

But that was who it was. That was the man he'd seen in the photograph. The man holding the cigarette for Daniel's wounded colonel.

When he'd stood before the girl for the third time, he saw anxiety cross the girl's face.

'It's only something I need to know,' he'd said. 'I'm not wanting to look.'

It took him a week to telephone the Crystal Palace number printed on the card she gave him. He'd been rolling the marble for ten minutes, from one side of the blotter to the other, to and fro across the inky map. It didn't roll smoothly, got caught on the roughened pink fibres.

'I'll dial the number the first time it runs straight,' he said.

But they are foolish pledges, those made against the spirit, because when the clear run came, he still couldn't nerve himself to it, and in the end he put the marble in his pocket, slapped himself on the cheek, held his breath and put his finger to the dial.

'Don't know that we have that information,' the voice said. 'Call again in half an hour.'

Daniel waited and ran his marble again. He watched the pigeons. They were beyond courtship now. He wondered how they balanced, heaped on top of one another on the window sill. Curtains of feathers rubbing up against the glass. The voice was more forthcoming when he called back.

'You'd be surprised, what we get asked,' it said, when Daniel explained once again what he was looking for. 'There's some think they can see a loved one in a picture. Not the real figures but, you know, their ghost in a corner or something. And others say we shouldn't be showing them at all because they're bad for morale when the country's got to be looking ahead. And you get them that can't speak at all, only cry. That's tricky, not wanting to hurt their feelings, but a job to do and so on.'

The voice was getting into its stride. The marble made another clear run and Daniel cleared his throat.

'Did you find a name for the one I mentioned?' he said, pitching his voice in at a pause.

'The two men with the cigarette, and the nurse?' the voice said. 'Yes.'

There was a long pause, so long that Daniel wondered if the telephone had gone funny. He noticed out of the window that the pigeons had finished. One was pecking at a piece of weed that had somehow found its way to this third floor window sill, while the other, as Daniel watched, flew out into the sky, its heavy body rising, soaring up. He was about to put down the receiver and dial up again when the voice returned.

'There's a letter of assurance here from a J. Hursten. It's definitely about that photograph, got the red tally number in the corner. Telling us we can go ahead and use it. We try to get them from all the private donors. Some of the photographs are official, but lots are taken by soldiers, nurses, what have you. They've sent them in to us.'

'Is there an address for him?' Daniel rolled the marble beneath his hand, its hard curve pressing into his palm.

Another pause, the sound of papers shuffled, and then the voice read it out, three lines, and Daniel pocketed the marble.

When his mother woke him, her fingers resting his arm, Daniel flailed out, catching her on the cheek with the back of his hand.

'Don't touch me! . . . Johnnie!', he yelled, or dreamed he had.

He was awake the second after and saw his mother's eyes wide, her hand to her cheek.

'Did I do that?' he said.

'You were dreaming. You said something, but I couldn't hear the words.'

'What time is it?'

'Your father is listening to the news. I have cocoa done.'

Daniel sat up, his body heavy with the dream. He nodded.

It was the dream he often had, never exactly the same, but near enough. He was standing at the end of a road, facing a hill. It wasn't raining, but the air was heavy, so dense that his shoulders were weighted down with it. Though he couldn't see what it was, he began striking down on something, a block of wood or a mound of earth, with an implement, perhaps a spade. As he struck, he could feel the impact through his arms and his shoulders. The spade became a rifle and he was striking a man while women and children watched him silently, and as Daniel beat down, the man stared up at him.

Then he was in a ditch which was also a truck somehow, and Johnnie was there (he was always there), and Will Savage and Cadet Charters, whose name Daniel had never even known before it was over, and George Spring. It was foggy, always foggy. Others too, but their faces slipped away from him as he woke. They were wounded, dying, and he wasn't, but he couldn't move, couldn't help them. He could see them all, their wounds, and the yellow gorse, the rocks behind. There were women holding the guns, two

22

older and a younger one with a small child at her skirts and a bigger, silent boy. They'd done the shooting. They stared at Daniel and as long as they looked at him, he couldn't move. One of the children was crouching near, arm reaching towards him, when his mother woke him.

Her fingers touching her face, Mrs Brown walked to the door.

'Did I hurt you?' he said.

She shook her head.

Downstairs, his father had lit the fire. It had rained hard in the day and now the air was sweet and cool and the sky clear to the stars.

'Fall asleep?' Mr Brown said.

Daniel nodded.

'Ought to get out more. Join a club. You'll never meet a girl, or anyone, always on your own. And we won't be here forever.'

Mrs Brown brought in a tray with three cups and saucers.

'Daniel had a nightmare,' she said.

'You could enquire at the library. We'll stop off on the way home. Debating society, philosophical society, something like that. They'll have information.'

'It might need more sugar,' Mrs Brown said, passing Daniel a cup and saucer.

'You used to like the tennis club, didn't you?' Mr Brown said. 'And the riding? All those friends you had? It wasn't only the sport.'

'I've forgotten the teaspoons,' Mrs Brown said.

Daniel hadn't told them about his telephone call. He had never properly talked about what it was like over there and they'd never properly asked him. He could imagine his mother. She wouldn't believe him. She'd want to take his part. And his father, shaking his head as if to keep out the sounds he didn't like. He'd say it was what happened in a war, though he'd never had to fight in one.

Opening the cutlery drawer, Daniel took out the teaspoons. He put one in his mouth and bit down. It was cold and hard against his teeth and a nerve sang through his jaw. He'd gone beyond the bounds and he didn't know how to think about it. He'd been

23

broken, but there was nobody to tell, and no way to get away from it. He took the teaspoons in to his mother.

When he had returned, before he said anything else, he'd told them they were not to ask what had happened, nor were they to tell anyone else anything they might learn. Most especially they were to say nothing to anyone in Ireland. It was a motor-lorry accident, and that was all. So they had never asked him. Instead they'd all busied themselves. Hidden like crabs in the sand, digging and shimmying, covering themselves over with the practical questions till after two years all that could be seen was hard shells.

How long would he be in hospital. Would he walk again. Who was the best doctor for his leg. For his shaking arm. Was swimming good. Was walking. Cycling. Which were the best crutches. Which the best stick. He'd need a steady hand in the family business. Of course, they knew he couldn't ride a horse. A good hand with a pen was important for business. A firm signature. What to do for the pain. And by the time it was safe to talk, and Daniel knew it was safe by now, it was too late. His parents didn't want to know.

Sometimes, passing other young men in the streets, he'd wonder whether they were all silent too, about what they'd seen, and done.

He waited till his parents were asleep before opening the front door. The moon was full, but still he had to take care, walking in the dark, the jolts and fissures in the paving stones seeming to rise and meet his feet. He lifted his stick from the umbrella stand at the last minute, and now, with so much else pressing, he was glad it could take some of the weight.

The river was up. You could smell it before you could see it. Even a few steps away, it looked still, unmoving, pools of shining dark under the gaslights. But leaning close over the railings, Daniel could see its force, its pull towards the sea. It was a spring tide and the water was very high. Daniel knelt and put his hand in, held it there till it was cold. When he lifted it to his face, it smelt of somewhere else. He went across the lock-bridge. No toll. This late at night you could cross the river for free.

He walked for a while towards Kew. Somewhere there were

lovers. Their voices hung over the water, ripples of laughter and soft noises fading as they reached his shore. The 'hooo, hooo' cry of a tawny owl ahead of him, and behind him the last train crossing the river towards St Margaret's.

Johnnie dared him once to cross the river on the railway bridge. Walk along the rails in the wake of a train. If another train came, you'd have to jump up on to the balustrade and dive into the river. They shook hands on it, 'a firm shake', Johnnie called it, which meant you had to go through with it. But when they pulled open the heavy cast-iron gate and crossed the grass, climbed over the wall and squatted just out of sight, waiting, fingers clutching tussocks of weed while a train went past them, then stood at the top, the rails still purring, and looked along the line of the track, the sleepers stretched out, away, like an endless ladder, then he didn't mean to, but his head went faint. And if Johnnie hadn't held on to him, he'd have run away through the thistles and nettles and dirty yellow flowers.

He held him just long enough for Daniel to find his feet again, and then Johnnie climbed onto the track and did it for him, his legs steady in a jerky half-run over the sleepers.

Daniel wondered whether Johnnie would have done the things he had over there. He wondered whether some of those things hadn't also happened in the trenches, though the men came back from that war as heroes.

Daniel walked as hard as he could on into the night, daring his leg to fail him, daring himself to go further. The tow-path was soft and quiet under his feet after the rain. Across the water, the herons hunched high on their island were silent. The night gathered and thickened around him. He had the piece of paper in his pocket with the address written on it and, as he walked, he knew that somehow he must set off along the sleepers and go there.

The sky was grey as the train left London and Daniel looked out through a window slashed by rain. As the train gathered speed, the drops were driven faster across the glass, chivvying each other. His father was surprisingly amenable when he asked for the holiday.

'I might be back in a day or two, might be longer,' Daniel said.

'Take as long as you want,' Mr Brown said. 'It's slack right now and the break would be good for you. Just check out the contractor for me while you're there.'

'I'm not ill.'

'No, but it's hard work, the business, and what with your leg.'

'And my leg is fine. It's just . . .' Daniel stopped himself. 'My injury,' he said. 'The day I was injured . . .'

'You offered yourself up,' Mr Brown said. 'Nobody could ask more.'

Daniel shivered. His father had no idea. Daniel didn't even know who was hurting whom. 'But what happened that day, what I told you wasn't . . .'

Again Mr Brown interrupted.

'Just don't go over it with your mother. More than she could take.'

So Daniel didn't try to say any more. And there was no point in being angry.

'Only thing might be,' Mr Brown said, 'to give her a call every now and then.'

'I was going to write.'

'Better for her to hear your voice,' his father said.

'Since I don't know that I'll find a telephone easily.'

'She doesn't trust letters much these days,' Mr Brown said.

'Of course,' Daniel said, and he bit his lip hard at his stupidity.

He heard the post arrive that day and went to the front door for it, shuffled together the letters, not looking at them, and returned to the sitting room. He handed letters and paper knife to his mother and she began to slit the envelopes. It was a habit of hers, to open all the letters in the pile before she began to look at any. She did it by feel, finding the envelope's top edge with her fingers and easing the tip of the knife under, then a swift pull to cut the paper. Usually she was talking as she did it, to Daniel or his father, or to the maid. Or she was reading, one of her library novels. Today, however, she wasn't talking. And though her eyes were open, she had the appearance of someone who is looking at another place entirely. Mr Brown was at the desk on the far side of the room with various pieces of official correspondence before him. His pen was uncapped and he had clean notepaper ready to use, but for the last half-hour he'd been reading the same piece of paper, his fingers tugging at his shirt cuffs, his right shoulder hitching every now and then with the slight tick that surfaced when he didn't know what to say. Except for the small crackles and shuffles of the coal in the fire, there were no sounds in the room. The clock was not wound, and it felt as if everything was suspended, like a breath drawn in that you daren't let out, lungs tight to bursting. And although it had only been two days, Daniel couldn't imagine how they would ever breathe again.

It was the third or fourth letter in the pile and Mrs Brown was putting the knife to it, her gaze still elsewhere. Daniel was watching her and as she let the letter drop onto the pile, it caught his eye. Mrs Brown reached for another, and Daniel picked up the dropped letter. He held it flat on his palm. It weighed so little. He knew his brother's writing as well as his own. Despite the masters' fierce efforts at school, Johnnie still wrote with his left hand and his writing was as unkempt and changeable from day to day as Daniel's was regular and precise. Although he didn't want to, although it was the last thing he wanted to do, Daniel could see Johnnie now, his arm caught tight in against his ribs and the paper turned sideways in the effort to avoid smudging. He imagined him seated, hunched, on a crate perhaps with the product stencilled on the side, 'Capstan' or 'Cadburys', his hands over his ears to concentrate, to block out the booming, battering noise he wrote was so hateful, so oppressive. He saw him pick up his pen and dip the nib, the ink bottle pushed into the mud at his feet, stroke the nib against the side. Then the quick rush of words, dipping the nib impatiently now, blotting the smudges with his handkerchief. Daniel could see Johnnie's bayonet leaned up against the side of the dugout, could see him tap a cigarette from his case, hitch it into the side of his mouth, just as Daniel would learn to do, cup his hand around the match and suck in the flame as if his life depended on it. Then pick up his pen again and write the address in capitals.

Daniel chuckled at that thought. He would bet that Johnnie had laughed as he wrote it. It was an old joke between them, that even Johnnie's capitals were illegible.

'Daniel?'

His mother's voice startled him and he was there once more, in that room that could never be warm again, his father standing at the desk, his mother with a pile of letters she couldn't bear to read.

'What are you laughing at?'

He held out the hand with the letter.

'It's from Johnnie,' he said. 'Isn't that funny? He's dead for two days and here he is, alive again.'

It was afternoon by the time Daniel arrived at his destination. He'd enjoyed the journey. It had been a suspension, like time out of place. He hadn't read the newspaper nor either of the books he'd brought. He'd barely even looked out of the window, as if just for now he would take nothing in, and he seemed to have passed much of the journey in a trance.

The air was colder up here, and fresh. The train had shrugged off the rain long before and now the sky was streaked with high cirrus cloud and the sun made long, late-afternoon shadows of the passengers on the platform. The station-master suggested a good inn and, once he'd seen Daniel's limp, drummed up a man with an Austin 7 to take him there.

'You're too late to see the best,' the Austin 7 man said. 'From the south?'

Daniel nodded.

'We start earlier up here,' the man said. 'Always have had the jump on you, doesn't matter if it's royalty or sheep.'

Daniel wondered whether the man was joking, or looking for a rise, but there was no change of expression, no sly look.

'What did I miss?' Daniel said.

'Best livestock this country can find.'

'I don't know very much about animals,' Daniel answered.

'Though I did use to ride before . . .' He gestured towards his leg. 'Except for birds. I know about birds.'

'So, what are you doing in town on market day, then?' the man said, but went on with a nod before Daniel had to find an answer.

'The Green Man,' he said. 'Rooms are reasonable and they'll do you a good tea, but you'll want to be careful of the smell,' lifting a finger to the side of his nose. 'They bring the cattle to the pens down the ginnel one side of the inn and the dung won't be cleared till the morning.'

The room smelt of beer and pipe tobacco and it looked out over the banked cobbles of the town square. Knots of men still stood about, cap brims touching, talking, Daniel supposed, about the price of sheep. Beyond, he could see the first rise of the moors, mauve and orange in the late sun, and the last swifts playing havoc in the sky.

A red and white quilt covered the bed and rag rugs were spread over the boarded floor. It was like somewhere else he knew, somewhere good. Daniel lay back on the bed, shoes kicked off, arms and legs spreadeagled, and listened to the bar below, people's voices rising muffled through the rugs. The man had been right about the tea. He'd eaten a vast plate of beef and potatoes, peppery swede, rhubarb and apple pie. Running his fingers across the quilt, he could feel the seams between the colours, and how, in alternate strips, one colour was more worn than the other, the fabric rubbed to strands in places. He remembered. It was Coolderry. The rug and the quilts reminded him of Coolderry.

He thought he'd walk downstairs and sit elbows out and friendly at a table and strike up easy conversation, buy a round, admire the local beer. Make believe he was the person he used to be and maybe it would happen. But his limbs were heavy and the bed was soft, and before he could prevent himself, he was wrapped like a caterpillar in a cocoon of quilt and asleep, rocked deep in anonymous ease.

The house was near the square, past the game butchers with its proud flock of dead ducks hanging line upon line outside, left at the auction house and up the hill, beyond the livestock pens, where

29

men were still busy with brushes and water, making the road run brown, and past a terrace of polished front steps. Daniel had scrubbed the night's lethargy from himself and he felt sure and sharp.

As he walked, he rehearsed what he would say. How he would explain that he'd travelled over two hundred miles to ask a question about two men in a photograph taken during a war that ended eight years ago. He had his sketchbook in one hand, ready to show.

'Keep as close to the truth as you can,' he told himself. 'Much easier that way.'

He was nervous, dry-mouthed, when he reached the house and he hesitated before walking up the path and pulling the bell.

He noticed the size of the house, its rough golden stone, the rise of windows high up to the dormers in the roof; the child's pram and the tricycle, abandoned on the front lawn; the flower beds full of stocks and lavender; the drive down one side and, just visible, a motorbike and sidecar. And later he would recall all this and think upon it. But right now the only thought he had in his mind was to ask his question.

He pressed the brass button and bells rang in different places. A dog barked. A moment's silence, voices far off, then footsteps. A maid opened the door, frowning, brushing off her skirts. Daniel could see a wide hall behind with chequerboard tiles, a table with a jug of flowers, and what looked like a train set half set out on the floor.

'I'd like to speak to Mr Hursten.'

'Mr Hursten is out at the moment.'

'I'll leave my card and call back later then,' Daniel said. 'Daniel Brown, if you could say that I called. What time is he likely to return?'

Sucking the air in through her teeth, the maid considered. 'Won't be till late in the day, I wouldn't think,' she said. 'And tomorrow being Sunday . . .' She began to push the door to.

Daniel wasn't sure why he shouldn't call on a Sunday, whether there might be some impropriety. It wasn't, after all, a business call, but perhaps Mr Hursten had religious convictions that made it difficult. He turned and walked back down the path.

'Janey, who is it?'

Daniel heard the voice before he saw its owner.

'It's just a man,' the maid said.

'Just a man for what?'

'Wants to speak to Mr Hursten.'

'Perhaps I will do instead,' and the door was pushed wide open again by a young woman with white hands raised before her, as if in surrender.

CHAPTER TWO

It started deliberately, Jude's finger framing. She'd set her fingers around what she saw: her bicycle, the dog, a man selling chestnuts, a woman with a pushcart. She'd make a rectangle, then draw them in closer, see how it altered things. When something caught her attention, she'd try to make a memory of it and she'd tell herself that when she had a camera, she'd take a picture of it.

Leo teased her at first, and her parents told her it looked peculiar, this girl too often with her hands before her face. But they became accustomed to it and then they stopped remarking.

She'd been an accident, an afterthought. She knew this from listening at the door. She hadn't meant to, but she'd heard her name spoken, her mother's voice in a room with the door nearly closed. Her mother had laughed. She'd been talking to Jude's aunt who had come to stay from her farm, bringing eggs and raspberry jam, and smelling of damp wool and the air beneath the trees.

'The last thing on my mind,' Jude's mother had said. 'A precious mistake. At my age, for heaven's sake,' and Jude, kneeling on the cold hall tiles, had heard her mother chuckle, and her aunt, who had no children, join in.

She went to find Leo then, and asked him what their mother meant, and he told her it served her right for listening at keyholes.

'Is that why she's so wrinkled?' Jude said. 'More than the other ladies?'

'What?'

'Because of the worry. At making such a mistake?'

'No, silly.'

'But other girls, their mothers aren't.'

'It's because she's older,' Leo said, with all the authority of the newly grown, and he stood up, tall above his ten-year-old sister and did his growl to make her laugh.

'And now I'm going to eat you,' and he bent down, put his hands around her waist and lifted her high so that she shrieked with pleasure.

Leo had given Jude the Kodak for a going-away present. A running-away present, he called it. And she shot everybody with it, unless they looked about to die.

In Belgium the men liked the camera. They'd lean up on a shoulder if they could, or grin and lift a fag to their mouth, or give the 'V' for Victory. 'Send it to the wife as proof,' they'd say, winking. Or 'Be sure and get my right side, it's the better one.' One man told her this as she pointed the Kodak and she couldn't tell whether he knew that his right cheek was only a bloody hole, whether he was joking.

But mostly it wasn't the men she photographed. It was herself, and Kate, and their *Poste de Secours*, their first-aid station. It was the ordinary that she wanted to capture. How they made their own particular ordinary in the middle of that particular horror. Still lives.

They'd fought their own battle for this place. When they first walked in, the village seemed little more than rubble with a church tower that stood incongruously alone and a bell hanging silent. Nobody wanted to be there, the war going on only yards away. They found themselves a carcass of a house, the enamel number plate still stuck on: 26. It had a dry, vaulted, brick-floored cellar, jars of jam and chutney still safe on the shelves. And in the parlour they found Christ still hung bleeding from the wall, which seemed apt, and so they left him there, safe right until the end.

There was a meal on the kitchen table, or what had been a meal before the rats had it. Plates, cutlery, glasses still in their places on the table, and spilt salt. Jude tossed some over her shoulder. Kate opened cupboards.

They occupied the house within the hour and often Jude came across something – a piece of ribbon, a spirit level, a child's bonnet – that made her stop and wonder.

The first days they had no more than they'd carried with them. A tin of cocoa, a box with bandages, swabs and dressings, some iodine, Lysol, a bottle of brandy, some morphine and syringes Kate had badgered from a doctor, two slabs of navy chocolate, some bread, tins of corned beef, crackers, a hurricane lamp, sleeping bags, bed rolls, disinfectants and a box of sanitary towels.

'Might have to use them as dressings if the other stuff doesn't arrive quickly,' Kate said.

They put their bedding in an upstairs room. Jude brushed the floor, laid out the bed rolls, put a candle in a pot and a mug of water at the head of each and their haversacks at the base. Kate mixed something in a bucket.

'Against the rats,' she said. 'Dettol and Keatings powder.'

'It doesn't look so dirty,' Jude said, as Kate soaked a rag in the mixture and made a ring around the bedding, trailing the wet rag across the floorboards.

Jude laughed. 'Our desert island.'

But that night it was Kate who slept soundly while Jude lay awake and very still, legs together, arms tight to her sides, and listened to the heavy scurrying. And in the morning it was Kate who was laughing.

'You look like a convent girl, laid out like that,' she said. 'No touching. The nuns would be proud.'

From then on, until the rat traps arrived, it was Jude who painted the magic circle, swabbing the mixture on to the floorboards as if her life depended on it.

Peter walked into the kitchen on their second day, stooping in the doorframe, their slender fairy-tale prince. He'd been seconded to them by a kindly major because of his nerves. He wasn't allowed to go home, he wasn't far gone enough for that, but he was more use to them in their house than he was in the trenches. So while

Kate and Jude unpacked, sandbagged the front door, checked their medical supplies, Peter lit the stove. He found a kettle, and a black pot and then he was away for slates. He never seemed to rush, but the pot was never empty, or so it seemed, and he was its tattered Cinderella.

With every pump smashed and every well blocked with rubble, for the first two weeks they took their buckets to fill from the ditches. The long ditches where, however often they were cleared, still the dead men lay.

'We're as good as taking our water out of dead men's bellies,' Kate said, and despite all she had seen already, the thought made Jude shiver.

She would scan as far as she could, to left and to right, searching out the signs of a body, a limb flung up the bank, the hump of a man's tunic, and then she would let her buckets fill and pray. And she thought that perhaps the gods heard her, because none of them fell ill with it. But though they boiled and re-boiled the water, still the taste remained, and the day that Peter cleared a well and gathered the first bucket of clear water, they toasted him with it.

There was wood everywhere for the burning. No shortage of fuel. Log piles, neatly stacked, at the side of most houses. And once these were exhausted, there were the broken houses to plunder. Chairs and tables, beams hanging from ceilings, crushed beds, some covered in rubble but with their counterpanes still folded, ready for the night. But it was strange, discovering the things they baulked at, and while Jude was happy to carry logs and pull down fences, she couldn't bear to split the broken legs from chairs; or tug the shelves from a kitchen cupboard; or wrench the boards apart of some old table, its heart already damaged by the shelling. Her fingers would rub rough on some grains of spilt sugar, or she'd see where a child had carved some letters or where some wine had spilt, and find herself close to tears. So she left this gathering to the others.

They found saws, their teeth oiled, and axes hung up on nails in abandoned outhouses. These peacetime tools were sharp, precise.

Kate cut her thumb, testing an axe blade. Jude would have liked to have sawn wood and chopped logs, but it quickly became clear that, together with the pot, this was Peter's province, and it wasn't long before he always had some handsome soldier, sufficiently recuperated, to help him in the long hours chopping and sawing in the outhouse.

Jude had been so young at the start and so ignorant, that she wondered at first why Kate had been willing to set this all up with her and not somebody more experienced. She could do very little by comparison. The motorbike was Kate's, though Jude rapidly learned both to ride and repair it. And although Jude had been to VAD training camp, she wasn't a trained nurse like Kate. When they met, Jude had been in Belgium for little more than a month, frustrated that she couldn't get closer to the action, frustrated with watching men die, not from their wounds but from the trauma of their journey away from the trenches, cold, exhausted, hungry, shocked. So when Kate suggested they do something about it, Jude leaped at the chance, and a month later they were there, in sight of no man's land, in the house that was to be their home for over three years.

Jude raised her age to get to the war, just like the boys she knew. Leo tried to stop her, and when he couldn't prevent her with argument, they tossed a coin over it. Heads she'd stay, tails she'd go. He tossed the coin, she picked it up. He should have known better, she told herself.

She took his old motorcycle jacket over with her and wore it all through. She said afterwards that she must have known, had some mysterious insight that she'd need it. It was too big, always sitting on her stiffly, a beetle carapace. But it didn't take long, over there, for the black sheen to rub away and soon there were cracks, fault lines, in the creases of the arms. Sometimes, at the end of a day and exhaustion riding pillion with her, the weight of it felt nearly too much. But if she opened the jacket and buried her face in the lining, through the dirt and the sweat she could smell home, so she wore it always, her familiar skin.

*

The farmhouse had been part of their inland sea, the nearest island on their watery horizon. Kate and Jude could see it, walls and roof, from their upstairs room. And when the waters were still and the sun shone, it rose out of its own reflection. But as the flooding finally drew back, a track appeared, first like a shadow and then, more substantial, lifting like a rift in the water's seamless cloth, linking farmhouse and village.

It was Peter's idea to go out there.

'See what remains,' he said.

'We know what will have remained,' Kate said. 'We've seen it dozens of times.'

He shrugged. 'I'd still like to see. It's eerie, having it out there unvisited. It deserves a bit of human sympathy.'

Jude laughed at that. 'I'll come with you,' she said, so, a week or so later, when they judged that the track would have dried enough, the two of them walked out there, Jude with her camera, empty haversacks on their backs, because, as Jude said, who knew what you might find, even in a house that had been all at sea?

On their way out, she took a photograph of the farmhouse, four-square in its watery domain, and much later then it was Elsa who asked, was this how Noah's ark had been?

A high tideline was visible round the outside of the house higher than Jude's waist, and the bricks were damp above it and still wet below. The windows and the doors were swollen and the paint was crawling off. Mud pressed itself up to the walls and rotted vegetation languished. Peter managed to open the kitchen door, and the two of them went in.

Little remained in the downstairs rooms. The furniture was gone, taken off, Jude imagined, on a cart like one of those she had seen so often at the fringes of this war, piled beyond hope with objects and people. Despite the flooding, squares of shade were still visible on the walls where pictures had been, and on a nail beside the door, two keys. A filter of silt lay over all.

They went upstairs, Peter into one room to exclaim at the view back, across the strange sea, she into the other.

'I can see our place,' he called out. 'Come and get a picture of it.

The roof. Your white cross. It's clear as day. I love it that you can't paint straight.'

Jude laughed and stepped further into a room with a small gilded mirror and a bed, all curlicues and little painted flowers that must have been unwillingly left behind. She walked past the mirror, catching a slice of herself, her jacket, her hands around the camera. They looked like a man's hands, strong-fingered, the nails clipped almost to the quick. Stepping back, Jude bent a little. She hadn't seen her face in a mirror for weeks, except in the tiny compact Kate had tucked into her kitbag, and you could only see one thing at a time in that, an eye, a cheekbone, your mouth. She stared at herself and wondered at how young she still seemed. She looked as young as the boys she nursed. Then she grinned at her own foolishness.

Jude took out her camera and stepped closer to trace the painted patterns and then, despite herself, despite all she had seen, she exclaimed, so loud that Peter came running.

'What is it?' he said.

In the centre of the mattress, her spine curved round, protective, lay a cat, dead for so many months, the skin of her jowl stretched tight against her jaw, her tabby belly fur dipped, hollowed out, her eyes two tiny raisins. And nestled in to her, three balls, one black, one tabby, one fiercely striped in grey.

'I don't cry at the men,' Jude said, 'but these.'

'If you don't know your arse from your elbow, then get out of the bloody kitchen.' Kate lifted the lid on the pot and the steam billowed up, blanched her face. 'Christ,' she said, stepping back.

'Mind him!' Jude shouted.

Kate gave a cursory look at the shape on the stretcher. 'He's dead to the world, not going to feel a thing. Come on, you stir it. Burn your own lips.'

Cautiously, Jude looked into the pot. 'Peter said half the liquid should have gone, and it should smell peppery.'

'And?'

'It does smell peppery. But maybe we ought to add a bit more water. There's only a few inches.'

38

'He'll murder us if we've ruined his stock.'

'Kate, we were busy.'

'I was busy. You were just doing what I told you to.'

'And you'd have thanked me if I'd been stirring the pot instead of passing you the swab?'

Kate made her way round the unconscious soldier and peered into the pot. She turned to Jude. 'I can't tell. Will he know, if we add more water?'

'He said to take the bones out, once it was done.'

'But if we put more water in?'

'What is it about you?' Jude said. 'Completely calm taking out shrapnel, stitching a wound, cleaning mud out of flesh, deciding what you can do to save a life, but when it's Peter's stock pot, you go to pieces.'

'Well, do we or don't we?'

'What?'

'Add the water, for Christ's sake. God, you'd think I'd have known better than to get stuck away in this hole with someone who conjugates Latin, rides motorbikes at daft speeds, isn't afraid of death and can't do a lot else.'

They'd been in the house four months and exhilaration had given way to exhaustion. Food was their calling card, and it had taken only days for word to spread amongst the soldiers. So every day now they fed soup and hot chocolate to a stream of men queuing with mugs. And every night, carrying heavy, steaming jugs, they made their way to the sentries in their dug-out outposts at the end of the world, looking out into the darkness, over the mist, over the floods. They'd hear no sounds except their breath, their footfalls. The quiet bark for the password, then a hand would appear and take the jug. They'd hear tin mugs being filled and after a few seconds the jug would be handed back empty, no word spoken, and they'd return. Sometimes a star shell would break above them and they'd have to stand stock-still and watch its cold light harden over the blank fields and dead water, the ruined buildings, then fall to the ground around them, before they moved on.

Sometimes by day the village was still shelled and you had to listen to the skies. But at night the ground was more treacherous than the air, darkness hiding the slurry and the shell holes. Still, Jude liked the night walk back through the village. It seemed less ruined when she couldn't see behind things. And she came to know the craters and the gashed walls, the piles of masonry and where the water spilled, and felt a growing ease with this shattered place. There was a single plane tree surviving on the main street, a strange, lopsided thing, but she noticed that it had managed some leaf buds ready for spring, and passing in the night, sometimes she'd put a hand out to touch the trunk, as if by accident, not wanting Kate to see her do it.

If the food was their calling card, then the cellar became their salon. They received all comers, day or night, the wounded and the dog-tired and the scared. Mostly the wounded came to them, but sometimes Jude and Kate would go out and help retrieve them, laying their stretcher down on the mud, and lifting the man on. At first Jude would apologize, each time the man cried out or jerked with the pain, 'Sorry. So sorry,' till Kate took her to task.

'If you say that once more, you can carry the damn stretcher on your own,' she said. 'Tell them something useful. That you love them, that you're their mother, whatever you like, but not sorry.'

The first wrench from the ground was the hardest, with the mud fighting them, gravity fighting them, with the sniper waiting for them to stumble into his sights, with the man's cries of pain to be left still, left alone, and always under their boots the horrid slush of war. Then they'd have the stretcher up to waist level, the handles rubbing into their blisters, pressing the blood from their fingers. And the weight of the man, and his boots and rifle, his uniform and tin hat, of the unsent letter and the dog-eared photograph in his pocket, the weight of all that expectation that gathers itself into staying whole, being alive, pulled their arms from their shoulders, bent them down, as they made their way over the cratered ground. And though there were times Jude's arms were shrieking with the strain of it and she thought she couldn't make another yard, still they never dropped a man.

40

Jude took the bones out of the stockpot and put them in a pail. Outside, the air was cold and the bones steamed. If you touched them, they felt like velvet after so much boiling. You could press your nail in.

With so many dead horses, there was no shortage of meat. You saw them everywhere. Sometimes a couple of dogs nuzzling at them or, at twilight, rats. Peter would go out with his axe and his knife when the shelling had been bad. Wait till the sky was quiet. He had an old tarpaulin with him and he only came back with the very fresh.

'Too risky otherwise. Don't know what else the rats have been in,' he'd say.

The Belgians were impressed. He cooked as well as a native. But he stopped telling the British soldiers what it was in the stew after one refused to eat a 'man's best friend'.

'You'd think we were cannibals, the way he carried on,' Kate said.

'What the eye doesn't see, the heart won't grieve over,' Jude said. And after that the men ate ravenously and only ever asked for more salt.

Jude picked her way down across where the garden used to be to the shell hole they were using for their rubbish, and tipped the bones in. She liked this chore. Except for these short times, carrying rubbish, or going for the turnips or potatoes, or spotting planes, she could rarely be on her own.

The first time she'd climbed onto the roof, it was to put back some tiles. Peter had no great head for heights and Kate was away with the ambulance. What with the shelling, there had been leaks since they arrived and they'd become canny with the buckets, but it was getting worse, so when Peter found a stack of unbroken tiles, the short straw fell to Jude.

They were red pantiles and they reminded her of home. She'd slung a satchel across her shoulders, leaving both hands free, and Peter had loaded in a half dozen. The ladder took Jude up to the gutter and then she had to hitch one foot up, wedging her boot toe against the gutter edge for purchase, and pull herself onto the roof. The roof pitched steeply and she had to be careful not to dislodge the tiles as she climbed. Keeping her weight forward and her hands out above her, bracing her legs and shoulders against the slip of gravity, she clambered up to the ridge where the worst hole was.

She looked down once and felt her muscles tighten. Then she thought of the cliffs she loved, the birds making their nests on the edge of nothing, and that steeled her. Replacing the tiles took only a few minutes and she was back down to collect some more. Peter stood at the base of the ladder, his hands gripping the sides, his face scrunched with anxiety.

'Stop standing there like some mother,' she said. 'Least nobody's trying to kill me.'

Peter shrugged.

'Have you always been like this?' Jude said.

'Yes, but it's worse when there are children around. I think you count as a child, though. God knows what'll happen if I have a child of my own one day.' He grinned. 'Though that is a bit unlikely.'

'You'll be a Nebuchadnezzar. On all fours.'

The next time up, her body was easier with it and she allowed herself more time, straddled the roof ridge and looked around. After all the rain it was a clear day, ribbons of cloud strung across. Near to, the village was laid out, houses with their insides showing, pieces of wall with tatters of wallpaper strung like bunting, rafters pointing all ways but across where the roof had been, mad spokes, all the savage work of the war exposed. In the far distance baubles of smoke hung rounded in the blue sky like decorations. And in between, she could see water and the lines of war. All was quiet.

'You can see everything from here,' she called.

'Come down,' she heard in return. And though she recognised the urgency in his voice, it was diluted and came up to her light, insubstantial.

The front line had shifted several times since they'd arrived. Now it stood farther off, but up here she could see right across the awkward criss-cross of trenches and earthworks, strange lumps and ridges from where she stood, over the coils of barbed

wire and into no man's land. It seemed as if the land stood waiting, awaiting. Nothing moved there, no man, no animal. Even the
wind seemed to have given up the ghost. She knelt down, her back
against the chimney. The river ran across the bottom of her view,
only a stubble of trees left to mark its course now. A heron
crossed the sky towards it, the heavy tread of its wings. When it
flew too close to the church tower the rooks came out to see it off,
flapping their black cloaks, pitching in sharp to harry it. The
heron lifted its heavy chest, turned a few degrees, and flew on,
steady, unhurried.

When Jude first heard the plane, it was a distant whine, high-
pitched, irrelevant. Sometimes they watched dogfights in the sky
here, planes wheeling high up, flimsy, like dancers, as if they had
nothing to do with the dirty mess on the ground. The plane came
closer. Jude stood up, tall, straight-backed, her arms around the
chimney. She couldn't see the markings yet, but it seemed to be on
its own, and it was trailing smoke and losing height.

'Get down,' Peter shouted. 'You've no cover.'

She shook her head. It was close enough now for her to see the
markings. The plane was German and it would pass dangerously
near to her roof. She had no camera up here to put between herself and this plunging metal bird. The whine had grown to
something ghastly, a sound that cut through the roof and shivered
the chimney bricks. Now she could see the pilot, his face white,
unseeing, locked in concentration, in the effort to fly.

The plane must have passed only twenty feet from the house
and Jude watched on, just long enough to see where it would end.

'Get the bike,' she shouted to Peter, who had come out again
and, with a last look, she came down the ladder.

It had landed in no man's land, in full view of the German gun-
ners, but they knew by now what Jude did, they were familiar with
the red crosses on her Matchless, her sidecar. And besides, he was
one of theirs. That first time the pilot was dead before she reached
him. He'd managed to make a landing of sorts, but the impact had
pushed the joystick too far into his chest. He was so fresh, in his
pilot's uniform, so unmuddied, unsullied, she thought he looked like

one of Leo's friends come to call, still barely shaving, a boy of nineteen or so. They buried him in the German corner of the churchyard.

From then on they kept the ladder handy for the roof. The German snipers never fired at them up there. And it became another place where Jude could be alone.

Since childhood, Jude knew she had never stood at the heart of things. At high school, she saw how it was done, the belonging, the groups and games, but she was one of those who stayed on the outside, unnoticed. At break times the other girls would glimpse a tall, slight figure with unruly dark curls at the edge of the view, her mackintosh half-buttoned against the wind, her tam-o'-shanter crooked as she walked around the playing field, or stood against the school wall, her shoulder blades in two points against the brick, and made pictures with her fingers. She only swam into full view if they were a girl short, when they might demand that she joined in with the game of tag, or held a rope for their skipping. And she would do so, but as soon as she could, she'd slip away again to the shadow of the wall.

'Take your fingers down,' Miss Bude, who taught history, would tell her when she came across Jude framing things, and she would whip her knuckles across Jude's hands so that they smarted. 'We must take part, Judith, as best we can.' And Jude would try her hardest for Miss Bude, who wept at the fate of Anne Boleyn and Lady Jane Grey and all the other lady victims of history.

Jude liked Miss Bude and she liked Miss Cupinall, who taught French, and most especially she liked the botany teacher, Miss Butterling, who took the girls deep into meadows of tall grass so that they could see for themselves trembling couch and rye, rattle, mare's tail, timothy and willow, and learn how various even the fields above their own town were. She laboured hard to remember the difference between St John's wort and saxifrage, or between loosestrife and creeping Jenny, propping her exercise book behind Leo's plate of breakfast so that he could test her as he ate his eggs.

But often, at school, her thoughts took flight. Seated at her desk in a classroom intent upon calculus or the Roman conquest, Latin

44

conjugations or the fate of the soul after death, Jude's mind would skip a beat and hang with the buzzing fly above the gas lights, or wriggle its way through the slit of open window and become lost in the toss of the leaves in the beech trees beyond the tennis courts. And when a question came her way, she found herself stranded, like the porpoise she had read of, lost up the river Thames, her body in one place and her spirit in another.

'But you're a clever enough girl,' her father would say perplexed, Jude's school report on the desk before him. 'I wish your mother were here to advise me.'

And he'd put a hand to his head and stroke his shiny, liver-spotted skull. Then, when she made no reply, he'd reach for his bowl of pipes and Jude, watching, would think how much she'd like to take a photograph, the angle of his head, the line of the pipe stem.

When Jude had first returned from the war, she couldn't bear to live in a house. Not Leo's, not anybody's. She didn't trust their steady walls. At the end, the hospital was tents. Solid, large, but still tents, which she'd been glad of. Then there were the trains, crammed, euphoric, and all the time, outside, the platforms with cheery people who only wanted to know you were alive.

Leo and Sally were on her platform, and their children, a baby in Sally's arms, a child with one hand tight in Leo's. Jude stood still as the train pulled out and away and wished she was not here.

Leo walked towards her, his small son tugging back, reluctant. The boy had Leo's hair, his walk.

'Jude,' Leo said, his face unsure.

'The journey was all right,' she said. She smiled at him. 'You've come with everybody.'

Leo looked down at the little boy, and over at Sally, holding the baby.

'They're the family,' he said.

She nodded.

'You look . . .' Leo said.

'It doesn't matter how I look,' she said.

45

Leo put his hand to his cheek, as though she had slapped him. Jude shut her eyes, watched the flash and dazzle of her own darkness. When she opened them, Leo was still there, and the little boy was on his way steadily back towards his mother further down the platform. Leo moved closer to Jude and lifted the haversack from her back.

'I didn't know Father was that bad,' he said. 'He didn't tell me. Didn't tell anybody.'

'Why?'

Leo shrugged. 'Maybe because of the war, all the young men dying. I don't know.'

'Was he in pain?'

'No. Just terrible fatigue. And of course he wouldn't listen to my suggestions, but then I didn't know how ill he was. Father had told the doctor not to tell me. I wrote as soon as . . .'

'Yes,' Jude said.

Leo put his arm around her, and standing on the platform, she let herself cry at last.

'You're home now,' Leo said, and his shoulder, where it was wet with her tears, smelt of milk, smelt of the baby over there in its mother's arms, waiting for its father.

They tucked her into their house, covered her with comfort, their questions hanging silent fire in the movement of their arms, their heads angled to listen better. But she couldn't tell them anything, not even that she was all right. She didn't want to, and so she left after two nights.

'You're not yourself,' Leo said to her. 'Jude?'

She shrugged. 'I have been,' she said. 'Be patient.'

She took a train and then a slower one, and a third, and walked the four miles to her Uncle William's farm. The short cut above the road was wet with rain, so that treading through the grasses and the buttercups, her boots darkened and she could feel the slink of her toes. Years back, she'd have taken the boots off, knotted and hung them from her neck, laughed when her aunt chided her for her bare feet. But she knew better than that now. You don't take off your boots, not unless you have to.

Her uncle offered her a cottage, empty until harvest time. But she didn't want anything so strongly fixed. She didn't know how he'd come by the caravan. The wheel axles were rotten, so it wasn't going anywhere, but still it wasn't rooted in. William said he'd fix it up for her, find her a horse even, if that was what she wanted. But she wanted only to be left there, and he did so.

They gave her food, William and his wife Joan — eggs, bread, meat, milk, vegetables — and every so often she'd go down to the farm for a bath.

'Let her be,' William said when she arrived. 'She won't let you be her mother. Nor me her father.'

There were the sores and scabs and her hair was cropped like a boy's. She liked to put her hand over it, the tickle on her palm. They didn't touch her, not even a stroke to the cheek, and her hair grew and the scabs became scars, some of them.

She knew that they wondered what had become of her. She could see them at it. She knew the girl they'd lost, the girl that they could wrap themselves around. The girl who'd visited them every holiday, copying them in their tasks, making a game in the midst of their labour. She'd seen her go, and somebody else grow up in her place.

That girl was a fairy-tale creature now, a mischievous will-o'-the-wisp who crept out of the mist and tugged William's arm as he walked to the cowshed in the early morning, or plucked at Joan's scarf as she bent to cut sweet peas. She haunted the place. They heard the odd tuning of her whistle in the distance, caught a glimpse of her dance, were sure they saw her disappear into the hay barn or heard the creak of her footstep on the stairs, tousled from a nightmare. But she wasn't there.

She was too tall for her aunt's, so she went about in her uncle's clothes, having brought nothing of her own beyond what she stood up in: his corduroy trousers, pulled in with a belt, his shirts, the cotton soft with age, the collars turned and bare, his ancient pullover darned in the elbows, his old boots when hers got a hole. She was at ease in these things.

A cat joined her in the caravan, a wild streak of a creature, as

unwilling to be touched as she was. It ate the same food she did –
meat, scrambled egg, bread soaked in milk – and slept at her feet,
but it wouldn't be touched.

The first time she noticed it behind her, a mile from the farm,
she thought it was chance that had brought her haphazard walking
and the cat's hunting to the same place. But when it happened
again, she knew it must be deliberate. The cat became her only
company, stalking her at an angle, as though it wished to persist
with the illusion that their proximity was accidental.

She walked for miles each day, her journeying sometimes taking
her so far off that she would stumble her way back in the dark, and
more than once she was forced to sleep the night curled into the
corner of a barn. She carried her Kodak with her and took photographs of the long views, the horizon, the hills rising on the
skyline. Her father was dead, her lover was dead, her closest friend.
And all the others. With so many gone, she needed to walk in an
empty landscape, needed to take her mind's eye as far away as she
could.

For a time, while she was in Belgium, Jude had taken photographs of hands. Her own, Kate's, Peter's, other soldiers', trying to
capture them in a gesture or going about some habitual movement,
peeling potatoes, lighting cigarettes, playing cards or rolling bandages, their precision, their delicacy. But there had been one young
soldier brought in, she could still see him come through the doorway, and he'd changed that. It was winter and very cold. The
soldiers were suffering badly from chilblains, their hands and feet
swollen and painful, and some had frostbite, so that at first she
thought that was this man's trouble. He stepped forward, eyes
wide, shocked, and held his gloved hands out to Jude, like an
offering, and if she hadn't caught him, he would have fallen to the
ground.

The soldier behind him told her that it was the left one that had
been hit, but that the young fellow wouldn't look at it even.

'He's too frightened,' he said.

Jude got the man on to a stretcher and gave him a slug of
brandy. Still he hadn't spoken a word. As gently as she could, she

began to cut away the woollen glove, and for a short moment she thought the injuries might be superficial. Then she saw that the darkness of the glove was made up as much of blood as of the dark blue wool. As the hand was uncovered, it became a mess of bone and blood. Two fingers were severed, the knuckle bones sharp white even in the cellar's poor light, and the flesh on the hand was macerated, raw. Woollen fibres were tangled into the mess of it all, so deeply threaded into the flesh, it was almost as though God had made it that way. The doctor would be here later, but she knew there was nothing he could do with this.

She was exhausted by the time she'd finished and though he was conscious, staring at the ceiling, still the soldier hadn't flinched, still he hadn't spoken.

'It's serious,' she said, 'but you should make a good recovery. I've cleaned it up pretty well. We'll get you back to the hospital tomorrow, and you'll be strong again before you know it.' And because he wouldn't speak and because she was so tired, she said, 'You're not left handed, I hope?' and still he didn't speak, but when Jude saw that he was crying, she was sorry for her facetiousness and she went and found the one who'd brought him in.

'He's not left-handed, is he?' she said to the soldier, who looked up at her over his mug of soup, and he shook his head.

'He's a pianist,' he said.

So later, in all her time on her uncle's farm, Jude never shot people. No bodies, no limbs. And when finally she came to leave the caravan, she threw away all the landscapes on the rolls of shot film, as she'd known she would.

Jude never found out how they recovered the motorcycle. She hadn't mentioned it. But one day William came to her door, waving a slip of paper.

'It's at the station,' he said. 'We'll go for it this afternoon.'

She waited for him to explain, and he handed her the slip.

'Matchless arrived 0600 hours. To be collected, Mr Emerson.'

'My motorcycle?' she said.

'We'll set off soon as dinner's done,' he said, giving a nod as if to confirm it to himself. And maybe she clenched her jaw and he could see that she was close to something, because he turned and walked away.

Kate's motorcycle. It was very dirty. It hadn't been ridden since. Mud, grit, oil, crud caked hard over wheels, forks, footboards, handlebars, sidecar. The same mud and grit. She didn't touch it. Just looked. When they got back, William wheeled it down from the trailer and into the yard. Strange, to see it there in the sunshine. As much as her, it had lost its place in the world.

The dogs sniffed it, though they didn't lift a leg, didn't mark it out as theirs, and the hens pecked around it, odd inconsequential birds. Sparrows sat on the saddle, chivvied around the sidecar. She waited, still didn't touch, and only at last when they'd gone elsewhere, when everything seemed to have gone elsewhere, did she go close and grip the handlebars, and allow herself to straddle the bike, and remember.

She'd ridden pillion for the first lesson, Kate yelling instructions to the wind and Jude nodding blindly, her eyes streaming without goggles. But there had been little time beyond that for the luxury of learning and already the following day, Jude had had to set off on the bike for supplies with Kate's injunctions still burning in her ears.

'For God's sake gently with the throttle,' Kate yelled after her, and then something that began, 'If you bring her back . . .', but by then Jude was beyond earshot, and looking in the mirror she could see that Kate had already turned back towards the wounded men in the cellar below.

'It's enough now,' Jude told herself in her uncle's yard, climbing off the saddle, and though she didn't know what she would do, she knew that she would ride the bike again.

She stayed longer on the farm than she could have believed, out and away from the returning world, and it took her a long while to get used to living in a house, to get used to streets and motor cars and drays and lorries. People, sounds, buildings seemed to press in very close and her reflexes, still strung along war wires, made her start and duck, so that she began to take her camera out with her again as a way of keeping her distance, as defence. Leo and Sally never pressed her about money, never asked her to find a job, but she knew before she was ready to that she must.

'But not nursing,' she said.

'Not nursing?'

Jude and Leo were sitting on the lawn in the garden, keeping watch over Elsa on the swing.

'No.'

'Because?'

She was fiddling with a blade of grass, stretching it between her thumbs, blowing at it.

'Kate taught me to whistle,' she said. 'She told me it didn't work with garden grass, but I didn't believe her.'

'Why not nursing?' Jude could see Leo's hand twitch. Seven years earlier and he'd have snatched the grass from her fingers. Seven years earlier and she was still a child and wouldn't have been able to answer his question. Jude rolled her shoulders. She could feel the muscles bunched tight.

'Because I couldn't do it like before. Matrons are much worse than generals. I couldn't obey all the rules. Couldn't stand being humble.'

Leo laughed. 'You could learn.'

'No.'

'And not teaching?'

'No,' her voice impatient.

'So, what then? There isn't much, not even factory work, now the men have returned.'

'I want something I don't need to care about,' she said. 'Do it and leave it.'

'Father thought you should be a photographer,' Leo said.

She shook her head. 'I couldn't be the kind I wanted to be.'

'You don't know that.'

'I do,' she said.

At the edge of the flower bed, missed by the lawnmower, she found a piece of rougher grass and holding it between thumb and forefinger, carefully she pulled it free of its sheath. Running her thumb down its edge, its bristles caught at her skin. She laid the blade flat against the side of one thumb, married her other thumb tight on top, lifted them to her lips.

The sound was oily and coarse, like a strange bird cry, and it took her back. She blew again.

'I know you've always said no before, but I could try to get you a job,' Leo said. 'In my company. Pay would be very low to start with, while you were training.'

'What kind of training?'

'It's mainly on the job, and some evening classes. Typewriting, shorthand.'

'So I'd be a shorthand typist?'

Leo nodded.

'They'd have known Richard.'

'Yes.'

Jude twisted the grass around her finger like a tourniquet, watched the skin whiten.

'Would they know I was your sister?'

'I could only get you an interview. They won't do favours. It'd be up to you, if they took you on.'

'I don't think they'd like my other skills,' Jude said.

'I don't think you should tell them. In fact you'd need to bite your tongue. You know that now, anyway. Yes, sir, and no, sir. And your hair. They'll probably ask you to keep your hair longer.'

Jude unwound the grass.

'But I want it shorter.'

'Why?'

'D'you remember when I got back, after the war?'

Leo reached over, put his hand on Jude's hair, the tight black curls, like his.

'That was because of the lice. You told me.'

'I liked it, too.'

He shrugged. 'Long hair dressed in a bun, or back with ribbon. Dark ribbon.' He pointed at Elsa, swinging, humming to herself. 'That length. And no rings.'

'Not even a wedding ring?'

'Only single women, you know that.'

'For God's sake,' Jude muttered, but not at Leo's words because he was right, she did know that. 'It took me half an hour once,' she said a minute later, in a different voice, 'and the brother standing by me, to pull the wedding ring from a dead man's finger.'

'Jude?' Leo said, uncertain, and Jude shook her head.

'Cobwebs,' she said, her voice breezy now, implausible. 'Anyway, how do you know so much?'

'I used to interview them,' he said.

Jude was silent, brooding.

'I don't much mind what I do,' she said at last. 'It'll be dull, won't it?'

'But you don't want . . .'

'No, dull is fine. What about the motorcycle?'

'To work?'

Jude nodded.

'No. Recreation only. Train to work. Besides, it'd be dangerous in a skirt.'

'You won't see me for dust at the weekends, then,' she said, flicking the grass away.

What shocked Jude most was that she got used to the office. At the end of the first day she was ready to leave, and again at the end of the week, and certainly after a month, and still after six, then a year, and so on. She couldn't quite believe that she had to keep going there. She felt like Elsa after her first week of primary school. Couldn't she stop now and go back to her play? But Jude didn't leave. She bit her tongue and kept her place.

Each morning she would tug the blue worsted suit from its hanger, put on the white silk blouse, the lisle stockings and sensible shoes, drink a quick cup of coffee and take the train into the city with Leo. She stood on the platform looking like anyone else while Leo flicked the pages of *The Times*. They didn't walk together beyond the station. You couldn't do that to work, even brother and sister.

The weather was hot those first weeks and by the time she

reached the office Jude's skin was sticky and she could feel the sweat beading under her hat and she was longing to pull off her gloves. Crossing Boar Lane, she'd walk up Park Row to George Street, one of such a stream of girls. She'd never have imagined there could be so many.

When she was a child and visiting her father, Jude had been scared of the revolving door. The way it seemed to suck people in, usher them secretly, never opening except when it was already closing. You might be squashed if you timed it wrong, or you might twirl and twirl, go faster and faster, be caught in the blur of wood and glass, and never escape. She'd always let her mother go first, and then wait for an age to go in, terrified. She'd wait so long that often enough her mother or her father would be spat out again to find out what had happened to her.

The room was large and bleak. High windows, which Jude was glad about, through which you could just see the tiling on the mansard roofs, a bank of filing cabinets along one wall, and trestle tables along the others. Twenty girls sat at twenty typewriters and now Jude was one of them.

The sea was like another field. A rising stain of green, thin-lined below the sky, tugging her eyes from the road. Leo had his arm out, signalling to stop, and Jude pulled into the side of the road behind him. She stepped away from the Matchless, the dew coating her boots. The air was still. She could hear the birds again. She pulled off her gloves and put her hands to her face, her cheeks cold and hard from the wind, her eyes still dazed. Her arms and legs were stiff and she teetered for a minute before shaking out the motion.

'You're determined to go up there?' Leo said.

'Yes.'

'If you wait, I can leave them on the beach and come with you.'

'I'd rather be on my own.'

'And if . . .' he fell silent at the thought they both had.

'Leo,' Jude said, a plea in her voice.

'I've made as much room for you as I can,' he said. 'I know you need it. But I can't stand and watch, if I think you're going to . . .'

'That's not what I want,' Jude said.

She could see his fists clenching. She knew that anxiety was seeded in his belly like a scatter of pearls, his muscles gathering around them. But she must go. She waited, and finally he undid his fingers and gave her a hug.

'You'll find us on the beach, then?' he said.

'Will you swim?' And her question made him smile. It was an old joke from childhood, when Jude was fearless and he was scared. 'Keep me some beer,' she said, 'and don't let the children out too deep.'

'I'll be watching for you,' he said. 'Remember.'

He blew a dandelion. 'She loves me, she loves me not,' but she wouldn't play that far.

'I'll find you by lunchtime,' she said and she started up the motorbike and there were no other rhymes in the world.

She was safe, watching the birds. Safe as houses, if she could face out her fear. She turned into the wind, the sharp, ammoniac air, and walked towards the cliff.

When they had come here as children, Leo would hold Jude by the wrist to stop her going too close to the edge. He'd plant his feet squarely, one hand holding her, so tight it hurt her bones, and the other clamped against one ear because of the din. There was the smell too, so he'd breathe through his mouth. Then it'd be a tug-of-war, she bracing her slight weight against him, trying to unbalance him and inch towards the cliff edge, and him with the bulk, standing stock-still. She didn't see the danger then, any more than his children could see it now, kept safe by his caution. But Leo didn't need to hold her away any longer, or even warn her.

The ground was uneven, humped up, so that Jude had to watch her steps, though there'd be nothing worse than bird shit to fall into here if she lost her footing. She left no footprints in the wiry grass, and the tiny cliff-top flowers – thrift and saxifrage, tormentil's fierce yellow, the purple pinheads of wild thyme – remained untouched by her boots, impeccable.

The noise was getting louder, a shrieking swell rising from the line where the land stopped. Birds turned above her and she could sometimes pick out their single cries before they dropped and dived down beyond her sight. The stench of birdlime burnt her nostrils. Far away on the sea, easy in the swell and break of the waves, clusters of razorbills and guillemots, puffins and kittiwakes sat high. And now she was close enough to see the cliffs, the smeared white of the rock, busy with the business of thousands of nesting birds. Close enough to see how far away down the sea was.

Before the war she had often come here with Leo. But since returning she'd been out only once. It was winter and she was on her own, wanting just to see the cliffs. But she was too scared to stay. The sweat poured from her even before she got close, and her heart pounded so that it hurt. That day she stopped fifty yards off and stared down across the meadow to where the land ended, terrified that if she moved forward another step, she would run and not stop, that she would have her last fling with the air.

'Richard,' she whispered, 'please don't make me,' and she stood, unable to move, until at last some cattle, unafraid of this stationary figure, grazed their way across her vision and she was able to turn and walk away.

Jude had no idea how Leo had known. She hadn't told him, but that evening he came and found her in her dark room.

'Things take a lot of time,' he said, 'especially these hard griefs. Don't hurt yourself, please.'

This second time, Jude was sure that she'd be able to manage it. Leo would be below, on the beach, and though he could prevent nothing, she'd be in his view. And far from being empty, the cliffs were so densely inhabited at this time of the year, she couldn't imagine tumbling over, into all those bird lives. Of course she didn't know if she could, but she was determined to keep her nerve if possible, at least for long enough to take some photographs.

She knew a place she could stand away from the edge, from where she could see a piece of the cliff face and the sea below, and she walked there slowly, keeping pace with her fear, marking the charge of her heart. When she arrived, she spent a few minutes getting her camera ready. Then, putting it down for now, she took out her binoculars and dared herself to look.

The relief was as palpable as the fear. She could feel it in her arms, in her stomach. She had survived and now she could let herself go.

At first, watching them, the birds looked chaotic, their flight random. As if they were caught in the sky together just for the hell of it, just to be suspended high above the water and in the face of the cliffs. But if she picked out a bird and kept her eye on it, refused to let her attention be drawn by another gull's fancy flightwork, or by another bird's sure fire pitch into the cliff, then she'd quickly see how concerted each was, how focused, so that they reminded her of the eight-fifteen city rush off the morning trams for work, except they were climbing the skies instead of treading the pavements.

In the war she'd taken photographs as still lives, intimate things to set against that vast, awful energy: their truckle beds, hers and Kate's, the lanterns on nails behind, Kate's diary on her pillow, the shelf with binoculars, photo frame with heads visible, an apple; or the kitchen stove, herbs drying above as if all were well, bottles and tins, tin spoons in a pot, a pan with steam. And she'd taken portraits. Kate mainly: reading, bandaging a man's hand, stroking the cat; or Peter at the stove, peeling vegetables, turning to the camera, grinning. And the wounded men, of course. Other, grimmer things too, sometimes. A skull in a ditch, two dead horses, a single flower in the rubble, the land besieged.

Now, Jude wanted to capture movement. To hold something still in the lens when all its impetus was to be away and gone.

Sometimes at home she looked at the pictures she took before the war, before she needed to try to keep things still. Not the ones in the albums, but those left loose. Took the box out from under her bed and carried it downstairs to the drawing room where the light from the windows was strong. She lifted off the lid and drew out an unruly pile, sharp corners pricking her fingers. Tom and

Elsa joined in if they could, closing their eyes tight and shuffling down in with their hands, playing lucky dip with the past.

They picked out photographs one by one and asked different questions of her.

'Why has the boy got his hat on? Whose dog is it? Why are they running away? Is it Grandma making stew? Who won the marbles? Did you comfort her, the girl crying?'

Most of the photographs she knew immediately, where she was, what the light was like, even sometimes what she'd wanted to capture. Though she wouldn't know what the dog was called or remember why the girl was crying, so she had to make that up. But there was one that Tom found one day, deep in the box, that she couldn't bear to speak of.

'Jude, why's the boy leaping?'

Tom was leaning over the photograph as if to interrogate it, and his voice was puzzled.

'And you've missed off his arms. And his head.'

Elsa looked up from her crayons, forehead pinched at the interruption, and leaned to look.

'It's not Daddy,' she said. 'He was never like that.'

And despite herself, Jude laughed.

'He was as thin then,' she said, 'but he could never jump that high, no.'

'That's our leaping rock, isn't it? He's doing it from there.'

'Yes.'

'I like this one specially. Who is it?' Elsa said, and before she thought to say nothing, Jude answered her.

'It's the boy who flew too close to the sun,' and she turned the photograph over so they could see the inscription.

'*Icarus, 1912*,' Tom read out.

There was so much more she could have told them. That he'd been a friend of Leo's, for example. She could have told them that. Or that he'd worked in their father's firm. Or that he'd worn a suit to work and was as slender as a reed, supple as a fish. She could have told them how he laughed and larked, told them his pranks. That he let her take photographs of him. Or that he'd shot his

58

share of the enemy, sometimes because they were shooting back and others because there were only so many prisoners you could take and what else were you to do. She could have told them that he couldn't weep at what he'd done, and that his letter to tell her of this had taken five weeks in the writing, each new start beginning with the words, 'I am still here'. She could have told them that he never got the letter she wrote in reply.

She could have told them that she loved him. And that it was only when he was gone that she knew how far from himself he had had to go.

She could have told them that when the wax melted and he fell, down onto the barbed wire, his face and leaping legs torn, and then fell still further into the mud and the filth, that then it seemed a terrible thing ever to look at him soaring so high, so that when she came home from the war, she took the photograph down and put it away in the box.

'Go on out now,' she said. 'Enough of the photographs.'

'But I haven't finished my picture,' Elsa said.

'Go on.'

'And I'd only looked at a few,' Tom said.

She picked up Elsa's picture and the box of crayons and put them in her arms.

'No,' she said, and they heard her voice, and went.

If Leo had been up here on the cliff, he'd have been telling her what kind of fish each bird favoured. How the black guillemots dive for molluscs and worms whereas the common guillemots eat sand-eels and sprats like the puffins. Or how the bigger gulls cruise the cliffs for other birds' eggs and chicks. Or how the biggest of the gulls had a wingspan of more than five feet and could swallow a rabbit whole. But he was on the beach, a tiny speck, and she was alone.

She'd been given these binoculars when it was all life or death. When she lifted them to her eyes, there'd be a few seconds, not more, when all she could see were the black rims of the lenses, everything blurry beyond. And now, years after her war's end, she could lift them and look and for a moment it wasn't the cliff, or the sea, or the children running far off, that she'd see drawing into focus. It was the mud and duckboards, and the grey pan of the sky, and the distant figures weren't moving, but too still. Then she'd focus and the squall of the birds would be back, veering into sight, and the cliff and the sea.

The birds dinned into her skull. There was no room for other sound or thought. There must have been a mackerel shoal close in to the shore, because suddenly the gannets were diving closer than usual, slicing into the water like bullets, worrying the sea to a froth, tugging the fish free. They dropped as fast as a stone. It was how they lived. Putting down the binoculars, she took up her camera. Usually they were too far out, but maybe she could shoot them today. The long, lazy beat of their wings, the arc of their flight, turning above the water, then dropping lower, circling tighter until finally the half-tuck of their wings, sharp-angled, and the drop. They were virtuosos of the dive.

But the trick was to catch the bird before it dived. It was like that half-moment before a man jumped from a wall, or ran between sniper fire, when his soul had already gone and it only remained for the body to follow. A moment when action and suspension were the same. But she couldn't get the timing right today, so instead she picked a gannet returning, watched as it hung in the air with its sliver of silver before dropping to its nest, running the gauntlet of hostile beaks. She followed the bird with her camera so it became the still point, its long, black-tipped wings caught in an upbeat, the world around a blur.

'Daddy saw you,' Elsa said. She looked like some kind of sea elf, a creature that lived in the seaweed and only came out at low tide, her slender child body pale and goose-fleshed, her long hair caught, salt-sticky, across her shoulders. She was dressed in a cast-off swimming costume of Tom's, which would always be too large for her slight form, and as she ran across the sand, the wet knitted wool dragged in the wind, so that she seemed to be trying to leave its clumsy weight behind her.

'He's cross, but if you look after me near the waves he'll be better,' and she took hold of Jude's hand and tugged towards the water.

Jude looked over at the cliffs, the birds only slight lines in the sky from here, then over towards Leo and Sally's windbreak, set up far behind at the back of the beach. Leo was pouring from a thermos, Sally was taking things out of a bag and Tom was heaping sand nearby, busy with barricades.

'He could barely have seen me from that distance,' she said.

Elsa shrugged. 'But you were too close. He said so,' and letting go of Jude's hand, she set off towards the sea, running and jumping, high-stepping and awkward on the hard, rippled ridges of sand.

So Jude took off her boots, slung them up the beach and followed, slow with her photographic lumber. Elsa was only knee-deep, jumping the wave frills as best she could. The water was warm and clear, rising over the sand. She turned.

'No crabs?' she said.

Jude shook her head. 'Not here. Too much sand. They like the rocks,' and Elsa nodded, and turned back.

The waves reached up, darkening Jude's rolled trousers. Elsa was crouched low, peering down, one hand cupped to her eyes as if she could see more clearly through the waves that way.

Jude looked across the sea to the horizon. The boats out on that line. If you were standing on their decks, there'd be noise and motion, the sea alive beneath and the wind loud, raucous in the sails. But from here they were motionless. And if her photographs were good, the birds would be caught there, impeccable, suspended in their fierce movement. It wasn't so hard to hold things still, and the water was gentle round her legs. The boats weren't moving and the sun was warm. She could stand here a while, it wouldn't hurt. She shut her eyes. Elsa had moved a little further off, body still hunched, still intent on looking. She was making noises, small sounds of pleasure. The sun was bright on Jude's eyelids, hot in her hair, and the water was smooth, a caress against her calves. She could be lost in here for now.

But then the dizziness came. With her eyes closed, her body began to lose up from down, to confuse sky and sea. And Elsa's noises became louder till suddenly Jude knew it was not pleasure. She opened her eyes. Elsa was screaming, shouting something, but not at Jude. She was shouting at the sea, standing motionless, her arms caught tight below her chin, hands over her ears, eyes staring out towards that same horizon.

'Elsa,' Jude called. 'What is it?'

But she didn't answer, didn't move her hands from her head, didn't stop her screaming. Jude waded towards her, the sea dragging at her, now that she wanted to move faster. As she came close, she slowed, and then it was that she felt the tickling on her feet. She looked down and even through the waves and flurry she could see them. Dozens of little crabs, skittering sideways on their way else-where.

Jude lifted up the little girl and carried her towards the shore.

'It's all right now,' she said. 'You're out of the water.'

Elsa made no sound.

'They couldn't have hurt you, Elsa,' she said. 'They were barely big enough to tickle.'

Still Elsa made no sound, only hung from her in a limp fury, and when they reached the dry sand and Jude set her down, she ran from her up the beach towards the windbreak and her parents.

Jude followed behind slowly with her boots and bag, and watched Elsa climb into her mother's arms. Sally had made a castle of her groundsheet. Towel heaps made boundary stones and Tom's sandworks formed the outermost defensive wall. Inside, she was surrounded by the clutter of the picnic and neat piles of dis-carded clothes, mackintoshes, books, hats, a cricket bat, the newspaper weighted with a stone, Leo's glasses.

Jude had reached the highest of the tide lines by the time Leo met her. The bladder wrack was brittle and sharp under her feet. Swarms of tiny flies settled like bloom. Setting down her burdens, she picked up a piece of driftwood, smooth and light, took the weed from it. Leo stood before her as if facing her down over something.

'She was terrified,' he said.

'I know.'

'You shouldn't have said . . .'

'I wasn't trying to deceive her,' she said. 'Crabs don't live in sand.'

'You always act as if you're the only one in the landscape,' he said.

He was angry with her.

'What shouldn't I have done, Leo?'

'You take things too close,' he said. 'I saw you up on the cliff. And then Elsa running back so scared.'

'I'm going back,' Jude said. 'I'll see you tonight,' and she turned back towards the path inland.

Leo followed.

'But you haven't had any lunch,' he said.

And she shrugged, and left the beach.

Jude took the thin road away, high over the wolds. She held the motorbike tight to the road, taking the corners sharp on the inside, accelerating out of the bends. This she could do. First she rode the eight miles to Rudston where she stood before the megalith in the churchyard. High as a house, like a vast spearhead, nobody knew how it had got there in a time when they had no wheels, no iron, no machinery for such grand display. An old woman was bringing flowers to the church. Seeing Jude, she came up and whispered to her.

'It goes down into the earth as deep as it goes high into the air,' she said.

Jude stood up close and pressed her hands against the rough grey stone, traced the carvings of the weather. Then she was back on her bike and into the hills, dipping into villages, Wold Newton, Foxholes, Butterwick, Helperthorpe, through East Lutton and turning across Thirkleby Wold to Sledmere.

The memorials were close to each other, within shouting distance. The one on the village green, needle-sharp, pointed to the heavens. Its brassy armoured saints, facing out from the panels, knew nothing of what had gone on. The other one stood beside a coppice of beech trees, as sturdy as the men it remembered, or sturdier, since they had died so easily. From a distance it looked like a core of ancient column, like something found in Rome, raised up on stone steps, guarded by four smaller pillars, and point-capped with a great stone bullet head. Up closer and its carving told a tale, spiralling down. First there were the farm labourers, men from this place, high up on the column, steady with their rakes and pitchforks, bringing in the harvest; stooks of corn, wagons high with bales. Then enlistment and farewells, the journey to the war in boats. There was the battle with the ugly Huns, their bayonets lanced towards the sturdy waggoners, bullets like large bees in lines above their heads, and still the waggoners stood firm, as unyielding in the storm of battle as they had been beneath sun and rain. And at last their return, to take up their rakes and womenfolk again, though in truth few of them returned.

Maybe it was a good thing, to mark it down like this, carve it in stone, even if it was nothing like. Something to stand in for it all, something you could come to and look at, trace with your fingers: the wagon wheels, the little dog chasing after, the scowling enemy, the neat bullets. Except it didn't do for Jude.

She sat on the grass and thought to herself that she should go home. The sun was hot, and she took off her jacket, laid it beside her like a torso, arms flung out. The smell of the warm leather was comforting. An old man came and stood before the memorial. He carried a vast horse mushroom in his arms, cradling it as if it were a baby. Putting it down gingerly on the grass, he stood. Or maybe he wasn't that old, but he had had a son die; she knew that. One of those sturdy young waggoners who had taken the bee-bullet into himself. Or it could have been the bayonet's jag, the Hun thrusting so hard that he'd made a hole in the boy's chest, and the father in his fields still sowing his crops for his son's return. The old man stood before the column of stone, not seeming to look at it, his cap pulled down on his brow, eyes to the ground. Then he walked around it once and turned to Jude and nodded and made a noise that was maybe a cry, or a greeting, picked up the horse mushroom, nursing it again, and went on his way.

The sky was clear as day, no clouds to cover the sun. She rode home and in the evening lay on her bed and watched her square of blue darken, and the swifts' mad flight give way to the jagged dance of bats.

CHAPTER THREE

It was a week after the trip to the sea and Jude's hands were white with flour when the doorbell rang. The bread got delivered during the week, but on Saturdays, while Leo and Sally went into the city on errands, Jude liked to make it with Tom and Elsa. It had become a habit with them and sometimes they would experiment with different shapes, cottage buns, plaits, little knots, and sometimes it would be just loaves.

Jude always had the children roll up their sleeves when they helped her make bread, and, making a pile of her watch and signet ring at the end of the table, she warned them about getting dough stuck in watches and rings when they were older.

"Specially you, Elsa. If it's an engagement ring, imagine. Dough in the diamonds.'

As she kneaded the dough, she rolled her shoulders. 'Like this, remember?' she said, exaggerating for the children, playing the fool, so that they giggled together, but under the heels of her hands they saw the dough become shiny, elastic, and so they copied her. Then she'd gather the different pieces together and knead them into one, put the dough in the large bowl, cover it with a dish towel and put it in the airing cupboard to rise.

When the doorbell sounded, Jude crossed the kitchen to the scullery steps.

'Janey,' she yelled down. 'Can you get the door? My hands are . . .', and Janey came up the steps, her face red with the steam from the washing, pulling off her old apron, rolling down her sleeves, wiping her brow, taking her time.

'Sorry, Janey, it's only that,' and Jude rolled her eyes at the children, their hands deep in dough.

But when Janey opened the front door, Jude could hear the colour of her voice, its sullen irritation, and so, with her hands still white, she left the children in the kitchen and went to see who it was.

'Probably a tradesman,' she said to them. 'So he'll need rescuing. I think Janey was out of bed on the wrong side.'

She stopped and turned around before going out of the kitchen door, doing it slowly to give them time, but still she caught them both.

'I told you not to,' she said, her voice mock-ferocious, which had Tom smirking, his fingers still in the dough, but Elsa near to tears, the white gobbet sticky between her fingers. 'Your mother will not forgive me, she says it gives you a bad stomach,' and then she winked at them and allowed herself the pleasure of Elsa's smile.

'Janey, who is it?' Jude called.

'It's just a man,' Janey said, her face sullen.

'Just a man for what?'

Janey had almost shut the door on him by now.

'Wants to speak to Mr Hursten.'

'Perhaps I will do instead,' Jude said, and she pulled the door open again.

The man was walking away down the path and Jude noticed that his right leg pulled slightly. He was young, not more than twenty-two or three she guessed, quite tall and slightly built, and smartly dressed.

'Can I help you?' she said, her white hands up before her.

He turned back, his steps first uncertain, and then, as if he'd made a decision, bold. His limp didn't sit easily with him. It looked like something he was still reluctant to give way to. He had his hat pulled forward so that it wasn't until she spoke again, and he lifted his head, that she could see him.

'Excuse the flour,' she said.

Her first sight of his face, she had to look away, pretend that something, a bird, a dead flower, had caught her eye. She bent and peered down at the flower bed, then stood, the blush still full in her cheeks.

It wasn't that she mistook him. She could see he was different. Not Richard. But he was the same height, the same build, and, she didn't know why, but there was something about the way he had lifted his head that reminded her so strongly, she felt as if someone had punched her in the gut.

Jude thought that this was a man who never rested. He didn't seem agitated, it wasn't that, but it was as if he couldn't see enough. She watched him look at her, his eyes, which were, as she knew they must be, the deepest blue, probing, enquiring, seeking out the details of her face, glimpsing down at her trousers, her shoes, taking in her clothes, her hair, her floury hands. He noticed her scratch at a scrap of dough on her thumb, he saw the curls of hair escaped from her scarf, saw how one of them tickled her cheek, making her twitch her shoulder against her face, then tuck it behind her ear, leaving a dab of flour on her ear lobe. She knew that he saw all these things, even as he took the step forward, even as he spoke to her.

'I was hoping to speak to Mr Hursten,' he said.

He spoke tentatively, but also with determination, as if this wasn't easy, but he would do it anyway. She noticed now, because he was patting it, that he held a small, leather-bound notebook in one hand.

'He won't be in till later,' she said, and she hoped he didn't want to sell something to her, because she didn't want him to take his leave.

'Perhaps I could explain to you, then,' he said, and she nodded. She liked his voice. It was deeper than she'd have expected, from such a slim figure. 'I won't take more than a minute of your time. It's about a photograph.'

He opened the notebook, flipping the pages over as he spoke. There were pages full of birds, pencil-sketched. Some pages seemed to be given over to details: wings, beaks, feathers, claws; and on others she glimpsed birds in flight, or plucking at a worm, or perched in a tree. The drawings were rough, often partial. Sometimes there would be a landscape added, some water, once she glimpsed part of what looked like a low cottage, all a matter of a few line strokes.

'Just a moment,' he said, flipping through. He held the notebook out for her to see. 'It's only a sketch,' he said. 'I got down what I could. I know it's a long shot, but I discovered that it was Mr Hursten who took the photograph, and I'm hoping he might be able to remember more about it.'

Jude looked at the sketch. It was nothing dramatic. One man lying on a makeshift bed, another in officer's uniform giving him a cigarette, and a woman in man's clothes with a scarf over her hair, standing to one side. She noticed that he'd drawn in the medal one man wore on his chest and that he'd put in the shelf behind, with the OXO box and the bottles. They made a pleasing shape. She'd seen that too. And though he had only drawn the bodies in roughly, he must have been at pains with the faces because she knew them for real people.

The man was still speaking, explaining that it wasn't that he'd been there himself, but that he'd met one of the men afterwards, telling her that he'd been too young for the war though his brother had gone, saying he was sorry if he'd intruded at a weekend and could he call back later to see Mr Hursten. And Jude was going through all the motions of listening, still holding her white hands out from her sides, stiffly, like one of Elsa's dolls, till finally he stopped and she could tell him that it wasn't her brother Leo's photograph at all and that, in fact, Leo was here all through the war, on account of his chest.

'Oh,' he said, and it seemed as if all his energy left his body in that small sound and he was reduced, caved in. For a moment it looked as if he might fall, and reflexively, she put her hand on his arm to steady him, which he bridled from and she cursed herself for her clumsiness. She was out of practice. She had been about to say something else, but she checked herself and asked instead whether he wouldn't like a cup of tea. The unsaid words burned like a hot branch in her stomach.

'If you don't mind the children and the dough. And please do tell me your name.'

'Daniel Brown,' he said.

'Jude Hursten,' she said, putting out her floury hand. They shook hands, which seemed to Jude a little after the event by now, and the flour made Daniel's dark cuff cloudy. She noticed him brush it off and she noticed him smile.

The children had grown tired of kneading. Elsa was shaping little snakes and hearts, and Tom had made a battlefield, two dozen knobs of dough in pitched warfare. At first they didn't see Daniel, intent within their games. Not until Jude lifted the kettle onto the hob and asked Daniel whether he'd like to sit down. They looked up then, at the strange man in the kitchen.

'Is he Mister Ictharus?' Elsa asked.

Daniel raised one eyebrow at Elsa and she giggled. Jude laughed. 'This is Mr Brown,' she said. 'He's come to look at a photograph.'

Elsa nodded and went back to coiling snakes, but Tom watched as the strange man pulled out a chair, sat down. Tom looked at Jude, as if for direction, and she shrugged, turned to find cups and jug.

'Why are you limping?' Tom said.

Daniel picked up a piece of dough. It gave beneath his fingers. He rolled it into a marble, placed it on the table before him.

'An old injury,' he said.

'In the war?'

'No.'

'So you weren't a soldier?'

'No, I was. But not in the Great War.'

'So you didn't know Jude?' Elsa said. 'Or Mister Ictharus?'

'Here, tea,' Jude said. This man had some mystery behind him, and she was intrigued. She put the cup down in front of Daniel and picked up the flour dredger, shook it into the bread tin. 'Tom, finish the game. If you knead the bits together and put them in the tin, your parents will never know they're eating a battlefield. And we can bake your hearts,' she said to Elsa. 'Maybe wrap the snakes around themselves, make coil buns?'

She sent the children out into the garden with biscuits and milk, then sat at the table. Her visitor had bitten nails, and a signet ring on his right hand. He was still rolling the lump of dough beneath a finger.

'You were in the war?' he said.

'I was a nurse. I took the photograph,' she said.

He didn't look up. Didn't lift his eyes from the dough.

'I'll have the negative somewhere,' she said. 'I could probably find it and make you a print. I might remember more, too, if I saw it again myself.'

He didn't answer her at first, only drank the tea down like a man with a thirst. He didn't lift his eyes from the cup, wouldn't catch her glance. Jude looked down at the table, noticed a scurf of dough she'd missed with the cloth. If Leo were to return now, he'd be angry with her for asking this man in. She could imagine what he'd say to her, privately, not in front of anyone. He'd ask her if she'd thought of the danger. He'd remind her of the stories you heard, about war injuries and shell shock leaving men changed. Aggressive and violent in their moods where they used to be calm and gentle. He'd ask what if this stranger had attacked the children, or herself? And she wouldn't have anything to say in her defence, except that he reminded her of his friend, whom she'd loved.

'Could I have some more tea?'

Jude looked up at his voice.

'I seem to be parched,' he said.

Before Jude's return, the side shed was the place they stored the apples. They laid them out on the *Leeds Mercury* in September, a little air between each to prevent decay spreading, and the apples would last till the spring. When she was little, Leo used to tease her that those last, wizened apples, with their liver spots and dense, soft flesh, were really old people, enchanted by a wicked witch, so that even now, as an adult, she found it hard to eat them.

They'd picked apples in Belgium, too. Somehow, in that blasted place, the grass was still green beneath the two surviving apple trees. Kate found a wide basket, like a cradle. The apples were small red globes, not like the ones Jude knew from home. She sat down, leaned back on her hands. The grass was cool, scratchy. It held tiny wild blue flowers, not violets or speedwell, ones she didn't know.

'Get picking,' Kate called, and so Jude picked up an apple. It was rotten, and black, where she hadn't seen, with ants. Parting the grasses, she tracked them, a wavery, determined filament, to their hole, the earth bunkered up in grains around it. The ants processed in, tugging their particles of rotten apple, storing up their future.

Kate was in a tree, her weight making the branch creak. It was old, its bark hoary and knobbled, dappled green with lichens.

'Catch,' she said, but the apples were raining, so many small worlds coming down on Jude's head, and she scurried about, with none of the ants' steady composure, to gather them in.

The photograph Jude sent back home showed Kate standing in the sun, the basket at her feet piled with shiny fruit.

'They'd never guess,' she said.

The shed was Jude's darkroom now, and still beneath the chemicals she could often catch the mulching smell of old fruit, old vegetables. She'd promised Daniel Brown that she would do her best to find the negative that day and have a print ready by tomorrow, so after she watched his tilting figure off down the path, and without allowing herself to think about what she was agreeing to, she went there. She could hear the children far down the garden and through the trees she could see the flash of the swing rope.

On Jude's fourteenth birthday her father had given her a camera, a Leeds plate reflex camera. Not a point-and-shoot Box Brownie, which a few girls at school had, but a proper camera where you had to make the picture.

'We'd decided years ago it should be now,' he said. 'At this age.'

'Even before Mother was ill?' Jude said.

He nodded. 'Even before then.'

It came with instructions which she memorised that same day and which even years later she could recall verbatim. The camera had black bellows with chamfered corners, a twelve-plate plateholder and a square back. The plateholder could go in either way: vertically for upright or horizontally for landscape pictures, and there were lines marked out on the viewfinder for both. Behind the lens there was a mirror at forty-five degrees, which reflected the view back on to the focusing screen so that when you looked through the viewfinder, the picture was the right way up.

Jude pressed her head in on her father's shoulder, the heat rising to her face, her eyes.

'Now it'll be a box in front of your face, and not just your fingers,' her father said.

She couldn't trust herself to speak. So she lifted the camera up and looked down through the viewfinder. She didn't know how to use it, but that first movement was enough. She knew in her bones, in her arms and shoulders, in her neck curving down and her fingers braced with the weight, in the pressure of the darkness on her eye, that she needed this for herself.

Mr Hursten bought *Photography for Novices: The Primus Handbook* by Percy Lund and they followed his instructions to the letter to make a darkroom. They made a screen, edged with green baize and covered with canary and brown paper for the bathroom window, and a developing table to sit on the wash basin. A cylinder of canary paper placed over a candle was a darkroom light. Then there were dishes, trays and tanks, racks, scales and solutions, printing tray and papers, and a stool to sit on.

At first Jude lost more photographs than she made. She used too long an exposure and the image was fogged, or too short and the shadows had no detail, or her hands were too shaky, or she cut off the head, or the feet, or the tail of the dog. So she read up in *Photography for Novices* on how to prevent flare, or to avoid 'soot and whitewash' and sat on her stool into the small hours and brushed and immersed, soaked and blotted till the prints were hung, like smalls, to dry. And soon what she took was good, and something very different from the pleasing views, or well-balanced portraits, or harmonious landscapes that Mr Lund thought suitable.

She took people unawares. Her aunt's hands on the kitchen table, the skin loose with age and dusty with flour from bread-making.

Her father, stripped to the waist, working in his garden, though it was his back that caught her eye, shiny with sweat, the muscles still ridged up like plough lines. Leo and his friend Richard playing chess, neither young man aware of the fifteen-year-old girl watching.

From her bedroom window she photographed the street below, the children playing out, as she and Leo were never allowed to do, their games between the gas lamps and the kerbs. The line of the rope in its high arc over a girl skipping; a boy after a ball, one leg stretched out, elbows wide for balance; a girl with a kitten, holding it high by the tail, its body twisting. She began to learn the geometry of captured lines. And she loved the alchemy of a world changed to black and white.

She found she could be invisible with her camera. She could be seeing, but not seen. Like an insect which impersonates its surroundings to fool predators, she could become the bark and leaf, the stick and the shade of the place, so that where before she had been timid, now she could be fearless. It was true, if she stood in the street for too long, people would start to ask her what she was up to, and little children would pester. But only for a moment, only till the adults checked their watch and hurried on; and the puppy, or the loose ball, or the muffin man, caught the children's eye, and then she'd be unnoticed again.

Daniel Brown was just a man asking about a photograph, Jude told herself. And all she was doing was making him a copy. It was generous of her, but nothing more. Anybody would have done it in her place. With the children's voices in her ears, still arguing over the swing, she went to open the darkroom door. A spider had spun its way across; the web was so fine it left no shadow in the sun, and no flies yet, or none that Jude could see. She thought at first that the spider was basking, but when she looked closer she saw that it was braced, legs tense. As she watched, it plucked at two spokes of web, waited a second, then turned and plucked the next two, waited, and turned again. It had made almost a complete circuit and she could see no flies caught yet to shiver at its tug, but on the sixth, the spider knew otherwise. It

74

plucked again at the web and then, too quick for Jude's eyes, it pounced.

The fly was a small one, its agitation barely visible, but the *coup de grâce* was performed with the aplomb you might expect for something more resplendent, a bluebottle or a bee. The fly was trussed and dragged to one side, tight into the joint of the door. Jude watched it all through, no corners cut by the spider in securing its dinner, before she opened the door, broke up the spider's pattern.

CHAPTER FOUR

Daniel returned to the house the next morning. He rang on the bell and this time a tall, big-boned man came to the door, stooping as if trying to be smaller. He put out his hand.

'Leo Hursten,' he said. 'I know who you are. It's been explained,' and he ushered Daniel in.

There was the smell of roasting meat, and he could hear a child's voice somewhere chanting a rhyme.

'If you could wait a moment,' Leo said, leaving Daniel in the hall.

The child's rhyme came closer. On the wall there were prints of Fountains Abbey and York Minster. The day before, at a loose end after his visit to the house, he'd taken a train to the moors and walked across the heather, found a stream and dipped his feet as he used to as a boy. So that today, after all that walking, his leg was very sore and he leaned heavily on his stick.

When the child appeared – he couldn't remember her name – she stopped her singing and looked hard at him, his stick, the angle he was leaning at.

'Why don't you sit on the chair?' she said, and when he had sat down, she nodded, like a job well done, resumed her rhyme and went on her way.

He heard doors open and close, felt the brush of a draught against his trousers, and Jude appeared. She walked into the room as though it were the place above all she needed to be. She wore a blue print cotton dress that caught and drifted at her hips, and the dark curls of her hair were loose, corkscrewing to her shoulders.

She flicked it from her face in a way that reminded him of a horse flicking its tail, something habitual and yet graceful. She was holding two envelopes.

'I've made your print,' she said without preamble. 'It's a good one.'

They sat in silence at the dining-room table with the photograph between them and Daniel wondered how to ask the questions in his mind.

'It is the one you were looking for?' she said.

He nodded. 'Yes.'

'And you know one of the men?'

'Yes. I know one. And the other, I think I've seen the other man, too.'

'Is he still alive? The one you know?'

Daniel shook his head. 'But he didn't die in the war. Not there.'

'And the woman? Do you recognise her?'

Daniel shook his head again. 'She's a nurse?' he said, a little unsure, because she wore no uniform.

Jude's questions had come thick and fast to here. She wasn't aggressive, but she wasted no time. Now she stopped, brought up short by Daniel's query. He recognised the look in her eyes and he waited.

Finally Jude nodded. 'I knew her very well.'

Daniel shifted in his chair. He leaned back and looked around the room. Strange, that his visit to the exhibition should have brought him here, to Yorkshire, to this room in a house in a place he didn't know. To this woman who was beautiful, but who either didn't know or had forgotten it. The room was hot, and he took off his jacket, pulled up his sleeves till the cufflinks were taut.

'So,' he said. 'Can I ask you? I know it's a few years back, and the war was its own time, but . . .'

Jude made no answer immediately. Daniel shut his eyes. He hadn't slept well the previous night and he felt bone-tired. It was a wild goose chase, this. Probably he should put away his boldness, take his leave and go back home.

When Jude started speaking, he thought at first she was talking about the children.

'They'd been playing on the see-saw earlier that same day, those two,' she said.

He opened his eyes, looked at her. She was still staring at the photograph.

'The see-saw?'

'We'd put it up beyond the house, on a bit of clearer ground. Peter's doing. He'd used a long, long plank, so you could go very high, and cobbled two saw-horses he'd come across. It was madness really, except no one ever did get hurt. Bruises, but nothing else. The newspapers wouldn't publish my photographs of the see-saw. It gave the wrong impression, they said. Leo sent them out to several. The Germans had a game with us sometimes, taking pot-shots at the man at the top. That's how close to the front line we were.

'So these two and a couple of others had been trying to bounce each other off. They had a fine game, and then it was back to the trenches, and later on it was the one brought the other in wounded. He was leaning for Pisa and his blood all over the other's uniform. He had caught some shrapnel in the stomach, the worst place, been stuck in no man's land a while. So we took it out and dressed the wound. And he kept on about the officer rescuing him and could we rinse his tunic.'

'Colonel Whittam,' Daniel said. 'He was the man injured. Except he wasn't a colonel then. So did you take the photograph that day?'

'The next, I'd guess. The fellow, Whittam, looks too perky, and he wouldn't have been good for much the same day.'

'Did you find out how he was rescued?' Daniel leaned forward over the photograph as if to see inside.

Jude pushed her chair out and walked to the window. Daniel looked at her. He tried to remember how she had looked the day before, but all he could conjure were her hands covered in flour, and an apron. And her hair. Those tight black curls.

'What exactly do you want?' She was up close to the window and her voice was muffled by the glass, so that Daniel couldn't tell her tone. 'I don't know what I think about you,' she said. 'Or only that it's strange, having you in my home when I know next to nothing about you. Or even why you're here. I didn't know quite what to say to my brother and his wife last night. And there are the children. It's not as if you're asking for something easy, is it?'

She turned from the window and looked at him, one hand in her hair as if wrestling with the dark mass of curls. He looked down at his knees. He didn't know how to answer her.

'Ha!' She was grinning now. 'There's a speech for you,' she said.

'You're right,' Daniel said. 'A strange man with a strange request. I might have done anything.'

'You might,' Jude said, 'though it wasn't that that was bothering me.'

'But you don't know. You can't tell from the outside what some-body might be. I know now the thing that I was dreading, the worst thing of all. That they knew each other, were even friends.'

Jude laughed. 'There's a problem with friendship? Anyway, I'm not about to start thinking you're a murderer or a kidnapper, if that's what you mean.'

'I should go,' Daniel said. 'Go back home and leave you be.' Jude looked at him nonplussed as he started to get to his feet. 'You've been very generous. Before I leave, could I buy . . .' and he nodded in the direction of the photograph.

'I didn't mean the conversation to take such a turn,' she said. 'I was only asking to know a little more about you. And you can't buy it, though I will give it to you.'

'Is that what you do?' he said. 'For a living?'

'I'm a typist,' she said.

'A typist by day, and . . .'

'What?'

'And in the war? What kind of a nurse were you, to be so close to the front line, and the see-saw?'

'We set up a first-aid station.'

'Who?'

'Me, and another nurse. Kate.'

'Is she a typist now, too?' Daniel's tone was facetious.

'No.'

Daniel paused before speaking again.

'You shouldn't be tapping keys all day. Not when you can take photographs like that.'

Jude put the photograph and the clipping back in their envelope. Then she opened a cigarette box, offered it to Daniel, who shook his head. 'No manners,' she said. 'I haven't even offered you a glass of sherry. Nearly noon on a Sunday.' She lit a cigarette and drew deeply.

Jude held the cigarette loosely. She'd smoked only half of it and Daniel watched the glow travel up towards her fingers.

'But you must explain more,' she said, 'if you don't leave.'

He wondered if the little girl had been listening at the door, to knock at this moment.

'Mummy wants to know, will your visitor be staying for lunch?'

'Thank you, Elsa,' Jude said. She turned to Daniel. 'Will you?'

Jude had no appetite for lunch and she watched the conversation around the table as if from another room, the voices – Leo's, Daniel's, Sally's – sounding far away and unconnected. Her mind was snagged somewhere in the photograph, caught on something, and she couldn't pull it free. From a distance she watched Leo carve the joint and count out the potatoes. He had the same way of doing these things as she did, she knew this without thinking. Steadying his feet and dipping his head as if to block out the world while carving, just as she had done over the live bodies jolted down into her cellar. To focus so that nothing else existed. Whereas this stranger at their dinner-table with his eyes that never rested, she would guess that his glance always went wide. He was talking with Sally now. She was questioning him. Safe questions: Where did he come from? Did he like the suburbs? Had he any brothers or sisters?

She watched him as he ate. One hand was tucked below the table, but the other, his left, had escaped and fidgeted with his fork, turning and turning it. She could see the muscles in his forearm shift, like lines of current in the sea. He had a high brow, the hair drawing back already, and more on one side than the other. That would impress Leo, she thought, who had a theory she didn't believe in about intelligence and the size of your forehead.

'Jude, please, would you mind?' Leo was handing her a spoon. 'Make sure you give them both plenty of beans.'

'And what do you do for a living?' she heard Sally asking bluntly, and his pause.

'He's a soldier,' Elsa said. 'It's why he's got the stick.'

Tom put his hand to his forehead. 'Stupid, the stick's why he's not a soldier.'

'Don't call Elsa stupid,' Sally said. 'And eat your beans.'

Jude noticed Daniel's small smile.

'They're delicious beans,' he said.

'They're Father's,' Tom said, and now Elsa rolled her eyes.

'They're not his. They don't belong to him.'

'He knows what I mean,' Tom said.

Jude heard Sally's voice grow stern, noticed Leo's brow, watched Daniel's polite ignoring of the family argument. She saw her plate of food, the meat and potatoes, the slight skim on the cooling gravy, the sliced beans. She saw the shape of her lip where the sunlight struck through her glass, the smear on her knife from the meat. She didn't want to be in the house, in amongst the family, any longer, and she thought that she would go somewhere after lunch where the light was sharp, somewhere which belonged to no one.

'I'm going to take Daniel up to the Rocks after lunch,' she said. 'He'd like to see them.' She looked at Daniel. 'You'll be all right, in the sidecar? Being tall, I mean?'

'Fine, yes.' His face was bemused, but he didn't ask anything.

'Can't we come too?' Elsa's voice was shrill. 'Daddy? Can't we go too? You could take us in the motor car?'

'Not today,' Leo said.

'But please. I want to show him the hermit cave.'

Leo shook his head and Elsa hunched over her plate and scowled. Jude wished the meal were over. Tom was lining up the food around his plate. She set her eyes on the far wall.

'Tom, please eat your beans.' Sally's voice was fiercer than the beans warranted. Tom put some in his mouth. He sat suddenly straight and tapped Daniel on the shoulder.

'And the leaping rock,' he said, his mouth a mash of green. 'Did she tell you about the leaping rock?'

'Tom, please,' Jude said.

'Did she tell you?'

'It wouldn't be something he could do,' Jude said.

'It's in her box of pictures,' Tom said. 'A man leaping from it.'

'Barely more than a boy,' Jude said quietly.

'But he died in the war,' Elsa said, cutting vainly at her meat.

'Mr Icarus?' Daniel said, but he didn't look at Jude, and he didn't ask her to explain.

It had only been at the last minute that Leo couldn't come too. Some business at home, he told Jude, and she and Richard should go on anyway, he'd squared it with Father. She was disappointed, but relieved, because she had something in mind that she wanted and she couldn't bear to wait for longer to try to achieve it. So she groaned for him, and felt glad for once to be a girl, whom business never detained. And it was only later she saw that it must have had to do with their father's last illness. That he would have known by then, though he hadn't told his son. So she had packed her picnic and her camera bag and gone to meet Richard.

'Leo can't come,' she said. 'So it's just me, unchaperoned, and my camera.'

'Of course, your camera,' Richard said.

They had taken the train as far as they could, and then walked. High cloud flattened the light. The landscape seemed subdued, suspended, as if the fields and the hedgerows were waiting for something to bring them to life. The camera bag was heavy and the strap cut into Jude's shoulder. On the train, seated beside one another, their hands on their laps, they had talked of anything. Of the *Titanic* and Home Rule for Ireland and votes for women. About war with Germany and Scott reaching the South Pole. But now, on the empty road, walking into the moors, everything seemed used up and so Jude was silent, at a loss, and Richard whistled a tune she didn't know.

They were nearly to the Rocks before either of them spoke. Jude glimpsed them through a break in the hedge a half mile ahead.

'So what's it to be this time?' Richard said. He had cut some grass from the hedgerow and now he draped it over his head. 'I'd be very fetching as a girl,' and he posed so that Jude couldn't help herself but laugh.

'A pity Leo won't let you take him,' he said. 'He hasn't given in?'

She shook her head.

'He was cross when he saw I'd shot him unawares.'

'So you'll have to make do with me. I'm glad I'm useful for something. Thank God I can strike such good poses,' and he affected to walk a tightrope before dropping the picnic basket and turning a cartwheel into the ditch, his body seeming to be all angles, elbows and knees, yet oddly graceful.

Jude laughed. 'I want to take you in flight,' she said. 'That's why Leo suggested the Rocks.'

'In flight?'

'Leaping. Close as we can get.'

He flapped his arms. 'No wings. So I'll be falling.'

'It depends,' Jude said. 'Whether you think you're falling as soon as you leave the ground. Even at the moment you're jumping up.'

'Like dying, then,' he said. Jude looked at him. 'As soon as we're born, we're on our way to it,' and he grinned, as if to disarm her, then set off striding on.

Later Jude wondered how it was that somebody who was just one part of your landscape could, so suddenly, fill the centre of your eye. She stood absolutely still on the road and, as though her gaze might consume him, she looked away from Richard's back, and down. An ant pulled an ear of grass over a twig and a moth paid homage to the ground, its yellow wings spread like a favour. Jude closed her eyes. The feeling in her chest was more like a fury than a pleasure and she clenched her fists, then followed after the slender form of the man she would have fly.

Four times Richard leapt, his feet bare, his shirt pressed tight to his chest in the wind, and Jude photographed him, his body high above the rocks. Each leap, he seemed balanced in air and there was time enough and more. But when Jude developed the negatives that night, setting the four plates to drain in the rack, she saw that she had caught him only once. She made the print, then knocked on her brother's door.

'Look,' she said, handing him the print, and Leo looked at the figure, no arms, no head, who seemed to be leaping at the sun. She watched him and saw that she had told more than she meant to of her feelings.

'Like Icarus,' he said. 'Be careful, Jude.'

Jude gave Daniel a pair of goggles and one of Leo's old sweaters, slipped her bag down by his feet and fitted the tarpaulin over him. He was embarrassed, she knew, by the intimacy this demanded, her fingers tugging the loops over the hooks beside his hips, her breath close to his face.

'It can be cold in that sidecar, even on a day like this,' she said. 'Especially with a strong wind.'

'Do you often do this with strangers?' Daniel said.

'I usually ask them to be wounded first,' she said with a laugh.

Away from the town, and even with the wind, the landscape looked slick with heat. Cattle swam in the grass and the sky was bleached of colour. The rocks were an island rising high above them until, at the last, the road dipped its head before turning and climbing to reach them.

Jude knew from Daniel's face, when he took off his goggles, that the ride had left him free, as it had her. She unhooked the tarpaulin, folded it to carry, and offered him an arm for climbing out.

'I used to feel like this, riding a horse,' he said.

'We can walk round to the top,' she said. 'There's a stile.'

Daniel nodded, and she wondered what it was she hoping for, bringing him here. They walked slowly round the lower rocks and Jude pointed out 'The Eagle' and 'The Camel', 'The Dancing Bear' and 'The Yoked Man'. They passed the rock she had stood below that day, waiting, with her camera ready, for the figure leaping at the sun. But she didn't name it to Daniel.

The wind was loud and warm around them, and the tossing air smelt of gorse and honeysuckle.

'There was a place in Ireland that I loved, made me feel like this,' he said. 'They were high up on their hill. Three stones only, and man-made, but ancient. You could feel apart, standing there beside them.'

'I saw a kite here,' she said.

'A red kite?'

'Thought it was a buzzard, that "wheeo" sound. But when I looked up, there it was. That forked tail. It was a day like today, and I watched it swing across the wind.'

She saw that he was flagging, leaning harder on the stick, studying the craggy ground carefully at each step.

'The other side of that rock,' she said. 'Tom's hermit cave.'

The ground was worn to dust, littered with sheep droppings. Jude spread the tarpaulin and Daniel sat down heavily, one leg out straight before him, the other bent up, and he looked out at the hill rising behind, the bent trees, the straggle of sheep, the gorse's sweet yellow. His fingers found a small smooth stone in the dust, and without even looking at it, he slipped it into his pocket. Jude squatted the other side, her boots flurrying the dust into heaps and troughs for a moment. She looked across at Daniel, this stranger she'd brought up here.

'That photo,' she said. 'What are you after?'

Daniel had moved barely a muscle, only his eyes blinking in the wind. She licked her finger, dipped it in the dust, a smooth grey oval, rubbed it away and settled down to wait. She didn't look across at him, but set her eyes to the hill. A flurry of little birds worried the gorse away in the middle distance, the size of sparrows, though they weren't. This time tomorrow she'd be at a typewriter in that high-up room, typing away as if her life depended on it, taking her lunch in a tea-shop with the other girls, boiled egg, treacle roll, scrubbing the ink from her fingers at night. That's something Sally wouldn't believe, what a dirty job it is, being a typist. Somewhere, thunder rolled and she noticed that the wind had dropped.

'We weren't allowed secrets when we were small.' Daniel's voice was quiet and steady. Jude looked over to him. Although she knew he was speaking to her, it was as though he were speaking to himself, his eyes focused on the grey rock. She waited for him to go on.

'It wasn't done. Mother told us that very clearly. Not if you were a little boy. And to be caught with one, it was worse than being caught with your hand in the biscuit barrel.'

'But I'm not your mother,' Jude said. 'And anyway the biscuit barrel loses its gleam once you grow up.' She stood up. 'I'm not leaving, it's only my feet are going numb.'

He smiled and looked down at his leg stretched before him, rubbed it absent-mindedly. She hoped he wouldn't go on with the childhood memory because she didn't feel very patient.

'All right,' he said, and now his voice was resolute, as if he'd come to a decision, and he looked straight across at Jude. 'I don't know what I know.'

The air hung very heavy and the clouds were banked high and rimmed with coarse purple. The sheep had gathered themselves into a corner and the air seemed suddenly full of tiny, haranguing flies. Jude shook out a cigarette packet, offered it across. Daniel shook his head.

'Against the bugs,' she said, lighting up.

'Ireland wasn't like the trenches. You never knew who the enemy was,' Daniel said. 'Or where. It was all hell let loose but you couldn't see it.'

'And Colonel Whittam?' Jude said.

'He was my commanding officer. He'd had a good war, though it didn't count for much over there. Maybe made things harder, though he was very clear to us. We were to obey orders, stick together, and let the politicians do the thinking. If we did that, we'd be doing nothing wrong, clean consciences. But it wasn't true. The men who thought it was important for the cause, what we did, maybe they've had a better time with it. But those things you do, the dirty things, they come out of you, but they still stay inside.

And they're in no cause, that's what's terrible, and afterwards all you can do is hide. Maybe that's what I've been doing.'

'You wouldn't be the only one,' Jude said.

Daniel looked at her. She had her head turned away. He rubbed his face. She was such a mix to him already with this reluctant vulnerability and her fierce directness.

'And the day I was injured, there's a thing that still troubles me, but it's the other fellow, the standing one. There's something about him. Though if I look at him full on, then it goes.'

'Where were you then?' Jude's voice was quiet, low.

'Cork. County Cork. For a year, just over, back before the Truce.'

'I don't know a lot about Ireland,' Jude said. 'But it didn't sound like an easy war to be fighting.'

'No.'

Jude turned and looked at him. He was defiant now, as though she'd said something to attack him, but his face, his cheeks and his eyes, looked hollowed out, emptied of something. She looked at her cigarette. She could draw one more lungful, and she shut her eyes, breathed in deep, felt her lungs fill with smoke. Sometimes she wanted to go back inside her old shell, become a snail again and look at the world from a distance, her eyes outside her.

'It was a bloody horror,' he said, 'and nobody over here knows a thing or gives a damn. And so far nor do I, except in my dreams.' He shifted his leg. 'Which is maybe just as well.'

Jude wondered what it was he knew in his dreams that he couldn't know when he was awake. She wondered whether Richard had had dreams like that. She flicked her cigarette butt into the dust.

'And now you've come all this way north to look out of the corner of your eye?' she said. 'You don't do that just because somebody looks familiar.'

She saw him pause and then decide something before he replied. She could see it in his face and the thought went through her head that she was noticing a great deal about someone she'd only met the day before.

'It's funny,' Daniel said. 'We used to call him "The Trout",

Colonel Whittam. Not to his face, but he knew it anyway. Partly it was because of his fishing, and partly his face. And now I'm on his hook and I can't get free.'

Jude knew then that he wasn't going to tell her. She didn't know what, only that he'd come to a decision and was giving her the easy story. She'd heard plenty of men doing that. It was a necessary part, an awkward part, of surviving. And if he wasn't telling her, she would do the same. She knew more than she would say to him about those two men.

The rain had started, coming straight down, steady, putting a veil beyond the rocks. Daniel looked out from inside their cave. The world beyond had gone dim.

'I came up here on a whim, I suppose,' he went on. 'Hoped that if I found the photographer, they'd remember something. Anyway, it's been a good excuse to get away from home.'

'Were you injured over there?'

'Motor lorry accident in the fog,' he said, too quickly she thought. 'Bloody Crossley! Invalided out, thank God.' Then he laughed.

'What is it?' Jude said.

'Actually, it wasn't an accident,' he said. 'It's just what I've always said. Got used to saying. Had to at first, and then it was just easier. A bit ignominious, if you're a soldier, but easier.'

Jude waited.

'It was an ambush. First time I've told anyone.'

'Even your family?'

He nodded. 'We were ambushed, and I was the only one, nearly, who came out alive. They left me for dead and they'd have hunted me down if they'd known I wasn't.'

'But not any more?'

'No. They've got better things to do over there now. But the letter that arrived nearly did for my mother. She thought it was to say I'd been killed. Couldn't open it, left it in the hall all day till my father came home. It's all she expects, all she's waiting for, since Johnnie died.'

'Johnnie?'

'My brother.'

'He was killed in the war?' Jude said, and Daniel nodded.

'So what will you do now?' she said.

He shrugged. 'Go home. And die for lack of air.' He laughed. 'I've got a bit of work to do for my father. And I'll get a train south on Tuesday.'

'A wild goose chase.'

'Dead end.'

She drove him back to The Green Man. He took off Leo's sweater.

'I'll send you my address,' he said, 'in case.'

Unsure how to take their leave, they shook hands on the pavement. Jude took an envelope from her bag.

'The photograph,' she said, giving it to him. And not knowing how to tell him that she'd known men like him, that she knew things went wrong in war, not knowing how to say that it wasn't something she usually did, taking men up to the Rocks, showing them photographs like that, not knowing what to do with the urge she felt to put a hand to his face, or his hair, to stand near to him and feel the length of his body against hers, not knowing what to do with the thought that she liked this man powerfully and the wounds and scar-tissue did nothing to diminish this, not knowing what else to do, she climbed back onto the motorcycle and was gone.

In the weeks that followed, nothing seemed to happen to Jude. Daniel sent his address, as promised, and his thanks. He made no mention of any photograph. It was a dull, formal note. He might more likely have been thanking her for her contribution to some charity drive, she thought, than for the time they'd spent, but she put the letter away carefully in a drawer in her room, pushing it back into its envelope, tucking it in under her writing paper. It seemed unlikely she would ever have reason to contact him again and the thought made her feel hopeless in her life.

The weather remained quite warm and she was exercised by the difficulty of not appearing at work with sweat rings under her arms. A girl had been dismissed the previous year for this. She had begun to take more dictation, now they had found out about her

French, and this made the job slightly less irksome. But still, if she stopped long enough to think, she couldn't believe that this was what she was doing.

At home she fended off the questions about Daniel, which wasn't hard since nothing had gone on, but still they made her very cross. It was an odd mission he'd been on, she told them, she couldn't help him further, and he'd gone home to his life in London. That was all there was to it. And having sent Tom off with a flea in his ear, made Elsa cry and snubbed Sally and Leo into silence over dinner, Jude thought that surely there would be an end to it. She even told herself that it was all no more than a curious quirk, a brief postscript to her war time.

Whatever it was that had brought Daniel Brown to find her, she knew it was something grave, even if he was telling her the truth and didn't yet know what it was himself. She knew the sound of it, recognised it. Richard's last letter had had something of the same quality. He had shot unarmed men, prisoners of war, men whose arms had been raised in surrender. He'd been under orders, he should have disobeyed and now he must live with it. But then he had died on the wire and she would never know how he might have lived with it, or how she might have done.

It wasn't just natural curiosity that made her hope she'd see Daniel again. Nor, oddly, was it only that she liked him, or pitied him. She had been let off the hook, spared something with Richard's death, despite her grief, and she didn't want to be. She didn't know what had happened to Daniel, or how far he had gone beyond the bounds of war. But she wished, whatever it was that had gone on, that he would break the silence.

CHAPTER FIVE

Some weeks went by and Jude's life settled again. It was Friday evening and she was going out. Elsa sat on the bed, swinging her heels. Jude sat beside her in her slip, unpinned her hair and started to brush it out. It spat and crackled.

'Can I do it?' Elsa said.

'If you're gentle.' Jude gave her the brush. With one hand on Jude's head, Elsa began to brush. Jude shut her eyes. It was an age since anyone else had done this for her.

'Who is he?' Elsa said.

'Martin Dawes. You've seen him before.'

'Is he your boyfriend? Will you marry him?'

'Elsa, for goodness' sake.'

'Does Daddy know him?'

'I've known him since I was five and we played tea-parties together on the lawn.'

'Did Daddy play too?'

'No. He broke up the party. And we went crying to our mothers and Leo got told off.'

'Is he coming here to get you? Will I see him?'

Jude wagged a finger. 'Don't mention the tea-party.'

Elsa giggled. 'What if I do? What if I say it to him when he comes in?'

'Then I'll do the same to you when you have a boyfriend.'

'So he is a boyfriend.'

'No. He's not.'

'He's Mr Ictharus's brother, isn't he,' Elsa said.

Jude turned towards Elsa, so that the brush caught at the fine hair on her nape.

'Ouch!'

'You moved. Anyway Mummy told us. She said he was very kind.'

'What exactly did she . . .' Jude said, then checked herself. 'Will you fetch the pins? On the shelf.'

Elsa had arranged Jude's clothes on the bed. Blouse with its arms out, skirt, stockings stretched like snake skins, wrap over the shoulders, paste-pearl necklace over the hollow of the neck, earrings each side of the pillow, shoes like clown's feet at the bottom.

'Now you can climb inside,' she said. 'Like a ghost, putting on a body.'

'Thank you,' Jude said, amused, disconcerted.

'Are they real pearls?'

'No. Paste. But pretty still.'

'Don't the earrings hurt, clipping on?' she said.

'Try them.'

Jude laughed as the little girl attached the first, wincing, solemn-faced.

'Pretty,' Jude said. 'Look in the mirror.'

The second earring tumbled from the bed and rolled underneath.

'I'll get it,' Elsa said.

She came out swimming, dust balls gathered in her hair like weed. She had the lost earring in one hand and something square and tarnished in the other.

'Look!' Elsa's voice was breathless. 'Buried treasure. What is it?'

'Let me see,' Jude said, stepping towards her. Elsa held her hand tight round the object and Jude smiled at the little girl's conflict, the right of possession at war with her curiosity.

'If you'll let me see, then maybe I can tell you.'

Elsa put the object down on the table. She rubbed at it, solicitous, and wiped the blackened finger on her dress.

'So?' she said, peremptory, and Jude stepped over to the table.

Where Elsa had rubbed, the metal gleamed and the beginnings of a pattern showed through. Jude looked and felt a small punch to her stomach. She picked it up and rubbed at the tarnish.

'You'll have your hand mucky for going out,' Elsa said, disapproving.

'Do you see now what it is?'

Elsa shook her head. Jude flipped open the lid.

'Oh!' Disappointment had winded the little girl. 'It's not gold then.'

'No. It's a . . .'

'I know. It's a cigarette lighter.' Elsa walked to the door.

'What about my clothes?'

'I'm bored. I'm going in the garden.'

'Leave me my earring then,' Jude said.

Zig-zags cut across one side of the tarnished brass, and there was a date, 1916. She turned it over, and on the other side were two clasping hands and a four-leafed clover.

'I know you,' Jude said, turning the lighter in her hand. 'And I'd forgotten you.'

So many men had made these things, she'd seen dozens of them: lighters and vases, cigarette cases, ashtrays. Peter had made a paper knife out of a piece of shrapnel and a lighter from German belt buckles, 'Gott Mit Uns' carved around the edge, and he'd taken home a dinner gong made out of a howitzer shell, though Jude couldn't imagine him using it in the little flat he'd described. But this lighter had been Kate's first, a gift from a wounded soldier, carved from a shell casing.

She should be dressing. She should be making her face up ready for the evening, preparing to smile, to be grateful.

Jude flipped it open and struck the flint, felt its soft grind. Kate didn't smoke, but she'd always carried a lighter for the men's cigarettes. Jude smiled. There had been a way Kate had of reaching forward with it, eyes almost averted, as if she were embarrassed at being brought so close to another person's mouth. And then she'd shut it off too soon, before the cigarette was lit, and have to start again.

'Don't whip it away so fast,' Jude told her. 'Let them get a proper drag.'

'I keep forgetting.'

'So take up smoking,' Jude said. 'Then you'd get the hang of it.'

'I don't like the smell.'

'It's better than most of the smells here.'

'But you don't stick them in your mouth and suck,' Kate said.

So Jude had had her practise. She'd lean across from her camp bed, cigarette between her lips, leering, and Kate, face set, stern, would try to hold the lighter steady, try not to jerk it away as Jude's face loomed in closer.

Jude stood the lighter on the table. 'Let's see if you still work,' she said, and found her lighter fluid, refilled the tank. She struck the flint again and the spark caught, almost transparent in the early evening sun. Turning her back to the sunlight, she cupped her hand around it and watched the steady flame.

She put the lighter in her bag. Checking her face in the glass, she went downstairs. Martin Dawes was waiting, smoking a cigarette with Leo in the garden. The evening was warm and both men were in shirtsleeves. Jude thought how solid Martin looked, how confidently he stood there, feet planted apart, one hand in a pocket, tipping the ash onto the lawn.

Martin offered Jude a cigarette, lit it for her, and she kissed him on the cheek, and remembered that he wore the same eau de Cologne as his brother used to, and then remembered, blushing, how his brother's cheek felt.

The men talked on for a few minutes, trading local business news, opinions on house building schemes. Jude watched Martin scuff up the gravel with his toe, brush the dust from his shoe. He had been kind to her after Richard died, Sally was right to tell Elsa that. The two brothers had gone to the war together and only he had come back. She'd never told him about Richard's last letter to her.

But it wasn't kindness that she wanted. When he turned to her, she smiled and nodded.

'We must go, or we'll miss the start of the picture,' she said.

'What is it?' Leo said.

Martin shrugged. 'What are we going to see, Jude?'

'*Safety Last*. A Harold Lloyd picture.'

'Enjoy yourselves,' Leo said, and waved them off as if they were going on a journey rather than a date.

The difficulty started at the cinema. They'd been to films before, sat side by side, knees together, hands in laps, only the accidental brush of an elbow or the passing of the chocolates to connect them, and Jude had been quite content with it. She hadn't minded the courting couples on either side, the shifting and shuffling, the rustle of petticoats as hands reached over the arm-rest and under the skirt; the heads caught kissing in the glow of the film romance. But tonight she did mind, though she couldn't have said why, and she was twitchy, uncomfortable in her seat.

'Do you want to leave?' Martin put his hand over hers on the arm-rest.

She shook her head and took her hand away.

'I hate leaving the pictures early.'

So they stayed till Harold Lloyd was down on the ground again and had Mildred Davis in his arms, then Jude was up and out, before the lovers around them surfaced.

'Where'd you get it?' They were at a corner table in Giacomelli's. Jude would have liked to go somewhere bigger, noisier, somewhere more impersonal, but it hadn't been up to her. Martin reached across the table for the lighter. He flicked it on, the flame lighting up his fingers. And off, and on, and off. 'Somebody else taking you out to the pictures? Man from the office, maybe?'

'You'll use up the fluid. I don't think there's that much in it.'

He turned it over in his hand. 'Not a bad piece of work. Though I did see better when I was over there. This one, it looks like it was done by an amateur.'

'I don't know who made it. Let's choose some food.' Jude put her hand out for the lighter.

Martin opened his menu.

'Rack of lamb for me, and why don't you have the sole,' he said and he flicked her menu shut and turned, his fingers raised, to catch a waitress.

'Martin,' Jude said, and he didn't answer, but perhaps he didn't hear her with his head turned.

'Martin,' she said, louder. 'I haven't chosen my food yet.' She opened the menu again. 'Give me back my lighter.'

He turned back to the table and, looking hard at Jude, put his hand out, palm flat. Jude took the lighter, put it on the table, and looked back at him.

'What's possessed you?' she said.

'You loved my brother,' he said, 'but it was me who came back.'

'And so?'

'And so maybe . . .' He tapped a finger on the table. 'I lost him too.'

'I know, Martin. I know it isn't only me. I'm sorry. I don't mean to sound as if . . .'

'So cut me a bit of slack, then. I know I'm not the same as Richard, but you could do a lot worse, so maybe . . .'

'I'll have the steak,' she said.

'You might love me instead,' he said. 'Perhaps we could comfort each other, that way,' and then he asked again, but quietly, as if to distract her from these words, 'Who gave you the lighter?'

'It wasn't Richard,' Jude said.

'I know it wasn't Richard. He couldn't carve his name on a tree, let alone . . . But your mind's elsewhere. You haven't been with me all evening.'

'We're friends, Martin. But I'm not in love with you, and even if I were, I wouldn't want you choosing my food.'

'And the lighter?'

'Kate's.'

Martin's face looked heavy in the shadows of the restaurant's half-light, his mouth dragged down, his eyes dull, though Jude couldn't tell if it was with mistrust or disappointment. He didn't look angry now, thank God, but she didn't know how to fend off his dismay. The waitress came with drinks and took their order.

'I was watching gulls and picking up pebbles.'

'You were what?'

'When she got gassed. I was on a beach. Photos to prove it. Seagulls like army majors, strutting on the tide line. Pebbles in the sand. I brought one back for Kate.'

'Why were you on a beach?'

Jude gave a sharp laugh. 'It was a gift. Kate made me a bet for my birthday, that she could fix the visit. "A bit of sea air," she said. So there I was breathing the sea breeze when there she was gasping for her breath.'

'You need a cigarette,' Martin said, holding out his packet. He reached over for the lighter, held out the steady flame.

But Jude, drawing fiercely on the cigarette, no longer saw him, or the restaurant.

Jude had been awake since the dawn. No need to be up early, it was a Sunday, but the routine was dug in too deep. She'd been staring at the cracks, a left-over habit.

The room they had had, she and Kate, had been on the first floor. Not as safe as the cellar, but that was always full of wounded men. Although they had sandbagged the house and stuck a large white cross onto the roof, it had been shell-damaged before they ever arrived and when the barrage began each dusk, the shells came very close. So they had put strips of brown paper over the worst of the cracks and each morning they would check to see if the paper had torn. It was a bit of a genteel farce, as Kate called it. Because there was nowhere better to go, and even if you could drive a coach and four through the cracks, they'd still very likely be sleeping in there.

The cracks on Jude's attic ceiling now didn't change. The three that made the boat, high-prowed, straight line for mast. And the sail, a stain where a tile had fallen two winters past and the rain had come through.

Jude could reach her boots with one hand, tied to the bedstead behind her head. Even up here, even these years later, she didn't trust them on the floor. Too many men had lost their heads with no boots on.

Over there she had been living so close to the front line, they

97

had called her skywatcher and given her the duties of it: a pair of Zeiss binoculars and a field telephone to mark out the progress of their planes. Up here in the attic was a square of blue. A safe sky, a cut-out square, no elbow-room any more for playful gods. There were only swifts this high up, their crazy shrieking, their mad speed. They made her gut tumble sometimes, they cut so close, but they never hit and they never fell, and she loved them for that.

She went downstairs quickly, in twos, then the three around the corner and a final two and two and one. Round the landing, listening for the family's sleeping sounds, and down again.

In the kitchen, the stove was warm still. She fed it, lifted on the kettle, squatted close, lit a cigarette and watched the steady stumble of the glow. The dog knew not to shift. Only let his tail bang twice on his basket and watched her with one eye. She walked across to the pantry, unlatched the door with its diamond peepholes. Such dull gleams inside. Such cool. No colours to surprise. Jars of Leo's jam and chutney, pickled onions lined the higher shelves, the marble slab so cold under her palm, it sent a chill along her arm. It kept the meat nice, kept the blood sweet, too.

Remembering was a strange affair. Jude made it a habit not to linger any more, but so much was inadvertent. She couldn't help it when her ears or fingers found echoes. Rummaging amongst the tins and packets, she found the bag of coffee beans and closed the pantry door. In Belgium they kept the coffee in the meat safe that Peter had devised. And in the winter months, they found a spot for it outside. She'd keep it in the refrigerator now, but Sally said it took up too much space. She spooned the beans into the coffee mill and turned the handle. The smell rose like a dream. Scooping the ground coffee into a small jug, she lifted the kettle from the hob and waited till it was off the boil before pouring the water in, just enough to cover the grounds. She found the strainer and a small cup, adding two spoons of sugar. Then she sat, head sunk over the cup, and breathed deep.

Once Jude had had a pile of different futures planned: scientist, photographer, aviator, explorer, journalist, doctor – she wasn't sure which would suit her best, and she'd talk them over with her

friends on the train home from school, her mind alive with possi-
bilities, her fourteen-year-old determination like a willow branch,
green and pliable, whippy and strong. Nowadays, when she saw
girls dressed in that familiar uniform – the green gabardine tunic,
black stockings she knew to be buttoned up high to a Liberty
bodice, square-necked tussore blouse, hat and gloves, even in
summer – she wanted to warn them, plead with them: be unrelenting and ruthless with your heart and with your mind; think
only of yourself.

'But your heart wasn't broken over there,' she said to herself. 'It
was the best time.'

Jude wished the children were awake and down, wished their
noise and demand would keep her from thinking. But it was still
not seven o'clock and, no need to wake them for school today.
Somewhere outside she could hear a bell, like the muffin-man's,
only it was too early. The day looked bright, clear. She'd take her
camera and ride up into the moors instead, catch the light breaking over one of the small high lakes maybe, or ride into the city.
She got out the bread and was parcelling some slices up in brown
paper when Sally came in, dressing-gown wrapped around her.

'You're up very early,' Jude said.

'He's snoring again,' Sally said. 'I stood it as long as I could.'

Jude laughed and took down a mug, poured Sally a coffee.

'Thanks.' Sally slumped into a chair near the stove. 'You going
out?'

'I woke before the crack. Thought I might take an early ride out.'

Sally took a sip, shuddered. 'God you make it strong.'

'Be back later in the morning.'

'Sit down a moment, have another coffee,' Sally said. 'Cigarette.'

'Now you've got me,' Jude said, smiling, and she poured out the
last of the jug, and lit up.

'How was Martin? The film?'

'The first became tedious, the second was good.'

'Poor Martin,' Sally said with a grin.

'Poor Martin!'

'How's the job going?'

Jude shrugged.

'I see you going off each day, coming back, but I still can't think of you doing that, even after all this time.'

'It's work,' Jude said. 'It pays me my pin-money. It pays you something, at least.'

'You don't have to do it,' Sally said. 'At least not for that reason. We'd all survive.'

'I can't allow myself to stop,' Jude said. 'Even though typewriting is deadly.'

'You've learnt shorthand as well, though.'

'Nearly as bad. I knew it after the first day and here I still am.'

'Maybe you'll have an adventure,' Sally said. 'Like in the romances.'

'You're still half-asleep,' Jude said, 'if you can talk about romance and typewriting in one go. Though I suppose I could use my gauntlets. Instead of wearing them to protect my blouse from typewriting ink. I look like some emasculated knight.'

'They're quaint.'

'Closest I get to an adventure.'

'What about a noble insurance manager,' Sally said. 'You know. You're called in to take down a letter and one look from those eyes, or on the stairs, you're walking up, gaze a little averted, demure, and he's rushing down and knocks you flying.'

'Did Leo ever behave like that?' Jude said laughing. 'Or have you taken to reading those novels. *Love's Ecstasy*, or *The Enamoured Virgin*, that kind of thing?'

'I read in a magazine that more couples are meeting in the workplace these days than ever before the war,' Sally said.

'We don't even use the same staircase as the men, Sally.'

'In case of what?'

'In case of God only knows. Spontaneous pregnancy, perhaps.'

'That's why you never bump into Leo.'

'I'm as fast as anybody, and I've been doing the French documents for a while, which is a bonus. But I'm not going to meet a husband there. I feel like I'm treading water. Three years of it now. Just keeping my head afloat with as little effort as possible.'

'But you mustn't let it be the death of you,' Sally said.

A thin ribbon of sunlight struck the far wall. If she put her hand up, Jude could break it, make a shadow jump on the wallpaper.

'I don't press you about things because I don't think you want me to,' Sally said. 'But I'm anxious about you. And you know what Leo is like. I don't learn anything from him.'

Jude stood. 'I'm going to go, while there's this early light.'

'Thanks for the coffee.'

'Thanks for putting up with me,' Jude said. 'Not easy, I do know.'

She left the house quietly and pulled her helmet close around her head. She would ride into the city, an act of defiance, not in her skirt and stockings and cardboard gauntlets this time, but in her britches, on her motorbike. It would be empty this early, the streets all hers.

Without the people, City Square seemed wide and free. The wind blew. The pigeons were still asleep on the statues, heads beneath their wings, like so many small grey boats. The air was so clear, Jude was sure she could smell the heather from the hills that rose behind. She walked across, exhilarated by the space and the light, by how different it all looked without people. She photographed the slender classical figures carved in bas-relief above the pilasters of the Union Life building and caught Time with his gilded scythe in her lens as the quarter hour rang out from the clock on Colonial Sphere Importers. The sun, still rising, cut between the buildings and across in a single narrow stroke, and standing in the bright line, Jude stared at her shadow. Crouching low she looked through the viewfinder, but the shadow was too long and she lost her head, or her feet, however she tried.

She felt like a child let loose in a sweet-shop, as if somehow the square, and all this space and air, had been given over just for her to see for these minutes, a reward for something. The blade of light stretched beyond her shadow over the far pavement and up the brick façade of Rathbone's Temperance Hotel. Through the ground floor window a figure was visible, a waitress laying for breakfast, and as Jude watched, a man in sober suit opened the front door of the hotel and stood looking out at the day.

Lifting her camera, she followed the light line up the building, across three windows, their curtains drawn, to the fourth floor where the sash was open wide and the net curtains were gusting out across the brickwork. She wondered why anybody needed net curtains up there, what on earth they feared might look in. The light on the hotel looked sculptural, and Jude wanted to photograph it. Setting her shutter speed and aperture, she smiled at the memory of Mr Lund, her first mentor, and his *Photography for Novices*. He would not have approved her subject or technique.

When she looked again at the hotel, a female figure had placed herself in the window on the fourth floor, head and shoulders visible, as if expressly for Jude's photograph. She readied her camera and was about to take the shot, when the woman moved, disappearing. Jude waited to see if she would reappear, and perhaps a minute later she did, this time with a white bandanna around her head. But before Jude could take the shot, the woman leaned forward, chin on the sill, and pulled herself up, so that now she was crouched there, hunched over her knees four floors up, the curtains blowing out like wings on either side, her skirts hitched to her thighs, the patent toes of her shoes glinting.

Jude breathed in sharply. The sight made her dizzy. She felt her heart thump in her chest. All was so quiet. The woman made no sound. Jude looked around, but the square was still empty. Breathing deeply, steadying herself, she lifted her camera again.

Gingerly, the woman stood up on the sill, one hand on the raised sash for balance. She brushed off her skirts, pulled her cuffs down straight, put a hand to her hair. And then she jumped.

'No,' Jude whispered.

For a split second, she didn't look like she was falling, but seemed to hang. Jude could see her mouth, painted red, and wide as if surprised. Then she dropped, catching a heel on the sill as she fell, so that she tumbled head over heels, her smoothed skirt, her petticoats rucked up with the speed of her fall, limbs akimbo, like a rag doll flung away by a child.

Jude took one photograph before she hit the ground.

Her bandanna, which had come loose from her hair, fell more slowly, dropping like a wreath.

In a trance, Jude walked closer. It reminded her of a battlefield, when the noise has stopped, figures making slow, tentative movements in this changed landscape. She took a couple more photographs: the waitress standing at the restaurant window, her face pressed to the plate glass; the man at the door peering round from his spot on the step, hand to his head scratching like Stan Laurel. The woman, fallen to the ground, seemed little more than a heap of clothes, and Jude was about to take another photograph when the man in the doorway yelled something out. She stopped, suddenly horrified at herself, and turned and ran. She knew that there were lots of things you shouldn't see, and one of them was a body falling through so much air.

CHAPTER SIX

It was Monday, early evening, when the telephone rang. Daniel was doing some work on the dining-room table.

'Hello, Twickenham one oh nine?'

'I've changed my mind. I know who the other man was.'

'What?'

'No question. It's probably not enough, but I'm completely sure.'

Daniel frowned. The voice was familiar. He waited for it to introduce itself, explain what it was talking about.

'Daniel?' It sounded both impatient and anxious, and now he recognised it and found his stomach leaping.

'You don't go for preamble, Miss Hursten,' he said, smiling.

'Mr Brown, I phoned to tell you something important. Given that you travelled over three hundred miles north in pursuit of my recollections, it doesn't seem particularly odd that I should get straight to the point in a telephone call. And if you persist a minute longer in calling me Miss Hursten, I shall put the receiver down.'

There was a small notebook next to the telephone, and a pencil. Daniel flipped the notebook open, ran his eye over a list in his mother's hand: A.M.: Change bedding. Flowers for John. Coffee. Letters. Sandwich lunch. Groceries, usual. P.M.: Rest. Tea with Marcia. Prepare dinner.

'Could you repeat what you said first?' he said. 'I wasn't entirely ready for it.'

There was a sigh at the other end, and then Jude's voice,

speaking slowly, clearly, so that he could imagine her mouthing the words as if to a simpleton.

'The man in my photograph,' she said, 'the one not wounded.' Already she'd forgotten about speaking slowly, her voice back to its usual pace. Daniel could feel the fear blooming in his stomach. He barely knew this woman. Did he trust her?

'He was from Cork. I don't know any more about him. But I do know he was from County Cork. I remember that because Kate made a joke about a wine bottle.'

'Not a very funny joke,' Daniel said.

'It didn't much matter,' Jude said. 'Any joke would do, there.'

The trip to Yorkshire had made Daniel's nightmare worse, and it had unlocked other things. He supposed they were memories, though to begin with most of them weren't things he even knew he'd noticed. There was the noise of the bees in the fuchsia hedges, so loud in the summer that he'd wanted to block his ears in the narrow country lanes, 'the boreens' they called them. Then, walking over the bridge to the station a few days ago, it had been the mud. The tide had been out and the estuary mud gleamed, swollen, smooth, the birds already busy in it. Always if he had a minute, Daniel would look to see what was there, the different birds dipping their beaks, and once he'd seen a dunlin far away from its beach and once a green sandpiper. He'd always liked the smell of it, sulphurous, slightly rank, touching the back of his nostrils. It was its own element. But last week it had made his heart race to smell it and he had hurried past, blocking his ears to the sound of his memory, giving some poor explanation to his father for his haste. The roar of lorries in the street, a cat wailing in the night, the flare of a gas lamp, the single clip of somebody's shoes walking past the house at night, the smell of kippers, or beer, boys pushing by him on his way home, the gardener's bonfire flaring late in the twilight – it seemed that almost anything could catch him out now so that he felt hunted by his own thoughts, on the run.

Daniel knew the nightmare well. It was always the same, more or less. Of attacking, then being attacked. Of striking hard, beating. His brother Johnnie. Then women and children with guns, and the boys he knew, Will, hurt, dying, and him powerless. Always the colours of the heather and gorse, the nubbly hills, rocks, mist, the air heavy with moisture. He'd been having this dream ever since he returned. Some weeks it would be night after night, other times he'd be free of it for a month or more. He knew his mother had heard him crying out, though she always claimed she couldn't make out what he said, and this worried him as much as the dream itself, which he'd almost grown used to.

But these other things, these memories, slipping into his waking mind, leaching like a dye into the fabric of his life, these were worse, these he couldn't prevent or wake up from.

He put the telephone earpiece down on the table, took a step back. He felt the coldness of the hall tiles under his shoes. Jude's voice went into the polished wood, tinny and incoherent, then stopped. He stared at the earpiece through narrowed eyes. It looked like a rat, the coil of its connection lying quiet across the table. Something hung in the balance. He had asked Jude to tell him if anything came back to her, sent her his address, his telephone number, and here she was doing so. He could either ignore what she had to say, or he'd have to do something.

When Jude started speaking again, her voice was so loud, she made Daniel jump.

'If – you – don't – reply – I – shall – replace – the – receiver – and . . .'

Reflexively he reached for the telephone again.

'Hello,' he said.

'I'm in the sitting room lighting a cigarette, and when my brother is angry, because he doesn't like the smell and he hates me smoking, I shall blame you.'

Despite himself, despite his fear, Daniel laughed. Something had been bridged, broached, since their meeting. Or maybe it was by virtue of their having met before, so that now they talked with greater familiarity than they properly possessed, and this surprised him. It pleased him.

'But there can't be many bugs in your sitting room,' he said, and she laughed, so he knew she remembered the Rocks.

'Bugs and nerves,' she said. 'Two of the best reasons for a ciga-rette.'

'Nerves? You didn't strike me as . . .'

Her voice broke in like rapid fire.

'Look, is what I'm telling you helpful or not?'

He didn't know what to say. Because if he told her yes, it was helpful, he knew he'd have to act, go over there, and he didn't know if he dared. But if he told her no, then she would replace the handset and that would be that, and he'd be standing in the hall on the cold tiles, his parents drinking their morning coffee on the ter-race and his head silting up further every day with these memories and nothing in the world to keep them in there even, but his life becoming like an echo chamber.

She didn't try to hurry him and he thought he could hear her waiting in this shared telephone silence. He pictured her, seated in a hard chair against the sitting room wall, the telephone on the floor beside her. She'd have her elbows on her knees and she'd be looking out, her body very still, brown eyes focused on something beyond the room, into that long, unkempt garden he'd only glimpsed. He imagined one of the children coming in, Elsa. He wondered whether Jude would brush her off, impatient with the interruption. Or whether she mightn't lift the girl onto her lap, almost absently, put her hand round Elsa's middle to keep her from slipping as she carried on the conversation. Because it was those two children, he thought, more than anybody else, except perhaps her dead lover, who held Jude's heart.

'What you've told me,' he said finally, 'the men that are dead aren't going to come back to life because of it. It won't make any difference to what's gone.'

He paused, and she waited. Then she asked, in a gentler voice than he'd heard so far, 'But will it make a difference to you?'

Jude wondered later whether Leo didn't know better than she did, what would come out of her trip south the weekend after. Daniel's request had taken her by surprise and she'd answered him before she had time to think, then written to confirm it, needing to send the letter as much for her own certainty as for his.

'In the spirit of enquiry,' Daniel had said, and when she told this to Leo, she didn't know whether or not she was offended by his roar of laughter. She'd found him in the vegetable garden, crouched down, picking the lowest runner beans, and when he'd straightened up to listen to her, she thought he looked like a green man, something wild, the last red flowers on the beans like a garland on his hair.

'I've never heard it called that before,' he said, and she would have taken offence, except that somewhere she knew the justice of his remark.

'I'm meeting him in Kew Gardens, which is near his home. And I'll stay with Peter, be back on Sunday in time to press my blouse for Monday.'

'You've spoken to Peter already?'

'He was intrigued. Wants to make it all into a detective story. Put me in some sleuthing hat and pipe.'

Leo picked up the trug, full of beans, and stepped carefully out, lifting each foot high.

'I need to do this,' Jude said.

'Whatever it is.'

'Yes.'

'We'll tell Sally it's an old school friend,' he said.

'Why?' Jude raised her eyes to his in question. 'Why not say who it is?'

'Daniel Brown worries her. She thinks he needs too much.'

'That's absurd. All he did was sit and eat her Sunday lunch. She seemed to like him.'

Leo put a hand up, stopped Jude's noise of protest.

'It's what she thinks.' Leo shrugged. 'And you like him, don't you?'

Jude took a bean from the trug and bit into it.

'He seems like a nice enough fellow,' Leo said. 'Clever. And troubled, but then who isn't after such times? Certainly a match for you, which is important. You'd never be able to bear someone too easy.'

'I'm going down there to try to help him with something,' Jude said. 'Not to make love to him.'

'Something's happened, Jude. Is it just because of this man turning up on the doorstep?' He shook his head. 'There's something very urgent about you.'

Jude didn't reply. She hadn't told Leo about the falling woman. She hadn't told anyone. When she'd come home afterwards, she'd pleaded a headache and kept to her room till late into the day. She hadn't thought much about what she was doing, but she'd found herself staring at the photographs from the war; at that desecrated landscape where she had been so powerfully alive, at Peter, at the wounded soldiers, and most of all at the friend she so loved.

'I know there doesn't have to be only one reason,' Leo said, 'and that sometimes you're the last person to know something about yourself.'

Jude tossed the bean away and spat the coarse, milky fibre into the grass. 'Anyway, needs too much what?' she said.

'You'll find out, perhaps,' Leo said and he got up and walked away back up the garden, swinging the trug and its lanky green load, calling up to the two children who were playing by the pond, and Jude watched him and envied his contentment.

She had her camera and a newspaper for the train south. Also a book. Jude wasn't much of a reader, but this would be a long journey, and Sally had persuaded her to bring it.

'It's about a girl called Ann Veronica,' Sally said. 'More your kind of thing than mine. She's quite determined to have her own way.'

Leo had lent her a book about war by George Bernard Shaw, but she'd left that one on her bed.

Jude opened the novel first, but the girl's gusty eagerness was oppressive and she put the book away. The newspaper told her that England had beaten Australia in the cricket, that you could see movies with sound now, 'talkies', and that the coal miners were giving the government a hard time. She folded the newspaper and looked out of the window.

It was hard today, sitting still for so long and she felt a terrible impatience brewing. The muscles in her calves and her arms were twitching and she couldn't let her eyes settle. Her gaze rested in some middle distance and the landscape passed beneath it. She saw the cropped fields shearing away under the hard summer light, the pools of cattle under trees, tiny men with carts and heavy-legged horses, the long, colourless sky. Kestrels hunched small on telegraph poles and rooks scattered, their messy black rise and fall like so many scraps of litter, and Jude wondered whether you could ever catch that motion in a photograph.

What was she hoping for? She didn't know, except to stave off the panic that beat against her ribs whenever she thought that her life might have settled now for good. She wouldn't think, tried not to think, about Daniel and the tall line of his body standing out-side her door, or his face against the rocks, or his voice, thick with uncertainty, asking for her help.

She took the Underground from King's Cross. When she had told the children of her trip to London, Tom had been uninter-ested, except on one point, which was that she might find herself taking an escalator. It was one of his four greatest ambitions, to take an escalator, and he managed his envy by requesting Jude to note down everything there was to tell about it. How high it was, how many steps there were, was there any visible machinery, and was a man with a wooden leg on the up as well as the down part?

'They'd need a lot of men by now, if they did that,' said Jude. 'Lots of the stations have escalators.'

'But there's loads without legs. And they might lots of them be glad of a job. And it's indoors, and no walking. Only standing.'

'Where did you pick this up? In the *Boys' Own*?'

'But it's true, Jude. They do pay men with wooden legs.'

'Why?'

'So as people aren't frightened, going on.'

Jude didn't press him further. And being in good time at King's Cross, she took the escalator down and then up and then down again, pausing after the second descent to write some notes for Tom and to try a photograph. She held the camera as steady as she could on a long exposure, but the ground shook with the rumble of the trains and the light was very poor, so she didn't hold out much hope.

She took the Piccadilly Line down to Earl's Court and changed there on to the District. The tube was crowded and she had to stand, her hand on the rail for balance. She looked along the rail at the half a dozen others gripping on and she wondered for a moment what had become of the young pianist.

The slender-fingered female hand, engagement and wedding rings dull in that light, nails manicured for battle, gripped close to the rough, broken nails and coarse skin of the labourer's; long, brown-skinned fingers made close companionship with the broad reach of freckled, ginger-haired fingers. Her own hand with its wide knuckles and nails cut short for typing, still a trace of engine oil beneath one, found common cause with an ancient fist, its knuckles swollen and pushed about with arthritis. Incongruous couples, and she wished she could have caught them in her lens.

Jude hadn't known she was holding her breath, but when the train surfaced, first at Baron's Court, and then properly after Hammersmith, she let out a tremendous sigh, and she felt as she used to after huddling in the cellar while the Germans sent their shells whistling around, which was a bit light-headed, breathy. Coming out at Kew Gardens, she fished a piece of paper from her pocket with Daniel's instructions scribbled down. She was to make her way to the entrance at the end of Kew Green and he'd meet her there.

Jude had no idea what she was walking towards. But what she did know, what had painted itself across the inside of her eyes on the journey south, was that she would do anything to break the toppling inertia of her life now. In the war she'd done this every day, walked blindfold towards things. Sometimes because she couldn't see how dangerous it might be, and sometimes because if she'd pulled the scarf from her eyes and looked straight out, she'd have been too scared to step forwards. Better not to see.

The war had been a very big adventure and she'd been at the top of the list. Better than in Tom's *Boys' Own* with its bareback riding and rafting and shoot-outs, she'd rescued men and saved lives.

And today, although the adventure didn't look so likely, walking towards the Royal Botanic Gardens along the pavements, past the quiet, tidy houses with front gardens and railings to keep things in, she pleaded with the gods to intervene.

He was waiting by the turnstile, leaning against the Opening Times board, watching the people file up and ratchet through. He didn't seem to be looking out for her, his head half-turned from the road, but when she was within a few yards, he stood tall and raised his hand. And though she had seen him from a distance, known it was him, still when he turned towards her, she felt that shock of the actual, a single pulse through.

She noticed how he moved, as though his limbs were connected at the joints with pins. Rusted pins, pushed in at an angle. So that his hand, raised in greeting, seemed ill at ease with his arm, and his arm moved oddly from his shoulder. She was moved by the sight of him, and taken aback by the range of her own feelings.

'So,' he said. 'You have come.'

'Did you think I might not?'

'It's a long journey to make, and . . .'

Jude shrugged. 'What would be good to see?'

'My mother says the lavender beds at this time, and the roses.'

'My grandmother kept lavender,' Jude said. 'Against a wall, south facing. A great bank of lavender, high up in Yorkshire. She'd cut it about now, put a vase in every room to keep the flies away.'

'Flies?'

'They don't like the smell. We used it in Belgium too. It's good for wounds.'

'Do you need to drink tea first?'

'No.'

They walked beside flower beds heavy with the day's scents, silent, both awaiting. The paths were busy with Saturday afternoon people. Fathers with little figures hoisted on shoulders, old women with bread for the birds, children bickering over hoops and ice creams, feeding squirrels, chasing squirrels, mothers wiping noses and mouths, couples wandering, fingers intent in one another's palms, oblivious or arguing. Daniel watched them, all the ordinary motions, all the ordinary pleasures and quarrels, and fought with the fear that cut like a band across his chest. The fear that these things were closed to him because he'd smashed them somewhere else, that he'd stepped beyond them.

He watched a boy peg a pebble at a squirrel and the father in his Sunday best cuff his son so hard across the ear, the boy stumbled. He watched a girl snap the heads from a line of proud daisies and felt his skin shiver. Jude bent to smell a flower and he looked at her, her elbows out, her dark curls tickling over her face so that she put a hand up to wash her skin clear. She was someone more at ease, he guessed, with larger movements.

Jude looked round at him and he saw her expression acquire that cast she must have learnt in the war, of solicitude, professional concern. And he knew then, somewhere behind his fear, somewhere behind the horror of what had gone on, that he wanted to know this woman when that guard was down.

'Let's go and talk,' he said. 'Sit down somewhere, under a tree where it's private.'

'The lavender?'

He shook his head. 'The perfume's too bloody strong.'

'Your leg's hurting,' Jude said. 'You should have said.'

Daniel stopped dead and faced her, very upright. 'No, it's not,' and he said the words so loud he made her flinch. 'My mother does that,' he said.

'Does what?'

'She tells me what's hurting.'

'My apologies,' Jude said, her voice clipped tight. 'I won't again. You can yell and scream all you want and I'll say nothing. I've heard enough men screaming in my time, for God's sake. It's nothing new.'

She didn't walk away, or cross her arms, but Daniel knew from the edge of her shoulder, from the fierce forwardness of her gaze, that he'd angered her. Things were pushing out from inside and he didn't know the limits of his own restraint. He must speak his mind to her soon, before the echoes got the upper hand.

'I suppose it is less than clever to compare a woman to one's mother,' he said, finding from somewhere a lighter tone, and Jude turned away to hide her grin.

'Especially,' Daniel went on, wondering whether she would baulk at his tone, 'when that woman has journeyed hundreds of miles to help one, and is so entirely unlike one's mother.'

'There's no need to become extravagant,' she said, still smiling. 'But let's talk.'

They had stopped in the middle of the path and people skirted them like a river round an island. They stood in a diamond of space. Daniel searched for a likely place to go. A little stand of trees ahead and to the right looked good, nobody near. He pointed to it.

'We could sit there.'

They walked past beds of red hollyhocks and blue cornflowers, past yellow sunflowers and stocks in every colour, and perhaps this blaze, which battered the eyes, explained why Daniel didn't notice the fuchsia until it was nearly upon them.

'Listen,' Jude said, walking closer, 'the bees. We had this in the garden, my mother loved it. Leo and I, we'd spend ages pulling off the flowers. There'd be this pinprick of sweetness if you sucked. He got stung once, doing it.'

She turned, but Daniel hadn't heard her. He had moved away and was leaning hard with one hand on his stick, the other clapped to his ear, like a man beyond his years, his eyes on the ground.

'Daniel?' she said.

'It's everywhere in Ireland, in the west,' he said. It grows wild there, the hedges are made of it. So loud. It crowds in on you from every side. They hack it back and it just grows bigger and bigger.'

He looked up and his eyes were scared.

'And you didn't ever suck the flowers,' Jude said, trying for lightness.

'I don't want to see it,' he said and, hearing his voice, Jude said no more.

They sat in silence beneath the tree, Daniel with his eyes on the ground, Jude looking out from beneath the heavy canopy. A woodpecker dipped between trees, laughing hard. Two stag beetles fought it out in brittle dance in the dust at Jude's feet, till one was tipped over onto its shiny back, legs jerking in the air. High and tiny, an aeroplane made loops, and in the distance, on the path they had left, people watched, a child tracing the O's with its finger to the sky.

CHAPTER SEVEN

Jude waited, and when Daniel finally started to speak, she leaned back against the rough bark and shut her eyes to the Saturday world strolling past. She'd come a long way to listen.

'I only just got to the war,' he said. 'By the skin of my teeth I made it. Got my commission, like Johnnie, was gazetted, did my training and got over there. My mother crying at the door, tugging at my damn coat.'

Despite the warmth of the day, Daniel pulled his jacket round him as if, even now, he could feel his mother's hands. Jude looked away. She felt as if she were witness to something private.

'So you went to France,' she said, 'you went into the trenches,' making her voice loud and solid.

'I couldn't stay, not with Johnnie dead. Every time my mother looked at me, she saw a ghost. I was in flight, for God's sake. I had to get away.'

Jude dug her toe into the dust, watched an ant divert its course away from the mountain of her shoe. She looked round at Daniel. He was staring straight out across the grass, for all the world, she thought, as if *he* had seen a ghost.

'But that's normal now,' she said. 'There are millions of men dead all over Europe, millions and millions of mothers, and wives, and sweethearts, and half of them seeing ghosts.'

'I wasn't frightened,' Daniel said. 'Not a bit. If anything I was stronger after Johnnie's death. Determined. I was going to be all the things he was. I'd got myself stronger, been lifting weights. And

116

now I was going to go to the Front and come home again. Not a telegraph for my mother this time.'

'So you did fight?'

Daniel shook his head. 'Got packed off to the front line and it was over. I never fired a shot, never even got to stand in a trench.'

'And then you left the army.'

'We had to wait for ever to be demobbed. Last in last out, and no war fought. It made some of the men murderous. I came home, and that seemed to make it worse for my mother than before. Johnnie had never come home. So now it was as if I was a ghost, but the wrong one. We did look alike, same brown hair, same physique, height almost, mannerisms of course. I'd see her staring at me, and ask if anything was wrong. Had I got a smut on my nose? Was my parting crooked? And she'd never answer, I don't think she heard me, but sometimes she'd come close and touch my eyebrows, or run her fingers through my hair, and it wasn't me she saw then, it was Johnnie.'

Daniel paused. He wondered, did she know she was the first person he'd ever spoken to of this, and he turned to look at her. She returned his gaze, made no effort to speak, and he thought that probably she did know. Somewhere far off behind them, it seemed infinitely far, he could hear a child's call, 'Catch me.' He gripped his arms tight, feeling the print of his fingers against bone. He was doing this well, telling it. He could do this, and he'd go on now.

'My friend, Will Savage, he'd got decorated in France, seen everything and was still alive. He was demobbed before me and we lost touch. Don't remember how we got to be friends, but anyway I bumped into him, in a pub off Oxford Street. I was in a suit, working for my father by now, and he, I don't remember, but he told me he was going to Ireland. They had problems there, violent rebels who'd stop at nothing and they were murdering policemen, causing havoc. So they were recruiting for a special force.

'We got to talking and he said to me why didn't I sign up too? Since I'd missed the action first time around. He said had I seen the adverts? They were offering a pound a day – a very good wage –

117

and they wanted ex-officers. They wanted them experienced, but seeing as they were hungry for men, he was sure he could talk them round to me. So I joined.'

'When was this?' Jude said.

'1920. Summer of 1920. I became a temporary cadet in the Auxiliary division of the Royal Irish Constabulary, but a soldier, as near as damn it. They gave us some training, six weeks in the Curragh, and a uniform, tam-o'-shanter beret with a little golden harp badge, and plenty of guns, and then they sent us south in our big lorries and none of us, not even Will, had a clue.'

'Was it like a war?' Jude said.

Daniel shook his head. 'We didn't know who the enemy was. We were meant to protect people. We were meant to make Ireland hell for the rebels to live in. That's what it said in the *Dublin Police Journal*, and so somebody wrote it out large on a banner and put it in the mess: "Make Ireland Hell for Rebels".

'I thought the enemy would wear a uniform. So you didn't shoot the wrong person. But you'd drive out of the barracks and there would be people in the town going about their business, men and women standing about on corners, and you wouldn't know what they were. Not even the children. Some of the women were friendly enough, lots weren't. But then you found out it was the friendly ones were carrying the messages for the men, or the weapons, and so you started not to trust anyone. You'd hear those voices, that accent, and think that if they spoke like that, they'd be bound to be out for you one way or the other. Men, women, children, priests, all of them. Christ, one fellow, he started searching the dogs for stuff.

'It made us scared, angry, feeling like that, and then you start seeing things differently, drinking to get your courage up and so things happen when you go out on patrol that oughtn't to. Things I wouldn't do, but I did them. And afterwards nobody says you shouldn't have, nobody punishes you. Everyone says it's what they deserve and we're only here to help them in this godforsaken place, or they say that they were the enemy and they had it coming to them, and so you say it too, and believe it even though you know it's not true. Not really. And then you do it all again, and again.'

'So you were a . . .' Jude hesitated.

'Black and Tan. Yes,' he said. 'More or less.'

Jude stood up. She walked away from the tree, elaborately stretching, and then back to it again.

'I never understood the nickname,' she said.

Daniel shrugged. 'Nothing special about it,' he said. 'It was the uniform – dark green and khaki. A bunch in Limerick went on a drinking spree early on, smashed things up, and they got named "Black and Tans" after a pack of hounds that went by that name there, and because of the colours they wore. And then the name stuck for all of us.'

'So you were one of them, and you got wounded over there,' she said.

'Yes.'

'And in between?'

'I'd like to say we were a little mad over there, some of the time. But that would be making excuses. It was horrible, what went on sometimes, and we were being told to do it, ordered, so we laughed and laughed. Harder and harder.'

'I know what men do in wars,' Jude said. 'I saw it for myself.'

'Saw it?'

'As near as damn it, yes.'

Daniel put his hand on his leg, felt with his fingers through the cloth of his trousers to where the skin was puckered, to where the ridges of scar tissue crossed his leg like so many fortifications. He'd kept it going up to here, but it was slipping, he could feel it slipping.

'And us meeting, it all has something to do with the photograph of two men sharing a cigarette that I took in Belgium in the Great War.'

Daniel looked up at her. She was staring at the tree trunk, one finger prising at the thick bark. He noticed how she lifted her eyebrows, when she said something that was especially important.

'It's strange, don't you think?' she said, raising her brow again.

Daniel didn't answer her question, if it was one. He looked away.

In the distance two boys, brothers from their matching clothes, were playing some kind of tug-of-war with a branch. The branch was slender and Daniel could see the white grazes where they had cleaned it of its shoots.

First, one boy would grasp it, both arms outstretched, hands placed firmly round the wood, and the other boy would try to twist and tug it from him, and then they would swap around. From this distance they looked like dancers. There seemed to be a rule to do with how far along they could hold the stick, so that more than once one of them overstepped the mark and they swapped. But then a dispute arose which neither had the will to resolve. They grappled for a time, then the larger boy let go of the stick and pushed his brother to the ground and the game was over.

'Things taste different there, the same things we eat here. Like the bacon except they call it rashers and bacon's something different. And the milk. And brown bread like a cow pat and a cross in the middle, which isn't like ours and not even made with yeast at all. One of the kitchen boys told me. The place is like that, things looking like they should be the same, but they're not, so you don't know where you are and you sit down to breakfast and it all looks about right and you pick up your knife and fork and cut something, put it in your mouth and it's nearly there but not. Except for Coolderry, and Horse Island.'

'Horse Island?' Jude said, but he didn't seem to hear her.

'At least they were good places. Places you could be in properly.' He traced the names on the grass, then tapped his head. 'That's where I try to go back to in here, every day nearly.' He paused. 'It's not nicer or nastier, the bacon, or the bread. It's just different. Foreign.'

Jude was looking at the bark she'd picked from the tree, how on the inside it was smooth and damp. Daniel put his hands down on either side of him, and rolled his shoulders round. Tension cut like blades down his back. Dropping the bark, Jude sat down. She didn't know what the names meant, and it wasn't the time to ask. She needed him to tell her about the photograph.

'Stop telling me about the bacon,' she said. 'And tell me what you need me to know.'

Daniel breathed in deep, making his head swim. He couldn't speak about the things he'd seen, the things he'd done. He wanted to, he hoped she'd ask him, demand to know, suspect him and interrogate. It was her fault if she didn't ask, because then how could he tell?

'What did you think when the journalists wrote about the Boche nailing babies to front doors? Did you believe it? Since you were there?' he said.

'No more than I'd believe it of our lot, no. I saw plenty of horror, but never anything like that.'

'But people go too far in war, that's what they do.'

'Killing other men is going too far,' Jude said.

'Yes, but not just that.'

'I didn't come down here to discuss the morals of war,' Jude said, because she couldn't bear to take it further now. She knew what he was asking her to do, but she couldn't be the bearer of his conscience. Only she wondered where his own revulsion was.

'All right,' he said, though he knew she was wrong. Absolutely wrong. And then like a man plunging from the rocks into an unknown sea, he began again.

'The man in your photo, the Irish man, he was a soldier in the British army, an officer. I know this because there it was in the exhibition, "Our Brave Men who Battle On". I saw it, and the camera doesn't lie. I stood and looked at him a month ago, and everyone else saw him too, arm around his wounded brother soldier, and I recognised him. And the old ladies went "Ah" because, look at that, they're sharing a cigarette and there's a smiling nurse standing behind and it's all like it should be and doesn't he deserve her smile, after all he'd done for his country . . .'

He paused. He was beginning to shout and he could feel the rage rise inside him, the mad rage in which you could do anything, to anybody. He paused. He must try to be calm. He was speaking too quickly and forgetting to breathe. His hand was a fist and something sharp was pressing into his palm. Slowly he breathed in through his nose and out through his mouth, like Will had shown him when they were on a raid. Opening his hand, he found a sappy piece of twig on his palm, its shoots making their prints on his skin, and he put it in his pocket.

He barely knew this woman but he needed her to hear him out. He mustn't scare her away, or not scare her exactly, because he knew already she wasn't the scaring type. But he mustn't revolt her either. He could feel his fingers tightening and his lips drawing back and the saliva becoming thick in his mouth and he didn't want to gouge at the earth or bare his teeth or become one of those figures you passed in the corners, flailing and spitting at the world. He looked up. He must remember. Here he was in Kew Gardens on a sunny Saturday afternoon with a pretty girl beside him, and over there families were promenading, and courting couples were looking at the flowers and each other.

'This is what makes me . . .' he said, and he spread his shaking hands out for her to see, palms towards the sky. 'It's like the duck rabbit picture. You look and it's a duck, you look again and it's a rabbit. It's both, but never both at once. One is the outside of the other and the other is the outside of the one. It's why I'll have to go back and find out, is it a duck I'll be shooting, or a rabbit? I saw him last month on the exhibition wall and he was a British soldier from the trenches. And before that I saw him, in Ireland, in the flesh, and he was dressed like a soldier then too.'

Daniel stood up. For some reason he couldn't say any more, and he rummaged in his mind for why. He wiped his mouth on his sleeve.

'My mouth is dry. I must find some water.'

He started walking towards the path. Jude sat watching him, unsure what was happening. Then she picked up her bag and camera and followed.

Later, that evening, telling her tale to Peter, Jude found it hard to describe what had happened.

'It was as if I wasn't there any more,' she said. 'As if he didn't see me, or the gardens, or the people walking about, or the birds, or ducks, or flowers. He didn't seem to see any of it, or only when it fitted to some other place that was in his head. As though he was in a different landscape. Different weather. He was walking that lopsided walk fast as he could, urgent, stick in one hand, and buttoning his jacket with his other, pulling up the collar as if the day had gone cold, and around him people were basking in the sun.'

Peter nudged Jude's cocktail with a finger. 'Drink, lady. Best Manhattan in town.'

Jude took a sip, looked around her. 'Classy bar. Is this your usual?'

'It is for now, till I get a better offer,' he said, smiling over behind her. Jude turned her head to see, and caught the barman's bow.

'Very nice,' she said and took another sip. She grinned, remembering the first time she'd met Peter, how cross she'd been when she thought he was making up to her.

'How did he get his leg injury?'

'An ambush,' Jude said. 'He told me that before. Said he'd never told anyone else before.'

'So you followed him?' Peter said.

'Of course I followed him, though I didn't try to catch him up. I thought he was making for the path, maybe going to the tearoom, because he'd said he was thirsty. But he crossed the path, people staring at him because he's going so fast, his head down, and muttering, though I couldn't hear what at first. There was a woman standing there and he brushed her face with his arm as he went past, didn't seem to see her.

'He was walking in a straight line towards these bushes. He could easily have gone round them, but he didn't, as if he didn't see them either. I was close to him now, almost as close as I am to that next table, and when we got into them, I could hear him fairly clearly and he seemed to be saying something about them. "Bloody bushes," he said, more than once, but as if he'd only just seen them, as if they'd jumped up and hit him.'

'Bloody bushes?' Peter said.

'Yes. And something about getting caught in the bush, I wasn't quite sure. He might have meant the ambush, I suppose, or the bushes he was pushing through.'

'But you weren't frightened of him?'

'After what we went through,' Jude said, 'you and me?'

'People losing their marbles is more frightening than them losing an arm or a leg. And it sounds like he came quite close. Though we did see some like that too, of course. And God knows what he'd got up to in Ireland.'

'It was as though his wound was still raw, still filthy from battle. As if nobody had taken a piece of lint and some iodoform and cleaned it yet. But no, I wasn't frightened. I was very curious. And cross. He'd stood me up, so to speak. Got me all the way down here and then walked out on me. And he was sane when he walked out, I'm sure of it.'

'Jilted lover, then,' Peter said. 'Is he handsome? Tall? Dark? Sharp cheekbones? Broad shoulders?'

Jude gave him a look. 'Not your kind of handsome.'

'So, tell me something.'

'He's quite tall, very slim, hair brown on the way to fair. The kind of hair that gets streaked by the sun. And eyes that change depending on the light. Green almost, indoors, but then blue outside.' She looked down at the table. 'Anyway, this is ridiculous because I barely know him.'

'So? I barely know him,' Peter said, tipping his head towards the barman.

'He gives you Manhattans. Daniel Brown has given me nothing but trouble. I can already hear Leo saying, "I told you so." And Sally being quietly right behind him.'

'So, he might be handsome,' Peter said, nodding to himself. 'And you don't really know how hurt, do you? You don't know how much he'd take.' He paused, thinking a moment. 'So, tell me the rest. After the bloody bushes.'

Jude put a hand to her neck. She was very tired.

'Cigarette,' Peter said. 'What you need now,' and he pulled two from a packet and stuck them between his lips.

Jude found her lighter for him. He lit them and passed hers across the table.

'Recognise it?' Jude said.

Peter turned the lighter over in his palm. 'It is familiar, but I've seen so many of them. Just about every soldier, every sailor I meet,' and he shrugged his shoulders. 'Kate's?'

'Yes.'

'And she didn't smoke.'

'No.'

Jude knew Peter was waiting, that he'd take his cue from her. But she didn't want to talk about Kate now, only to say her name out loud, remember her for a moment.

'Do you want to finish your story?' he said.

'There's not much more to tell,' Jude said. 'He was walking through some oak trees, me still just behind, and he stopped short, turned and looked at me. He'd seemed very nearly mad in all this, but when he looked at me, the madness was gone and he was absolutely sane. He said, "I have to go now and I'm sorry to have led you such a poor dance. Perhaps if we'd met at another time . . ." and then he walked away.'

'And you didn't try to follow him?'

'No.'

'That's not like you.'

'It was clear he didn't want me to. And he seemed very sane then. So I just walked round the gardens for another hour or more, and then I came to meet you.'

Peter stirred the last pale dregs in his glass, drank them off, more as if it were a pint of beer than a cocktail, Jude thought, and set the glass down. He looked over to the bar, but the barman was busy flirting with another customer, a thick-set man in a smart suit.

'He'll want to be careful,' Peter said in a low voice. 'They have them undercover in places like this.'

'Can we go back to your flat?' Jude said. 'I'm very tired.'

Peter threw another look towards the bar.

'And I want your full attention,' she said. She pushed her glass towards him. 'Finish mine for me?'

They could hear the telephone bell ringing as they came up the last flight of stairs, but by the time Peter had the door open, it had stopped.

'They'll try again if it's important,' he said. He sat her down on a chair in the kitchen, put on the kettle and took out the cocoa tin.

'In memory,' he said, holding up the tin. 'Also, you look done in. When you've drunk it, I'll make up your sofa.'

The cocoa nearly made Jude cry, so she held her face just above the mug and made something of a dance about the steam from the mug scorching her face, to hide the flush that tears brought. They sat either side of the red oilcloth, hands clasped round mugs almost as if in prayer.

'Do you remember Kate working out one day how much cocoa we'd made? How many gallons, and then how many bathtubs, and then a swimming pool, and so on,' Peter said.

'I told her she was making it up, and she got cross.'

Peter laughed. 'You were like a couple of sisters with your squabbling. Always nit-picking down in that cellar. Real nits too.' He got up and went out, came back carrying a small hinged leather photo frame, which opened to show three photographs.

'I have this on my bedside table,' he said, passing it to Jude.

She opened it and smiled. Peter had taken the middle photograph. She remembered him doing so. It was her birthday, nineteen years old, and they had had a picnic. She was lying on a piece of tarpaulin, and next to her was Kate. They were laughing at something. Kate had a wine bottle in her hand, and Jude had her arm round Kate's shoulder. They looked so young and so carefree, and in the distance behind them, just visible, was the outline of the broken church tower.

Flanking this was a photograph of Peter at the stove, head turned towards Jude's call, caught by surprise, wooden spoon in his hand, his mouth open for retort. And on the other side a photograph Jude hadn't known of. It showed her in profile, Kate's greatcoat wrapped around her, britches and boots, white headscarf gathered and tumbling down her back like water in spate, binoculars raised towards who knew what.

'You look so beautiful,' Peter said.

Jude laughed. 'In the greatcoat and boots?'

'Then and now. You should be in love.'

'Perhaps I am. Perhaps I have been,' Jude said, a finger to her lips so he wouldn't ask more. 'Anyway, what about you?'

Peter started to wash out the saucepan. She watched him, his economy of gesture, his grace.

'I used to love watching you cook,' she said, rolling her head forwards, trying to ease the tension in her neck.

'Do you want a bath? Plenty of hot water here. I've got some lovely bath salts.'

Jude laughed. 'That bath,' she said.

'Four of us to get it into the room.'

'The two inches was heaven, and us so prudish. Funny, the pair of us dealing with wounded men all day and night, we must have seen everything there is to see. But it's not the same, the other way around. And then you brought us champagne. There was more champagne than there was hot water.'

'Champagne in tin mugs.'

'I hadn't been in a bath with someone else since I was too young to remember.'

'Somebody to soap your back.'

Jude looked down into her cocoa mug, her throat suddenly tight again.

'Jude?' Peter's voice was tender, soft.

'That's why I keep the photographs at the bottom of the box,' she said. 'And why I haven't been in touch very much.'

'So as not to be reminded.'

'Yes.'

'So many deaths,' Peter said.

'It's just the two that I can't bear.'

'Kate would understand.'

'I was picking up pebbles at the seaside and she was drowning in her own lungs.'

'You couldn't have saved her.'

'I know,' she said.

'The people we love die. And in the war, too many of them die, for all of us.'

127

'I know, but she was one of the people I knew. Me especially.'

'I never met Richard, but I remember the letter arriving,' he said. He covered her hand with his, stroked her fingers. 'That's when you stopped sky-watching.'

'I lost my head for heights. It just happened.'

'That still the same?'

Jude nodded.

'I think you need to do something differently,' he said at last. 'This new friend of yours, what's his name?'

'Daniel Brown, but he's not a friend. Not yet.'

It was getting dark, sapping the colours from the kitchen. Jude saw Daniel crossing the grass, moving away from her, his hobbled walk, his blind distress.

'You think that there's something about him. Something beyond his madness, or sanity, illness, whatever it is,' Peter said.

Jude nodded again.

'What does he look like? Will you tell me now?'

'He reminds me of Richard. Same way of moving, despite the limp. There was something awkward about Richard, and yet he was so athletic.' She thought a moment. 'He was like a colt. Barely grown when he died.'

'And you like him, don't you? This Daniel?'

Jude shrugged.

'I thought so,' Peter said.

'I like the way he listens. And I want to hear what he will say. And he looks like a man who wants to be freed,' Jude said.

'From his body? His hurt leg?'

'From his mind.'

'So is that what made you come down and meet him? Because it wasn't just the colour of his eyes.'

'I needed a change.' Jude gave a rueful grin. She couldn't answer him, not tonight, not quite yet.

Peter shrugged. 'All right then. What will you do if he contacts you?'

'I don't know,' she said.

'Which is unlike you. The whole thing is very cloak and dagger.'

Peter put his arm around Jude's shoulders. 'That's enough now. You're exhausted, and I'm going to tuck you up like I used to. We'll talk in the morning.'

She was so tired, Jude barely took in Peter's flat, its high ceilings and battered cornices. She didn't know why she'd left the sitting room door ajar, but last thing before she slept, her eyes drifted over the slender slip of light, like a soft searchlight, that threw itself in from the hall and she thought how simple it would be to close the door against it, and how hard.

Jude had told her boss she had to come to London for the final illness of an elderly uncle and so could she please have Monday off in lieu. An elderly uncle, even a very ill one, wouldn't usually have been enough to gain the day, but when Jude mentioned the will, they were very understanding. And she'd never missed a day before, not in the four years she'd been working there.

'So is it me or Daniel Brown who's the uncle?' Peter said when she told him this.

'Well, there'd be no point touching you for any pennies, would there?' she said. 'And frankly, after yesterday, I don't know whether I'll ever see Daniel again.'

'You might be glad of that,' Peter said.

'No,' she said.

They had a leisurely Sunday, beginning with a slow breakfast and, after a short discussion which took them nowhere, an agreement to avoid, if possible, contentious conversation. So instead they walked through the Sunday city talking of plans and aspirations, of Peter's hopeless romances and Jude's dream of travelling round Europe on her motorbike with her camera, of leaving one life and beginning another. They remembered the funny and the terrible times in the war, and they didn't talk about Daniel or Kate.

Jude was exhilarated by the empty city, and, determined to walk free from her ghosts for this short time, she began to photograph the Sunday figures: women in hats returning from church, a wandering dog, a man on his own with a placard, railing against the secular hordes who were nowhere to be seen, a figure visible through an open window sipping from a glass. But she hadn't noticed how her eyes were drawn upwards until Peter spoke.

'What's so fascinating about the tops of the buildings?' he said. 'That's all you've been looking at this last half hour.'

And as he said it, she saw again the woman crouched there, saw her lean into the air and jump.

'It's something,' she began, and then she stopped. She didn't want to talk of it now. 'It's a bad habit,' she said. 'Something I'm trying to stop doing. Let's walk in a park now instead. I won't be tempted then.' And shaking her head at his raised eyebrows, she packed her camera away into its bag, took his arm and tugged him into a stride, till he laughed and rolled his eyes, and he didn't ask her more.

After lunch, they went to the movies, bickering all through *The Thief of Baghdad* about Douglas Fairbanks' costumes, which Peter coveted, his body, which Jude thought handsome and Peter did not, and his swordplay, which neither were that excited by. So that by suppertime Jude was feeling much more relaxed, as Peter had predicted, but also as if something important might be slipping by.

'Perhaps I should telephone Leo,' she said. 'See whether Daniel has been in touch.'

'Don't,' Peter said. He opened the oven door, peered in and shut it again. 'Rice pudding's ready.'

Jude looked at him amazed. 'Yesterday you were the one saying I should have followed him in Kew Gardens.'

Peter put his finger to her lips. 'But you needed the rest today. And if you telephone now you'll undo all that, whatever Leo tells you. Anyway, there's nothing you can do between now and then.'

'Then?'

'Tomorrow, once you're back home.'

Jude groaned. 'I hate having pipe dreams. Makes going home harder.'

Peter opened the oven door again and the kitchen was filled with the smell of cinnamon and nutmeg. Jude took two spoons out of the drawer and they set to, breaking the thin skin of the pudding, then dipping their spoons deep.

'You mustn't stay a typist,' Peter said.

'But I can't do anything else that pays.'

'Nursing?'

'God, no! I've been spoilt for that. I couldn't bear being told what to do by one of those starchy buggers. They wouldn't accept any of what I did in the war, I'd have to start and train from scratch.'

'You sure of that?'

Jude nodded. 'I checked a few years back.'

'And why not photography?'

'That's something I would love to do.'

'You know you're good at it, all the pictures you took in the war. So?'

'So the war was a unique thing. Terrible. But women did all kinds of things they'd never been allowed to do before, and then the war stopped and that was it.'

'But it's not like being a train driver or an engineer. You don't have to stop taking photographs just because the war's stopped, do you?'

He looked at Jude, waiting for an answer. Abruptly she stood up and, going into the hall, she rummaged in her bag. She came back into the kitchen holding a manilla envelope and pushed it across the table.

'I saw this happen. I took this, and I don't know why, but it's what made me call Daniel Brown.'

Putting aside his bowl of rice pudding, he opened the envelope and pulled out a photograph. Smoothing the crumbs from the table, he put the photograph down before him.

Slowly, beginning at the bottom edge, he moved a finger, tracing over the black band of border until it reached the falling woman: her diving arms, the flounce of her petticoats caught upwards in the fall, her face, eyes shut, mouth tight, her hair. Then it moved on, so slow now that he might have been marking out each brick on the building, till it reached the window where the waitress stood, just out of focus, staring out, while just above her, beyond her sight for just a split second longer, a woman is falling to her death. His finger stopped, and he circled the waitress's head.

'Almost my first action photo,' Jude said.

'You being sarcastic?'

'Am I ever sarcastic about myself?'

'You wouldn't want to be her, would you?' he said, and though his tone was light, she saw that his eyes were worried.

'No,' she said. 'I wouldn't.'

'That's all right then.'

'I want to be the one with the camera,' Jude said.

'You caught her in flight,' he said.

'But not like taking birds.'

'It's extraordinary. Terrible.'

'It was just chance, my being there. I was looking for something different, but then she climbed out and . . .'

'What made her jump?'

Jude shook her head. 'I only took the photograph.'

'So do it again. And again. Become a photographer.'

'But I don't want to take pictures of children, or dogs, or newly-weds. And that's what women photographers do if they're lucky, that's what's considered suitable, not women caught plunging to their deaths. Oh, and the royal family, and military occasions, strangely enough. Over here, anyway. I couldn't be a photo-journalist, though that's what I was in Belgium. At least not with an agency.'

'So break the mould. Be the first.'

'And all the time I'm trying to break the mould, what do I live on?'

'Be the waitress too. Get a job in a restaurant. You could share with me, here,' and he waved his arm with what struck Jude as touching largesse.

'On your sofa?'

'It'd be fine.'

'And if you had a friend back?'

'As long as you didn't try to pinch him.'

Jude laughed. 'And if I wanted to have a friend back?'

Peter threw up his hands. 'Well, don't smoke a pipe then. No dreams. But anyway come back and visit me sooner,' and he reached across the rice pudding, tugged Jude's hand across the table and lifted it to his lips.

'If I weren't . . . you know,' he said. Almost coyly, Jude thought.

'Except you're not my type,' she said with a grin.

Lying on the sofa that night, Jude thought about the conversation and wondered if Peter was right. That it was better not to have the pipe dream, if you never did anything with it. Still, his was the easier one she thought, as her mind stumbled into sleep, the right man rather than the right life.

Peter's voice woke Jude. He was speaking to somebody, and she realised that the telephone bell in her dream had been real. It was the middle of the night and he was standing by the hall table in his pyjamas, his body still hunched over with sleep but his voice with a note to it that had Jude entirely awake even before she'd fully remembered where she was. She'd heard this accent before, when they'd received casualty warnings before a bombardment. Then, too, Peter's voice would become clipped so that you might almost mistake it for hostility if you didn't know him.

'Yes . . . yes, I understand. She did see him, yes. I'm not in a position to answer that. No. She is, yes. No, I can't do that now, but if you give me your telephone number, she will speak to you in the morning.'

Her eyes narrowed against the light, Jude pushed open the sitting room door.

'Leo?' she said.

Peter put a hand over the receiver. 'It's his father,' he said. 'He's disappeared.'

'Who's disappeared? Whose father?'

'Daniel Brown's father.'

Jude shut her eyes, shook her head to clear it. She put her hand out for the telephone receiver. 'Let me talk,' she said.

Peter handed it to her, disappeared to the bedroom and returned a moment later with a dressing-gown, which he draped around her shoulders, and a sweater for himself.

Jude leant down to the mouthpiece. 'Hello, this is Jude Hursten.'

It might have been Daniel speaking, the voice was so like his, urgent, desperate in tone.

'Our son went to meet you on Saturday? He said he was meeting you?'

'Is that Mr Brown?' Jude said.

'Yes, yes. Daniel's father. We don't know what's happened to him.'

Jude looked down at the floor, at her feet pale and distant. She shivered and crossed one foot on top of the other for warmth, feeling the floor dust rub across her skin.

'I met him in Kew Gardens on Saturday afternoon, and he left me there at about half past four.'

'He wouldn't say anything to us afterwards. Not a word. Only packed up a few things and left.'

'What things?'

'His passport, and some money. I don't know what else. He took a small suitcase.'

The thought crossed her mind that this wasn't usually how you met the parents, and she swallowed a smile. She looked over at Peter, squatted down, his back against the kitchen door, his head slumped. She watched him put a fist to his sleepy eyes and was struck by a wash of affection. At that moment he looked to her just like her little nephew Tom and she wanted nothing more in the world than to put her arms around him and take him back to his warm bed. The telephone earpiece was hard against her ear.

'How did you get this number?' she said.

'He's not with you then?'

'I haven't seen him since I left Kew Gardens, but it was only on Saturday.' Jude looked at her watch. It was one o'clock in the morning. 'A day and a half ago. How did you find me here?'

'We telephoned your brother. Woke him up, I'm afraid. Please, Miss Hursten, Daniel has never gone like this before, even in the worst times after Ireland. We're beside ourselves.'

Jude could hear another voice weeping in the background, Daniel's mother she supposed. She put her hand over the receiver and looked across at Peter. 'What should I say?' she whispered.

He looked up at her, his eyes alert. 'You could meet them tomorrow?'

'But I don't know what's happened to him.'

'Perhaps you could find out.'

'I have to get a train north.'

Peter looked at her again, not speaking.

Jude took her hand off the receiver. 'I don't know that there's anything I can do to help,' she said, 'but . . .'

There was silence at the other end of the line, a breathing, waiting silence.

'I could visit you tomorrow morning, perhaps? He might have returned by then anyway, and if not . . .' Jude left the sentence unfinished.

'Thank you, yes,' the voice said. 'Thank you. Perhaps ten o'clock? We're at the end of the District Line. Richmond. If you take a cab from the station?' And as if anxious to finish the conversation before Jude could change her mind, Mr Brown gave out an address and said goodbye.

They were waiting for her, the front door opened, ready before she was through the gate, so that she had to push away the feeling that she was in some sinister folk tale from which she'd never emerge. Mr Brown was tall and slender like Daniel, and dressed with more care than his son. He shook Jude's hand and showed her into the drawing room. Once again it was a sunny day, but a fire was burning in the hearth and the room was sweltering.

'She feels the cold so easily now,' Mr Brown said as Jude sat down. 'She's just going to bring in some coffee. You would like some coffee?'

'Thank you.'

Mr Brown nodded.

'You haven't heard from him then?' Jude said.

Mr Brown shook his head.

'And friends, family, nobody else has?'

'We don't see very many, we're quite private, cosy I suppose. Just the four of us, three now since John.'

'Daniel told me of his death. I'm very sorry for your loss,' Jude said. She waited for Mr Brown to ask her how she'd met his son, where she lived, anything, but he said nothing more, only walked to the door.

'I'll just help her in with it. Sent the maid home today. Easier if we do it ourselves, these awkward times.'

Left alone, Jude looked around. The room had all the usual paraphernalia – easy chairs, a sofa, rugs, mantelpiece with clock, photographs, some ornaments. Jude looked at the photographs, Daniel in his family, his dead brother. The last showed John, smart in army uniform and proud as punch. There were a few pictures on the wall and a newspaper and a couple of magazines on the side table, just what might be expected. But there was something about it all that at first Jude couldn't put her finger on, something which, despite the blazing fire, left her spirit cold. She sat down on the sofa and narrowed her eyes like she did when sizing up a photograph. Sometimes it made things clearer, brought them out of the shadows. Now it made her see how carefully the room had been arranged, everything lined up, from the objects on the mantelpiece, each equidistant from the next, to the pictures, to the armchairs which were at matching angles before the fire. Even the hearthrug fronds reached to exactly the same place beyond the fireplace. The curtains were tied so that each had the same number of folds in the hanging, and the books in the shelves looked as if they had been arranged by height.

Sitting still in the midst of it all, Jude felt her skin flinch and she got up and went to the window, looked out at the garden, at the trees and the shrubs, at all there was to see that was alive and unruly, till the door opened again and Mr Brown came in with the coffee tray, followed by his wife.

If Daniel had his father's voice, he had his mother's eyes, the same blue, the green blue of the sea before a storm. But unlike her son, who looked around so restlessly, Mrs Brown seemed like someone who couldn't afford to see anything more. Her eyes were cast down, as if the pattern in the carpet held some solution, so that apart from the brief glimpse Jude had on shaking her hand, all she could see of Mrs Brown's expression was the slight movement of her mouth as she opened it to drink the coffee and, in the end, to speak.

'Thank you for coming,' Daniel's father said.

Jude gave a slight nod and sipped the weak coffee and waited.

'My wife doesn't agree with me, doesn't think you could help, feels we should keep it in the family. And maybe she's right, I don't know, but if there's the slightest chance . . .'

'What makes you think Daniel might need helping?' Jude said, keeping her voice impartial as best she could. 'He's only been gone since Saturday afternoon, and he is an adult.'

Mr Brown looked over at his wife, but she kept her eyes on her lap and said nothing.

'I don't know what he has said to you,' he said. 'I don't know what it is he thinks he's seen in your photograph. But lately he's been having dreams, violent, disturbing dreams, about his time abroad.'

'In France?' Jude said.

'In Ireland. And not only in his sleep. Talks about people not being what they seem, about needing to know things, needing to go back. And when he's not speaking like this, or muttering rather, he's more and more withdrawn. You ask him a question and he doesn't answer. And he can't bear being in the house.'

'He was a little jumpy in Kew Gardens,' Jude said carefully.

'He wouldn't speak to us afterwards. Twenty minutes, and then he left, not uttering a single word.'

'So, where do you think he might have gone? What might he have done?'

And when Mr Brown looked at her, Jude knew his worst fear.

'But he took a suitcase,' she said, and suddenly she had an idea as to where Daniel might have gone. It was just the germ of an idea and she said nothing aloud. She didn't want to raise their hopes or fears, nor her own.

So far Mrs Brown had sat motionless, but now she raised her head and stared at Jude.

'What did you say to him? To my son?' she said quietly.

'I didn't . . .' Jude said.

'It's your fault,' she said, very calmly, just as if she'd said it was a fine day, her hands gathered on her lap, though Jude could see that her fingers were white in each other's grip. 'He was doing quite nicely till he met you, you and your picture.' She turned to her husband. 'We had everything nicely set up, didn't we, for him? Really quite nicely, all the wars over with.'

'My dear, I don't think we can blame Miss Hursten,' said Mr Brown. But Mrs Brown seemed not to hear him, or at least not to heed him. Standing up, she set her cup and saucer on the tray and left the room, shutting the door behind her.

Mr Brown walked to the window, stared out.

'Did he say anything, in Kew Gardens, that might have led you to think that he wasn't well? Or did you have any kind of disagreement? I'm sorry my wife spoke to you like that, it's just that we are at our wits' end. I need to be calm, not least for her sake, but we don't know what to do.'

'What about the police?'

'We thought about that, but unless we think Daniel's done something wrong, broken the law, or . . .' He tapped at the window glass. 'The river's just behind us. They pull people out every year. Not usually up here, usually further in to the city.'

'He didn't say anything to me that made me think that,' Jude said.

'But what did he talk about? You were the last person to see him.'

'He did say a bit about Ireland, about the food tasting different.'

This made him laugh, and Jude had a glimpse of a different man.

'He had my wife cook him bacon every day for a week when he got home,' he said. 'He couldn't get enough of the taste of it. Even staying with the Murrays, the food didn't taste like home.'

'Irish friends?'

'Not exactly, no, but they were very kind to Daniel. My wife's sister, Daniel's aunt, was at school with Moira Murray. She said they'd be happy to have him visit during his time there, if he was stationed near enough.' Mr Brown fell silent.

'And he was? Stationed near enough?' Jude said after a minute, prompting.

'Yes. They live in a place called Castletowne, which I gather is in a pretty corner of the west. And Daniel stayed there quite a bit. Coolderry House.'

And Jude nodded, and kept her face still.

Mr Brown's suggestion that she look in Daniel's bedroom took Jude by surprise.

'How could that help? I don't know him very well,' she said, uncomfortable with the thought of such unsolicited intimacy.

'I know it's a strange thing to ask. Snatching at straws really. It's only, we don't have people into the house, and nobody who knew him, maybe you might notice something we've overlooked.'

So, for the sake of his desperate father, Jude agreed. She stood in the middle of the small room and looked at Daniel's neat white bed, pyjamas laid out at the foot, his wardrobe, his bookshelf with its books, not arranged by size, his writing desk, the half dozen school photos on the wall. She looked for the disturbed, desperate man she had met and she looked for the man, still mysterious to her, that she found so compelling. But the room gave nothing away.

Mr Brown pulled open one of the desk drawers. 'I'm afraid that I've had a look at the letters,' he said. 'Didn't like doing it, but, anyway, there was nothing recent, apart from your letter of course. That's where we got the telephone number from. I hope you don't mind.'

Jude inclined her head in a way she hoped signified neither offence nor acquiescence.

'So, you never found out what happened to him in Ireland? Contacted the Murrays, perhaps, in case they knew more?'

Mr Brown shook his head.

'Daniel was very clear about that when he got back. He was all those months in the hospital, you know. He couldn't tell us any-thing for military reasons, and we were to say nothing to anybody else, even if they asked, and especially if they were Irish. So when

139

the Murrays wrote, concerned as to Daniel's well-being, we didn't reply. Terrible, not to reply to such a letter. But Daniel had been adamant. So fierce.'

Mr Brown fell silent. Jude pointed at the drawer of letters.

'There was nothing in there that might help you?' she said.

'They were mainly letters from John. A couple from us, when he was in Ireland. Some postcards from school friends. Nobody he has seen for years. But you could look at them, if you wanted.'

Jude was beginning to regret coming. Despite her deepening conviction about where Daniel might have gone, there was nothing she could do in this house, and she was seeing too much, too much of these people's pain.

'I think probably you'd have found anything important,' she said. 'I should go now.'

They stood uncertain, neither quite sure how to take their leave, Mr Brown rolling gently on to the balls of his feet and then off again. He put his hand out, and Jude, thinking that it was probably more appropriate to shake hands here, in Daniel's room, than on the doorstep of a house that could bear to let nothing in, and noticing how well-kept his fingernails were, was lifting her hand in response when there was a scream downstairs, and the sound of breaking glass.

Jude had a thorough acquaintance with breaking glass and this sound, she knew, was of something small, a glass probably. But what was disconcerting was that the scream had come first. She watched Daniel's father rock backwards and turn towards the door in a single fluid motion, the sounds tugging him as a magnet tugs at iron filings.

'Don't go before I return,' he called back to Jude.

'No,' she said, because under the circumstances she couldn't very well say anything else.

Sitting down on Daniel's white bed, the door pulled to, and though she could hear sobbing below, Jude felt calm, dispassionate. Her disquiet at being so close to this family's grief dropped away, rushed down the stairs with Mr Brown, and she looked around the room as if for the first time.

'There must be something to find,' she said, and she went to take a closer look at the desk.

But Daniel's father had been right. Old letters from other people held no clues, and there was nothing else in that drawer. She pulled open the others, but they had little in them beyond the usual detritus: old fountain pens, a cricket ball, writing paper, school fixtures diaries, penknife, feathers, a few toy soldiers, an old school timetable.

She went over to the wardrobe, opened the door, her reflection swinging away in its mirror. A few suits hung hollowly, below them several pairs of shoes, so that they looked together like puppets with no strings. There were four broad shallow boxes stacked beside the shoes. Jude lifted one out and its lightness surprised her till she lifted the lid. Inside were birds' eggs, each caught in its own false nest and neatly labelled.

At the back of the wardrobe, braid catching the light, Jude could see an officer's uniform. A string of ties hung across the door, and as she pushed it to, they swung in easy motion, several getting caught in the lock.

She wandered over to the bookshelf and glanced at the titles. An abridged Gibbon, some Greek philosophy, Nietzsche, a few novels: Dickens, Henry Dana, Kipling, Rider Haggard. In the centre of the shelf were the two volumes of Coward's *Birds*, a book Jude knew of but did not own. At a loss in this room, she reached and pulled out Vol. I. Opening it randomly, she glanced through the pages. There were dates and locations written in beside some of the bird descriptions: Mothercombe, Aug 24, 1920. South Downs, Feb 16, 1924. Timoleague, Dec 12, 1920, and occasionally the comment, 'sketch made', and she remembered their first meeting, Daniel's notebook, full of wings and feathers. It was in putting the volume back that Jude noticed the diary. She had to push Nietzsche and Plato hard up against Kipling to make space again, and as she was slanting Coward's *Birds* Vol. I back in to the shelf she noticed what at first she thought might be a sketchbook, placed flat to the wall, as if in hiding.

It was a slender volume bound in imitation red morocco, and inscribed on the first page in careful hand.

Occasional Diary
Belonging to Daniel Frederick Brown
June 1920

Turning the page, there was a drawing of a wading bird, and behind it, barely sketched in, a ruined tower. Beneath this: Castletowne, Jan, 1921. She flipped to the end of the diary. It seemed to break off and the last pages were empty, but at the back there were lists of birds and plants, some with place names and dates beside them. Jude was about to read the first entry when she heard Mr Brown's footsteps on the stairs and, without a qualm, she slipped the book into her bag.

He came in, diffidently, almost as though it were her room.

'I'm sorry,' he said. 'It was only a small breakage.' He was silent a moment, rubbing absently at his right hand. 'There can't be anything really that you . . .'

'I can't promise anything,' she said, 'but . . .'

He put his hand to his head and Jude watched a thread of blood well up and trace itself across the knuckles of three fingers.

'You've cut yourself,' she said.

He nodded.

'Have you got some disinfectant?'

'It's only that I don't know what to do, and if you were to think of anything?' and Jude nodded, then shook her head.

CHAPTER EIGHT

Telling Peter, Jude didn't know where the decision had come from, except that she knew she had made it with absolute certainty, that this was what she was going to do. When she got on to the tube at Richmond, she hadn't known, but by the time she reached Regent's Park, she had come to a decision.

'You barely know this man from Adam,' Peter said. 'He's disturbed, shell-shocked very likely, maybe violent, and he's been a Black and Tan. I'm not even sure that you're in love with him. Not with the man himself. And now you're proposing . . .'

'Not proposing. I am going.'

'All right, at the drop of a hat you're going on your own to a country you don't know, that's just come out of a war with England, to rescue him. A bloody tricky needle in a dangerous haystack.'

'Yes. That's about it, except for the rescuing.'

Before negotiating her way into the hotel kitchens to find Peter, Jude had used one of the telephones in the lobby to make a call. The telephone booth had a door with glass panels that folded shut, so that you could see the comings and goings, but not hear them, and it had a gilt chair upholstered in maroon velvet. Jude sat down, sinking into the plush, and shut her eyes. This softness was seductive and for a moment she imagined never getting up, but the telephone rang. Her call had been put through.

She would have preferred to speak to Leo, but he was at work and hard to get hold of. So she was telephoning home to Sally instead.

'It's Jude here,' she said. 'I'm still in London.'

Sally's voice was anxious. 'You're not ill?' she said.

'No, I'm well, but I won't be back today. And I've decided to leave my job.'

Jude was glad she was sitting down to say this. She felt her legs go shaky. She'd decided what to say and rehearsed the words on the tube, but still it was different speaking them out loud, to someone else.

'You've decided to do what?' Sally's voice sounded rushed and impatient.

'Could you tell Leo I'm leaving my job. I'll write properly when I get back, but if he could please send in a note for me tomorrow.'

She could hear Sally breathe in deeply, but she said nothing.

'I'll be coming home, probably tomorrow, for a short time anyway. I'll explain as best I can then,' Jude said.

'Is it that man?' Sally said.

'It's not what you'd expect.'

Sally sighed. 'No,' she said, 'of course it isn't.'

'Sally,' Jude said. 'Would you?'

'I don't want to be picking up your pieces again,' Sally said, and Jude hung her head as if she were a child, although Sally, hundreds of miles away, could have heard only the silence.

Eyes straight ahead, walking confidently and quite as if she knew her way and had an appointment, Jude bluffed her way through five sets of double doors to reach the kitchens. Peter's kingdom. She stood inside the last set, winded for a moment by her own decisiveness. The room before her seemed to stretch for-ever, a domain of scrubbed wood and marble, black ovens squatting like chiefs, shelves full of pans, bowls of vegetables, tubs of herbs, pots of spices, things waiting for their moment under tea towels, and all around figures wrapped in white aprons ministering, pouring, stirring, chopping.

The air was warm and moist, and as Jude crossed the kitchen, scouting for her friend, different smells gusted across her, garlic sautéing, bread dough, rosemary, cinnamon, charging her taste buds, making her mouth water. A boy swabbed at the quarry tiles with a mop, and Jude tapped him on the back.

'I'm looking for Peter Davis?' she said. 'He's a chef de partie.'

'Sauces,' the boy said, pointed Jude across to one side and put his head down to his swabbing again.

Peter had his little finger in a small pan when she found him, a young commis chef standing anxiously beside him. He looked like someone tasting wine, rolling the flavour round his mouth, sucking in air, before nodding.

'Butter needs to be a fraction browner,' he said, 'otherwise good.' Then he turned and saw Jude. She saw the surprise in his eyes, but he didn't say anything. Instead, after taking a long look, he asked her whether she'd eaten anything since breakfast.

She shook her head and would have spoken, but he put his hand up.

'After I've fed you,' he said. 'Tell me then. If it's this important, you need fuel first.'

He took her over to the ovens and lit the gas under the smallest burner.

'Omelette,' he said, and she leaned back against the chopping block and watched him in his element, just as she'd watched him in the cellar years ago, his movements, then and now, both fluid and utterly efficient.

'I'm on an early shift today,' he said. 'Once I've finished prepping, we can talk. And I'm not on tonight.'

Reaching for a bowl on the shelf, he took a pinch of fresh herbs and sprinkled them over the frying pan.

'Cheese?' he said, and she shook her head. 'Good girl. It's often what they want out there, but it buggers up an omelette, I think,' giving a shrug and a grin.

Pulling a plate off one of the piles stacked below the prepping tables, he folded the omelette over on itself and slid it onto the plate. Shouting out some instructions to the commis, he signalled to Jude.

'The vegetable store,' he said. 'We can sit in peace there,' and he led Jude over to a door in one corner.

145

It was cool and smelt of earth. They sat on sacks of potatoes, and when Jude had finished the omelette Peter set the plate down on one side and crossed his arms.

'So?' he said.

'So,' Jude said, and she told him everything, and then she told him of the decision she'd come to. 'These places. Horse Island. Coolderry, which is a house. They were important to him, and he spoke as if they were connected. And then, when Mr Brown mentioned this place, Castletowne, of course I don't know, but if I had to guess, I'd say that wherever they are, these names, that's where he'll have gone.'

'Why?'

'Because he spoke of them as good places, refuges. In Kew Gardens he talked as if in the grip of something terrible that had happened over there. Not being ambushed, and not his injury. Something that gave him nightmares, that was still pulling him in. And set against the nightmare were these places. Coolderry House, Horse Island, that he tried to return to in his head instead.'

'That was talk,' Peter said.

Jude shook her head.

'I think he will break out of his mind, whether he goes there or not. And I'm sure he's gone there for real.'

Peter took her hand, squeezed it. 'Why do you want to do this?'

Jude looked down at the cool, dark floor. 'I don't know. Superstition, maybe. There were things Richard wrote about to me, I don't know what to do with them, and he died before I could find out. Daniel Brown's a haunted man too. Perhaps I don't want to find out too much about his ghosts before I have to, in case it stops me doing something.'

'I think you should let it go. I know you're drawn to him. Whatever you say, you are, and it's great to see you so alive, but it might be very dangerous. He's in a pickle and you barely know him. You made no promises. And you've got your own life to live.'

'That's exactly why I can't let it go.'

*

He argued at her nearly all the way back to the flat, telling her she didn't know what she was going into, that Daniel was a virtual stranger, that he might be violent, crazy, impossible to find. That her guess might be wrong, and he might turn up at his parents' house tomorrow, that she would do better to forget all of this, that it was a mad quest, a piece of folly, that she was only doing it because she was frustrated with her own life.

Jude listened as they walked through the commuter crowds, jostled for space in the underground lift, stood sardined on the tube, elbows in one another's faces, and mostly she agreed with him. And by the time they reached Peter's flat, he knew he couldn't dissuade her.

'It's for myself as much as for any thought of rescuing,' Jude said. 'Same as in the war. I'm not pretending to much virtue.'

Three storeys up, she looked out of Peter's kitchen window, beyond the patch of garden belonging to downstairs, beyond the garden wall, to the cemetery. They'd be shutting the gates soon, but she could see a few people still wandering under the angels' long, stony shadows. Peter put a sheet of paper and a pencil on the table.

'Since I can't dissuade you,' he said, 'make a list, and I'll make toast.'

They covered everything they could think of. What clothes to take, money, travelling as a woman, priests, the journey to Holyhead, the IRA, what story to tell, what to do in an emergency.

'Send me a telegram, or call me. Doesn't matter what time. Reverse the charges.'

'I'm going to go as soon as I can,' Jude said. 'By the end of the week, I hope.'

'Can you get the money released that quickly?'

'Leo will loan it to me if necessary. He's got the same legacy.'

Peter raised his eyebrows. 'Even if he doesn't want you to go?'

'I think so. No point in making bad blood between us.'

'Even though it could be dangerous.'

Jude rolled her eyes. 'It won't be the first time. I'm very well used to bullets and bangs.'

Peter sat down opposite and buttered some more toast. 'Don't be flippant. You know I don't mean bullets and bangs.'

'Well, I'm probably safer as a girl than as a boy.'

'I bet you don't know any more than I do what it's like in Ireland now or what he's like over there, if he is. But if he was a Black and Tan he can't have been a very gentle chap, and they won't be best pleased to have him back.'

'Which I'll find out soon enough.'

'Sherlock,' Peter said, knocking a cigarette from his packet and passing it to her. 'So bring me back some Powers, since you won't be stopped. A big bottle.'

More than anybody else, Tom knew why she was going. She hadn't told Tom and Elsa much, only that she was going to go to Ireland on her motorbike to search for someone whom she thought had got lost there.

'So why don't they ask somebody the way?' Elsa said.

'It's not that kind of getting lost, stupid,' Tom said.

'Tom,' Jude said, 'she's younger than you.'

'But it isn't,' he said, and then seeing his sister near to tears, he sighed and tried to explain. 'You know Elsa, it's like playing cowboys and Indians and you're lost in the desert and I know where you are really, you're up on that bit of wall in the corner, behind the greenhouse. But in the game I have to make up clever ways for you to come down all by yourself and get to the stockade.'

'But who is it that's got lost?' Elsa said. 'Not any of us. Not Daddy 'cos he's at the office, and Mummy's gone to buy some muslin. And not Martin because we saw him yesterday.'

Tom shook his head in exasperation.

'What about Grandma and Grandpa then?' Elsa went on. 'Or the man Jude took to the Rocks, with the stick?'

'Or Elsa's Mister Ictharus?' Tom said. 'Are you going to say everybody we know who it isn't? What about Father Christmas, or the Hound of the Baskervilles?'

Elsa's lip began to quiver again.

'Actually you're right, Elsa. It is the man with the stick,' Jude said.

'He was called Daniel,' Elsa said.

'Why does he need to be found?' said Tom.

'I won't know that till I find him,' Jude said, and both the children seemed to think that that was enough of an answer, or at least they didn't ask any more.

Jude stood against the ferry rail and watched the gulls pitching and scavenging in the wake. Her camera was packed away deep in the sidecar down in the hold of the boat, so she couldn't step aside behind the camera's eye, and she had just to look. She had sat in the saloon for a time, but there seemed to be a great many commercial travellers tucking into their dinners and the smell of the lamb chops became too much. She was better off outside, watching the wind suck at her cigarette and the light drop out of the sky.

Leaving had been easier than she'd anticipated, except with Leo. He didn't try to argue her out of it, as Peter did. Instead he sulked, more as though she were his eldest child than his sister.

'But we've made every allowance for you,' he said. They were picking raspberries for supper, and all Jude could see of him was the top of his old straw hat. 'The darkroom, your comings and goings, not expecting you home for meals.'

'You have,' Jude said, 'and I'm very grateful for all you've done, making your home mine too.'

'I don't want gratitude,' Leo said, 'but I do expect you to have the same consideration for us as we have for you.'

'Leo,' Jude said, 'this has nothing to do with you or with how you've been. It's nothing to do with all of this, the house, Sally, the children. It's separate,' and even as she spoke, she knew that that of course was what he resented.

'We do everything for you and then you go and you shove it back in our faces,' he said.

Jude said nothing.

'I don't expect there's anything I can do to stop you going.'

'No, there isn't.' She put down her bowl of raspberries and walked round the canes to his side. 'But you are my family. You know that. You've been father and mother to me since they both died. I'm not shoving anything back in your face, and without you, God knows.'

She sat down on the grass.

'Please?' she said, patting the place beside her, and after a moment of hesitation, Leo sat down, arms folded over his chest.

'I have to do this,' she said. 'Not only to try to help Daniel Brown, wherever on earth he is, but also for Richard, and most of all for myself.'

'You can't bring Richard back by saving Daniel,' Leo said.

'I know.'

'Then . . . ?' Leo looked round at her, a question on his face, but she shook her head.

'Don't ask me now, because I can't say. But I promise I'll explain when I come back.'

They sat on in silence till Elsa came with a message from the kitchen requesting raspberries.

After this conversation, Leo fussed around Jude like a mother hen, which she was glad of, bringing back purchases of maps, waterproofs and warm socks, all a girl could need, even helping her concoct a story about what she was doing, travelling in Ireland alone.

Jude wondered whether Daniel had been on this boat, or whether he'd taken a different route back. If, that was, she was right about his returning. But her hunch was strong. She was certain she would find him in Ireland. She put a hand to her breast to feel the diary, tucked away safely in an inside pocket. Though she had a Baedeker in her bag, who knew but that this little book might be her most important guide.

The sky was overcast and it was nearly dark on the deck by now, and getting cold. Looking down a last time over the rail, Jude could see only sharp glints from the sea, all else black. She turned towards the light and looked in at the saloon.

The chops had been despatched, the glasses of porter refilled, sluicing and slopping with the slant of the boat, and there was an air of thrusting bonhomie, visible even from the other side of the

150

porthole. A band of exhaustion tightened across Jude's shoulders. Though soon she would have to be a gregarious and affable self, and she would do it very well, for now she wanted nothing more than to nurse her solitude, so drawing back from the glass, she went to find her cabin.

The lower berth was already filled, its occupant lying with the blanket pulled high to her chin, eyes tight shut, dark hair tethered in a net like a separate creature, Pierrot face in the night cream. Jude got ready for bed as quietly as she could, and was climbing up to her berth when the Pierrot spoke.

'I have the cotton wool taken out now, so I'll be hearing you better.'

'I had hoped not to have woken you at all,' Jude said, stranded on the ladder.

She took a step back down, because it seemed uncivil to carry on climbing up.

'Ah, I was only just in myself,' the Pierrot said. 'Catherine Whelan. Pleased to meet you.' She waved the cotton wool. 'Against the engine noise,' she said. 'Would you want some yourself?'

'Jude Hursten,' Jude said nodding. 'Cotton wool?'

'Yes.'

'Thank you, but I like the engine noise. It soothes me. Sorry to have woken you. Goodnight.' And retreating up the ladder, she grappled with the sheets, which seemed maliciously tucked so as to prevent entry, and finally slid between them and slept.

FLIGHT

CHAPTER NINE

Daniel sat on the tube to Paddington staring at the map, staring at the lines reaching out this way and that, to Bow Road and Hounslow Barracks, Finsbury Park and Golders Green, as if they were straining to leave the centre, to unravel.

It was so different, going to Ireland without a gun, as if really he were in disguise.

He knew that the Murrays couldn't solve his problem, but he needed a safe place to go to, and their house, Coolderry, above that stretch of sea was as safe a place as he knew. Probably he should have telegraphed them, made sure his visit would be all right, made sure they were still there, but he had decided that he should just act now, no prevarication, no forward planning. And if, when he arrived, they had left and their house had gone up in the Troubles, then he would walk in the rubble and cold ash, with the rooks behind in their stand of pines and the herring gulls shouting above the sea and his next move would come to him.

He wondered what Jude had done, after he'd left Kew Gardens. He was sorry he'd left her like that, but he'd walked very fast until he was sure she wasn't following. It made things harder that he liked her, though what on earth she thought of him he couldn't say.

When she'd come towards him at the turnstile, he'd felt proud that this beautiful woman was coming to meet him, and even with everything else crowding in, he'd wondered whether people might think she was his girl, fiancée even. She moved so surely, as if everything she did rose from a clear decision. The way she walked, turned her head to look around, even the way she fished in her bag for something, and it wasn't that she was entrenched, only that she knew what it was she was moving towards.

If his mother were to meet Jude, he knew she'd say afterwards that she was a man's woman, which was a way of saying she was too forward in her own bearing. And his father would talk even harder than usual, about world affairs or cricket, or the state of the roads, to veil his unease in the face of such strong definition. Daniel knew all too well where Jude had gone since her war and, standing there in Kew Gardens, waiting for her to see him, and even in the midst of his own confusion, it crossed his mind that he'd like to be there when she walked back in from outside again. He'd watched her smile when she saw him and it had made his skin jump.

On the train from Cork a couple sat opposite Daniel, a woman in a blue cloak and an older man. The man had mud on his boots, and his hands were resting flat on his thighs as though he had been taught to sit that way in public places. The woman was crying a little, wiping her eyes on a corner of the cloak. The man leaned forward, tapped Daniel on the knee.

'No basket,' he said, pointing to the woman.

'No?' Daniel said.

'He was the last, we've just seen off. We didn't take the train with the others, but he was our last, so we've been to see him off at Cobh. We watched him into the ship, and he was holding the basket, waving to us with the other hand, just as if he was off to Cork for some business.'

'Oh,' Daniel said, unsure what response the man wanted.

'They said it would be better with the war over.'

'The war?'

'Against your lot.'

Daniel looked down at the floor. The boards were scuffed. If you ran your hand along them, you'd fetch up with a splinter. The man doesn't know, Daniel told himself.

'And it isn't? Over?' he said.

'It's a great thing to have the British gone, no offence, and to have the next madness over, thank God. But there's still nothing to

156

be done for work, and so the young ones, they've no choice but to leave. Always the emigration.'

'I'm very sorry,' Daniel said, but as he spoke, he knew the apology was for something more, something that he'd never yet dared face. And he felt the fear rise, because he had breached his own defence, coming back here.

The man shook his head. 'No, no. I'm only telling to explain about the basket . . .'

'I am very sorry,' Daniel said again, and he thought, I have kept this from me, kept it away with my injury and my fury. Now what will I do?

'Because you might be wondering, otherwise, though maybe not, being from over the water and things done differently there,' the old man said, and from the way that he stopped talking, Daniel saw he was expected to answer.

It went through his head that he would go mad. He knew that a terrible thing had been done to him, and he had come back here because of it. But there was something else looming, that he'd kept his eyes averted from all these years till now, and sitting opposite this old couple and riding across this landscape, he couldn't do so any longer. He'd done nothing to injure these two particular people, nothing to harm them, but it might as well have been the old man he'd arrested; it might have been their son he'd pistol-whipped or their daughter he'd burnt out; it might have been their family he'd looked away from as the boys obeyed orders. In the name of another man's order, he had done what no man should and he didn't know how to stand before it now.

The woman had dried her eyes by now and was staring out through the window.

'Be quiet, Dennis, for pity's sake,' she said. 'Going on about the basket. It's a wonder I haven't sent you over the water too,' and she turned her head and looked at Daniel gravely.

'From England,' she said, a statement and not a question, and Daniel nodded. 'Whereabouts?'

'London.'

'We've relatives in London. In the north of the city. Kilburn.'

'I'm from the south. Twickenham.'

'So it's your first time over here, is it?' the man said.

'Is it so obvious?' Daniel said, bringing out a hollow laugh from somewhere, for it felt to him as if his guilt must be written on his skin.

The man tapped himself on the chest. 'I've an eye for such things. Are you going a long way?'

'Castletowne,' Daniel said, and the woman nodded as if he'd just confirmed something she already knew.

'And then home to your mother?' she said, the words tugged from her as if she couldn't help herself but ask, and when Daniel nodded, she turned her face to the window again.

The man had been filling his pipe, tamping down the tobacco. 'Is it family you've got here?' he said.

Daniel could smell the tobacco, its sweetness filling his head, familiar, conjuring something.

'I don't know,' he said, and maybe it was the look he had, but they didn't ask him more after that. The woman looked on out of the window, the man attended to his pipe, and Daniel shut his eyes and pretended sleep.

The train ran across rough land. There was Cork city; there were small towns, Crookstown, Macroom, Bandon, Dunmanway; villages occasionally, a string of buildings and a creamery; sometimes a smallholding, dogs chasing the train, wild-haired children waving, shouting, their mouths wide in silent cries, the smell of turf in the carriages. But always the land threatened, rough bog, rocks, hills dense with gorse and heather, the metal gleam of surface water catching the shadow of the train as it went past.

Daniel sat, eyes closed, and clutched at the straw of his sanity.

The weather had darkened by the time the train reached Skibbereen, a soft rain gentling the edges of buildings. Before leaving the train, the woman found an umbrella and the man buttoned his jacket high into his neck. Relieved to have something to do, Daniel took out his cape and pulled on his hat. He thought it was about five miles to Castletowne, and he'd already decided to walk, ignoring the ache in his leg, always stronger

158

when it rained. Stepping down from the train, Daniel turned to the woman.

'Where would be best for something to eat?'

She seemed to look him up and down before answering, as though they hadn't already met.

'You'd better try Becher's,' she said.

Daniel put out his hand. 'All the best then.'

And she nodded, her lips in a tight line, and maybe it was just his mood, but Daniel thought something in her eyes had gone hard. He turned to her husband, but he had his back to them and was deep in conversation with a man in an overcoat. So Daniel left them and went on his way.

He ate dinner at the hotel in the plainest of dining rooms, its walls a pale yellow at the wainscot rising to a deep brown near the ceiling, the air very slightly rancid with the decades of tobacco smoke, a single glassed-in trout – fifteen pounds in weight and caught in the Ilen river on 29 February, 1904 – eyeing him as he ate the food quickly, cutting the meat up into equally-sized pieces, breaking his knife through the potatoes' coarse skin into the floury flesh, scooping it up with his fork. He had forgotten these potatoes till now. They didn't exist in England, and if he hadn't been so hungry, he would have left them on his plate.

'I must be crazy, to be coming back,' he thought, and his heart began to race and his palms became sweaty. He had to do this and it made him very scared.

It was still raining when he left Becher's. He shook out his cape and was about to fasten it around his shoulders when he looked at it with horror.

'Christ almighty!' he said below his breath.

Pulling the cape off and gathering it in his hands, he stared about him, but nobody seemed to have noticed, and he opened up his suitcase and stuffed it inside.

'Bloody fool!' he said, because it was his Auxiliary cape he'd been wearing, as clear a badge of office as pulling on the beret and pointing a pair of revolvers. Perhaps that was why the woman on the train had gone cold and the old man turned away with no farewell. And if that were so, he'd been lucky to get away with nothing worse than a woman's contempt.

Leaving the town with its Weeping Maid of Erin and its grey, weeping houses, his spirits calmed and he set his mind to the road and the effort the walk demanded. He would not think for now. Twice, carts slowed to offer him a lift; one stacked high with turf, the other with two milk churns, some hens in a basket and two sheets of corrugated iron. And both times Daniel returned their gestures and smiled and waved them on saying thanks, but he could do with the air, and both times it brought a laugh and an exclamation about the weather, then a flick of the whip, the donkey's reluctant hooves striking up a quicker pattern and slowly the cart would pull away from him.

Now he was back here, on a road like the road in his dreams. Rough banks of hedge with swags of mombretia, ditches full with clear ochre bog water and dense with tiny yellow flowers and wild watercress; fuchsia in its violent red and the endless, heavy hum of the bees; the coarse fields with their boulders and yellow blaze of ragwort, and the rain falling through the still air so that he could smell the damp wool of his jacket, so that his shoes squeaked. But it was better, this, to be able to see and touch and smell it than have it slip around him like vapour. So as he strode on, his suitcase clutched as tight as any weapon, though he was frightened, he felt clearer in his mind and he was sure he'd been right to come.

He passed cabins and farmhouses where dogs barked to kill, a shrine in pastel blue and chipped shells, the Virgin reaching out her arms, prayers tied to her wrists, her elbows, and cold candles guttered out on stones. And after a couple of miles, above the smell of burning turf, he could smell the sea. He wouldn't see it until he was almost there, but the brine in the air was enough to lift his head. Things steadied with the thought of it. The road turned and twisted as if reluctant to arrive and then he saw ahead the plain, straight steeple of the Catholic church on the crossroads. It was only another mile or so to the village, another half mile beyond that to the house. A flock of sheep came wailing and bleating

160

towards him, two boys and a dog chivvying. Daniel stood still while the sheep shoved their way by him, their wool pungent, mud-smeared, baubled on their rumps with droppings.

The sheep past, the boys were close in their ragged trousers, shirts and grubby waistcoats. One lifted arm and stick in greeting. But before he'd said more than a word Daniel was reaching round to his shoulder, pulling for where his rifle should be, the suitcase hitting against his legs so that he stumbled and fell on to the wet tarmac, his hands still grabbing air, thunder in his ears, a shout swallowed in his throat, till suddenly everything went still and he heard the sheep again and above him stood just a boy in torn trousers.

'Yous all right?' the boy said, putting out his hand.

'Lost my balance,' Daniel said, and the boy nodded, raised a finger in farewell and turned back to his flock.

He didn't let himself think about falling, about losing his footing on a wet Irish road, about what he'd seen in the boy's raised arm. Instead he set his mind to the house on the hill and the path down to the beach, to the little boat, to those two people who, he was sure, could help him somehow.

Passing the church, Daniel soon came to the long hill down into the village. His leg was sore and he winced, walking carefully. He recognised the tumbled gate that led up to the standing stones on the crest of the hill. Mr Murray had taken him there, and to the hill fort opposite. You could see the whole of the peninsula from it. They'd stood there in the long shadows of early evening and Daniel had joked that he could hide out in the fort and never go back.

Down past the long wall, then he'd turn off to the right and though he was going slowly, it would only be another ten minutes' walk.

You couldn't see the house from the road. There was a short, winding drive dipping down in amidst the rhododendrons, oak trees behind, and then, magically, a glimpse of the sea, before you saw the house. It was nearly teatime by now. The rain had stopped and there were breaks in the cloud letting lines of sunlight through. Daniel turned through the gateposts. The gate had been painted since he'd last been here, and the hedge had been clipped recently. He made himself walk slowly. Wild strawberries grew on either side and he stopped and gathered some, carrying them in his cupped palm. As he came around the corner, though he knew it would be there, his heart leaped at the thin lip of blue beyond the green of the lower meadow, before it was hidden again by the out-buildings and then by the house.

It looked just the same. Except it was summer now and it was almost too pretty. Old roses flowered up the walls, the beds on either side were full of blues and yellows and in front of the house nasturtiums tumbled in a riot of orange and red. A black Labrador lay in front of the house. It got up and wagged its tail. A woman in a faded dress and wellingtons, her greying hair slipping from its pins, bent in front of them with scissors, snipping, and she stood and turned as Daniel approached.

'Daniel! My God!' the colour draining from her face, and he saw her drop the scissors which bounced on their points like a dancer, before lying, legs akimbo, on the ground.

'I'm sorry, I should have telegraphed, or written, but it all hap-pened so fast.' Daniel put down his suitcase and put out his hand. 'I'm glad to see you again, Mrs Murray.'

She took his hand, and then drew him closer, gripping him by both arms, holding him.

'We thought you were dead,' she said at last. 'No word, ever. I wrote to you, and your parents, and your aunt. And Joe spoke to the police in Cork, and the barracks, and nobody would tell us anything.' She shook him again, as if for good measure. 'And now, here you are, in the flesh.'

'I couldn't . . .' Daniel began.

Mrs Murray put a hand to his lips. 'Later. Come inside. I must find Joe.'

They gave him tea and buttered barmbrack, sitting on the terrace looking out to the sea, and talked of the weather and what the farmers were saying, and how the fish were running. The sky had cleared and there was no sign of the earlier rain clouds, only wisps of high cirrus streaked across the blue. The air was warm and the sea was calm in the estuary, smooth except for the wash of a couple of boats making their way out to fish, or gather in lobster pots. Though he knew from their faces that they were worried about him, Daniel was relieved and grateful that they didn't demand any explanations. Not yet at least. And when he spoke finally, he didn't try to explain anything, but only asked if he could stay with them a while.

'There's something I have to do. I'm not safe from things, but I believe I'll be safer here than anywhere else.'

'We've already discussed it, and you can stay,' Mr Murray said.

Daniel breathed out. He hadn't known he'd been holding his breath. 'Thank you.'

'Only thing is, if you want any supper, you're going to have to get out and catch it,' Mrs Murray said.

'It's still a rising tide, so we've a good chance with the mackerel.' Mr Murray pointed. 'You see where the water's ruffled? That'll be a mackerel shoal, on the hunt for sprats. Sometimes the sprats are so desperate, what with the mackerel all around them like tigers, that they'll throw themselves up on the beach.'

'How many did you find inside one that time?' Mrs Murray said.

'Last year it was. I was over a shoal and caught ten in about five minutes. No point taking more, we can't use them. And I was gutting them in the boat, throwing the heads and bits over the side, and the largest of them had fifteen sprats inside him. None of them eaten yet, lying there end to end. Like sardines.'

Daniel had been in the boat before, though not in the summer. He knew nothing about sailing, little about the sea, but Mr Murray had taught him which sheet to pull when he shouted out and Daniel had loved getting lost to the wind and the water and the demands made by the sails. This time Mr Murray took them across and beyond Horse Island before letting the sails flap and handing Daniel a spool wound round with fishing line, and knotted on the last length with a series of hooks, small weights and spinners that fractured the sunlight as the two men unpicked the sharp points from one another, then unwound the lines over the side of the boat.

'Let out most of the line and keep it taut against your finger,' Mr Murray said. 'So you can feel if there's a tug. And pull it gently every couple of minutes, to keep the spinners moving. It's the light they're drawn to, they gulp at the spinner and then they're hooked.'

It was just as Daniel thought nothing would happen that his line began to jerk.

'It's tugging,' he yelled.

'Wind it in then.'

Watching the surface of the water as he wound, the point where the line dipped down and out of sight, Daniel waited to see what he had hooked, and when he reached the end of the line and there were four floundering bright-eyed fish, their bellies iridescent green and blue, he felt his eyes fill with tears and he turned back to the water and peered at its sheer surface and let the spray wet his face so the one salt was like the other.

The fish gasped and bled for air on the floor of the boat, tossing and flipping and staring, till Mr Murray cleaned them with his penknife. Two sharp strokes into the gills and he flung the head high to a waiting gull. Then another stroke to open the belly, tugging the guts out quickly with his fingers, dragging his hand over the side of the boat to wash them free. When the fish were safely in a basket, lidded against the hovering gulls, he turned for home.

'Four's enough for tonight.'

That evening the Murrays talked about many things: their daughter Isobel, Mrs Hewetson and the St Barr's Flower Committee, the old dog, and the kittens born in the hot press. And Daniel caught the look that Mr Murray gave his wife at least twice in the evening, and he caught her slight shake of the head, so that still they didn't ask him why he'd walked down the drive that day.

Daniel ate and drank like a man not knowing where his next food would come from. The mackerel was good, and the cabbage. Mrs Murray brought in a glass bowl of gooseberries and another of whipped cream. Mr Murray talked a little about the hotel trade, that it was picking up, now their own wars were over.

'Thank God you'd retired before it got really bad,' Mrs Murray said.

'And I'm hopeful. More visitors again, the new government being seen to govern.'

Mrs Murray rolled her eyes. 'Though we can't expect them to do anything for the likes of us. Most of them are IRA men. They'd rather see us burned out than help us out.'

'That's not quite fair,' Mr Murray said, patting his wife's hand. But she pulled it away, and Daniel could see the rage far back behind her eyes.

'We're as Irish as they are,' she said. 'But they'd be rid of us if they could. They've been rid of a fair few already.'

'There've been terrible things on both sides,' Mr Murray said. 'And now . . .'

'And now they have it that we've only been out for ourselves. They tar us all with the same brush. If you're a Protestant, you're the enemy.'

'Come on love, the people who know us think no differently than they've ever thought.'

Mrs Murray looked round at her husband. 'I was in Mr Moriarty's last week and I'd to wait a while for my order, and Mrs Moriarty was cutting a ham. Mrs Moriarty, whom I've known since before this century began. She asked after Isobel and I said how they weren't so happy in England and were thinking of moving to Canada. And she said, all tears and sympathy, how it must be sad, people not wanting you wherever you went. Then she said, was it enough ham she had cut.'

'Darling . . .' Mr Murray said.

'Don't darling me. I've never done a thing to hurt Mrs Moriarty. Any of them. They're no better than peasants, treating us like that.'

'Moira!' Mr Murray's voice was severe. 'We have a guest at our table.'

After a pause, she shook her head and nodded. 'Hard times, and you don't want to be hated.'

They ate in silence for a few minutes, before Mr Murray spoke again, and he must have had a different kind of nod from his wife, because this time he asked Daniel a question.

'What about you?' he said to Daniel. 'We thought . . . we guessed you'd been injured over here, and when we didn't hear, no answer to our letter, we assumed the worst. Is that where you got the injury to your leg?'

All the way here – on the train, and the boat across the water, and the next train, and walking, and then arriving – all the way he'd thought he might not be able to do the next thing. But he had, and he'd arrived here. As fiercely as he could, he'd kept his mind on this place – sea, trees, birds, these two people – and kept at bay the fury tied inside him like a knot. But something else was lurching in his gut now, something he could control even less than the fury. He put his hands to his head, over his ears, he hunched his shoulders, as if he could shrink, as if he could make himself disappear.

'An accident,' he muttered, 'motor lorry accident.'

'Don't ask any more,' Mrs Murray mouthed at her husband, and he nodded.

'How are your parents?' he asked, and Daniel told them how his mother was and they nodded and looked sorry.

'Do they know you're here?'

'I'm going to write. Tomorrow.'

'It must be hard, being the only one,' Mrs Murray said.

'That's why I went to Ireland, partly,' Daniel said, still speaking as if from behind some barricade.

'But not why you came back?' Mr Murray said.

'No. Not why I came back.'

'That was the motor lorry accident.'

For a minute, Daniel didn't answer. Something was unravelling, and he didn't know if it was inside him, or, like some white, swaddling cocoon, outside.

'No,' he said at last. 'It wasn't an accident. It was an ambush. And I couldn't tell you then, even that I was alive, because it was too dangerous. And maybe it is now, too. But I can't hold things

166

in any longer now. The worst of it, do you know the worst of it?'

The two people either side of him waited, their faces still.

'It's Johnnie, and Will and . . .' Daniel shrugged. 'Can we talk of something else now?' he said, his voice, to his surprise, sounding calm. So they changed the subject then, and the three of them laughed at the dog, sleeping with her paws over her eyes, and after a few minutes Daniel uncoiled and picked up his spoon.

'So how's your father's business?' Mrs Murray said at last.

'I'm working for him now,' Daniel said.

'I remember you were in several minds about that.'

Daniel nodded. 'My leg . . . well, it put paid to the other minds. And now.' He stopped. The gooseberries were green in their bowl, the cream was white. The two people looked at him, waiting. He could see their faces, and beyond their faces the window and the darkening summer light. The sun had dropped beyond the line and the colour was gone from the day, things changed to black and white. He had to speak to them, but he was so tired, and it was so hard to get his tongue to make the right movements. Words were beginning to come out wrong and he feared what he might say.

'I will have to,' he said, and even this took the most terrible effort.

'You need to rest,' Mrs Murray said. She turned to her husband. 'It was too much, taking him out in the boat today.'

She went round to Daniel and squatted on the floor beside his chair.

'I'll take you to your bedroom. You should sleep now. Whatever we all have to say will wait.'

The room they gave him faced the hill. She told him that as she led him up the stairs. 'It's like being in the trees,' she said.

'I might dream loudly.'

'Do you want us to wake you?' she said, understanding.

He nodded. 'If you can.'

The Murrays agreed between themselves that for now they would try to keep Daniel's presence in the house quiet.

'He is so changed,' Mrs Murray said.

'What if he needs a doctor?'

'If he needs a doctor, then we'll have to trust Dr Ross. He met him of course, the first time. But otherwise, let's wait till we know why he's come here.'

'Lizzie will be tricky. We don't want the wrong people knowing about him. It could be dangerous.'

Mrs Murray thought for a moment. 'We'll send a message saying we've come down with something. Flu.'

'She'll still want to do the laundry.'

'So we'll leave it in the porch. For her well-being. And we'd better cancel bridge, and the Mahonys. They were coming on Saturday.'

'You don't think it's a girl, do you? Daniel's problem.'

Mrs Murray shook her head. 'I wish it were, but I think it's a different kind of pain. I'm not sure he knows it all himself.'

'It's the Troubles, isn't it? That's why he's come back. It's something to do with that, with his injury maybe, something to do with over here.'

'He'll tell us when he can because it's burning a hole.'

He was quiet that night, and still into the morning he slept. He slept throughout that day, rousing somehow only to drink some water, and the Murrays kept watch. He was, for the time being, safe to surrender.

CHAPTER TEN

Catherine Whelan was still sleeping the next morning, a gentle chug of a snore slipping between her lips on each breath, when Jude shut the cabin door behind her. She'd been woken by the change in the engine sound, and when she stepped out on deck, she knew why. The ferry was turning away from the sea, turning into smooth-skinned water, past two hulking forts high on the headlands and into another country. Jude shivered. The sky was pale and clear, the sun still a small flat unremarkable circle. Mist hung above the water and she could hear the plash of oars in the water somewhere, though she couldn't see the boat. The shores were wooded, here and there a break in the trees and a low cottage, a thread of smoke from the chimney, or the glimpse of something much larger. A couple of men huddled at the rail, their hat brims touching, muttering important things to one another and not looking at the scenery, or noticing Jude in her britches and her boots. Otherwise Jude was alone. Soon she would have to decide what on earth to do next, and somehow keep faith with herself that this was not all a piece of folly. She turned away from the waking landscape and pushed open the deck door.

She was on to her third cup of coffee by the time Catherine found her.

'You're visiting Cork, then?' Catherine said, sitting down opposite.

Jude nodded. Catherine Whelan was younger than she'd first thought, now her mask was removed, barely a woman yet.

'Family?'

'Work,' Jude said. She'd thought by now about what she'd say to this young woman. 'Photographs. Birds, chiefly. I'm a photographer. Started during the war. I'm on an assignment for some magazines.'

'Oh,' Catherine said, her voice rising with curiosity. 'The Irish birds'll be different from the English ones, then?'

'It's more to do with the landscapes,' Jude said. 'They're keen for me to show off the Irish countryside, remind people what a beautiful country it is, especially after . . .'

'It'll take more than a few photographs to do that,' Catherine said, her voice suddenly sounding older than her face seemed. Then, like a clown, she buttoned on a different expression. 'Anyway, you'll have to come and have something to eat with my family,' she said, 'and I'll show you the sights. I'll write you out my address.'

'It's very kind of you, but . . . I'm not sure of my schedule,' Jude said, but Catherine waved her down.

'No, you must,' she said. 'We have the best cook in Cork, and I'll be offended if you refuse. Anyway, are you not eating now?' she said, sitting down opposite.

'I've eaten,' Jude said. 'You?'

Catherine shook her head. 'I'll wait for the solid land.' She looked hard at Jude's sweater, at the leather jacket bunched over the seat beside, then up at Jude, her forehead creased in a question.

Jude smiled. 'My motorbike's down there with the motor cars,' she said. 'Hard to ride it in a dress.'

Catherine leaned over, glimpsed Jude's britches and her eyes widened.

'Of course it is,' she said, and she looked down at her own clothes. 'I can see that would be something of a problem.' She thought for a moment. 'So it's for getting around to see the birds you have the motorbike, is it then?'

'That's right.'

'They'll be all over it when you bring it onto our street,' Catherine said. 'And I'll be splitting myself looking at their faces when they see you're a girl.'

'Have you been away for long?' Jude said.

'It was my sister's lying-in. She has a nurse with her, but she wanted someone from home. So I've been over helping. Her first.' She opened her handbag, fished out an envelope and passed it to Jude. 'Such a dote,' she said.

Jude took out a small photograph. It was slightly out of focus, which, having no passion for babies herself in general, she thought helped endear, and the baby was so swaddled that its eyes were only just visible below its bonnet. She nodded and smiled.

'Sweet,' she said. 'Where does your sister live?'

'London.'

'And she's well?'

Catherine nodded. 'It's a girl, a strong one. Esther they're calling her, and both of them fine. Three weeks ago today.'

She stared out of the window, then pointed. 'Spike Island,' she said, her voice suddenly lower and darker.

'What's that?'

'A cousin of mine was in there for a while. Possession of a firearm, enough to put a man away then.'

Across the water Jude saw a series of low grey buildings. 'It's a prison?'

'A military prison. Your lot still have it.' Catherine got to her feet. 'Let's go outside, I'll point you out a few things.' And without waiting, she was weaving through the tables and pushing open the saloon door. So Jude followed.

'Now enough of all that,' Catherine said in a breezy voice. 'That's Cobh, used to be Queenstown,' pointing. 'The *Titanic* set off from there. And it's where we do our emigrating from.'

Jude saw a town of grey stone rising steeply up the hillside above the water, lines of tall terraces, and in its midst a great church with a vast tower high above the roofs.

'St Colman's cathedral,' Catherine said, pointing. 'You'd be a Protestant, wouldn't you?'

'I haven't been to church for years,' Jude said. 'I don't think I believe in anything very much.'

'Then you'd be a Protestant.'

'Yes, I suppose so.'

171

Catherine nodded, something confirmed, and pointed towards the shore.

'We're headed up the Lee at last. We'll be in soon enough now and I'll be on the tram and home. Are they putting you up somewhere proper, your assignment people?'

'My assignment people?'

'The ones who want the birds.'

'Oh, yes. Yes they are, for a night at least, though I don't remember the name of the hotel.'

Catherine looked at her doubtfully. 'But you're sure now? You've somewhere to be going to?'

'Yes, sure.'

'Well so, here's my address. It's in Sunday's Well, north of the river, but it's near in. Anyway, you have your motorbike to be getting about on. You'll come and have some supper with us tonight. My mother will be delighted.'

If a tall man in a heavy tweed suit hadn't come up at this point, Jude thought later, she'd have had to have made up an excuse very fast to get away. She needed to collect herself, and she couldn't with Catherine pointing out every bend in the river. She'd have been getting her to go to Mass next thing.

'Why, Catherine! Such a thing to meet you here. I spotted you over my fried eggs,' he said, pointing back towards the saloon window. 'Whatever are you doing, so far from your mother's apron strings?'

'Dr Kelleher!' Catherine said, turning to the figure bearing down on them. 'This is my new friend, Miss Hursten. Dr Kelleher. Our doctor, before he moved on to grander pastures.'

Jude looked up at a face whose ruddy complexion looked more like a farmer's than a doctor's, but whose broad smile didn't conceal the sharp quiz that was in his eyes.

He held out his hand. 'She's always a one for the flattery. You'd want to watch her if you were a fellow,' he said.

'She's here to take photographs,' Catherine said. 'They want to see our birds now back in England.'

Jude gave a laugh and nodded. His handshake, like his smile, was both firm and somehow interrogatory.

'Well, good,' Dr Kelleher said. 'So whereabouts are you headed for?'

'Tonight, no further than Catherine's house and supper,' Jude said, matching his jolly tone with her own. 'The Irish living up to their reputation for hospitality, and I'm not even off the boat. If you'll excuse me, though, I ought to check my equipment,' and she was walking towards the saloon door before she'd even finished her sentence.

'Come at six, then,' Catherine called. 'And watch out for the Cork drivers. They're the devil. Specially the ones with a donkey.'

Two hours later Jude lay sprawled on a pale green needlecord counterpane and marked out the cracks on the ceiling. Daniel's diary was beside her, but her thoughts were rushing and she told herself that she needed to steady them before she opened it again. It had been so straightforward, getting to here, as if some powerful external momentum had been driving her forward. But now, lying on this bed in the middle of this noisy, foreign, unknown city, she felt beached.

A travelling salesman in the ferry hold had recommended the hotel just as the boat was docking.

'Try the Victoria. Clean, very reasonable. Bang in the middle of the city. You can put your motorbike in their yard, too. It's full of hens, but safe from little fingers. Patrick Street, opposite the Ulster Bank, perfectly safe these days. Ask for a room at the back though. It's noisy at the front.' And then, looking at her in her britches and her boots, he'd said, 'But you want to be careful what you get up to over here, you know. The Pope might not like it.'

And she was going to ask him what he meant, but then they opened the hold doors, he started up his van and it was too late.

There were no vacant back rooms in the Victoria, but Jude didn't mind being at the front, all the bustle of a city at its business below. She listened to the sounds: tram bells, the clip of heels and horses, motor cars, women's voices, a child wailing. It was so close to home, almost like England, and yet so foreign. The voices had a different rhythm, different tune almost, and though she'd barely

173

spoken to anybody here yet, hers felt a heavy, blunt thing beside this other, quick music.

She wondered now whether this was a fool's errand, a mad journey she was making. And to busy herself, and stop herself wondering further, after writing out a list of errands – maps, provisions, postcards, telephone call to Leo – she packed the diary into a bag and went out into the city.

An hour later and she was done. Three postcards lay stamped and ready on the table in front of her. Peter's with a stout Irish man in tailcoat, worsted stockings and knee-breeches, puffing a clay pipe and making eyes at a pretty Irish girl in a shawl; Tom's showing another stout Irish man driving a jaunting-car over boulders and upsetting his tourist passengers; and Elsa's with the same figure again leaning over a pigsty and a bubble over the pig's head saying, 'Oh no, not that old tale again'. Leo had been called and her bag was heavy with provisions and camera film.

She sat by the window in the Pavilion restaurant and looked out at the people on the street, her gaze catching on different figures: the black-shawled woman staring in through Lipton's window at the bacon cuts; the young men heading in beneath the Bar Billiards sign; the mother with her daughters in hats and gloves; the boy peddling string with a grin; the man up a ladder pasting 'Wolsey Underwear' to a billboard; the old man filling a clay pipe leaning up against a cart, cap pulled low, fingers shaking. And all around them, the crowds busy about their day.

A waitress brought her a huge lobster salad. Finding herself in something of a holiday spirit, Jude brandished the nutcrackers and broke open the thick shell of the claw, laying bare the soft pincer within. The lobster had come with bread and butter, thick slices, different from any bread she'd had before. It had a rough brown crust and a soft, moist, yellow crumb. It was delicious. As she buttered it she remembered Daniel telling her how different the food was here, so that he had craved the tastes he knew. She drew out the flesh and dipped it in the mayonnaise.

Jude hadn't opened the diary since the day she found it in Daniel's room, and though it was less than a week ago, it seemed

174

like a lifetime. She'd told herself she had enough else to organise, and till she got there, there was nothing she could do anyway. Now, though, she knew she'd been putting it off. She needed to face out her fear of what she would find in there. She wished Peter was with her, to offer up sardonic asides if it got too much. But she was here alone and she needed to find any clues she could about where Daniel might be and why. So she took the diary from her bag and put it on the table. She'd open it once she'd finished the lobster.

They were building something huge across the other side of the broad street, she could see it in between the trams. Men with winches lifting great blocks of stone, others hunched over holes, a crane swinging out over the Tivoli restaurant, over the busy pavement, another over boards for 'Paddy's whiskey' and 'Jacobs biscuits', and a clutch of little boys, all knees and elbows, agog at it all, who made her think of Tom.

'What are they putting up?' Jude asked the waitress.

'They say it'll be the grandest shop in Europe,' the waitress said.

'Who's building it?'

'So my da swears, there's money gone in from over the water, though I don't believe a word of it.'

'Over the water?'

'Guilt money from your lot, but very hush-hush. It's a fellow he knows in the pub works on the site and he overheard the foreman, you know how they make them travel, those stories,' and Jude nodded. 'Says it's your government in England has put it up, but he doesn't say it in the kitchen or my ma'd have him. She says she's had her fill of the Troubles and there's to be no more mention in her house. Now, will you have anything else?'

And lifting the plate of lobster shell from the table, the waitress swung away. Jude looked again out of the window, taken aback by her own forgetting. She'd seen the photographs in the papers, it couldn't have been much more than four years ago, 'Cork city ablaze'. She even remembered having an argument about it with Martin.

'Good propaganda for the IRA,' he'd said, facetious, grinning, but still, and she'd been outraged, which was what he'd wanted.

'Lloyd George sent the Black and Tans over as thugs. They've been burning homes ever since they started. And now this, now they're burning cities.'

'The photo could be of France or anywhere,' he'd gone on. 'Piles of rubble and burned-out buildings. And anyway there are some saying the Black and Tans didn't light the fires but were trying to put them out.'

Jude wanted to ask the waitress, did she see the burning? And the Tans? Was her family involved? She wanted to ask this young girl in her pinny and starched cap, who was just then walking so carefully to the table in the corner, her tray heavy with plates of oysters and pots of tea, what she thought of it all, and did she hate the young English men who burned her city and terrified her people, one of whom Jude had come to find.

She sat back in her chair and checked her watch. It was two o'clock. She had as long as it took. Weighting the diary open with the sugar bowl on one side, salt cruet on the other, she started reading, writing down notes in the 'Bells of Shandon' notepad she had bought for the purpose: names, places, important events, questions as they occurred to her. She didn't notice the waitress returning.

'Will you have something else? Tea maybe, or coffee? We do lovely coffee.'

Jude started and shut the diary, tipping over the salt cruet as she did so. Pinching up some spilt grains, she flicked them over her shoulder.

'Superstitious,' the maid said, smiling.

'Doesn't work though,' Jude said.

And only once the coffee had arrived and the waitress had gone did Jude begin her reading again.

Feb 21st, 1921.
    5.30 a.m. Rain still. Very dark inside barracks, what with shutters and shell boxes. I think it makes men worse.

You can feel the pressure building, especially when you can't see the sky. Two or three of the lads very nervy, out for blood. I don't think they've slept much. They say they know who the Shinners were. They say Smith was shot in the back. I saw his body when they brought him in last night. I couldn't say for sure.

There'll be a fishing trip.

Jude looked up from the words, at the bustle, the people eating and drinking. Daniel might have sat next to any of these, might have passed the time of day. She was glad she was reading this in a place where people were doing ordinary, busy things, and not on her own. Looking back down at Daniel's small, neat script, she thought how innocent the words would look from a distance, to a passer-by. Their tidy sentences and paragraphs, all the dates underlined, no crossings-out, proper punctuation. She sat up straight and rolled her shoulders, tried to ease the tension, then went on reading.

It certainly makes you angry, and when you thought you were trying to help them. Not the out and out Shinners, they're the enemy, but the women, and the little boys that sit on the walls watching. Because they're as likely to be up to something as the men. Duguid came in shouting about how he was going to shove his hands up the next lot of skirts he came to, orders or no orders, and then about what he was going to do with what he found.

They're signing out ammo, so we'll have to go into the town and let them know what's what. Col. Whittam ordering us to use restraint, but you can see he doesn't believe it. Reminding us about firing in the air, firing at windows. A child was injured last month, and some cows. Those Shinners will have gone by now, they'll be in the fields or the hills, or gone to the city. So we'll have to bring in others.

1.00 p.m. What a fishing trip. I was right. There were only the women left. We searched the places pretty thoroughly, O'Connor's house and shop, the other fellow's farm, and only found a cousin, a boy about fifteen, hidden out in the pigsty. All the men had gone, both the fathers. A few bits got broken, some windows of course, whatever Col. W says. Behave like pigs, treat them like pigs, Will said, which I was surprised at. It's a sign of the pressure, I suppose. It gets to all of us. Still, for corner boys and rustics who barely know a rifle from a hurley stick, they do enough damage. It's no wonder our boys retaliate.

I'm in the mess upstairs, in my corner. Jumbo is sprawled on the table next to this diary, his tail flicking at my pen as if it were some aggravating insect. He's my favourite of the barracks cats.

The boy is downstairs, he's Col. Whittam's, so he should be safe enough. There's a couple of others brought in who are already on our lists, so they're bound to know something. He's got them downstairs too. I can hear them when somebody opens the mess door. He's not being very gentle, but then they weren't very gentle with Smith.

Jude put her hand over the page and shut her eyes. This had been written by a man she thought she liked, by the man she was searching for. He had sat at a table, stroked a cat and written paragraphs describing what amounted to torture. Torture he was justifying as tit-for-tat. Jude's heart raced, and she made herself breathe deep and slow. A girl was discussing her trousseau at the next table, how many nightgowns, how many handkerchiefs she would need, and Jude listened in for a few minutes before opening her eyes and making herself return to the page.

Col. Whittam has sent notice to both families to vacate their premises. I don't want to be on burning duty, I hate it. You get drunk on it, shouting and roaring with the others, and these pathetic figures standing there in the street, watching their home burn, women and children again usually, and you loathe them and their men who've run and hidden, and then afterwards you're left with a horrible taste in your mouth. Maybe everybody else feels like that too, but you don't talk about it so I don't know, even about Will. The enemy does it back, of course, but still it doesn't seem right.

There's been stuff at home in the papers again about over here, but they should come and see for themselves. I don't know where they get their information from, but it's not from us. It's enough to drive a bloody conchie to violence.

I'm 4–I up over Will at billiards. I've got the hang quicker than he has of playing the tears in the felt. No word on when it will be replaced, but we've got the glass back in the windows, so better light, which makes the shots easier.

Nothing from home still. I'm worried about Mother.

Passes out are cancelled for now, so no fish and chips, even if they do taste like they're fried in engine oil. Will said they wrapped his in the IRA propaganda paper one time. It's written *An t'Óglach,* but I don't know how to say it. So he says he read all this IRA propaganda, made-up victories and arms hauls, but I don't believe him. Too risky. The shopkeeper would've been shut down, gaoled for it at the least.

Everyone's getting more pent up. It must have been easier in the Great War. A proper enemy, and the women and children properly innocent.

Except for the Murrays and Coolderry and Horse Island, the sea, the birds, I wish I was out of this godforsaken country.

This latest mess makes real fishing look more unlikely. I was hoping to go there in three weeks. But even Castletowne might be too dangerous now. For me and for the Murrays. Prods are fair game for the Shinners anyway, though Mr Murray said not a single person in their vicinity had been attacked so far. If I go I'll have to be incognito somehow.

There are stories of IRA reading all our mail. One Auxie being told by a Shinner on the street that his mother had died before he even knew it himself. Don't know whether to believe it, except that worse has happened that I know to be true, so why not.

Some of our boys very keen on confetti at the moment. That's what Will calls it. Getting blind drunk then driving through town shooting off at the bushes, trees, bog, spraying bullets at everything. There are accidents of course. Lots of damage to property. A little girl with two bullets in her leg, a man killed working in a field. He only had a spade. They've had a dressing down for it, but Col. W will do what he can for them.

For as long as she was reading it, if she pretended the diary was nothing to do with her, treated it like a novel, or a newspaper, written by somebody she had no knowledge of, Jude could read the entries through. The lists of food, the numerous so-called fishing trips, the burnings and brutality, the anecdotes, the searching for Shinners, the broken 'bits', as he liked to term Irish property. But as soon as she stopped, the horror came in and she felt her bile rise. Who was this man? This callous figure who could write about bullets as confetti and children as less than innocent. Jude didn't recognise him, didn't know how to put him together with the man she'd taken to the Rocks, or even with the haunted man she'd met in Kew Gardens.

She became quite ruthless to get through it, banished her thoughts, her fears, and in this way she read it all right through.

The waitress brought her another pot of coffee, and then one of tea, so that by the time she was finished, Jude felt awash. Outside, shops were beginning to close, tired shop girls rolling down shutters and lifting grilles into place, and the water wagon was laying the day's dust to rest. 'Wolsey Underwear' gleamed out whitely opposite, its glued seams smoothed, and there was a new trickle of young men, still in working clothes, disappearing under the Bar Billiards sign.

Jude looked at her watch. It was nearly five o'clock. Catherine had asked her for supper at six. She was numb, unable to take in what she'd read. Even within the diary she couldn't connect one Daniel with another, he seemed so different at different times. And the man with blue eyes that were also green, with his twitches and his lame leg who had knocked at her door, it seemed an age ago, though it wasn't more than a couple of months, he was somebody different again. She remembered Richard's letter. He'd shot defenceless men and he couldn't weep. Closing the diary, she put it in her bag and, one hand on the table to steady herself, she got to her feet to go.

CHAPTER ELEVEN

The hotel yard was locked and the man with the key, having fed the hens in the yard, had gone to feed his own when Jude went to retrieve her motorbike. So she took the tram to Catherine's house in Sunday's Well. She had posted her mail in the pillar box on the corner. A scratch in the green showed the old British red through, and the 'V R' and its royal insignia was painted over but still clear to see.

The sun was setting and the river had turned black, slick as oil. Jude sat and shut her eyes. Exhaustion hit her, piled itself on, pulsing through her skull, pressing at her eyes, crushing her shoulders, turning her stomach over. She should look out of the window, watch the scruffy boys at their errands and the girls in their layers of skirts slowing their step at last for the young men who hung about the quays, and the women tugging barrows and the men walking home from she didn't know where. She should look up at the city, at Shandon's steeple high and white above. The busboy in the Victoria had already told her about the bells.

'It's a Mr Meredith you'll want to find,' he told her. 'He's the bell-ringer. He'll do just about anything you'd want, "The Harp that Once", "Oft in the Stilly Night", "The Last Rose of Summer". You can hear them across the city.'

'What would you ask for?' Jude said, and the boy replied that he'd ask for 'The Croppy Boy', though he'd never heard it played on the bells, and Jude said she didn't know that song, at which the boy nodded as if he knew that.

But now it was evening and too late for the bells and anyway Jude's eyes were closed as the tram made its way, her thoughts drifting away from Cork city and the busboy and the bells of Shandon. She was horrified by what she had read. But the harder thought, the one she was keeping at bay, would push from her mind for the evening, was what on earth she was doing here, pursuing the man who had written those things.

She'd asked the tram conductor to let her know when they had reached the nearest stop to Catherine's address, and it was now that he tapped her gently on the shoulder.

'There's the convent there, and beyond is the gaol. You'll be somewhere near the two of them.'

The Shandon bells struck the quarter as Jude climbed down from the tram. The steeple reminded her of some building blocks Tom and Elsa used to play with. You could stack them, each one smaller than the one before, the yellow on the red, red on green, green on white and so on up, and make a steady tower.

She could smell roses somewhere in the air, though none were visible, and horse dung, familiar smells, but not enough to reassure. She'd give her eye teeth right now to be stacking building blocks, or anything that went one upon the other upwards.

Jude wished Kate were here, or Peter. She felt very much alone on this hill above Cork city, all high walls and secrets, the night coming on, on some crazy adventure to find a man she barely knew who'd been involved in God knew what, and in a country she didn't understand.

Five minutes later and Jude had found Catherine's house. It stood at the end of a tall, grey-plastered terrace, long thin gardens sloping away down the hill towards the river far below. Through the front window she could see somebody at the piano, and a somewhat thumping rendition of 'Für Elise' made its way through the window.

The door was opened almost before she'd knocked on it and a diminutive version of Catherine in a faded print dress and bare feet stood before her, grinning.

'You'll be Catherine's English friend from the ferry boat,' the girl said. 'The one with the motorbike,' and she peered out into the street.

'I came on the tram,' Jude said.

'They'll never believe me now,' the girl said, her face glum as quickly as it had been bright.

'About what?'

'That girls can ride motorbikes, they'll never believe me, Frank and Dermot. You have got one?' and her tone was both questioning and accusatory.

'Next time, I promise,' Jude said. 'And you can have the first side-car ride, if your mother allows.'

'Really?'

'If your mother allows.'

The girl nodded, grinning, and took Jude's hand. 'I'm Martha Whelan.'

'Jude Hursten.'

A square woman bustled up at this point and gave a rough curtsey to Jude and ttched at Martha, pointing at her bare feet.

'It's our guest, from England,' Martha said. 'With the motorbike, only she hasn't it with her now. Will I go on and tell Mammy?'

The woman patted the small girl on the head.

'Put your sandals on and take our guest in. I'll go and tell the mistress,' and still without saying a word to Jude, she was gone.

'Catherine's been in such a tizzy, with having you to supper, we've hardly heard a thing about Daisy's baby. Mammy had to have a word,' Martha said, taking Jude's hand.

'I'm sorry,' Jude said.

'No, no. Mammy's very glad. She loves to have guests. It's only with Catherine back from England and sounding like she knows a thing or two above. It's a stir to her. She says she's been boiling bacon since before Catherine was even a spark in the eye, and if Catherine would like to do something useful she could go and lay the table, which is already seven, and then Dr Kelleher coming, though he might be late, with his house calls. Catherine said you'd met him on the boat.' She paused for breath, then finished up. 'Of course, it's the cook who boils the bacon, but I suppose it's Mammy tells her to.'

Listening to this little girl's chatter, Jude felt a dart of home-sickness. Martha must be about Elsa's age and for a moment she would have given anything to be back at home with Elsa and Tom, and not heading off on this strange pursuit, even in the company of such small and charming strangers.

Martha's speech had brought them through a hall, which seemed only just to contain the hats and coats, cricket bats, hockey sticks, umbrellas, skipping ropes, hoops, school satchels and bowls of flowers that were hung, leaned, hooked and piled, and past two steps down to the kitchen. Even with the door closed, a delicious steam, sweet with cloves, issued from in here.

Martha pushed open the sitting room door and Jude followed her in. The room was high-ceilinged, papered in a Japanese style, with windows showing onto a long garden bounded on each side by a high wall. Far down it Jude could see fruit trees, and nearer to, a boy, older than Tom, intent with a stick of some kind. Although it was summer, a fire was burning in the hearth and a woman sat on a sofa before it, darning, a heap of stray socks in a basket at her feet.

She got up as they approached, wiping her hands on her skirts as though she had been cooking, and put a hand out to Jude, meeting her with a strong smile.

Jude's first thought was that Mrs Whelan looked like a woman who was used to meeting her troubles face on. Something to do with the way she squared her slight body as if making herself ready, balanced like a dancer.

'Welcome,' Mrs Whelan said. 'I see you've had a somewhat formal introduction to the household.'

Jude laughed. 'It's very kind of Catherine to invite me, but I hope it hasn't been a trouble to you.'

'Not at all. Will you have a glass of sherry?' She beckoned to Martha. 'Be a great girl and bring us some sherry. Very carefully.'

The little girl nodded slowly, importantly. 'Which glasses is it?' she said. 'The ones are all jagged, or the ones like the communion cup?'

'Like the communion cup, but little,' Mrs Whelan said, showing with her fingers how tall, and Martha nodded and was off.

'Catherine says you've an interesting job to do over here,' Mrs Whelan said, 'photographing our birds and such like.'

Jude nodded.

'And that you've come on a motorbike?'

'I have. I've ridden it since the war.'

'The European war?'

Jude nodded again. 'Actually, I wondered, would you have any objection to my giving Martha a ride in the sidecar another time? I promised I'd ask.'

Mrs Whelan studied her guest. 'Is it safe? Have you had any accidents ever?'

'None on the motorbike,' Jude said. 'It's as safe as a bicycle.'

Martha returned with the sherry and glasses, slow-stepping into the room, craning her head over the tray to avoid tripping, picking her feet up elaborately high. Jude watched Mrs Whelan pour the sherry. Though her daughters were dark, she was red-haired and in that evening light her skin seemed translucent. Her face was angular, pale, cutting different planes as she moved and the shadows around it shifted. Something in the way she moved reminded Jude of Kate.

'I'd love to take your photograph,' she said, the words coming out before she had time to consider them, and for a moment Jude felt a pang of guilt. As if, even though Kate had died all those years before, this new adventure broke an old pact of intimacy that Jude had kept in trust all this time.

'My photograph?' Mrs Whelan sounded taken aback, and Jude was annoyed at herself, because perhaps professional photographers didn't say things like that.

'I'm sorry. That's very rude.'

'No, no, it's not rude. Just surprising.'

'The light at this time, in this room. It'd be good for it. Perhaps when I'm back in Cork?'

'It might be raining then,' Mrs Whelan said. 'But I'm flattered. I'd be curious, to see what you made of me. So you've been here a

186

quarter of an hour, and you're going to take my photograph and give my children rides on your motorbike. Tell me this isn't how you usually meet strangers?'

And Jude couldn't begin to answer her, because Mrs Whelan was right, and she didn't know how it was that this strange quest to find a missing man should make her so forthcoming, and she put the thought by, as something she should think about when she was on her own later.

'So it's your first time over here?'

'It is,' Jude said, and after a little more small talk and with the sherry drunk, Jude was despatched with Martha to the parlour while Mrs Whelan checked the progress of the dinner arrangements. The pianist, a girl a fraction taller than Martha, had moved on to somewhat frantic scales. Catherine came in, proprietorial, with fresh lipstick, and kissed Jude on the cheek. Then she turned to the pianist.

'If you play them slower you'll learn them faster, that's what Ma says, and could you stop now, so our guest can sit till supper.'

The little girl stopped playing dead, mid-scale, slid down from the stool and without a glance at Jude, stalked from the room.

'That's Mary,' Martha said. 'She's a year and twelve days older than me, and very good at the piano playing, but she's the worst of the tempers, and she hates to be commented on. D'you know who they are, though?' and Jude was nonplussed till she saw that Martha was looking at the pictures above the piano.

Jude walked up closer. There were some nondescript water-colour landscapes – the Italian Alps, the Killarney Lakes, the Lake District – and a couple of horse races, together with some photographs of young men in teams, a rugby ball sitting proudly between the legs of the captain. Somewhere in all that burly good cheer, Jude thought, must be their father. There was another photograph of men in lines, this time in police uniform, their buckles catching the sun, and flanking the lot, one on each side, were two portraits of historical-looking men.

'So do you know who they are?'

'Do I know who which are?' Jude said.

'There's our papa,' Catherine said, pointing to a figure sitting smart in his police uniform.

'Now you have to find him in the rugby,' Martha said, 'and no help from us,' and Jude did so easily, struck by the girls' likeness to their handsome, dark-haired father.

'But do you know who those two are?' Martha said then, pointing at the small portraits.

Jude looked at them, not allowing herself to look at their names, then shook her head.

'You don't know?' Martha said. 'Truly?'

'No,' said Jude.

'So then, that's Daniel O'Connell, and that's Robert Emmet and they are both Irish heroes, but I don't remember which came the first.'

Between the two of them, the two girls told Jude all she could possibly need to know about the family before the bell was rung for supper. And Jude listened as it was spilled out before her, and it filled up her head and, for now, kept at arm's length the dark material of Daniel's diary.

'Our papa was in the Force,' Martha said.

'That's the RIC,' Catherine said, 'except it isn't called that any longer. It's the Garda now.'

'Anyway, he was a policeman.'

'He was a District Inspector,' Catherine said grandly.

'But he died,' Martha said. 'How long ago was it he died, Catherine?'

'Five years,' Catherine said.

'I'm sorry,' Jude said. 'That's very hard, to lose your father so young. Do you remember him well?'

'I helped him put on his uniform,' Martha said. 'That was my job. And I got to put his cap on him.'

'Quite a responsibility,' Jude said, thinking the little girl couldn't have been more than three years old.

In the silence, Jude could hear the boys arguing outside the door, then just thuds as they fought.

'And once when I'd the fever, it was in the night and I was

allowed to sit up with him while he had chops and tea and then he went out. Mama didn't like him having chops and tea because it's what the constables ate and he wasn't one, he was higher up. But he said it was what he liked and he should be the one to choose.'

'Martha,' Catherine said, 'there's no need to be saying all of that.'

'And he didn't die in the Troubles,' Martha went on, and as she spoke, she hit a piano key again and again. 'And it wasn't the IRA that killed him. He had a weak heart and he was after chasing somebody one night and in the rain, and it shouldn't have been him doing it. It's the wet that did for him, and Dr Kelleher won't deny it either, and he should know.'

'I'm sorry,' Jude said.

Martha jigged on the sofa next to her. 'Play something, Catherine, please? Like Ma said, to entertain.'

And Catherine turned to the piano and played till the bell sounded.

Jude enjoyed supper. It was loud and genial and she was treated both as an honorary member of the family and as somebody who needed to be looked after, not understanding the customs of the place, especially by Martha.

'You should eat the cabbage with the bacon,' Martha had instructed her, 'it's how God intended, is what our papa told us.'

There were arguments between the boys about cricket and hurley, whatever that was, until Catherine rounded on Dermot.

'The way you go on, you'd think there was nothing in the world but hurley,' she said, rolling her eyes. 'You'd think the Holy Father played it the way you go on.'

And then Mrs Whelan intervened, and Jude sat back and enjoyed it all and missed Tom and Elsa in equal parts, until the door bell rang.

The table changed with Dr Kelleher there. It wasn't that he demanded anything, as far as Jude could see, or that he expected anything particular from the children. But she noticed how each of them tried to impress him in their different ways. So Dermot sat straighter and finished his vegetables and Frank announced that he knew how to do long division and that he'd come nearly top in the Latin test. Martha had taken Dr Kelleher's jacket from him and Jude could see her trying to hang it on a peg in the hall, jumping with the jacket above her head, till Mrs Whelan sent Frank to do it for her. And Mary, seated next to him, got him salt and pepper and the mustard pot, chivvying up the table to have them passed along quickly.

Mary and Martha especially, the youngest of the children, seemed not just anxious to please the doctor, but wanted to press in on him, get as close as they could. More, Jude thought, as if he were a father returned, rather than a family friend.

'Your first day in Ireland began fine on the ferry this morning. I hope it has continued that way,' Dr Kelleher said.

'Yes, thank you.'

'Not so many birds in these parts for you to snap, though.'

'It's not only birds I'm wanting. But anyway I plan to head off into the countryside tomorrow.'

'Ah.'

There was something in Dr Kelleher's tone that Jude couldn't make out. Not that he didn't believe her exactly, but certainly some element of suspicion.

'And tell me again what you're taking them for?'

'It's a commission from a picture magazine. They want to run a piece on the landscape of the British Isles. So landscapes and some animals.'

'You must be a very good photographer. Can't be an easy world for a woman to make her way in.'

'No, it isn't. But I've known it's what I want to do from very young, and then I took a lot of photographs during the Great War, just as an amateur, I was nursing in Belgium, but it still helped, I think. My name got around a bit, I made some contacts. One of the very few for whom the war brought good fortune amongst the bad.'

She felt dizzy, tipsy almost, as though she had drunk far more than the one glass of sherry. What was strange was that it felt so easy, to make up this story, exhilarating. As though by saying these things, she was making them so. As though she were making up for herself someone else to be in the world. 'But be careful,' she told herself, 'or he will find you out.'

'I don't suppose you've any with you, though,' Catherine said. 'Magazine photographs, I mean?'

'No, I haven't.'

She had Daniel's photograph in her bag, though. What she thought of as Daniel's photograph, of the two men sharing a cigarette and Kate standing behind. And a few others from the war, and a couple of birds in flight she'd taken recently, that she'd stuck in the envelope too, she didn't quite know why. Old times' sake, maybe, the war ones, though she winced at the thought. So on the spur she decided to show these around the table. After all, Daniel had been stationed in County Cork, and if his Irishman, as she thought of him, if he'd been important, he might be well known. His photograph might have been in a newspaper. Somebody might recognise him. She opened her bag and took out the envelope.

'But I have got a few other photographs. A couple of birds, gannets, I took recently, and a few that I took in the war.' She passed them to Catherine. 'The war ones are snaps really, amateur things,' she added, swallowing with pleasurable ease the small bubble of embarrassment she felt at her white lie.

'You were nursing over there? In the European war?' Catherine's voice was sharp with excitement.

'I was.'

'Your mother let you go and do that?' Catherine said.

'My mother died while I was still at school. And my father couldn't really stop me, not when so many young men were joining up to fight.'

'Girls get up to all sorts these days,' Dr Kelleher said, looking at Mrs Whelan, and Jude was conscious of another conversation going on at the table, one she was not privy to.

Catherine glanced for a second at the gannets and then pored over the wartime shots as though if she studied them hard enough, they might yield up the key to her ambition.

'Come on and let the rest of us have a look,' Dermot said, and reluctantly, Catherine passed them round, the bird photos first, and then, one by one, the others.

Jude sat watching. It was uncomfortable, being viewed like this. But if she was to play her part properly, she supposed it was something she would have to appear used to, so she tried to look relaxed and bit her tongue. Sat on Catherine's left, Dr Kelleher was the last to see them. Frank had wanted to know what kind of rifle the soldiers carried, which she couldn't answer, and Catherine asked whether she'd seen men die, to which she said she had, and women too. Dermot asked her how fast she rode her motorbike and she explained that it depended. That if you had a wounded man in the sidecar, you went slowly so as not to bump him, whereas if it was just you, and you were trying to avoid being shelled, you went a good deal faster. She told him that she'd had to ride across the fields once, the road being blown up, and that some of the shell holes were so big, half the size of this room, and filled with water, that you might disappear for ever at night if you weren't very careful.

'Like Doctor Foster who went to Gloucester,' she said. 'We were forever stepping in puddles up to our middles.'

Dermot listened gravely. 'That's nothing,' he said. 'We've those all over in Ireland. Isn't that right, Dr Kelleher?'

'Well, there are still holes in the roads, certainly,' Dr Kelleher said laughing. 'I don't think we'll have them smoothed over in a hurry. But they're not the kind from the Tan war any more. Those have been mended now, and they weren't shell holes. Trenches more often, and made on purpose. Miss Hursten wouldn't have been able to skirt round those on her motorbike. That was the point of them.'

The photographs had reached Dr Kelleher by now, and Jude, her thoughts drifting back over that drowned Belgian landscape, was only half-watching. She could smell it again, riding on the road to the village, where, even in the cold air, behind the water there was the sweet, rank smell of rot. She saw the pale light over the flooding, ruined farmhouses like islands in the watery plain. Cows like floating balloons, dead fish breaking the surface, their white bellies to the sky, and sometimes a dead soldier lifting the flat line of the strange inland sea. Occasionally there was a burned-out motor car, the passengers still sometimes seated, unrecognisable, unmistakable, or the humped-up body of a horse or a sheep, clumsy in death. And if the sun broke through and the light sharpened, then visible on the horizon was the low line of trees that hid the German guns. Jude could see their tongues of fire across the flood waters, and the shells digging geysers, throwing columns of water into the air, the filthy spray falling like stones, hurling fish on to the sodden land.

'You look as if you've seen a ghost.'

Jude started from her reverie. It was Mrs Whelan speaking, but not to her. Mrs Whelan leaned across the table and tapped the doctor's hand. He looked back at her blankly.

'Dr Kelleher?' she said.

He turned abruptly, and stared at Jude.

'You're not staying long here?'

'I'll be off tomorrow,' she said, waiting, wondering if he had more to say, if perhaps he had recognised somebody.

'Not planning any photographs of the city then?'

'She's going to take Mammy's photograph,' Martha chirped and Jude felt herself blush, though she didn't know why.

'I am,' she said, 'but that'll be on my return through Cork. I did think I'd take a few of the city early tomorrow, before going,' Jude said, unsure of his tone, unsure what he wanted.

'In which case, perhaps you'd let me be your guide,' he said, in a tone that had more aggression than courtesy in it. He shuffled together the photographs and handed them back, his eyes all the time on Jude, not giving them another look.

'I was going to go out at about seven-thirty,' Jude said.

'That'll be fine. We'll meet underneath Father Mathew.' Jude looked blank. 'It's a statue further down Patrick Street, near the river.'

'So who was he?' Jude said.

'A big temperance fellow,' Catherine said, 'and the statue was put up as a reminder.'

'And does it work?' Jude said.

'Not at all,' Frank said. 'As Father always said, the statue is a beacon to the porter drinkers of Cork,' and Catherine scowled and everyone else laughed.

'All right,' Jude said to Dr Kelleher, 'seven-thirty tomorrow.'

'Could I come too?' Catherine said, grinning, perky.

'No,' the doctor said, so abruptly that Jude saw Catherine's chin quiver, and the girl said nothing more. Something had altered his mood, but Jude could see that he wasn't going to say what. He got to his feet.

'I'd better be going.'

'But you never go till much later,' Mary said. 'And I'm to show you my piano piece, and Dermot, he's . . .'

The doctor shook his shoulders, as if to shrug the children from him.

'No, it's bedtime for me now, if I'm going to be on my toes first thing tomorrow.'

'But you've not had any pudding,' Martha said, tugging at his sleeve. 'You never go without pudding.'

'Let go, Martha,' he said.

'Martha, go and get ready for bed,' Mrs Whelan said severely, and Martha did so without another word.

CHAPTER TWELVE

Daniel had made a flag for himself on Horse Island. A spindled, bleached branch as the pole, bark worried off by the sea, knots standing proud, and on top his shirt, though it didn't blow out much that day, there being so little wind. He didn't put it up on the beach because nobody must know he was there. But if he climbed up the rocks at the back of the beach, he could follow a sheep path through the bracken and broken stone walls to the middle of the island. So he'd carried the flag in and stood it where it couldn't be seen, anchored with stones.

The sheep were in a sorry state, their torn wool hanging like bandages beneath them. They didn't like to go down to the beach either. They were anxious. Daniel tried not to look at them, always turning this way and that, jutting their heads, rushing off one after the other through the bracken.

If there'd still been horses, then he could have caught one and ridden it bare-backed when danger came. But there were no horses on the island any more. Mr Murray said it was the good herbs they used to bring them over for. Good herbs for sick horses. They'd leave them here a while, then fetch them back. Daniel wondered what a horse would look like in a boat, Mr Murray's boat for example. It would look too tall.

He stood up on a piece of wall and looked out across the channel. Birds hung above the woods and he could hear a cuckoo. The fishermen were long gone on the early tide, he'd watched them leaving when he woke. But he counted three yachts moored, nobody visible on them, and a few sailing boats. Near the mainland, a dinghy with some boys larking about. He imagined boats tip to tail across the sea, from there to here, a sick horse in each and a man pulling the oars.

They'd wanted to make the Irish horses sick. Will had shown him a sheet of paper.

'Don't ask where I got it,' he said. 'Read it.'

<u>Glanders in Horses: Propaganda Directive No. 16.</u> He remembered the number. He hadn't known what glanders was. But Will had known. The island herbs wouldn't have been enough for those sick horses. He'd told Daniel about abscesses and ulcers, the skin swelling and bursting with pus, suppurating, and then the muscles and the joints and finally pneumonia.

'Most don't survive,' Will had said, 'it's a horrible death. Two weeks or so it takes. And it's very contagious. Even humans sometimes.'

Directive No. 16 had been very practical. How to doctor a bag of oats with a hollow stick and microbes, and how it might help to turn the war for the British.

'Turn the war how?' Daniel had said, and Will had looked at him scornfully.

'Because of their passion for horses. To break their spirit.'

At the far end of the island the watchtower on its cliff faced out to sea. It was round and had no roof now. He stood in the middle of the circle and looked up at the blue sky. A blackthorn bush was seeded up at the top, its trunk making a loop around the stones, and there was ragwort in the window-hole. The light was very clear and Daniel could stand inside the doorway and look far out over the water. That's where the Spanish ships had come from, the Armada. They'd been fleeing, at their wits' end. But it wasn't out there that the danger would come from now. If Johnnie had been here, and not dead in France somewhere, they could have split the lookout and one of them fished or slept while the other watched. It was easier having Johnnie in his mind when he was on the island. He could imagine him here. Johnnie would have understood this place.

He made a den inside the bracken so nobody could see him, and slept. In his dream everybody was a horse except him. Will was, and Colonel Whittam, and there were horses with glengarries on their heads, and others with slouch hats and overcoats. Then the shooting started and there were horses wounded and dying all around him, his friends. And other horses, foals and fillies, looking on, holding the guns. Then a piebald foal lifted a hoof towards him and raised a rifle, and Daniel sat straight up, back tight away from the foal, hands to his face for protection, because everything was touching him, his neck, his hands, ankles, arms, scratching, tickling, and the air was murmuring. He opened his eyes and the air grew green and quiet. He sat till his heart had calmed, then crawled out of the bracken and lay on the grass above the rocks.

'I am awake now,' he said. He was thirsty and took out the thermos of water Mrs Murray had packed for him. Then he ate a sandwich and three plums.

He had brought nothing to Ireland for the birds, so Mrs Murray had found him a notebook and soft pencil and he had Mr Murray's binoculars for the day. He was careful with the binoculars. If the lenses caught the sun, the dazzle would betray him. A flock of choughs wheeled above the woods across the water, their 'keeow' calls soft at this distance, then scattered as a peregrine winnowed its way high into the sky before making a lazy glide across the canopy. Sitting far back on the beach, he watched the oystercatchers, their red bills and red legs, as they hammered limpets from the rocks and dug in the sand for worms. They stood in lines at the low tide, facing out to sea, waiting for the water.

The water was cold and very clear. At one end of the beach there were sea urchins in the deeper pools. Daniel saw a small starfish. If he needed to, he could fish for mackerel off a rock, or collect winkles and boil them in sea-water over a fire, pick out their insides with the hoof pick on his penknife. Johnnie should be here too, but he wasn't.

Daniel stood very still in the shallows and after two minutes or so small fish began to nuzzle round his shins.

The tide had gone right down and begun to rise again and the wind was rising when he saw the boat coming to get him. He crouched behind a rock until he could see the colour of the hull. Mr Murray's boat was painted green. Once he knew it was green, he rolled his trousers up and stood up to the knees, waiting for Mr Murray to come and take him off.

CHAPTER THIRTEEN

Jude was woken early the next day by the sound of the water pipes, which groaned and rattled under the floor like hard-done-by ghosts. She surfaced from sleep slowly, remembering where she was. The day was bright. She could hear the rattle of carts, the occasional shout, something foreign in the rise and fall of the voice.

She found that one of her arms was above her head, dead to the world, and until she put her other hand up and felt it there, fingers caught between the bars of the bed head, she couldn't work out where it had gone to. Easing the hand free, she lifted the arm down to her side. The blood surged back so that she wanted to clench and grip, clutch against the feeling returning. She'd woken like this so often, she should be used to it by now, but she still found it strange. She would go to sleep lying on her side, legs drawn up, arms between her knees, wrapped around herself, and wake to find herself undone, reaching away.

As the feeling returned, Jude caught up with the waking day. She remembered now and her stomach clenched. She was meeting Dr Kelleher this morning.

She took pains with her hair, and put on her prettiest blouse and a skirt, though she would change out of both before the journey. For half a minute she wondered at herself. This wasn't a date, for God's sake, so why was she dressing up? And it occurred to her that it wasn't so much the doctor she was dressing up for as herself. As though she wanted to give herself the pleasure of her own beauty.

'You need some air,' she told herself then. 'Clear the cobwebs,' and she shook her head at the thought and lifted the heavy sash open to the day.

Jude was early to the statue. She had paid her bill at the hotel and packed her things. The motorbike was ready, she had checked the tyres and the oil, and as soon as this meeting with the doctor was over, she'd be away.

The morning light was grey and the sky low, the air was heavy and damp. She had her camera bag slung on her shoulder, but the light was too dreary even to pretend to be a photographer. She'd thank Dr Kelleher for his offer to show her around and then she'd take her leave. Politely, but definitely. The Whelans had been wonderfully hospitable, just what she'd always heard about the Irish, but she was less sure of the doctor. He wasn't being hospitable, and she didn't think he particularly wanted to show her the sights of his city. He made her uncomfortable, aware of herself, though she couldn't say why.

She looked down the empty street. A few boys were unlocking grilles from the shop fronts. It was nearly seven-thirty. Father Mathew held out his hand in bronze benediction above her and the pigeons slept on between his feet, heads curled into their chests. She sniffed the air and remembered the ditty Dermot had come out with last night.

> The smell from the river is something wicked, how do
>   Father Mathew stick it?
> Here's up 'em all says the boys of Fair Hill.

The song was right, Jude could smell the river this morning. She looked over across the bridge and up towards Patrick's Hill. There was one figure walking towards her and before he reached the far side of the bridge, she knew it for Dr Kelleher.

He walked with his head down as if deep in thought, nearly bumping into a woman pulling a barrow over the bridge, and when he was close enough for Jude to see his face, she thought he looked tired, as if he hadn't slept. He had his jacket buttoned against the early morning chill, but she was fairly sure he was dressed in the same clothes she'd seen him in at the dinner table the previous evening.

She felt a rush of pity, like the prick of so many pins against her neck, across her skull, and she could smell from nowhere her father's study. Her father had retreated there when her mother died and she would come to find him, to bring him to the dinner table or tempt him with a piece of warm toast, stepping into a fug of pipe-smoke, old tweed and the aniseed balls he had her buy for him by the pound at the grocer's shop. Now she felt it, obscurely, for Dr Kelleher, but as a woman, not as a child.

Ignoring Jude, the doctor lifted his arm wearily and saluted Father Mathew.

'I swear I haven't taken a drop in days,' he said.

Then he turned towards Jude and nodded a greeting. 'Good day,' his tone curt, his lip curled in something between a smile and a grimace.

'Good morning.'

'Ready to snap?'

'It's kind of you to meet me. I'd have telephoned you if I'd been able.'

'Why is that?'

'Well, the light's very poor this morning, not good for the kind of photographs I want. I haven't that much time so it'd be better for me to be on my way and I'll try to get the photos on the way back.'

Dr Kelleher made no immediate reply. He had taken Jude's elbow while she spoke and walked her down towards the bridge. She hadn't tried to break his grip, but his fingers were pressing into her arm. It wasn't aggressive, but it was very definite. When they reached the edge of the river, he stopped and they stood, unspeaking, staring at the grey water. Jude watched a crate float towards the bridge on the tide. Two gulls sat on the lettering, the remains of which read 'RY'S TEA'. As the crate slipped beneath the bridge, the gulls lifted from it, wheeled high and dropped down to perch on the limestone posts that ran, joined by an iron rail, along the river's edge.

'You'll walk with me a little way because I'm going to show you something,' Dr Kelleher said, and as he spoke, he pulled at her arm. Jude looked at his face. It was stony, his eyes hard, his mouth in a thin line.

'You're holding me too tight,' she said, and the doctor loosened his grip, but he didn't let go.

A tram rumbled over Patrick's Bridge, sleep-eyed people staring out at the couple walking by the waterside. Across the river, above the blue-slated roofs and the threads of smoke, the bells of Shandon tower rang out the quarter, and elsewhere other bells clanged and echoed.

Steps cut down to the water, a flight and a landing and another flight, and two boys hunched over a fishing line halfway down, heads intent. They passed an old woman with a basket of cabbages and two younger women hurrying. One of them muttered something to Dr Kelleher and tugged at her skirts in a kind of half-curtsey, and he gave a curt nod in return. They were approaching a large building which Jude thought must be a church, the curve of a chapel facing towards her.

'The Opera House,' Dr Kelleher said, and Jude saw that the near end was a box office, posters pasted up on the wall for *The Scarlet Pimpernel* and *Macbeth*. A little further on and he stopped, letting go of Jude's arm. Stepping away, she watched the gulls gyring, arguing in the sky. Dr Kelleher paced behind her, chinking the money in his pocket. She wondered whether she was frightened by him, and couldn't decide. Turning back she looked up at the Opera House, its bulk, its Doric columns and high balustrade.

'You brought me to see this?' she said, because although it was an imposing building, she couldn't believe he had gripped her arm so tight to bring her here, and she was bewildered.

The doctor looked pale, but she couldn't tell if it was just the early light. And his bigness, his bulk, which she had found overbearing before, now seemed hollow. As if somewhere inside that large suit a much slighter man was camping out.

'You don't get much of our news over there,' he said, gesturing with a thumb down the river, towards the sea. 'Your newspapers have got more important things to write about, of course. A whole empire. We're just the nearest scrap of it. Most of them think we should be cut off and pushed far out into the Atlantic, and of course I don't agree with them, but I can't say I'm surprised. Not when you look back at it. They've always thought of us like that.'

'But you've got your own government now,' Jude said. 'And the British troops have gone, most of them. You won in the end, didn't you? More or less?'

Dr Kelleher shook his head. 'I shouldn't have begun like this. Stupid of me. You'll read the *Manchester Guardian*, I'd bet.' Jude nodded. 'Which is better than nothing. But anyway I'm getting off the point. I have a story to tell you. It came to mind when you showed us that photograph of the wounded man yesterday evening.'

'You know the men in the photograph?' Jude couldn't keep the excitement from her voice.

'I didn't say that.' Dr Kelleher crossed his arms and, leaning forward into the iron rail that ran along the river's edge and staring down at the water, he began.

'It was a winter evening, not late, but dark. About five years ago, that'll be all, but it was just before the Auxies, the Auxiliaries, burnt Cork.' He looked at Jude. 'You knew about that?'

'I read about it in the newspapers. We were shocked.'

'And did you read about the Secretary for Ireland, Hamar Greenwood, claiming in your House of Commons that the citizens had started the fires? That it was nothing to do with the Forces of the Crown? Even suggesting that the fire leapt over the river on its own to set the town hall ablaze?'

'Did you see the fires?'

'You couldn't not. The sky red and the noise of the blaze. The smoke. Terrible. And Greenwood, a Canadian, for the love of God. You'd think he'd understand a bit more than the rest of them.' He gave a short laugh. 'There's an expression over here now about tall tales: "Don't tell a Greenwood". But you won't have heard that one.'

'No,' Jude said. And then she asked: 'Did they arrest any of the men, the Auxies?'

Dr Kelleher snorted. 'Did they fly and go to heaven? Of course not. They just moved them up to Dublin. And a friend up there wrote me that he'd seen them patrolling on Patrick's Green with burnt corks in their glengarries, boasting of it.

'But anyway, this night was before the burning. I'd been working all day, my surgery off Paul Street, people with nothing except a pile of poverty and illness. My housekeeper was gone home. She was always gone early those days, to be back before the curfew, my dinner left in the oven ready. I'd just set it on a tray with a glass of stout, to eat in front of the fire. I'd turn on the wireless, shut out the day. I remember it was lamb chops. Then there was a knock on the door.

'A certain knock, two raps, then three, I'd know what it was about. There wasn't a week went by at that time without me opening the door at night twice, sometimes three times. The woman on the doorstep was a messenger. Moira Sullivan. I knew her face, she was part of the Sullivan clan from around Grattan Street, the "Marsh". She said could I come at once, and sure enough it was an address over there. Broad Lane, the other side of the river. She was to take me. I told her to come in a moment while I found my shoes and bag. She stood in the hall, and I could see she was shaking.

'They always wore long coats, those women, and you didn't ask what they carried underneath. But the Black and Tans and the Auxies weren't allowed to search women, or priests, so they were the ones could act best as couriers, weapons and messages. As dangerous a work as anybody's.

'I asked her if she'd met anyone and she said no, but she'd heard a patrol over near North Gate Bridge. She thought they were heading across towards Blarney Street. I asked her, could she tell me the problem, and she said it was two men shot. One in the face, alive when she left, the other a wound to the shoulder but bleeding badly. She asked for a drink of water, which I got her, and then we went.

'We crossed Patrick's Bridge fine. The night was dark but clear and there was quite a moon. It would have been better if it had been raining. It would have put the Tans off their roaming and maybe this would be a different tale. Anyway, we turned onto the quays and there was nobody about, not even a dog. We'd got as far as the Opera House, just where we're standing now, when a band of Black and Tans appeared. They must have come down Half Moon Street, and normally you could hear them a mile off, but this lot were quiet as mice. Five of them.'

Dr Kelleher stooped and picked up a pebble. 'I don't suppose you've ever met a Black and Tan,' he said.

Jude had been listening so intently, the question made her start. She didn't want to answer it. She remembered Daniel telling her in Kew Gardens and how she'd walked away for a moment. Dr Kelleher threw the pebble far out into the water where it disappeared without a ripple and she realised that the question was near enough rhetorical. That he certainly wasn't expecting her to say yes. She shrugged, hitched up her camera bag, which was beginning to weigh heavy.

'What did they look like?' she said.

'Brutal. Hung about with weapons, sneering. Revolvers on each hip, bandoliers of ammunition slung across their chests, muskets, hand grenades in their pockets, as they liked to let you know given a half chance. Less than half.'

Jude nodded. She couldn't imagine Daniel dressed like that, couldn't imagine him pointing a rifle or pulling the pin on a grenade. There were a dozen things she'd have liked to say, to ask, but she bit her tongue.

'And this lot,' the doctor said, returning to his story, 'soon as they saw us they started singing, just quietly.

We are the boys of the RIC
As happy as happy can be.

'I tell you, that singing was far more frightening than any roaring, and I'd heard them do that too.'

205

The pantomime English voice Dr Kelleher sang the words in made Jude's skin crawl. She could hear Daniel's accent, and her own, inside it. But surely Daniel Brown couldn't have done this kind of thing?

'Then my messenger started to panic,' Dr Kelleher said. 'I could hear her, her quick, short breaths. I could see her hand clutching at the front of her coat. So I took her arm, told her to breathe deep and slow, told her I'd do the talking, and by the time the Tans were close, she had calmed down. I told her it'd be a night in gaol at the very worst, fool that I was.'

The camera bag had become too heavy. Jude set it down on the cobbles and put her hands on one of the posts. It was cold and stony under her palm, soothing. She turned away from the doctor and stared up the river. The sun warmed her back and cast a long, slender shadow before her. He was silent for what felt like an age but Jude knew it was probably no more than a couple of minutes. It was extraordinary, to be standing by the river Lee in the middle of Cork city early one weekday morning when she should be jostling her way to work. Standing there listening to a tale that made the hair on her neck rise as if it were the most normal thing in the world.

When the doctor began to speak again, she was sure she heard a catch in his voice.

'I could have told you any number of stories,' he said. 'Terrible things. I saw terrible things. You do as a doctor, and in a war . . .' He spread his hands on the rail, pressed them down. 'You'll know that. But this was one of the worst, and I didn't even see it happen, and anyway I couldn't prevent it.'

Jude turned back towards Dr Kelleher. It had taken her by surprise, seeing him like this. She had guessed him for a grimmer man last night at the Whelans', someone more inured to human suffering.

'I always found it easier to be in the thick of it,' she said. 'At least then I could see where things began and ended. Wounds, pain. If you're not there, if you only hear about it, then your imagination can pick up and run off with you.'

Dr Kelleher looked at her and then he smiled, as though, in the middle of his tale, she'd reminded him of something.

'You must have been so young,' he said.

'No more than the boys. And it was a very different war,' Jude said. 'But you were going to tell me a particular story.'

He clenched his eyes shut, and opened them again. 'Yes. The Volunteer, the one with the shoulder wound, that's what I had to tell you about.'

'But what about the woman? And the Black and Tans?' Jude said.

'You see, that's so often how it was. All the people who suffered by the by. Not the Volunteers, I don't mean them, though they did of course, they got shot and wounded, tortured, imprisoned and killed, but they were soldiers, IRA men, they expected it. But the women who knocked on your door after curfew, they'll never make the history books.'

'What happened to her?' Jude asked, trying to keep her tone gentle, but she had to know now.

'They walked up to us like a posse of tomcats, those Tans. That swagger.' He almost spat the words. 'Said what we were doing out after curfew, did we know the penalty, sneered at us. They were drunk, of course, I could smell it on them even before they got close. I kept my voice calm, explained that I was a doctor and that the woman had come for my help, someone in her family was ill. I think I said suspected scarlet fever, something catching anyway.'

'Did they believe you?'

'They wouldn't let Moira Sullivan come on with me. That was the thing. And they wouldn't let me stay with her. There was an argument between them about who was staying and who going, so that for a moment I thought maybe we'd be able to get away, if they all started fighting. But then one of them fired his revolver in the air and that quietened them.

'She was shaking like a leaf now. I think she knew much sooner than I did what was going to happen.

'Two of the Tans came up and shoved me away from her, demanded to know where was I going. So I had to think fast and give a false address. Someone I could trust to guess what I might be up to and to play along. I told them the number of a house on Henry Street, just off Bachelor's Quay, near Broad Street, and they marched me away. The last I saw of Moira Sullivan that night, she was standing with the Tans around her, her arms wrapped around her coat, her face white under the moonlight.'

'And afterwards?' Jude said.

'I saw her afterwards, but she couldn't bear to look at me.'

'They'd beaten her up?'

'They hadn't touched her face. Left her unmarked, the bastards.'

Dr Kelleher bent and picked up Jude's camera bag, toted the strap on his hands like a man playing 'Guess the Weight' at a fair, swung it gently to and fro.

'By the time I got to them, one of the Volunteers was dead. The other one, I patched him up and he survived. Went on to fight another day, as they say. He's a bit of a famous fellow in Ireland now.'

Dr Kelleher looked hard at Jude. He still held the camera bag but he was swinging it violently, the strap flat across the pads of his fingers. Any minute, the momentum would take the bag beyond his control, it would drop onto the cobbles and her lenses and maybe the camera itself would be smashed.

'Please put the bag down,' Jude said.

'Tell me what you're really doing over here. Because I don't think you've come over for the birds and the bees, not really, have you?'

'It's not the whole story, no,' Jude said.

'It's got something to do with that photograph you passed around last night.'

Jude nodded.

'I think we should go and sit down somewhere and order tea, maybe some toast, be civilised about it, and then you can tell me what exactly it is that you're after,' Dr Kelleher said, and he hitched the camera bag over his shoulder.

So Jude ended up in the Pavilion restaurant again, making small-talk with the doctor while the waitress, a different one, brought tea and a shiny silver-covered dish to the table.

'I love being served toast,' Dr Kelleher said, lifting the lid on the dish. He seemed less angry here, but perhaps it was just because he was seated, and no longer swinging her camera close to oblivion.

'Do you see?' he said, and easing his butter knife below the piled slices, he prised up the base and gestured to Jude to look. 'To keep them warm. A *bain* of hot water.'

They ate several pieces in a silence Jude found to be strangely companionable. Sipping tea and spreading jam, the doctor seemed more like a bluff, genial uncle who might be enquiring after her well-being, than the steely adversary she knew he was. But then he put down his teacup and wiped his mouth with the napkin and she knew the interval was over.

'So?' he said.

Jude gathered her thoughts and decided she'd counter his question with one of her own.

'Was one of the men in the photograph the man you went to help that night? The man with the shoulder wound?'

'And what do *you* know of him?'

'You said he became a hero. If he's still alive, then it's very important that I find him.'

'Why? How could it be so important when you don't know a thing about him? Not even his name?'

There was no trace of the uncle about Dr Kelleher now. He sat back, arms crossed, ready to wait for as long as it took, and he didn't take his eyes off Jude. She was pinioned to her seat. She decided there was nothing for it but to tell him as much as she could and hope to God she hadn't misjudged this fierce man.

'Perhaps I could tell *you* a story now,' she said, putting away the photograph.

The doctor refilled her teacup, and then he nodded.

Jude fished her cigarettes and lighter from her bag. 'Do you mind if I smoke?'

'They'll make you cough,' he said. 'But go ahead.'

209

She lit up and took a pull, enjoying that first full tug in her lungs.

'May I have a look?' Dr Kelleher said, pointing to the lighter. Jude passed it to him. 'Where did you get this?' he said, tracing the four-leaf clover with a finger.

'All right,' she said. 'My story. I was in Belgium nursing for nearly four years. Set up a first-aid post with another nurse. Hundreds of soldiers came through it, Belgian and British mainly, most of them so young, many of them horribly wounded. Those with minor injuries, if we could patch them up and send them back into the trenches, we did. And they'd take whatever we could send them back with, pathetically grateful, a slab of chocolate, a new pair of mittens, or just a full belly. They didn't hate the enemy, most of them. There was far more resentment against the top dogs, Haig and his cronies. They were the ones carrying on this war. They were keeping the men in the mud and the horror.

'But not all of them were wounded. Some we just fed, we had Peter for that, a wonderful cook, or they came and slept like the dead in our cellar. Lines of palliasses. Kate, she was the other nurse, and I, we had our camp beds in our own room but as often as not we never made it into them. We had fifty hot water bottles to fill some nights. Soup and cocoa to an endless stream of men. I must have taken hundreds of photographs, of anything and everything. Kate at every kind of task: brushing her hair, changing a dressing, winding bandages, digging potatoes, on her motor-bike. And Peter, cooking, grinning usually.

'I took a photograph of two officers in a British regiment, one wounded, the other a friend, sharing a cigarette. For me that's all it was. A photo of two friends in wartime. There were piles of others. This one was nothing special.

'I did know one of the men a little, enough to say hello to in the street, if there had been a street. That was because he and Kate, they flirted a little over the dressings till his friend was patched up, and so I remember him. I knew he was Irish, and there was a joke about a wine bottle so I remember that he was from Cork, but that was all.'

'What happened to Kate?' Dr Kelleher said. Jude looked across at him. The question had surprised her.

'Kate?' she said.

'You mention her a lot.'

'She died. Gassed.'

The doctor nodded. 'Not your fault then.'

'No.'

'So go on about the photograph,' he said.

'An acquaintance of mine saw it in an exhibition a month or so ago, and it meant something very different to him, and that's what I'm trying to understand. He didn't explain it to me properly but it was obviously important. The last time I saw him he was very agitated, and now he's disappeared. But I think he's come to Ireland, and the photo is all I have to go on.'

'I'd like to see it again,' Dr Kelleher said.

Jude opened her bag and took out the photograph, passed it to him. 'It's like looking at a riddle,' she said.

He studied it, then set it down on the table.

'Your acquaintance,' he said, 'what does he have to do with the man in the photo? Why do you think he might have come here?'

Jude lifted out another slice of warm toast. She needed to steady herself, do something ordinary, and the only thing available was spreading jam. She took her time, bit and chewed, sipped at the tea, which she noticed now was the deepest brown.

'You make it very strong over here,' she said, swirling her teacup. A few dark grains eddied to the surface and sank again.

'It'll be Barry's, the tea. Best tea in Ireland. Anywhere.'

A man in a double-breasted suit came over to the table and greeted Dr Kelleher. Introductions were made, 'Miss Hursten, photographer from England, Mr Flynn, my friend and lawyer,' the men exchanged a few hurried sentences, agreed a time for a meeting, and with a brief nod of departure, Mr Flynn was gone. Dr Kelleher looked across at Jude again.

'So?' he said.

Jude didn't want to mention the diary.

'He spoke about a place in Ireland that he loved, Coolderry, in

Castletowne, and an island, Horse Island, places where he felt more at ease than in his own home, and something he said makes me think he may have gone there now.'

Dr Kelleher sat perfectly still, waiting.

'He came to know these people a few years back,' she said.

'During the Troubles?'

Jude nodded.

'So he was here during the Troubles.'

'Yes. And that's when he met the man in the photograph, though I don't know what went on between them.'

She knew so little. Only that Daniel had been injured in a motor lorry accident over here, that he still walked with a limp and that the sight of that photograph had driven him to strange and disturbing lengths. She was sure he had come to Ireland, sure he'd gone to Castletowne and Coolderry house, and that if she could find him, she could help him.

'If it was during the Troubles and your man is English, then whatever went on, it won't have been very pretty.'

'No,' Jude said.

'He was a Black and Tan, wasn't he? That's what you're finding so hard to tell me.'

'He told me he was an Auxiliary.'

The doctor chuckled. 'An Auxie. Worse and worse.'

'What's the difference?'

'Not much. The Auxiliaries had to have been officers. There's many thought they were worse than the Tans. What was his name?'

'Daniel Brown. I don't believe he's done the kinds of things you described.'

The doctor shrugged. 'Are you in love with him?'

'No,' Jude said, too quickly, she knew at once.

The doctor gave her a long look. 'So why the mission? It's a big thing, to drop your life and come looking for a stranger in a foreign land.'

'Nobody else can come looking for him, and I've nothing to lose. I'm worried for his safety.'

'With good reason,' Dr Kelleher said. 'An ex-Auxiliary wandering the Irish roads. He won't find many friendly faces if they know what he's been up to, and they'll probably guess soon enough, and once they do, he'll find worse than scowls coming his way.'

'So I'm realising.'

'And you're over here as his Don Quixote.'

The waitress came over and Dr Kelleher ordered another pot of tea. 'If you're going off into the wilds later, you should build up your strength,' he said. 'What about joining me in a full breakfast? You've told me the worst, so your stomach should be calmer.'

Jude grinned and nodded to the waitress.

'Will you be wanting them fried, poached or scrambled?' the waitress asked.

'Poached, thank you.'

Once the waitress was gone Dr Kelleher resumed. 'So will your man be looking for this fellow?' he said, pointing to the standing soldier, leaning over with the cigarette.

'Would he be hard to find?'

'I'd say not. He's a bit of a hero in these parts.'

'Can you tell me his name?'

Lifting his hands to his head, the doctor rubbed across his face, as if to wake himself from something.

'If I hadn't met you on the boat with Catherine, then we wouldn't be here now. You'd have gone off happy this morning to find your friend, and I'd have got up and sat with the *Examiner* and a pot of tea for half an hour and then sauntered out to open my surgery and greet the first of my ill flock. None of this would have been brought up today and I've only myself and my fierce curiosity to blame.'

'I'll be gone from the city very soon,' Jude said. 'And then you can put me from your mind.'

'Maybe,' he said.

The waitress came with their food and for a few minutes they welcomed the distraction that the eggs and rashers, sausage and tomatoes brought.

'There's no point my not telling you his name,' Dr Kelleher said finally, 'because you could find it out soon enough. You could

213

stand on the pavement in Patrick Street waving that damn photograph about and somebody would tell you within five minutes that the Irishman in the British army uniform is Matt Walsh. They might think he was in fancy dress, but they'd know the man.'

'Matt Walsh,' Jude said. 'I've never heard of him.'

'But then you don't know much about Ireland across the water, do you.'

'So what's he famous for?'

'Well, not for serving in the British army. There'd be quite a few would be surprised to learn about that, though I'm not, and he's not the only one in the IRA by a long shot.'

Dr Kelleher wiped a last piece of brown bread around his plate and gathered his knife and fork.

'Not that he'll have hidden it, but sure, I didn't know about it till yesterday when I was passed your photograph. Gave me a bit of a stir, even so,' he said, putting a hand to his chest. 'And he's a well-known figure in County Cork now. A business man. Building business. Respected. And still a fearless Republican. Fought the British and opposed the Treaty. Was gaoled by everybody. It'd do him no good if this picture was put about. I'd be wondering what was going on myself, if I hadn't heard the tale from you.'

Jude drew on her cigarette. 'Fought against the British,' she said. 'After fighting with them. Does he hate us then?'

'Have you noticed us hating you since you arrived?' Dr Kelleher said sharply.

Jude felt her colour rise. 'No, of course not. Stupid of me,' she said.

'He's famous for an ambush,' he said flatly. 'He fought all the way through, like Dan Breen or Tom Barry or O'Malley. You wouldn't know who they were. But it was the ambush put his name up in lights.'

'What happened?'

'An IRA flying column took out an Auxiliary patrol, two lorry loads, sixteen or so men, in West Cork. All the Auxies were killed except the Commanding Officer. He was wounded as I remember, and shipped back to England smartly, else the IRA would have finished him off. He'd seen too many of them. Anyway he killed himself not that long afterwards.'

'And Walsh?'

'Walsh was the commandant of those boys. The brains behind it all.'

The waitress came to clear the plates, and Dr Kelleher fell silent. Jude reached into her bag for another cigarette. She put it between her lips and struck the lighter, holding it before her and watching the pale flame. The pulse beat in her neck, and her scalp prickled with apprehension.

Dr Kelleher's voice took her by surprise. 'If you're going to light that nasty bit of tobacco, do so. Or have you hypnotised yourself?' he said.

She started, jabbing the lighter away from her, extinguishing the flame.

'Did nobody else survive?' she said.

The doctor shook his head. 'Which is quite something when you think that the Auxies were all armed to the teeth as usual. The Column had two killed and several wounded. One of the lads killed, I know his family. He was the eldest son, a good boy.'

Jude lit her cigarette. 'A good boy?'

'Your Auxie friend was probably not so very nice when he was over here,' Dr Kelleher said. 'Why don't you ask him a few questions when you find him, about what he got up to in our country.'

'So the man you went to help that night in Cork, the one with the shoulder wound,' Jude said, ignoring his last remark, 'that man was Matt Walsh.'

'It was.'

'It's been quite a piece of luck, meeting you, then.'

'Why?'

'Because it turns out you know one of the men in the photograph.'

'Luck has a smaller pond over here. Sure everybody knows everybody. Still, I'm sorry I haven't shown you the sights of Cork. Though it hasn't been an utter surprise to me that sights aren't your first reason for coming over here.'

Jude laughed. She put a hand down to her camera bag. 'Since I've got my camera with me, could I take your photograph? It's not only a front, the camera story. Outside, beside Father Mathew perhaps, or the river?'

Dr Kelleher tugged at his collar, brushed at a crumb on his waistcoat. He smiled.

'Next time, maybe,' he said. 'And if you're going to go searching people out,' he said, 'you'd maybe want to broaden your story. Make yourself more of a journalist, wanting to write stories about what's become of the heroes perhaps. And have yourself working for an American outfit. We love America here, and they love us. And they've buckets of money to spend sending ignorant young new women journalists over the water with.'

'You're out to help me now?' Jude said.

'I'm not going to stop you, am I?' Jude shook her head. 'So then, I might as well give you some tips on surviving.'

Jude put her hands on the table. 'Thank you,' she said, grinning. 'And I'll work on my story.'

'I'm old enough to be your father,' the doctor said.

'My father is dead,' Jude said.

'Well, maybe that is a small mercy for him, God rest his soul. Here's another tip. My last for today. The ex-Auxie fellow you're wanting to find, he might be sorry now for what he did then, and you might be the judge of that. For me, I'll leave God as judge. Forgiveness is hard when you've seen what they did, though I'll do my best if I have to. But even if the fellow is sorry, truly sorry, be as careful as you know how. Because what happened over here, it'll have found out a danger in him and that won't ever leave.'

Jude stared at her fingers. The doctor's words took her back to the afternoon in Kew Gardens, and the terror, or violence, that loomed behind things for Daniel, and she knew he was right.

'Now, my guess is you've a last favour to ask me,' Dr Kelleher said. 'So I'm going to make mine first. If you've the time down there in West Cork, would you be able to take me a few photographs?'

'Of course,' Jude said. 'What of?'

'It'd be for my pleasure, nothing more serious, a hobby I have. Ancient stones.'

'Ancient stones?'

'Stone circles, chamber tombs, wedge tombs, ring forts. Ireland's full of them.'

'You want me to photograph any I see?'

Dr Kelleher laughed. 'No. There's a particular stone circle called Drombeg. I've been there, but without a camera. You should go there anyway, it's an extraordinary place. Two miles east of Glandore.'

'I'd be delighted,' Jude said. 'I can include it in my photo-essay of Ireland.'

Dr Kelleher nodded briskly. 'Now you have got a last question, haven't you?' he said, in that cheery voice Jude associated with doctors who, having given the gravest news, finish off by asking if you've been to the pictures lately.

'Yes,' she said.

'So ask away,' he said.

'If I needed to contact Matt Walsh, where would I find him?'

'And you don't know yet if you do need to, because it depends on your friend?'

'Yes.'

The doctor looked at her and she met his gaze. Reaching down to his jacket on the back of the chair, he tugged a prescription pad and pen from the breast pocket. Although his hands were as big as the rest of him, his fingers were deft, their movements elegant as he opened the pad, uncapped his pen. She noticed the pale hairs along his finger, and his broad, scrubbed doctor's nail. When he held the pen, Jude saw that the middle finger of his right hand lifted crookedly above the others. It must have been broken at some point. He wrote down two addresses and the name of a town, Liscool, on one sheet.

'This is mine,' he said, pointing to the first address, 'and this one, if you go to Liscool and find Paddy McCarthy, he'll take you to Walsh. McCarthy's the man you need. A draper now. A draper then, come to that. Lives up the hill.'

Tearing the sheet out, he handed it to Jude, and on a second sheet he wrote a note of introduction.

'I have met the bearer of this note, and I trust her. Please answer her questions if you can.' And he signed it Dr Frank Kelleher.

'I've given my name,' he said. 'But go carefully! There's a lot you'll be treading on.'

CHAPTER FOURTEEN

Daniel returned to the island each day, going out in the morning and coming back before the sun went down. It was a good place to keep things at bay, better than the mainland. And he could take precautions, now he knew its topography. Be master of it. The weather had been steady, with some sun and no rain. But when he woke on his fourth morning, the sky was black and heavy and the wind rising. He knew that he must have had the dream again, he could feel it in his limbs. Beyond the window the trees were flailing, as if something was beating at them again and again and they were trying to get away.

Down beyond the garden, the sea was grey and coarse. The seagulls flew into the dark sky like bright, white scissors, cutting the air to shreds. He saw a hare cross the corner of the lawn, lean-limbed, its hind legs lifting high, loping slowly, then stopping to tug at some green delicacy.

The last time he had been here, on a weekend pass out from the barracks, he had come in towards the kitchen one day to find both dogs, shut out, standing faces up to the back door, tails still, noses quivering. Inside, Mr Murray was skinning a hare, peeling the fur from its haunches. A white bowl of blood was at one end of the table and the air was thick with the smell of it. Daniel had watched for a minute, though the smell made him nauseous. Something about the creature's limbs seemed too human. He had nudged the bowl of blood so that it swilled slightly, leaving a filter of pink against the white sides.

'It's very red,' he'd said.

'Of course it's red,' Mr Murray had said, snipping the fur from the ankles with scissors.

'No, but redder than a rabbit's. More like a man's,' he'd said, and Mr Murray had stopped snipping and looked up at Daniel. 'I mean it looks more like a man's than an animal's,' he'd said, and then the smell had been too much and he'd left the room.

This fourth day, Daniel found Mrs Murray in the scullery, putting some roses in vases.

'I want to go to the island today,' he said. 'Take a tent, food, stay a night or two.'

Mrs Murray shook her head. 'It's going to pour, and there's no shelter.'

'But I need to go,' Daniel said.

'Why?' Her voice was curious.

'Well, there's the bracken, which is good and deep, and the watchtower, though it doesn't face the right way any more.'

Mrs Murray snipped the rose stems at an angle and trimmed the lower leaves. 'Doesn't face the right way?' she said carefully.

'And there are fish of course, if I took a line. Water might be a problem though. I'd have to take a few bottles. I didn't see any springs.'

'Have you had some breakfast?' Mrs Murray said.

'I'll eat a lot. Stock up.'

Mrs Murray cooked him up a big breakfast, and she must have called Mr Murray in from somewhere, because they were both at the table as he ate, just drinking tea. They didn't say much, didn't look at him much, but he had the feeling they were watching him more than they were doing anything else.

'The hare on the lawn this morning? It wasn't like the last one,' Daniel said, in what he thought was a conversational tone. 'I couldn't bear the smell of that one, do you remember? And the colour of the blood? But the hare today was alive so I could only smell the air.'

'I don't remember the dead hare,' Mr Murray said.

'Well, it doesn't matter.'

'Daniel,' Mr Murray said, 'you've come here straight from England. That's right, isn't it?'

220

'Took the first train from Cork,' Daniel said, smiling.

'And you've been working in the family business till just the other day.'

Daniel nodded. 'I've been doing quite well. I think my father's pleasantly surprised.'

'Not recuperating recently? Or resting? Or . . .'

'No. Did a deal last week, and the pigeons just beyond the window, then the lift down, with the concertina doors and the soft dust, and the girls with their able bodies and umbrellas, to meet my father.'

'But when you left Ireland the last time, you were badly wounded?'

Mr Murray's brow was very creased, and there was something about his tone that bothered Daniel. As if he was listening, but hearing different words. Daniel picked up his teacup and took a sip. His mouth was dry. He would try to be very clear.

'I was months in hospital and by the time I came out they'd stopped fighting the British and turned on each other. But I couldn't talk about it. It was too dangerous.'

'Even in England?'

'Yes.' Daniel thought a moment. 'It's all right now, I think, and that's why I've told you, but then, it was too dangerous. And it was easier for my parents that way. After Johnnie's death, my mother couldn't bear to hear about the war. Any war. And I didn't want to think about it either. So I never told them what happened, and they don't want to know any more.'

'And you?'

'Look at me, still can't walk properly,' Daniel said, and he did another smile. But he didn't like this conversation very much, so he asked them about something that had been puzzling him.

'It's much quieter here. What's happened to your pretty maid? And your friends calling in? You haven't had arguments? Fallen foul of something?'

Mr Murray laughed and shook his head. Then Mrs Murray put her hands on the table, as if, Daniel thought, to show that she wasn't holding a gun.

'You're going to have to tell us why you've come back here,' she said. 'For your own safety, and maybe for ours, you're going to have to tell us.'

A cold wave spread beneath Daniel's skin. He'd been careful, he thought, he hadn't seen anybody, not anybody he knew, coming here.

'Has somebody asked for me?' he said, and he saw a look pass between the Murrays.

'No,' Mrs Murray said. 'Nobody. But we're worried. Your distress. The dreams, the sweats, that you want to hide away from everything. We're going to ask Dr Ross to come and see you.'

Daniel shook his head. He picked up his teacup, but his hand was shaking, making ripples, so he put it down again.

'You haven't sent the letter to your parents yet, have you? Telling them you're here. Safe.'

'I'm going to,' Daniel said.

Mrs Murray shook her head. 'That's what you said the first time we asked, but you still haven't. We'll post a letter tomorrow. Either the one you'll have written by then, or one of our own if you haven't.'

One hand resting on the table, Mrs Murray carved an endless figure of eight into the tablecloth. She looked across at Daniel. He watched her fingernail circle and circle. She was waiting. He wondered how much it mattered what he said next.

'Why on earth have you come back?' she said.

'My parents never replied to you because I told them not to. I told them it would have put me at risk. That the IRA would have come and found me if they'd known I was alive.'

'And would they?'

'Perhaps in those first months, I don't know.'

'Why have you come back, Daniel Brown?' Mrs Murray said again, her voice hard. 'Because your story isn't clear. You don't have your facts straight.'

'There's a question in my head, it's been there since that day, only mostly it's been like a spirit or a mood, taken the form of something else, so that I've thought I was going mad at times. But now I know that it's a real question about a real man.'

222

'So keep it in your head.' Mrs Murray's nail pressed hard into the cloth. 'And go home.'

'I can't. And since I got here, other things keep pushing in at me. Things I have to answer to. Things I've kept at bay these years, never let in.'

'People won't want to know about your past here,' Mr Murray said. 'And for your own safety, it's better they don't.'

'They don't want to know in England,' Daniel said, 'and I don't want to tell them.'

'In England it's because they're ignorant,' said Mr Murray. 'But over here it's because they're exhausted with it. There are too many wounds. Ones you can see and ones you can't. First fighting the British, then turning inwards and two years of civil war. Brother fighting brother, towns and villages torn apart, so much hatred, bitterness.'

Mrs Murray's finger stopped. 'You're too soft, Joe. Too soft to say what it's like, seeing your country turned over to thugs and corner boys. Because that's what's happened. We know people whose families have been here for hundreds of years. They're Protestants, but they're as Irish as anybody is, and they've been burned out of their homes, turned off their own land by a small bunch of bully boys carrying hurley sticks and shotguns. We know people shot in their beds for nothing more than being a Protestant. I don't say that Daniel's lot always behaved as they should, but to make out that the IRA always had right on their side.' She shook her head. 'We'll see if you're right, Joe, or whether we don't end up like so many, and have to throw in our lot here, in this country that we love.'

Daniel put a hand to his collar. It was chafing. Mrs Murray's speech was confusing. He didn't want to think about all the other people. He didn't even want to think about the Murrays. It was too much already just thinking about himself, about what he had done, what had been done to him.

'Does it matter as much, if you didn't mean to do something?' he said.

There was a long pause before Mrs Murray answered him.

'What do you mean?' she said, her voice careful, alarmed.

Daniel shook his head slowly and fiercely from side to side, as though trying to shake something free inside it. 'I'll go out to Horse Island,' he said. 'Clear my head.'

Mrs Murray didn't answer, only put a tray on the table and cleared his breakfast things. He saw that her hands were shaking.

'It was warning shots, when we fired in the air,' Daniel said. 'Let them know we were there. We were always out in the open, you know. Not like their lot. But the women would be squawking, like the hens, and the kids with their wide eyes. They made you angry, looking at you like that. Waiting for you to be angry and so you were. And the men. You didn't trust a man with his hands in his pockets. They want us to believe them, they can walk with their hands out.' Daniel pulled his cuffs up his wrists. 'Look, see? Nothing. Simple, isn't it. Keep your hands empty in the day, go to bed at night, and then we'll believe you.'

Mr Murray had stood up too now, and he walked round the table. He was walking slowly, as if he were in the woods and stalking something, Daniel thought. He stood behind Daniel's chair and Daniel felt his hands, very light, on both his shoulders.

'Come on,' Mr Murray said. 'We'll get some air.'

'But what happened when my leg got hurt, we didn't hurt the kiddies and the girls and the women like that. They didn't need to do it.' Daniel stopped and put his hands to his ears. 'Oh, God! Oh, Jesus! The Trout, Mr Murray. I have to fish. It's what I've come for. To fish for the fish. I'll have to do it soon.'

He felt Mr Murray's hands under his arms, holding him firm, lifting him up.

'Fishing's a good idea,' Mr Murray said, 'the weather looks right with the rain coming. I think the wind will drop. We'll go inland, take rods.'

Daniel turned towards the door. Mrs Murray stood there.

'I wouldn't tell my own mother,' he said.

She moved aside to let him by.

'I'll find you an oilskin,' Mr Murray said, 'and boots. It's going to be wet.'

224

Daniel went up the stairs. He heard their voices below.

'If you wait ten minutes I can hard-boil eggs. There's some cold meat, apples fresh off the tree, a bit sharp, but very tasty, thermos, fruit cake.'

'Sallin Lake, not a half hour's walk away.'

'But if you're not back by four, I'll telephone Dr Ross, or the Guards.'

'Is he safe?' Mr Murray said.

'Do you think he should be?'

'What he's saying? It's frightening. I don't understand what's gone on.'

'Nor does he,' Mrs Murray said. 'He might be in more danger if he did.'

When he heard both of the Murrays go into the kitchen, Daniel came down the stairs again. The dog lay on the rug in the middle of the hall floor, legs outstretched as if she were running lying down. She thumped her tail, but Daniel made no gesture towards her. He didn't want the dog following. He opened the front door.

Outside, the rain had begun. The wind had dropped. Daniel walked up the drive and out on to the road. He would go in a straight line from here.

He climbed the wall opposite into a field. Cows stood in one corner under a small tree. They didn't move except to turn their heads and watch him walk across. He crossed another wall, dislodging stones. It was raining steadily. The ground was hard after the days of sun but already it smelt of the wet. He walked across two more fields and then the ground rose, awkwardly, as if it had been heaved and piled. His straight line took him up, so he climbed. The thistles grew to four feet and the ground bucked and split invisibly beneath the coarse thick grasses, so that several times he had to brace himself from falling, making his bad leg ache and throb. More than once he nearly turned an ankle. Larks taunted him, singing high in the air as he stumbled near their souls. He had found a lark's nest once in the ground, its dappled brown eggs nestled in a hoof print, and seen one high bird dip away in the sky

225

and stop its song. Linnets sang in the gorse, finches flashed and stonechats jigged and jerked their warning dance, *tsak tsak, tsak tsak*, pleading.

The Trout had swum in a straight line out of the ditch. Daniel had seen him. He'd risen to his feet and climbed up out, trailing weed from his greatcoat, walked through the fog and straight at the hill, just as if he knew where he was going. After that Daniel had shut his eyes, because you couldn't play dead if you were blinking, though everyone was gone by then. But anyway it was easier to shut them against the burning in his leg.

There had been the marching and the songs before, some of those men their voices shaking, as whose wouldn't be after what they'd done. He'd recognised one of the songs. They'd found a copy of it under the floorboards during a house search and they'd made the lad in the house sing it. He'd had a lovely voice, which Will said was proof of him being a rebel.

Remember Comrades of Ireland,
As forward to Victory we go,
That England, the Tyrant of Tyrants,
Has Mercy ne'er shown to the Foe.

They'd taken the boy in for knowing the song. They hadn't found anything else, no guns or grenades. Not even a pitchfork out of place. But he'd known the song and it was enough.

'Bloody corner boy,' Will had said, just like Mrs Murray. 'That's what they all are. Thugs. Never done a full day's work. Spend all their time scheming against us and practising their bloody songs. Pretending to be soldiers.'

But the corner boys had got Will. Shot him clean in the head, Daniel found that out later, while the Trout swam away.

Daniel stopped climbing and stood up straight. Behind him he could see over the land to the sea. The rain was coming down steadily and you could barely see where the sky ended and the sea began.

CHAPTER FIFTEEN

When Jude went to retrieve her motorbike from the hotel yard, she found hens pecking around the tyres and a skinny boy, all knuckle and knee, in an old cloth cap, and a filthy waistcoat, leaning over the sidecar. He was fiddling with something and after the conversation with Dr Kelleher, crazy fears ran through her head.

'Leave it alone,' she shouted. 'What the hell are you doing?' and she tried to pull him away. But the boy seemed unperturbed and for an answer only wriggled from her grasp and leaned further over. Then he reached both his hands in to a dipped corner of the sidecar tarpaulin, drew them out full, and stood up triumphant.

'See,' he said and showed Jude a clutch of eggs.

The boy kept one egg, and the others he wadded round for her in a piece of old cloth and they were stowed now in a corner of the sidecar. It was something she'd learned to do in France, drink raw eggs. Even better when Peter had whisked them with brandy and sugar. She smiled at the memory. Kate's agonised gargle, her throat gagging at the texture. And though she knew it was absurd, she felt that the eggs were intended.

The journey demanded all Jude's attention. She knew she would have to stop and think about things, make some decisions, decide how to approach Daniel, if she found him. But for now it was a relief to have to concentrate on the road. She took the long straight road west out of Cork. It ran close to the river. The rain was still holding off, and away from the city, under the high grey sky, the surface of the river was smooth and very green. Swallows dipped and men fished, the curve of their mackintoshed backs visible above the water. There were a few clutches of buildings flanking the river on the far side: a waterworks with tall tower in pretty lines of red and white brick, and then a long line of grey buildings, all turrets and gables and hundreds of mullioned windows, which Jude assumed must be a hospital. Then she thought that over here it might equally be a convent.

Two miles out and the city was behind her. There were fields with cattle and cottages, single-storey, white-washed, occasionally a house with a few sycamores or poplars on either side. Jude felt her body ease against the bike. It was a relief to be doing something she understood so well. This she knew how to repair.

Jude stopped in Ballincollig to check her map. The long grey wall of the military barracks ran down the right side of the town, and she noticed the young soldiers keeping guard at the gate in their Free State uniform, and the tricolour flying above. It would have been only a few years before, when Daniel was here, that it would have been a Union Jack and English troops, lads with broad Derbyshire or Yorkshire accents perhaps, and now they were Irish boys. Passing them on her bike she gave a half salute, and one didn't move a muscle and the other grinned.

The motorbike was a good place for thinking. In Belgium she'd found solutions to all sorts of difficulties while bringing in wounded men or collecting supplies, and now Jude's thoughts went back to Daniel.

His diary, and Dr Kelleher's words, had sickened her. But she saw before her again the stranger who had come to her door that day and smiled when she'd dusted him with flour, the slender, nervy figure who had eaten Sunday lunch with her family just as if he were her beau, the first man since Richard she could imagine saying anything to, who had sat with her in the shelter of the Rocks. The same frightened, wounded figure who had walked away from her in Kew Gardens.

The road became rougher as Jude rode further away from the city, and it took all her concentration to avoid the worst of it. She passed men with hoes and forks on their shoulders, an occasional cart or a bicycle, women who stood to watch her, hands on hips. They'd lift a single finger in greeting as she went by, and she quickly learnt to return the gesture. Children shouted out and dogs ran behind the motorbike, yelping wildly, grey ghosts in the dust thrown up by her wheels. Deep ditches shaded into the sides of the roads, brown with bog water and edged with green plants Jude didn't know the names of.

She rode on to Macroom, some twenty-five miles out of Cork, and found a garage on the South Square. The man who came to the pump was singing something. Jude couldn't hear the words, but it sounded like a ballad.

'Lovely day,' he said to her as he unscrewed the petrol cap. 'You on your way somewhere else?'

'Yes,' Jude said. 'You have a handsome town here.'

'It is,' he said. 'And more so with its ruins. Picturesque, you might say,' and he looked at her quizzically. 'English?'

'Yes,' Jude said. 'What are the ruins?'

The man nodded to the left. 'Go on up there and you'll see, through the gate, the far side of the town hall.'

Although she was anxious to get on, Jude was curious about what the man had said. She rode slowly up one side of the square. Ahead of her was a turreted, castellated lodge. Leaving her bike outside O'Leary's Hardware, camera over her shoulder, Jude walked up to the broad gateway beneath. She ignored the old woman who had set down her basket of tinned pilchards and cabbages the better to stare, and the inevitable small boys appearing as if from nowhere to gaze at the motorbike.

Beyond the gateway was the blackened shell of what must have been a forbidding castle. Jude walked up close and rubbed a finger on the wall. It fetched up soot. This wasn't an ancient ruin, the kind you find in history books. It was a recent ruin. She looked through a window cavity. There was a damp mass of stone and rotted plaster and tangled metal which must once have been balustrades. No roof left, only sky. Wild plants had begun their travels, but the castle could only have been burned a few years before. Jude thought back to the petrol man, his words and his manner. She saw that they were meant, however courteously, as a lesson to her. This would have been an English castle, and it must have been burnt by the IRA. She took a few photographs of the eyeless hulk, of the slender green snaking its way round the twisted ironwork, and then returned to her bike.

Ten miles on and the road was rougher still and muddy. She stopped to clean her goggles, cutting the engine, and the quiet filled her head. It was still one of the moments she liked the best, disconcerting and exhilarating, when the blast of her own noise stopped and slowly, as her ears adjusted, the rest of the world came in again. From somewhere she heard the sounds of a cart, and otherwise nothing but the wind pressing against the gorse. The road ran straight here, through the bog. Jude looked back towards the ruins of a house just passed. Some words had been painted on to the gable end, white lettering dashed on in slanted capitals:

REMEMBER THE DEAD.

Finding her camera, Jude took a photograph. It began to rain, softly and thoroughly, and Jude stowed the camera quickly and climbed back on her bike. Soon the dust was exchanged for mud.

The route had looked straightforward on the map, but Jude discovered that signposting, even on main roads, was very intermittent. Several times she had to ask the way. Nor was it an easy matter, once she had found someone in this empty country, to understand what they said. Although they seemed to speak in the same accent as Dr Kelleher or Catherine, it was so much faster and in such an intense singsong that she didn't know where the important words fell.

The rain had been unrelenting and Jude was soaked. Her face was cold and her hands were stiff, fumbling with the tarpaulin rope to find the eggs. The road had been climbing for a few miles and she could see that it dipped down ahead. There must be a view, but with the rain driving across like mist, she could see

nothing beyond. Dirty sheep knelt at the roadside like suppli-
cants.

Jude picked up a small stone and, very carefully, cracked the top
of the first egg. She put it to her mouth, and prising the shell open,
she drank down the egg white before it spilt. The yolk lay alone in
the curve of the shell, a deep orange. Jude stared down into it, this
piece of dense colour in a landscape washed into greys and dull
browns, then lifted the shell to her lips and felt the yolk slip across
and break over her tongue.

She felt better. Making a rudimentary shelter with the tarpaulin, she unfolded the map and checked her position. She was less
than ten miles from her destination, she thought. There was a lake
marked very near, virtually reaching to the road, and though she
couldn't see it from where she stood, she decided to look for it
before going on.

'It'll warm you up, at the least,' she said to herself. 'Even if you
don't find it.'

Tucking the map away, Jude leaped over the ditch and clambered
down the bank. She could just make out a line of rushes about
forty yards away. The lake would be there. Stepping down, she
thought onto solid ground, a cushion of bright green mosses and
tiny flowers, she found herself ankle deep in brown water. She
pulled her boot free from the suck of the bog and managed to
plant it on one of the coarse grass tussocks that grew proud of the
moss. Then, keeping her arms wide for balance, she stepped from
hummock to hummock towards the rushes.

'Miss Barnstaple would be proud of me,' she muttered, remembering the broad calves and the long suffering of her school gym
teacher.

The lake was like a haunted place. Rain stippled its surface but
otherwise nothing moved. A bird cried out like a lost soul somewhere in the reeds. Bulrushes stepped their way into the deeper
water, haughty, erect. Jude stood still and stared, waiting for something, some motion, some action. But nothing came and suddenly
she was unnerved and turned, leap-frogging the bog back to the
road and her motorbike.

By the time she reached Skibbereen, Jude was cold. The rain was still falling steadily, her jacket and britches were heavy and wet, and, despite her balletics, the bog water had seeped in through the lacing on her boots. When she stood down from the bike again, she couldn't feel her toes. Two raw eggs had been fine for nourishment but they had done nothing to warm her, and she went in search of hot tea.

The rain had stopped when she came out of the tea room. Thin beads of sun made the wet streets gleam. She walked back towards the bike to see a group of boys gathered around it, laughing and daring the tallest of them, who was straddled over the saddle, leaning into the handlebars, vrooming like someone half his size. As Jude approached, swinging her hips, he started up and swung off.

Pretending she hadn't seen him on the bike, she took out her helmet from the sidecar and laced the tarpaulin tight.

'Mother of God, it's ridden by a girl,' one of them said.

'And a pretty one,' the tall boy said, not quite below his breath, and Jude felt herself blush with pleasure.

'Could you tell me if there's a garage near here where I can fill up with petrol?' she asked him.

His bravado crumbled into incredulity.

'It's not ever yours,' he said, and when she nodded, his mouth dropped.

'And you a lady,' he said, shaking his head, and the other boys followed suit. 'English though,' he added, as if this explained something, and they all nodded with him.

'I'll give you a ride if you'll direct me to the garage,' Jude said, and she watched his face break into a grin.

With the boy on behind her and wearing her helmet, his hands gentle round her waist, Jude rode through the town, turning left or right at the tugs on her sleeve. He was, she suspected, taking her on the long route to the garage, down any number of tiny streets with streams running by and old women in black and children scattering at the sound of the bike. But that was fine. Now she'd got this far she found she was nervous, and happy for any excuse to delay the last leg of the journey.

The other boys were already there, out of breath, waiting, by the time they reached the garage, and they greeted their friend with claps around the head and punches. When she set off, they saw her away with shouts and laughter.

She thought how strange it was that she'd come to a foreign country and found herself more at ease with people than she often felt at home. These boys, met for five minutes, the Whelans, even Dr Kelleher. But maybe that was why it was like that over here. Because nobody knew her, not even Daniel, if she ever found him. She had no history. Nothing was assumed, and for now she could leave behind the warring in her own heart.

And something more she felt too, which was more like the dawning of some new sense – and it came back to her in the strangest flood of emotion how she had felt that afternoon alone with Richard and him leaping. She had felt herself stretch and unfold then, and this now was something like it again.

The road to Castletowne gave nothing away, not even a sight of the sea. Although the tea had warmed her, Jude found the five miles or so exhausting. Her muscles ached and she could feel the pressure in her neck rise. She longed to be off the bike. Every pothole, every stone jarred and it seemed a miracle she'd had no puncture on these rough roads.

She kept her eyes forward. She wouldn't let herself think about what might happen next. What, for example, she would do if Daniel were not there? Or what she should say to him if he were? She'd never been good at prepared speeches, always come last in school debates. So she'd have to trust to her native sense now.

There was a steep hill down into the village and finally, churned and frantic, the sea beyond. Leaving the motorbike at the top of the hill, Jude walked down. She didn't have an address for the Murrays, but she guessed from Daniel's diary that the word Coolderry, his good place, was probably the name of their house, and she knew they had a dog and a daughter, and that they'd owned a hotel before retiring. Somebody would know them.

Twenty minutes later she had address, directions and quite a lot of information about Mrs Murray's deficits as a flower arranger,

233

the unruly nature of their dog and the more interesting fact that they had reportedly come down with flu, or so their girl had said.

'My God, you're such a good liar,' Jude told herself. 'Who'd have thought you'd find so much to say about roses, let alone the ecclesiastical virtue of the chrysanthemum?' and she muttered her thanks into the damp air for all those times when Leo had bored her silly with his flower talk.

The house was a short distance outside the village. Fifteen minutes walk, her informant, Mrs Hewetson, had told her, but which Jude reckoned for ten, if you weren't carrying quite so much weight forward as Mrs Hewetson. Anyway, after some deliberation, she decided to ride there. She didn't know why, but she wanted to be sure she could get away quickly if she needed to.

Jude found the house easily. The name Coolderry was carved onto a piece of slate beside the gates. She coasted down the drive, then cut her engine and sat in the silence. Now she was here, she realised she had no plan or thought as to what she would do next. A Labrador came round the side of the house barking, tail out high behind. It stopped a few yards from the motorbike and threw out short, aggressive yelps. Jude swung her leg over the saddle and stood away from the bike.

'Hey, come on now, boy. You're not so different from Rex.' Jude put her hands out flat towards the dog. 'Only you're a girl I see now. Didn't notice that at first. Shouldn't make those assumptions.'

Reluctantly, as if being coerced, the dog walked towards her, gingerly, as if the gravel was glass. Jude stroked down between the dog's ears and along her back. Her fur was warm and smooth. When the dog leant her weight against Jude's legs, she accepted the invitation and gently scratched the dog's ribs. Just now she missed home powerfully. Leo and Sally, her high bedroom, Rex, and most of all the children. She didn't hear the man approach.

'Who the hell are you?' he said, and Jude jumped, as if she'd been caught out at something. He called to the dog, who slunk straight to him, tail between her legs.

Jude straightened up. He was a tall, thin man dressed in old corduroy trousers, a gingham shirt, sleeves rolled up to the elbows, and a sleeveless Fair Isle sweater. His hair, still thick on his head, was white though his broad moustache was still black, and his arms and face were weather-beaten and freckled. He had the bearing of an army major and she was tempted to click her heels and salute, but she checked it and introduced herself. If this is Mr Murray, she thought, and if Daniel is here, he might have mentioned me, and she watched to see if his expression changed with her name. But he showed no sign of recognition, only folded his arms and stood waiting.

Jude thought of making something up, some other reason that had brought her to this corner of this country and down this particular steep drive. 'Landscape photographer' seemed thin, now she was in the landscape.

'I'm looking for someone,' she said.

His expression didn't change, but Jude saw that he became very still.

'You're looking for someone?' he said back, and she knew that he was buying time.

'Yes.'

'Well, I'm afraid there's only my wife and me here. The O'Connors are further on, a hundred yards or so, and there are the Rourkes. They're another half mile. But as you can see, we're very out of the way,' and he waved an arm around abruptly as if the trees and rhododendrons could demonstrate how far out of the way it was.

Now it was Jude's turn to pause. The dog stood between them, her velvet ears twitching, wagging her tail in a desultory, uncertain way, as if unsure where to bestow her favours. Whether with her master who was clearly out of temper, though not usually a jealous god, or with this stranger who had arrived so loudly but stroked her so gently.

'Excuse me,' Jude said, 'but you are Mr Murray?' and when he nodded, she said, 'I'm looking for Daniel Brown.'

When she looked back on it that night, she couldn't remember Mr Murray ever saying out loud that Daniel had been there. It was as if it became a known fact between them without being spoken.

The dog made up her mind and picked her way across to Jude, who stroked her absently and waited. Mr Murray put his hands to his head, then dropped them to his sides.

'You'd better come in.'

CHAPTER SIXTEEN

There was a large brown pot of hot tea already at one end of the kitchen table and two cups poured, and at the other end two mackintoshes flung across, and a torch, a package of sandwiches, apples, a thermos and a haversack. Mr Murray pulled out a chair for her.

'My wife will be here in a moment. I know she'll say you should eat something before we set off.'

He poured another cup of tea and put two eggs in a saucepan.

'Set off?' Jude said.

'To look for Daniel.'

'Oh?'

'You're right, he has been with us, it must be a week now. Just arrived here one afternoon, on foot for God's sake, with his leg . . .' He shrugged, and Jude nodded.

'But he's not here now,' she said.

'No. The last few days, he's taken to walking off,' Mr Murray said. 'And of course he's a grown man, but . . .' and so much hung in the 'but'.

'I know,' Jude said.

'So, I must find my wife, explain things,' and he left the kitchen.

The dog sat beneath the table with her head on Jude's lap but Jude wasn't fooled by cupboard love. She stared ahead, her eyes resting on the canvas of the haversack, seeing nothing. She should be looking around, getting a gauge, but just now she was too tired. She could hear Mr Murray's voice in the hall, and another voice that must be his wife's. There were footsteps, and Mrs Murray came in.

She nodded a greeting to Jude, put her hand on her shoulder, as though they were old familiars.

'Joe says eggs are needed,' she said, and Jude warmed to this woman immediately, and she understood. That there was too much to be explained, that, at least for now, just this time in the kitchen perhaps, much must be taken on trust. She liked this woman, she liked her sureness.

Mrs Murray boiled up two eggs and cut bread.

'Irish eggs are very good,' Jude said, remembering her earlier two.

'It'll be the moisture in the air,' Mrs Murray said, and Jude couldn't tell if she was joking. 'You'll be tired. It's a devil of a road in spots, from Cork. Maybe you'd be better waiting here, while we go?'

'No, I'm fine.'

Mrs Murray found her some dry clothes.

'You won't mind trousers, what with the motorbike?' Jude shook her head. 'Only they'll be more comfortable.'

Mr Murray was to go up the hill behind the house, and Mrs Murray and Jude would head off towards the standing stones. They'd all get back by seven latest, they agreed, and if they hadn't found him, then they'd set out and search again.

The two women walked in silence at first, finding a shared pace, eyes to the ground to keep their footing. The clouds had cleared for the late afternoon and the sun sent long slender shadows out from the walkers. Jude wished she had her camera with her. They crossed several fields, scrambling over the walls, avoiding the brambles and gorse as best they could, stopping every while and scanning the landscape, searching.

'Perhaps we should call out?' Jude said at last, staring across the rough country. 'You could hide for ever out here.'

'No,' Mrs Murray said. 'It makes him dig in deeper. We've discovered that already.'

'Has he been gone long?' Jude said a minute later.

'About six years.' Mrs Murray laughed abruptly. 'No, since breakfast,' she said then. Mrs Murray walked on more quickly now, and despite being at least thirty years younger, or so she guessed, Jude had to work to keep up.

'Has he . . .' Jude stopped. 'How is he?' she said then.

Mrs Murray halted mid-stride and looked at Jude, hands on her hips, breathing deeply. For a minute or so she didn't speak, only fixed Jude so intently, that Jude had to stare back. It was the first time she'd had opportunity to look properly at Mrs Murray, so quickly had things gone since she'd arrived there. Her face was as weathered as her husband's, perennially brown, Jude guessed, and lined. But whereas his seemed cut into by the natural elements, sun, wind, rain, hers was the face of someone who had worn her emotions close to her skin. Even as they stared, Jude watched mistrust, fear and curiosity cross the older woman's face.

'Perhaps you should tell me,' Mrs Murray said at last. 'Perhaps I'd like to ask you a thing or two,' catching her breath, her voice rough. 'You've arrived out of the blue at our house on a motorbike looking for Daniel. Who are you? We don't know anything about you, or what you are to him. Why on earth should we trust you?'

Despite her efforts, Jude had caught her hand on a bramble a little way back, and she picked at a thorn in the side of her thumb. She could see the black nub of it, but it was in deep. She wondered how much she should say. Mrs Murray waited, her eyes never leaving Jude's face. Jude pressed her teeth against the thumb and squeezed it till it ached. She could feel the thorn with her tongue tip, but it wasn't coming proud. Letting go, she made her decision and for the second time in as many days she told a virtual stranger the story of her photograph. Even as she spoke, it crossed her mind that she had left behind more than she knew when she crossed the water, and for a moment she felt light-headed with exhilaration.

When she had finished her tale, Mrs Murray didn't say anything for a minute. Then she nodded.

'We're nearly to the Three Fingers,' she said. 'Let's climb up to them first, in case,' and Jude understood. Daniel might be there, and if he were, then things would go another way for now.

The fingers stood in a line on the crest of a hill, slender, tall and rudimentary-looking. On one side the hill sloped down and away, and looking across Jude could see over to the peninsula, right out to where the ocean met the sky. There was no sign of Daniel. She put a hand to the middle stone. It was cool and coarse against her palm, the lichen tickling slightly.

'They make you want to stand as tall,' Jude said, 'or to hold on to them. Put your arms round,' and she reached her arms out around it.

'They've been here for over three thousand years. There used to be four, but our local lady of the manor, she fancied it for her rockery.'

Jude laughed. 'I can imagine Daniel here.'

'It's where I first met him,' Mrs Murray said. She leaned back against one of the stones. 'I knew Daniel's aunt, Charlotte's sister, though we hadn't seen each other for years. It was Christmas letters, that kind of thing. Then in the midst of these troubles, Charlotte wrote asking if her son could look us up, if he had opportunity. He was coming over to be part of the new police force. And we wrote back and said that he could, if he was careful. But we didn't hear anything from him, and to be honest, it was relief. The more we heard about these Black and Tans and Auxiliaries, the worse they sounded. No better than the IRA lot, and many were saying worse.

'So one day I'd come up here, just for a walk. It was a day a bit like this, the clouds clearing near the evening. Joe didn't like it, me going for walks then. He said it was too dangerous. But I couldn't bear not to, and besides, he was being over-protective, which always brings out the bloody-minded in me.

'I was standing here, right by the stones, so I saw him coming. He had a lovely bearing on the horse, that's what I noticed first, so fluent. And I think I knew before he reached me who he was.

'When he asked, very politely, for directions to my own house, but as though we were standing on Patrick Street, or Stephen's Green, I couldn't help laughing, and then he laughed too.'

'What chance. What a strange meeting,' Jude said.

'In the middle of the Tan war. One of the worst times. And you didn't mix with people like him, Auxiliaries and Tans. Or the military. You didn't even give them directions, not if you could help it. Even in a place like Castletowne which has more than its fair share of men who've given their best to protect the British Empire, and where you'd never hear the Angelus bells ring, even here people had been shot for less. Found in a field, or under a bridge, a card around their neck, 'Convicted spy'. It was different elsewhere, maybe in Wicklow or Galway, Sligo perhaps, but not around here. Besides which, most of the Black and Tans were ruffians. They were as bad as the other lot. Thugs. They'd come over here for a free-for-all, courtesy of the British Government. So it wasn't a good idea, us meeting Daniel.

'He was joy-riding that day. Shouldn't have taken the horse, though he said he was given the wink by his superior, and he got lost. Then finding he was close to Castletowne, he'd remembered our invitation. It was a bloody stupid thing to do, and he knew it. He wasn't in uniform, but it wouldn't have taken more than a few words for anyone to guess what he was up to over here.

'I can still see Joe's face before I introduced them. He was angry enough to hit me, bringing a Tan into the house. But then I told him who this was, and Daniel asked him something about fishing, he'd noticed the rods in the corner of the hall, and that was that. So simple. There was no question after that but that we'd be friends. Joe and Daniel had a way of understanding one another, it was more like father and son. Joe would have loved a son. And Daniel was so affectionate with me. Always found something to bring me, a little gift.'

She looked over towards the sea, her eyes reaching back.

'It was Turkish Delight one time, from Hadji Beys, and chocolates another. Then he started bringing me things he'd found. From anybody else I'd have been offended. Strange gifts. Bunches of flowers, not garden flowers, wild flowers. A smooth stone, a robin's egg, grasses one time. I asked him what their names were, but he didn't know. Only things he did know about were birds.' She paused. 'And you think you can rescue him?' she said.

Jude blushed. 'Or myself. I don't know, or both.'

241

'It's better if you're not here only for him,' Mrs Murray said. 'Or else he might take too much.'

Jude nodded.

Mrs Murray laughed. 'He used to eat me out of house and home. Never seen anyone eat so much. Only having had a daughter, I'd never met ravenous boys.'

'They were like that when I was nursing,' Jude said. 'Once they began to recover, we couldn't give them enough to eat.' But she wanted to hear the rest. 'So it was dangerous then, having him to stay?' which was disingenuous, because she knew the answer.

'Terribly risky, we all knew that. Even in our house, which is fairly isolated. Surrounded by woods. You might get men, armed men, at your door at any time. They'd demand food, shelter, guns even. And there was a levy made, a gunpoint levy, especially on Protestants, and most of us paid it. Stupid not to. We did, certainly. A man not two miles away refused. He was warned twice. Then they burnt him out. He's living in Berkshire now, I heard.

'Anyway, Daniel would come, not that often, every month, six weeks or so, and stay overnight. And right from the start, we had an unspoken agreement. As long as he was with us, we'd none of us mention the Troubles. He'd be distressed when he arrived sometimes, abrupt, black-browed, but we never crossed that line. It was the only way we could all keep it going.'

'You never asked him what he was doing, when he wasn't with you?' Jude said, and after all she'd heard from Dr Kelleher, she couldn't keep the incredulity from her voice.

Mrs Murray looked up, stony-faced. 'We should be getting back,' she said. 'If Joe hasn't found him, we'll have to be out again.'

'I'm sorry,' Jude said. 'I'm coming to all of this fresh. It's only after what I heard in Cork. About the Auxiliaries, and the Black and Tans.' And Daniel's diary, she thought. There's enough in that to sink a strong man. They couldn't think his hands were clean, surely.

Mrs Murray stared at her, such fierce scrutiny, Jude felt as if the older woman was sucking out and testing her very marrow.

242

'You don't know any better, do you?' Mrs Murray said at last, and Jude breathed out with relief, as if she'd been allowed to live after all. Not waiting for an answer, Mrs Murray went on. 'This is an exhausted country,' she said. 'Things have been done, terrible things, that nobody can think are right, and by all sides. I could tell you some tales, true ones, to set against whatever you've been told about the Tans.' She shook her head. 'Though what you heard was probably no more than the truth.' She paused. 'If you know Daniel – which you must do surely, to come all this way – do you think he's a brute?'

Jude ducked the question. 'Tell me what happened next,' she said.

The light was closing in, collapsing and confusing distances. An owl started up, and only the swifts were left, high up in the last of the sunlit air. The two women set off back, walking in silence for a time, and then Mrs Murray told the rest.

'I think it was his visits with us that kept him sane. Towards the end, for sure.'

'The end?' Jude said.

'We never knew what had happened to him. He just didn't turn up again. He'd arranged to come, and he never appeared and he never called. It happened once before, and he managed to send us word. They were sent out on a last minute patrol that time, all leave cancelled. But no word this time. Then we read about the ambush in the *Irish Times* and it was his division, and put two and two together. There'd been a lot killed and they gave numbers and no names, so we couldn't be sure, but he had to be one of them, it was the only explanation. We wrote to his parents, and his aunt, but never heard back, though now he's explained why that was.'

'And then he turned up again last week,' Jude said.

Mrs Murray nodded. 'Looking like a ghost. A limping, hunted ghost. I can't bear it, seeing him. I'm worried he'll do something terrible.' She looked at Jude. 'And I tell you, when we find him, if I think you're making it worse, or putting him in any further danger, or distress, I'll see you out of my house, whether I like you or not.'

And she strode on, not waiting for Jude's reply.

Mr Murray had already returned when they arrived back at the house, and he shook his head when he saw them.

'We'll have something to eat first,' Mrs Murray said. 'We'll need the energy. No point in getting exhausted.'

'And then?' Jude said.

He told Jude about Horse Island.

'It didn't occur to me earlier, God knows why not, but he might have taken somebody else's boat and rowed out. I checked and ours is still there. Or swum even. It's not so far if you walk round a way first, though with his bad leg, God knows, and it's a falling tide and there is a bit of a current.'

Mrs Murray cooked an omelette, and after they'd eaten, they gathered lanterns and walked down from the house and round the headland before dropping to the beach and searching out the darkness where the island lay, peering for any sign of a fire. But there was no sign. Only the sound of the water sipping at the shore and the whistle and spit of beached seaweed.

'Can't we go out there?' Jude said.

'Not in the dark. It'll have to be first light tomorrow.'

And so they were making their way up the path when they heard the dog. She'd been with them down on the beach, dragging out driftwood branches even in the dark. But now she was somewhere beyond and below, giving long yelps that echoed over the water, then silence, then yelping again.

'Would you ever tell that dog to be quiet,' Mrs Murray said. 'Call her, Joe.'

But she wouldn't come, and only carried on with the barking.

'She couldn't be chasing rabbits this late,' Jude said.

'She's down by the water. Near the tower, I'd say. Sounds like something's alarmed her,' Mr Murray turned to his wife. 'Why don't you go on up, and I'll get her.'

'I'll come with you,' Jude said, and so she and Mr Murray made their way down again, all the while the dog's yelps getting louder.

'What's the tower?' Jude said.

'It's ruined. Part of the lookout system going back to the time

244

before the Protestant plantations. To keep out the French, or the Spanish, or the pirates, which I suspect often came to the same thing. There's one on almost every headland around here.'

They came out of the woods on to another beach. The sky had cleared of all cloud and the moon shone down on the water, its thin silver light cutting across the black sea towards them in a fading arc. They trod through the dark mass of the tide line and out on to sand. The dog was visible now, standing at one side of the beach, barking at nothing, Jude thought, or nothing she could see. Small rocks and stones skirted with seaweed littered the beach, and Jude walked carefully. It would be easy to trip here and turn an ankle. She thought it must be the effect of the moon, but sometimes as she stepped, the beach seemed to glisten for a moment.

Mr Murray went off to the right, towards the tower, and Jude walked towards the dog. At first she thought the dog was barking at a rock. But as she walked past and on, she saw it was no rock but a man. And as she drew closer still, she knew that it was Daniel. He was crouched down, sleeves pulled up to his elbows, scrabbling in the sand. This time she was sure, there were sparks, like light, where Daniel's hands disturbed the sand, and as she watched, he tugged at some seaweed and flung it away, and it shimmered in the darkness.

As if relieved of responsibility once Jude was there, the dog gave up her noise and trotted over towards Mr Murray, and now Jude could hear that Daniel was breathing heavily. Coming close with the lantern she bent towards him, slowly, not wanting to alarm him. As she watched, he picked out what looked like a small flat piece of shell or stone. Rubbing the sand from it, he put it into his pocket, then started scrabbling again. He didn't seem to have noticed her.

'Daniel,' she said softly. 'Daniel.'

He paused, fingers in the sand, and looked up. 'Hello, Jude,' he said, and she had a strong sense of *déjà vu*.

'If you shut off your light, you'll see the phosphorescence,' he said.

'What are you doing?' she said, and he put his hand in his

pocket and brought out a piece of broken china, white in the lantern light.

'Feel,' he said, holding it out.

She took it. It was smooth, edges worn by the sea.

'You can't see the patterns in the dark,' Daniel said. 'They throw them into the tide once they're not wanted. But at least the sea is softer with them than the earth. Better than the bottom of the garden.'

'Not wanted?'

'Damaged, chipped. Limping a bit,' he said.

Jude couldn't see his expression in the darkness. She couldn't tell whether he was joking or serious, or even how far he knew what he was saying.

'It's dark, Daniel,' she said. 'Night-time. The Murrays, me, we've been very worried.'

'They're all over the place,' he said. 'Everywhere. Like cockles. If you know where to pray, you can dig and find them.'

'Pray?'

'To the Crom Dubh. An Irish god.'

She heard Mr Murray approach, the dog at his heels.

'Jude?' he said.

'Daniel's here.'

CHAPTER SEVENTEEN

Daniel knew it must be drawing close, the end to all this, because Jude arrived. He didn't know how she could be here, but it didn't surprise him.

When she found him on the beach, he showed her a piece of the china, but he wasn't sure whether she liked it or not, because it was dark.

He wanted to talk to her, explain himself, tell her about the island, but Mrs Murray insisted on everybody going to bed. She was fierce about it. It would all wait until the morning, she said. Before he fell asleep, he thought he heard their voices downstairs, and his name spoken several times. But the day had been long, and he was very tired, and he fell asleep very quickly.

In the morning the sun made the edges of the curtains sharp and drew a line up the rag rug and across the quilt on his bed, catching the white then the red then the white. Daniel's leg ached. He would go out to Horse Island today and take Jude with him. Next best person since he couldn't be there with Johnnie. At least you went in a circle if you tried to walk away there, and the bracken and tumbled walls slowed you down, not like the grass in Kew Gardens. And though he didn't know how, he was determined to call a halt to his travels. His head was weary. He longed to make a peace.

Downstairs, Mrs Murray had her arms full of flowers, tall flags of irises, delphiniums. Outside Mr Murray was sitting astride the bike and Jude was crouched beside. They were deep in conversation about camshafts, gearboxes and internal expanding brakes. Leaving them to it, Daniel went and sat on the terrace, his back to the wall of the house, and waited. The pulse of pain in his leg was strong today, a sign of tiredness. He sat very still, turning his piece of china between his fingers, and watched blackbirds tug worms from the lawn. They were like magicians, he thought, with their silks.

Mrs Murray brought out a jug of coffee and then he watched her bend to her roses, her secateurs like angels of mercy, cutting the dead from the quick. The air was so still, not a breath of wind, it would make hard work of their sailing later. Beside him, a butterfly clipped to the wall on the threads of its toes felt the sun on its back at last and shook itself awake, opening its wings coyly like a courtesan with her fan. Daniel shut his eyes against it. He could see too much today. Listening to the soft, clean cut sound of the secateurs, something became clear to him. Perhaps it was his exhaustion that freed him, perhaps it was the butterfly's spread, perhaps it was the secateurs, or perhaps it was just that it was time now. He wondered a little behind his shut eyes, feeling the gentle sun on his eyelids. And when they were all seated finally, Mr Murray twitching his old panama against the sun, Jude wiping at the oil on her hands with a rag, each drinking their coffee, Mrs Murray's secateurs laid on the ground beside her, Daniel opened his eyes and stared across the garden to the sea beyond. If you painted it now, he thought, it would be the thinnest line of paint, not even enough for a bird to dive into. Then he spoke.

'I don't know what happened in the ambush,' he said. 'But it is what I need to know. And I don't know, coming here, whether I'm running away from something or towards something, right into it, full-face, not even a hand up to protect.'

There. He had begun it.

'You want to talk about it now?' Mrs Murray said, and Daniel nodded.

'It was the photograph that set it all going?' she said. 'The one in the exhibition, that Jude took? Because it showed two men sharing a cigarette?'

248

He nodded. She said it so bluntly. 'Those two men,' he said, and now he felt cold, so cold in the sun.

'Daniel.' Jude's voice cut in. He took his eyes from the line of the sea and looked across at her. She wanted to rescue him, but he couldn't help. He wished he could hold on to her voice, keep it right there in his head, this good voice. He was falling in love with her, which wasn't why she was here at all.

'Tell us what you did over here,' she said. 'What happened that day.'

Daniel's stomach clutched. These were the wrong words for her voice. He turned his head, put her out of his sight, but she went on speaking.

'Don't run away.'

'It wasn't me who ran,' he said.

'But it was somebody else?'

'Can you imagine a fish running?' he said, and he turned in his chair and looked over his shoulder at the wall. The butterfly was gone. He put a finger to the plaster. It was a bare place to sleep away the night.

They were talking about him, over his head, behind his back, the Murrays, Jude. He turned back to them and he made his voice light, like the shiver of wind on water, like the flour from the dredger sifting down the first time he'd met her.

'What do you want to know?' he said.

'What do you mean, about the fish?' Jude said.

'I told you that, or I told somebody. It's what we called him, the Trout. Colonel Whittam.' Daniel looked back at the butterfly's wall. 'Well, it was because of him, I suppose, that we called the actions fishing trips.

'He liked to go fishing. Fly-fishing. So we got to calling it fishing, what we all did. Fishing. We had to be fierce. Keep down the natives,' he said with a laugh. 'Fishing.'

Mrs Murray picked up her secateurs and went to the roses again. Jude watched her, her movements brusque, jagged.

'I'm going to go and meet someone who was there, at the ambush,' Jude said.

Daniel shook his head. 'Everyone's dead. My brother Johnnie

first, in his war, and then everyone else in mine. Whittam was the only other one to get out, and he killed himself three years back. I told you that already.'

'I'm going to meet somebody from the other side,' Jude said. She waited, but he said nothing. 'Matt Walsh. The man in the photograph. The Cork man.'

'I'm very cold,' Daniel said. 'Let me go in.'

'I looked after him. He brought his friend, Whittam, in wounded and I fed him hot tea and wrapped a blanket round him and kept him from the war for a few hours.'

'I'm against the wall, aren't I? Not warming my wings at all.' He rubbed his hands together.

'Please, Daniel. I need to know what happened,' she said.

Mr Murray got up and went inside. Jude picked up her coffee cup. Her hand was shaking. Mrs Murray stood, staring at a rose bush. Daniel rubbed at his leg. His skin was in pinpoints. Mr Murray came back outside with a rug, and he put it over Daniel's lap, put his hand for a moment on Daniel's shoulder before sitting back down.

She knew it was her imagination, but Jude could have sworn that everything stopped in the minutes that followed. Not just the people, but the whole world. Trees, wind, birds, bees. That they all stopped what they were doing and turned to Daniel, waiting.

When he began to speak again, it was in a different voice, a practical, matter-of-fact voice, as if the words weren't really coming from him, but from someone else, someone speaking through him. He stared out from his chair towards the roses, but Jude didn't know what he was seeing. His hands rested flat on the rug, fingers still, no twitching.

'There'd been a burning,' he said. 'A farm and all its buildings. An official reprisal, I don't remember for what, but we went a bit wild. You know how the IRA used to cut off a girl's hair, hack it from her head, if she was thought to be walking out with one of us? That was the first warning. Will had been seeing a girl in the town and they'd done it to her, and the night of that particular burning he was still very angry about it.

'The family was in bed when we arrived and we hammered at the door, then opened it and marched in. A man came down to us already pulling on his trousers, and when Will read off the order, he didn't say a word, only disappeared and was back again with two sons. They went past us and outside and were rushing to the live-stock. We didn't bother to tell them we'd be taking the livestock too. Instead we went on in to the house, had a look around. It was cleaner than most, and there were some nice things.

'The girl must have been seventeen, eighteen years old, pretty. She came down still in her nightdress while we were rummaging. She started pleading with us. Her grandmother was upstairs, and frail and ill. Couldn't we wait till tomorrow? Or let them bring a cart for the old woman and take her somewhere else? But we had our orders, and you couldn't trust them, not even the young ones. We'd been tricked like this before. So Will told her no, the house was to be burnt in fifteen minutes and everyone was to be out by then.'

'It was official, this kind of thing? You had orders to do it,' Mrs Murray said, 'official orders?'

Although Daniel didn't respond and went on with his account, hands still flat to his lap, Jude saw his index fingers start to twitch, as if jerked up and down on a string.

'It was easy for my brother, stuck in his trench. Easy. No girls or old women. His fault I ended up here. If only he hadn't died.' He paused, then went on. 'The girl got angry then. She was abusive. The language coming out of her was shocking.

'I think it was the foul language that did it for Will, because one minute he was listening, and the next he'd gone and found a kitchen knife, a blackened ugly thing, and he grabbed the girl's hair and started slashing at it. What with her struggling, it's a miracle he didn't catch her on the neck, but me and Duguid managed to restrain her and then Will did his business. When we let the girl go, she rushed back upstairs and we followed her and there was the grandmother, just as she had said. And when Will saw her, he started yelling again, over and over. "Out! Now! Out!" And the old woman didn't say anything, didn't move from the bed, just stared at him. Then there was this smell and she'd wet herself and worse.

251

The girl was sobbing, trying to get a sweater, a coat on her. But what with the hair cutting and so forth, there was no time left for niceties and in the end we had to drag the old woman out, because she wouldn't let us carry her, the girl sobbing behind. I don't know what happened in the yard because I was busy with the petrol by then, but Will says the old woman had a fit. Anyway she died.'

Jude heard Mr Murray's gasp, the exclamation swallowed in the throat, and she kept her eyes on the sleeping dog, its paws running to nowhere inside a dream.

'It was quite a job to throw everything into the fire. Feeding troughs, horse harnesses, tackle, plough, scythes, hay rake, even the milk churns. But our orders were for everything, so everything went in. Then some of us went off searching for the men. I was relieved to be away from the blaze. We found them quite easily and Duguid and Charters took them off to the barracks for questioning and I was left with a couple of others to bring the cattle back. The horses were gone.

'Some of us thought it was a good sign, things going so quiet those next weeks. That they were frightened at last. But we should have known. So it must have been a couple of weeks later that we were on the road between Dunbeg and Clonnacook, two lorry-loads of us, eighteen men. It was dusk, teatime, and foggy. That's what I was thinking about when it happened, I was thinking about a cup of tea. We'd been out on patrol since before dinner and nothing found, nobody sighted, and nearly back at the barracks. Another quarter of an hour and I'd have my mug of tea. Will Savage was seated next to me and George Spring across. Colonel Whittam was up in the front, in the cab with the driver. You couldn't have much of a conversation in those Crossleys. They were too noisy, what with the wind. And that day we were all cold and weary. There was a fine rain dropping, like a mist, and our mackintoshes were saturated, our britches sodden and heavy on the legs.

'We turned a corner and there ahead, in the middle of the road and waving his arms up and down, was a British soldier. I didn't notice him because of the mist, till the lorry slowed.

'There was nothing we could have done. You couldn't tell him

252

for a rabbit, or a duck, and nobody even raised their rifle. He was a soldier, dressed as one of ours, as far as you could see in that light; khaki trench-coat, steel helmet. And when we were twenty, maybe thirty yards away, he lobbed a Mills bomb into the cab.'

Daniel stood up, the rug falling to the ground, then reached down and picked a small stone off the terrace. The others watched in silence. Swinging his right arm, he threw the stone in a high arc over on to the lawn.

'Like that,' he said. 'That's how you're taught to throw them. As if you were an off-spinner. That's what they told us.'

'A what?' Jude said.

'An off-spinner,' Mr Murray said. 'Slow bowler. Cricket.'

'And it must have happened in a split second,' Daniel went on, 'but I had this thought. Which was what a good cricketer he must be, because he had a lovely action with that Mills bomb.'

Daniel stopped talking again. He picked up another stone and threw it, then another, his face blank, giving nothing away. Jude could hear the wind in the yew tree and she could feel the blood banging in her fingertips, she had them gripped so hard around the struts of her chair. She hadn't noticed it before, but now she could smell Daniel's cologne, and something else, something she knew from the war, which was fear: an acrid, sharp sweat smell.

'Sit down, Daniel,' Mrs Murray said. 'Don't throw the stones any more.'

And he sat down again, gathered the rug across his lap, and went on with his story.

'He lobbed the Mills bomb into the cab and it exploded. I found out afterwards they did the same to the other lorry. We swerved and the Crossley nose-dived into the ditch, its back end reared up, and next thing I'm scrambling out over somebody who isn't moving, I don't know who it was, trying to find my feet, my boots sinking into the bog, the gorse up against my cheek, and brambles, so that I was finding thorns in my skin weeks later. And finally I made it up on to the road and took cover round one side of the lorry. It's all hell let loose there, men firing down on us from both sides, they're high up on the hill, behind rock outcrops, behind the wall on the far side of the road. Some of us are injured. Freddie Charters screaming blue murder. His neck is spouting blood so that I get a mouthful as I lift my rifle. I don't know how many of us are wounded, or dead.

'It reminds me of those playground games of tag we played at school. I was often the last boy left in then too, because I was quick on my toes. Nimble. Anyway, they were putting out some stiff fire from the other lorry, which was skewed across the road, but from where I was, I couldn't see how many men. I got down behind the Crossley and shot at the figures on the hill as best I could, and there were a couple of others with me, three at first. Colonel Whittam, who'd made it out of the cab, and Will. He was with us. And Springer, but he caught a bullet quickly and I took his rifle.

'It was the first proper action I'd seen over there, that wasn't raids and old women. I was firing like the blazes, wild with it, yelling. One of theirs fell forward wounded, and before they could pull him off the heather, I got him in my sights and finished him. But there were far more of them and it was obvious they'd got the better of us, they were gaining ground. So Colonel Whittam shouted at us to surrender. He threw down his rifle, and we did the same, me and Will, put down our rifles, put our hands up. Four sets of hands went up in the air from behind the other lorry. We counted them.

'The rain was falling harder by now, stair-rods, and we stood there, our hands in the air, while they scrambled down towards us, fifteen or twenty of them, rifles pointed, but not firing. The hardest thing I've ever had to do. Stand like that. Seven of us, with our arms in the air, and the rest groaning, writhing on the ground, or still. The leader, and I knew by his dress he was the man who had flagged us down, shouted to his men to take our weapons. The light was getting bad by then, so it was hard to make out the faces you knew, let alone theirs.

'They put all the weapons in a pile on one side of the road. The man who took mine, he must have been about my age and he wasn't wearing any kind of uniform. He had a cloth cap and a heavy farming jacket, a thick scarf wrapped around and tucked

254

inside, and when he checked my pockets for bombs, I could smell the wet wool of the scarf. His hands were scratched from the hillside, like mine.

"They had us disarmed and the main man was yelling at us to stand all together. They were prodding us into a group with their bayonets and rifle points, just like my man must have prodded his cattle. We were scared to hell by now, some of us crying, it might have been me, it's hard to know what I was doing and what I wasn't. Colonel Whittam was standing stock-still, mouth open. Will was muttering over and over, "Christ, not me, Christ, not me, Christ, not me.""

Daniel's fingers were dancing as he spoke now, jerking, and then it was his hands, pattering on the rug in a muffled tattoo. Jude got up and crouched beside him. She put her hands over his. His fingers were cold, white below the nails.

'My dream is about this. It comes back again and again. The stretch of road, the corner, the rocks and gorse, the lorries. It's never exactly the same, and it's not how it really happened. There are women and children there, and my brother, Johnnie. And each time when I wake up I think that if I could only remember properly what did happen, then I could be rid of the dream. But it's all so confused.

'Anyway, it was certainly quiet suddenly. After all the noise, grenades and firing, men shouting. We were surrendered and it was quiet. Even the men on the ground were quieter, not groaning so much and I loved it. I stood there, my comrades wounded, dead, around me, and I fell in love with that silence. I didn't ever want to move. Saying it now, just thinking about it, I can feel it again.'

His hands were still under Jude's, and she could feel them relax, his fingers unclench.

'It was quiet as the grave, and then all hell let loose. Suddenly the Shinners were firing at us. Taking aim and firing. For a moment I didn't understand what was happening. They'd just disarmed us, so we hadn't any weapons. I must have looked daft down their sights, my mouth hanging open amazed. I can see one of them now, he had the shakes badly and he was firing his pistol into the air like a mad thing, laughing wildly. Then I got shot.

'One minute I was on my feet, and the next I didn't know where I was or what had happened. I thought my leg had caught fire. There was water seeping in under my collar and my face was pressed into the bog earth. I managed to turn over, so I was looking up, my leg screaming with pain, my mouth screaming with pain, except that I must have been silent, because otherwise I wouldn't be here now. The shooting went on, the noise, and I shut my eyes. Can't have gone on for long though, minutes, not more, because the Shinners were always so short of ammunition, they wouldn't waste it. But it might have been for hours for all I could tell. Then it stopped. It was quiet again, only I was in pain inside it this time.

'A man was standing above me. I knew he must be on the road, which meant I was in the ditch. So what I could just see beyond, because it was very misty, was the hillside opposite. I could hear his voice, it dropped down to me in bits and pieces, and some bits I understood and others I didn't. And I could smell his cigarette. He was laughing. It was a hard bark of a laugh. And yelling. Yelling at somebody, telling him to get on and shoot him, not to be a coward, and he'd match the shot with one of his own, so I knew he was the commandant. I opened my eyes and looked up. He wasn't looking at me. His cigarette stood out from his lip and his pistol hung from his fingers, its nose pointing, aimless, straight down at my head. He had a wound on his hand, because I got drips of his blood on my face and they tickled. I knew then, as if it was the only thing I understood in the world, that I must play dead. Not move. Keep my eyes shut, keep still, despite the fire from my leg pushing up through me, despite his blood.

'I heard a shot and the commandant above me shouted out "Yerra, boy" and laughed, and then kicked at my ribs with his foot. I didn't move, didn't shout out. "This one's gone," he said. "Only the boss left, and he's mine."

'I could hear Whittam somewhere close to me. It was his voice whispering. "Get in the ditch," the commandant said to him. He told him to face him with his left shoulder. Then he said, "Play dead when I've shot you," and he whispered something, which I couldn't hear. It seemed a sick kind of joke to tell a man you're about to kill to "play dead". There was a shot, loud, close to me, and I felt Whittam slump in the ditch, some part of him pressing against my leg, so that I wanted to scream out with the pain. He didn't move then.

'That was his parting shot, the last one fired. He had them drilling and singing before they left, and there was his laugh in between it all. I was in and out of things, what with the pain and loss of blood, but I still remember the song,' and staring ahead, Daniel intoned it:

> '"Remember Comrades of Ireland,
> As forward to Victory we go,
> That England, the Tyrant of Tyrants,
> Has Mercy ne'er shown to the Foe."

They were singing and marching and wheeling, their boots crunching close, and away again, and close again. One of them was sick nearby me, I could smell it. Then they were gone and it was all very quiet, not even any groaning left.'

Daniel fell silent, and Jude, her hand still over his, felt his body slump, felt his exhaustion.

'But he wasn't dead,' Mr Murray said. 'Whittam.'

Jude glared at him. 'Give him a moment, for God's sake,' but Daniel cut across her, shrugging off her hand.

'No,' he said. 'He wasn't.'

'So?'

'The ravens made him move.'

'The ravens?'

'They were there so quickly, but then they like their meat warm. Johnnie used to write home about the French ravens. He would watch them hopping about beyond the wire amidst their spoils. He said it made him murderous.' He laughed.

Jude nodded. She remembered the ravens, and the rats, and the dogs. It was men who had done the killing. The animals were only going about their ordinary business. But it was repulsive when that business was the flesh of dead soldiers.

'That croak,' Daniel said. 'You can't mistake it. I opened my eyes and one was standing just above me, jutting out its beard, giving me the eye.' Daniel stuck out his chin. '*Cruck, cruck,*' he said, making his voice deep, hoarse. 'Like that. It hopped out of my sight, towards Whittam, and that's when I knew he wasn't dead. Maybe it even pecked at him, I don't know, but he cried out. "Off me, off me," something like that. The raven flew away, the lovely black green of its feathers. Colonel Whittam began muttering and sobbing.

'"Everybody dead," he kept saying, "everybody dead", and then all our names, our full names, like a roll call, reciting them. He was shaking, I could feel it. Then he got up. "Go straight, just go straight," he kept saying. When he started climbing out of the ditch, I opened my eyes. He was holding his shoulder, the blood pushing between his fingers. He walked across the road and up the hill opposite in a straight line, into the mist, then he was gone.'

'Why didn't you tell him you were alive? Call out to him, something?' Mr Murray said.

Daniel shrugged. 'I don't know. Something spooked me. And the next time I saw him was on the boat to England. I was on a stretcher bed. He came to see me, with his shoulder strapped. He told me I'd been very brave. He said it was a relief to think I'd been unconscious once I was wounded at the ambush. He'd thought I was dead. And I said I had no memory of it.'

'Why?'

'Because I didn't want to, I didn't want to remember. But it hunts me, and now I think I know why.'

'And did he believe you?' Mr Murray said.

'It doesn't matter whether he did or not,' Daniel said, 'because what matters is what I saw in that photograph.'

'What did you see?'

Daniel was shaking. 'I saw him sharing a cigarette. I saw an Auxiliary sharing a cigarette with a Shinner.'

'The man with Whittam is Walsh, the commandant,' Jude said in a low voice.

'But it wasn't in the Irish war,' Daniel said. 'That hadn't even

258

happened. They were still in France. So he knew that man before he ever got here. Ask Jude,' he said, his voice rising. 'Ask her about the two of them.'

Mrs Murray stood up. 'It's enough for now,' she said. 'Joe? Jude?'

Jude hadn't felt it before but suddenly she was exhausted, and the task before her seemed very heavy, and for the first time she was scared. She walked off a little way, down onto the lawn. The grass was deep. She stood and stared across the garden, its colours coming in like balm. She tried to stop thinking, to let her mind rest.

The Murrays were talking behind her, their voices just sound from where she stood.

What do they think I'm doing? she asked herself. What do I think I'm doing? I'm not some bloody knight on a white charger. Crouching down, she laughed at the thought, and laid her hands out flat on the grass, felt the blades tickle her palms.

'Jude,' Mr Murray called down, 'we thought we'd take you out to see Horse Island, Daniel and I.'

'Where?' she said.

'It's only ten minutes in the boat,' he said. 'Before anything else happens.'

CHAPTER EIGHTEEN

They all knew it to be a reprieve, the trip to Horse Island, and already, walking down to the boat, there was a mood amongst them which reminded Jude of the end of school examinations. Something had been faced by them all, the consequences couldn't be known yet, and in the short meantime, they would go to a place apart from their troubles, not quite a dreaming place, but not the hard day either.

Daniel was sure that Jude understood about the island. Crossing to it, she did look a bit green about the gills, as his father would say, the little boat lurching across the water. But once they were there, she was in her element. The way she crouched to the shingle when they arrived and ran her fingers through, and below into the finer sand, and picked between the stones and put one in her pocket. He liked the way she used her hands, and then, when the thought crossed his mind that he'd like her hands to touch him, he didn't banish it, as he might.

Mrs Murray had offered Jude a pair of boating pumps, but she said she was happy to go barefoot and Daniel stood in the shallows, his stick sinking into the sand, and watched her, arms around her camera bag, dance up the beach, where the rocks had gathered all the heat of the Irish sun, up towards the tideline and into the shade.

Jude and Mr Murray pulled the boat up high and Mr Murray secured the painter beneath a rock. He sat down.

'I'll stay with the boat,' he said. 'Perfect opportunity for some peaceful reading,' and he pulled a book from his pocket.

'So you'll have to show me the island then,' Jude said to Daniel, and he smiled and took her hand.

'Just to steady me,' he said.

They climbed high over the rocks behind till they reached a plateau of wiry grass, and then they sat for Daniel to rest his leg. Jude watched Mr Murray turn a page, watched him rub his fingers over the smooth silver curve of his rock. She watched as three oystercatchers gathered their wits on the wet slope of sand beyond, and she took a shot of them before some unseen danger caught their eye and they rose with a cry and cut low and straight between the waves for another shore.

The clouds drove across the sky and the sun was fierce between them. She photographed Mr Murray and the boat, then turned towards Daniel.

'Tell me about something,' she said, and as he began to speak, she photographed his face.

'I know the names on the island,' Daniel said. 'All the names. The flowers, the ferns, the herbs for the horses. They all still grow here. Mr Murray told me and I wrote it down. Tormentil and lousewort, bird's foot trefoil, silverweed and tufted vetch, thrift and lady's bedstraw, spear-leaved orache and samphire.'

Jude smiled. He sounded like Tom, like a child, eager to show off his knowledge. Then she remembered the lists of plants and birds at the back of his diary.

'The herbs?' she said.

'They used to bring sick horses here. Bring them and leave them for a while. The herbs made them well again.'

'Do they still bring them?'

Daniel shook his head. 'Too much other sickness now. It's no time for horses.' He got to his feet. 'Come on and I'll show you.'

They followed a narrow trail through hummocky grass and high bracken, crossing crumbling drystone walls, and every so often Daniel stopped to point out some fronded stem, or a small flower, or he picked a leaf and placed it on Jude's fingers, telling her to rub it and smell.

'Sorrel,' he said. 'Thyme. So close to the ground, you only know

261

it when you've trodden on it. Yarrow. Scabious. Sheep's bit scabi-ous with the little flower, and devil's bit with its jagged root.'

And all the names gathered in Jude's head like a strange song.

Daniel walked slowly, securing the ground with his stick before each step. Walking behind, Jude watched the injured stoop of his shoulders, the burden of his past leaving his body awkward, uncomfortable. And yet when he lifted his head and looked around him, or stopped for something particular growing, she glimpsed a different figure. Someone alive to the world, someone sure and eager, fiercely curious.

She thought that they were not so unlike in that way. She too was trying to lift her head and look around her again, to let go of a piece of her past so she could walk in the present.

They walked along the dipped spine of the island. It was warm beneath the sun, protected from the wind, with its own gathered perfumes from the gorse and the bracken, the heather and thyme. Jude felt protected here, as if for this brief time she could leave her journey behind, and Mr Murray, stroking the rock, deep in his book, would be gatekeeper, holding all beyond at bay. She felt her shoulders lift and she breathed deep into the briny, sweet air.

'Look here,' Daniel said holding his hand out, and there was a fine, white, bleached bone, curved into different planes so that however he held it, it tipped on his palm between points. Jude took the bone between her fingers. Its edges were like pinpricks, and it was very light. It was hard to imagine something this delicate clothed in flesh and fur. She lifted the bone to her face and stroked her cheek with it, very gently. A sharp line of sensation made her scalp quicken. She gave it back to Daniel and he put it in his pocket.

'Only a rabbit,' he said.

Cliffs rose steep at the island's end, the black rock, cut in vast diamonds, shouldering itself against the dint of the sea. As the island turned away from such exposure, the cliffs gentled them-selves a little, allowing small ledges for seabirds and rifts and gullies for plants and lichens in grey and green and yellow. Up here, out of the island's protection, the wind beat in fiercely, barracking

Jude's ears. Though she had stopped a safe way from the edge, still she crouched down. She didn't take her camera out.

It was easier, close to the ground. She looked over to Daniel. He too was crouched, but she saw that he had gone further than her and that now he was up at the edge, close to it, reaching his hands out to where the grasses gave way, and as she watched, he leaned into the sheer air.

Ice covered her skin and she saw the woman at the window, the woman climbing out and stepping forward, stepping off, she felt herself lifting the box to her eyes, framing it, her arms like lead, and she closed her eyes against the pit in her stomach, against the tumble of her heart, but she couldn't bear it, and she opened her mouth and yelled across the wind.

'Daniel! No!'

When she opened her eyes, he was turning back to the land, smiling, beckoning. She shook her head, and so he stood and walked across to her.

'All right?' he said.

'You were too close.'

He frowned, not understanding.

'To the edge,' she said.

'I was quite safe,' he said. She didn't answer. 'There's samphire growing on the cliff. I wanted you to see it.' He knelt down and looked at her more closely. 'You're sweating.'

'It's a hot day,' she said.

'But it's not that,' and he reached out and touched her brow. She didn't pull away. 'What are you afraid for?'

She stared out over the water. Unobserved, Daniel looked at the profile of her face. He noticed the small mole below her ear, and the dent of a scar above her chin, perhaps from chickenpox. He noticed that she had a slight bump on the bridge of her nose, which he had thought entirely straight. He wanted to touch her face with his fingers again, trace it, and the thought came to him that his looking at her now was as a lover might look and he felt a blush wash across him. He turned away and looked at the spread of the island.

'We must go to the tower before we leave,' he said.

Jude faced back in towards him. Two tears were scudded across her face, but he couldn't tell if it was the wind or some grief that had drawn them from her. He touched her cheek lightly.

'Your skin is gone rough with the salt,' he said.

'I'm glad you brought me here,' she said, getting to her feet. 'Thank God we don't have to deserve somewhere like this.'

Although Jude had glimpsed the tower from the boat, up close she understood why Daniel had insisted they must go right to it.

'Mr Murray said it was built as a beacon for boats,' Daniel said. 'But I'm sure it was in case of a marauding navy too. A watchman would be stationed here and he would send a signal – light a fire perhaps. You'd see it for miles.'

Jude stood at the centre of the tower and looked up at the walls, rising to the circle of blue above. She laid her hands on their stone.. The pieces were roughly cut, bedded in crudely. A swallow dipped in and down from the sky and pecked at the mortar before winging away again. She could still feel the touch of Daniel's finger on her cheek, and she knew she didn't only want to rescue this man. She saw how the lichen had gathered on one side only.

'You've been out here often?' she said.

'As often as I can.'

'Perhaps we'll come back here afterwards,' she said.

'After what?'

'I'm sorry about before,' she said. 'My shouting, on the cliff. I used to go to great heights, but not now. And other people, unless I am caught out, I can't watch other people.'

She could say nothing directly. She feared for too much. This man had woken her to herself as nobody had since Richard, since Kate. And yet the story that was unfolding around him was so horrible, she didn't know, at the end of it all, what she would be able to bear. Whether she would be able to bear the loving of him.

She looked out across the water. The current lines twisted away and the cloud shadows chased across, and it struck her, what an extraordinary point she had come to in her quest for the dragon.

An insect crawled across one foot and the sun warmed her shoulders. She lifted her camera to the view.

'Queen of all you survey,' Daniel called to her. She looked over at him. He had walked forward from the tower towards the cliff. A safe distance from the edge, he put down his stick and stretched his arms out on either side.

'Mister Icarus,' she called back, smiling.

'The photo,' he said. 'I remember. I don't think Elsa would let you call me that. Anyway, I'm a cripple,' he said, grinning back.

'I don't mind about your leg.'

'I don't mean my leg.'

'Well, I can't fly either,' she said, and she turned and walked back towards Mr Murray with his book and the beach.

That evening, they made a plan. It wasn't complicated, and it couldn't be hard and fast, because they had no idea what would happen. But in two or three days' time Jude and Daniel would set off for the town of Liscool. Jude would have Dr Kelleher's letter of introduction in her pocket and, though only he knew it, Daniel would have a knife in his.

'There'll be a Protestant church in the town,' Daniel said. 'Drop me there and we'll agree a time to meet up.'

'What'll you do while I'm trying to find him?' Jude said.

Daniel laughed. 'A few more hours to kill won't hurt. Read the gravestones, count the dead. And if you do find him and he talks about the ambush, ask him whether they killed us all. Every last man. You must ask him that.'

And after they had discussed a little more what Jude should say, Daniel took his leave, exhausted by the day, leaving Jude and the Murrays still talking by the fire. The murmur of their voices came up to him, and he was comforted before he slept.

He woke without dreams, feeling calm, a still point. He mustn't allow his feelings in now. Mustn't allow himself to think about Jude, for instance. About the way she raised her eyebrows when she was saying something important, or about the curves her body made, or about how she twisted a strand of hair in her fingers when she was listening to someone, and then, before replying, would tuck it behind her ear. He made his thoughts narrow.

It was then that he went and found Mrs Murray's knife. He took it from the shed. It was the one Mrs Murray used on her plants. He sharpened it on the whetstone outside the back door and wrapped a handkerchief around the blade. It fitted his pocket nicely. But he didn't mention it to anyone, reasoning to himself that it was no different to carrying a penknife, and he'd left his penknife in a drawer in Twickenham.

After that he walked on the beach, nodding a greeting to the man further out with his fork and his bucket, but he kept his hands clean, away from the stones and the weed.

Soon he would see if it was a duck in the picture, or a rabbit. He would have liked to have had a gun in his pocket. The Webley .45 would have been best, like he'd had with him that day. But the knife would have to do. He stroked the handle with his thumb. The wood was smooth, warm. He'd keep it with him till the time came.

Jude set off that day to find Dr Kelleher's stone circle, determined to get him the photograph he'd requested of her. She was glad to be on her motorbike, glad to be on her own. The day was overcast, not what she wanted, but Mr Murray had said the cloud would break later. Her route took her along narrow lanes cut down into the riddle of tiny fields, which would open out like magic to reveal deep, wooded estuaries and, the tide out to sea, an expanse of mud shining beneath the cloud. The journey was short and she stopped only once, to photograph a man at work digging worms, solitary in the mud sheen. She was glad of this task, that had nothing to do with her, that demanded her skill, and that left her alone. She brooded as she rode. The typewriting offered that, she supposed, but she so hated the work, whereas this she loved, catching things in her camera, and she could do it.

Dr Kelleher had told her no more than the name of the place, Drombeg, and the Murrays, busy with other things, had simply given her directions, and she'd no idea of what would be there. So to find a perfect circle, a crown of fourteen ancient stones high on a ridge, with the sea beyond and the hills behind, took Jude's breath away. A flat stone lay recumbent at the heart of it, and Jude sat here and waited for the sun. Her thoughts drifted, not along the ferocious currents of yesterday, nor into the life she'd lived in the war, but back to a conversation with Peter in London. Break the mould, be the first, he'd told her. Do what is necessary to make the life you want. And it came to her, sitting here, that she would, now. That this photograph for Dr Kelleher would be the first she took not just pretending to be a professional photographer.

When at last the sun came out, Jude took her shots and she knew they were good. Then she stood a last time at the centre of the circle and made her own pledge. She would not forget the past, nor ignore the needs of the present, but she would risk making her own future. The bike was hard to start, it began to rain and Jude surprised herself by coming close to tears. Then she reminded herself of her new resolve and she grinned at the drops and kicked the bike, which sputtered into life and she rode back in.

CHAPTER NINETEEN

The town was grey and the sky was grey. Grey stuccoed houses with empty windows and dirty fan-lights. There was nothing to lift the spirits, no hills, no sea. No children even, being still in school. The streets were quiet, only a few women here and there, and a few dogs arguing the toss in a corner.

The Protestant church stood at the bottom of the town, near the river. It might as easily have been in Yorkshire as in Ireland, Jude thought, as she watched Daniel through the lych-gate, Mrs Murray's packet of sandwiches tucked under his arm, her camera bag over his shoulder. All being well, they would meet here again in two hours' time. Then she turned her attention to her task.

Dr Kelleher had been clear in his instructions: she was to find Paddy McCarthy first, and he would take her to Matt Walsh.

She left her motorbike outside the Catholic church in the town square. As she dismounted, a priest appeared at the top of the church steps, arms folded comfortably beneath a substantial belly. She nodded a greeting, murmured a 'Good morning Father,' which she thought was the right thing to say, but which was not returned, and she walked away with his eyes burning a hole in her back.

'Another bloody raven,' she said below her breath.

After some wandering and a few enquiries, Jude found McCarthy's Drapers, white lettering on a chipped red board. It was between O'Halloran's Bar, with its two bottles of Murphys and several tins of fruit in syrup in the window, and a shop called Leahy's, which gave no sign away as to what it might contain. The street led straight up the hill from the square and ended, as far as she could see, in a field. She wished she had her camera with her, though she knew she was right to have left it behind with Daniel. She mustn't let herself look away from people's words today, and the camera lens would have tempted her.

A faded poster propped up in the shop window showed a line of little girls in white frocks and behind them a smiling nun. An ancient mannequin, gender indeterminable to Jude, modelled something that might be a summer dress, one arm flung upwards, the other adrift on the floor.

Pushing open the door, she stepped down and into a small room. The walls were lined with bolts of cloth — different degrees of grey, black and brown — that reached high into the gloom. A long wooden counter, the brass yards inlaid, stretched across the width of the shop. More bolts of cloth lay on shelves at the back, and a tall ladder stood ready for climbing. Nobody was visible, but there was a large bell on the counter. Jude rang it, and listened.

From somewhere distant she heard the sound of doors opening and closing, then footsteps, and as they came closer, a voice calling out.

'Just give us a minute, for the love of God. It's not you already, Nellie, is it?'

A head came around the door, mouth wide in a smile, blue eyes bright with anticipation. Catching sight of Jude, the mouth, open ready to speak, clamped shut.

'Good day,' Jude said.

'So it's not Nellie,' the head said. 'Excuse me,' and disappeared.

Jude ran her fingers through a bowl of buttons that stood like sweets on the counter and waited. A minute more and the door opened again. This time the man stepped into the room, sleeves rolled up, measuring tape around his neck, shifting his shoulders beneath his braces. Even under the yellow gaslight Jude could tell he was blushing.

'They were twisted,' he said apologetically. 'And I couldn't reach around to them. If you'd been Nellie now, I'd have had you tweak them for me. But you being a stranger, I couldn't very well . . .'

269

'Nellie?'

'My daughter,' he said, as if that were obvious. 'But she's a while before she should be home for her dinner. You're not from these parts though? And I'd say you weren't here to buy some yards of cloth?'

'No.'

'So have you lost your way, maybe?'

'No, not exactly . . .' Jude said. 'I've been sent by a magazine, an American magazine, to write an article. It's going to be called, "Where are they now? The Heroes of the Irish War of Independence."'

'Oh,' he said, 'all the way here to Liscool,' and something in his demeanour changed and he seemed to grow several inches. 'So you're a lady journalist, then?' Jude nodded. 'That's a new one on me. Haven't met one of you before.' He looked her up and down. 'Is that why you're dressed . . .'

'In trousers?'

'That, and the rest.'

'I came here on a motorbike,' Jude said. 'Not safe to ride one in skirts.'

He shook his head. 'No, no, I see that,' he said. 'Did you leave it somewhere, then?'

'Outside the church.'

'And the priest. He didn't happen to catch a sight of you, did he?'

'As a matter of fact he did.'

He ran his fingers over the top of his head, as he must have done when he'd had hair there to run them through. 'He won't have given you a smile then, I'll be guessing.' Jude laughed, and shook her head. 'That'll be us done for the next two Sundays. Three even. We won't hear the end of it, a lady in man's dress.'

Jude put out her hand. 'Judith Hursten. Pleased to meet you.'

'Paddy McCarthy,' the man said, putting out his, and they shook. 'Pleased to meet you, Miss Hursten. And the magazine is paying you?'

'Yes.'

'All right so. But it's just writing is it, for the magazine? No pictures?'

'I was going to come to that later,' Jude said. 'I've arranged to meet up with my photographer later on.'

McCarthy nodded, and was about to speak again when something made him pause. Picking up a pencil, he jabbed it at the counter. 'This is what I don't like,' he said.

'I'm sorry?'

'This mistrusting of people. I'm no earthly good at it, but I've to do it or where would we be?'

Jude waited while McCarthy made a few more desultory jabs. Then he looked at her in what she took for a stern expression, because he pursed his lips and narrowed his wide blue eyes.

'How do I know you're telling me the truth?' he said, pointing the pencil at her, and a moment later, as if embarrassed by his suspicion, added, by way of explanation, 'You weren't here in the bad times, you see, and they're not long over.'

'You mean the Tan war?'

'No. That was bad, very bad. But it was worse afterwards. Not just in Ireland, but in this place, Liscool, this very town, and Nellie only a tiny creature. We had men take up arms against their own brothers. Blood against blood, can you believe it.'

'And now?'

'And now there are men won't come to me for the cloth for their Sunday suits, and no more will their womenfolk. But Nellie plays with their daughters, so . . .' He laid the pencil down. 'So that's why I must be careful of you,' he said. 'Because it would take less than a poke to stir up the hornets' nest again.'

Jude reached into the inside of her jacket and brought out the note of introduction Dr Kelleher had written for her what seemed a lifetime ago. She put it on the counter.

'I met Dr Kelleher in Cork last week.'

McCarthy picked it up and read it, then he smiled again.

'And he's done it on his own prescription pad, so it must be bona fide,' he said, shaking his head admiringly. 'He's a clever man, that Doctor.' He handed the note back to Jude.

271

'So ask away,' he said.

'Dr Kelleher gave me two names,' she said. 'Yours and Matt Walsh's.'

In the pause before he replied, Jude thought how much hung now upon this name. And yet when she took that photograph, he'd been nothing more than another young soldier, barely more than a boy. A smile for the camera and then the temporary comfort of her cellar retreat: a blanket and hot soup and the brief reassurance of a woman's arm around his shoulder. He'd been no revolutionary then, no violent figure in another man's horror, no hero.

'Your man saved Matt's life,' McCarthy said. 'Did he tell you that?'

Lost in recollection, Jude started, then nodded.

'He said he'd patched him up.'

'Risked his own life to do it,' McCarthy said. 'They had Kelleher in their sights, the Tans, and a doctor could be arrested, not reporting a gunshot wound to the police. But if he hadn't got to Matt, Matt would have died. And if he'd died . . .'

During the journey Jude had brooded on how to come to the point. Whether to break in slowly or go straight for it. But McCarthy had done it for her.

'Tell me about the ambush,' she said. 'In your own words.'

'The Clonnacook Ambush,' he said.

'Is that how it's known?'

'It's famous across Ireland.' His voice was thick with pride. No shade of doubt that Jude could hear. 'Eighteen of theirs dead against one of our fellows, died of his wounds, God rest his soul, and three others injured. But they're right as rain now.'

'And Matt Walsh was your leader?'

'Our commandant, that's right. One of the best men you'll ever find. It was his plan, and it was him got us out afterwards. A bloody hero, he is.'

'So he's famous in these parts then, is he?' Jude said, remembering again the exhausted, frightened boy she'd seen him as in Belgium, neither hero nor villain, just alive.

'He is. And a big man still. A TD. We call him the Boss around here. He has a building firm now. Finger in all the pies, looks out for his own, too. He'd never let me go without, or any of the boys, not if he could help it.'

'What's a TD?'

'A Teachta Dála, a Deputy of the Dail. Like your MPs in Parliament.'

'Why did Kelleher send me to you first?'

'Liaison officer,' he said proudly. 'He's a very busy man. I'll vet a person, and sometimes they won't get to meet him.'

'You censor them?'

'I do. If I don't trust their motives.'

Jude thought it better not to pursue this, and she returned to the ambush.

'So what happened at Clonnacook, what was it like?'

'Did you not read about it before you came here? Look it up or something, whatever it is your lot does?'

'It is what I'd usually do, you're right. But when they gave me the assignment, they said: "Just go and find those men. No homework first." That way, it'd be fresh to me, I'd hear it all for the first time straight from the horses' mouths, if you'll excuse the phrase.'

McCarthy laughed. 'Horses is fine. The life of Ireland, they are.'

'So, will you tell me about it? In your own words?' Jude said.

McCarthy looked down at the ground and Jude waited. Finally he looked up, and shook his head.

'You should hear it from the Boss,' he said. 'He knows how to tell it straight. I'd misremember anyway. I'd be making mistakes. It was very foggy that day. Besides, it's him you've come for,' and he got to his feet, as if to end all discussion. 'I'll take you to him now,' he said. 'Then I can show you something of the place. It should be a good time of day to catch him.'

They set off at a brisk pace, not back into the town, but up the hill towards the fields. Jude could feel her pulse quicken. She was getting very close now. For a minute or so McCarthy didn't speak.

But once they had reached the top house and rounded the corner, he slowed down.

'Father Lynch never comes this high up the town,' he said. 'His heart.'

'The priest?'

He nodded. 'It was a queer time,' he said.

'During the Tan war?'

'It's funny still, hearing it called that. And there's even some calling it the Revolution now as well. So I heard, anyway.'

'Why funny?' Jude said.

'We'd call it "the scrap", if we had to call it anything, or the Troubles, sometimes. By way of a joke, I suppose, whoever said it first, because it wasn't a scrap of course.'

'How was it queer?'

'This farm,' he said. 'Looks well enough, doesn't it? Prosperous enough, certainly. Man called Joe O'Leary, it's his. In the Troubles, he'd pay up his dues when we asked him, but he didn't want to be bothered with us more than that. Not if he could help it. But you know what brought O'Leary over to us lock, stock and barrel? It wasn't men being killed, imprisoned, out of his own town, not even families being burnt out, or lootings, or creameries burnt to the ground. It was the strangest thing.'

McCarthy paused his story to climb over a wall. He was nimble, which was not a talent learnt as a draper, Jude thought.

'So what brought him over to you?' she said when they were clear and into the next field.

'They destroyed his mare.'

'They did what?'

'He'd taken his mare to be serviced by a stallion. A beautiful chestnut filly, high-spirited. He had high hopes for her. And the Tans arrived and drew their guns. Made the groom serve her with the other stallions stabled there too. All seven of them. She was ruined by it and he came home a changed man. He let us use his outbuildings as our bomb shop after that.'

'You sold bombs?'

'Made them. Incendiaries, grenades, mines. A home-made

business it was. We'd two boys were the chief bomb-makers, there were weeks when they barely left the buildings. But when the heat was on, the rest of us would lend a hand.'

'Walsh?'

McCarthy shook his head. 'He hadn't the patience for it. Nor the fingers. But I was good.'

It shocked Jude, to think of the men making their own bombs, though she couldn't have said why. She looked across at the low, whitewashed buildings, hens pecking outside, wagtails courting in the afternoon.

'You made them in there?' she said, pointing.

He nodded.

'The bombs you used against . . . against the British?'

McCarthy looked at her incredulously. 'Soldiers, Auxies, Tans, yes,' he said, his voice hard. 'And they used theirs against us, against the Irish people and on our own soil.'

It had been Daniel Jude had had in mind, but she realised she must be careful. She was walking in a minefield, she thought, smiling slightly.

'So you were good at it,' she said.

'I was,' and McCarthy looked at her, as if waiting for his cue.

'Tell me something about it,' she said, appeasing.

'All right, so I often cooked the eggs,' McCarthy said, in a voice that might have been talking about calico or tweed. 'Grenades. That's what we called them. Eggs. You were best doing the same thing each time, it got quicker that way. We'd use old Mausers to make them out of for the grenades. Clean the cartridges out with nitric acid, then cut them smaller, file them down. There was the wadding, cotton, cardboard, and the explosive. And then there was the cap last of all, drops of warm shellac for that. You had to be so careful with the explosive, gentle it in. I remember this fellow came up from Cork city to teach us, O'Faolain he was called. He told us: "A single grain might make twenty yards of difference in the cast, so weigh out the grains, for God's sake!" And it was him told us the trick, heating the caps on a hot plate, over a Bunsen.'

'It sounds very dangerous,' Jude said.

'It was. And there were men blew themselves up, working in bomb factories. It was the care made you good at it, and I was always a careful man.'

'And you kept all these mines and grenades in those outbuild-ings?'

'There's a souterrain. We stored our ammunition in there. But one time I was thawing out gelignite in a pot on his stove, and the Auxies came by.' McCarthy began to laugh.

'What happened?' Jude said.

'They looked through the door, thought I'd turned into a woman of the house. Made a couple of lewd comments and left.' McCarthy was still laughing. 'What did they think I was stirring, the porridge?'

Jude laughed with him, but she thought of Peter, stirring a pot all that time in Belgium and nourishing men, not blowing them up. He must have fed Walsh, for God's sake. She shook her thoughts clear.

'And it was all because of his mare?' she said.

He nodded. 'Yes. We didn't even know what it was had brought the change of heart at first, whether to trust him right out. It was a groom at the stables told the story and it came back to us here. So then Matt asked him was it true, and O'Leary, I saw him, he was about in tears at the mention of it. Anyway, it was a great place for us because except for that once, it was never searched. Don't know why not.'

McCarthy had led Jude up around the top of the town and down again by now, across fields full of unstartled, heavy-uddered cows, along a deep boreen running with water and smelling of wild mint and manure, and finally out into some rough pasture beside the river.

'Over the river and we're there, safe,' McCarthy said, and he led Jude across a narrow hump-backed bridge no more than a quarter mile away. She could see the Protestant church from there and she wondered how Daniel was doing his waiting.

Walking quickly along the edge of the town, down one street and up another, McCarthy took Jude round the side of a tall house, one of those she'd seen on her way in with its fan-lights and tall Georgian sash windows, and the only one with impeccable woodwork and fresh pointing. Behind the house was a small, neat garden, and beside it a large, brick outbuilding.

'It's likely he'll be in there,' McCarthy said. 'It's where he runs his business from,' and he walked over to the door, turned the handle and ushered Jude before him.

CHAPTER TWENTY

Jude had been waiting for this moment for days, imagining it, fearing it, wanting it. She'd argued and pleaded with and yelled at the man who stood before her now, a clipboard in one hand and a fountain pen in the other, caught mid-sentence, looking over towards her, his eyebrows raised in polite query.

The last time she'd seen him, almost ten years earlier, he'd been dressed in a tattered, bloodied uniform, his skin darkened with his weeks in the trenches. He'd been gaunt then, shocked, exhausted after bringing in his friend, and for all his bravado in the day, in the dead of night he'd been no more than a boy. And Jude, who was no older than him, had done what she'd done for so many fearful, exhausted boys, holding his hand, cradling his head and stroking his hair for a time, whispering to him that it would all be all right and to sleep now. And like so many others, in the morning he behaved as though the night had never been. But she understood that, that saving of face.

Now here he was, a big, filled-out figure in a well-cut suit standing tall before her, and he'd put on weight, his face full where it had been hollow. He'd grown a moustache, a small block of orange-brown on his upper lip, and he'd lost some of his curly hair. And at a side-table, like some strange simulacrum of her old self, of the person she'd been no more than a couple of weeks earlier, sat a woman, poised before a typewriter, head turned at the intrusion, hands ready over the keys.

Jude felt McCarthy's hand on her arm, pulling her forward,

278

heard his deep breath before he spoke. 'He's nervous,' she thought.

'Hope we've not caught you at a busy moment. This is Judith Hursten. She's a journalist, come from America to write about the Brigade.'

McCarthy stopped and waited. For a long minute Walsh didn't reply but stood looking at Jude so that she wondered whether he'd recognised her. And when he did speak, it wasn't to her, but to the typist with her hands suspended.

'Just finish off by saying that unless payment is forthcoming within the next week, and I mean that I have the money in my hand, then steps will have to be taken. And then if you'd like to make us some tea, that would be grand.'

Walsh's office was ordered and functional. Shelves of labelled files around the walls, two geraniums on the window sill, a small shelf with technical books, another with a large tape measure on its wooden reel, three spirit levels, a set of callipers and a clutch of sharpened pencils. There were some architectural drawings on the main table, and as he spoke, Walsh folded these into a tidy pile. There was no dust.

Only when the typist had left the room, glaring at Jude as she went, did Walsh speak again.

'So, Mack, a lady journalist, eh? What have you been telling her about then?'

McCarthy had picked up one of the spirit levels and he was tipping it, this way and that, watching the bubble float its way from one end to the other.

'I told her she'd have to hear it from you,' McCarthy said. 'It was you she'd come to find. Dr Kelleher gave her your name.'

'An honourable man,' said Walsh, almost, Jude thought, as if he were crossing himself. 'And he gave you my name, did he? Have a seat then,' and he pulled out one of the chairs and motioned for Jude to sit.

She busied herself getting out notebook and pencil, pulling in her chair, writing his name at the top of a fresh sheet.

'Who sent you?'

'An American magazine.'

'Name?'

'*Griftner's Monthly*,' Jude said, straight off. 'You'll have heard of it, I expect. It's very big over there.'

Walsh nodded. He wouldn't risk losing face, Jude thought.

'And what do they want from me?'

'I'm writing an article. "Heroes of the Irish War of Independence". About the men behind the myths. So I've come to you. I've a photographer with me too, but perhaps we could come to that a bit later.'

There was a knock at the door and the typist came in with a tray of tea things. Jude could see she was hoping to stay, but Walsh ushered her out again quickly and nodded at McCarthy to pour the tea. Picking up the spirit level, he replaced it on the shelf, in its space between the larger and the smaller one.

'Attention to detail. Something I'm very good at. As important on the column as it is in the building trade.'

'The column?'

'Flying column.'

Jude nodded. 'Of course.'

'So, putting aside the photograph question for now, what do you want to know?' he said, jostling the papers on the table, aligning them again.

'Tell me about yourself,' Jude said. 'Childhood, family, that sort of thing.' She needed to spend more time in the room with this man, try to find his measure. He was so different from the figure in her snapshot, the boy with the dirty, tired face and the cigarette. This was a man who knew he was a leader, who knew he was in charge, in control. A man who would flick his ash on to a dead man's face, or so Daniel had said, and the thought went through her like a pulse of electricity.

'There's nothing to tell,' Walsh said. 'I'd no more than an ordinary childhood.'

'Nothing that might have told us what was to come? That you'd become a leader?'

'Commandant,' McCarthy put in. 'He was the Commandant.'

'The title doesn't matter,' Walsh said, and Jude noticed

McCarthy's face widen in surprise. 'We boys were all in it together.'

'But you were the boss. We knew that from the start. Still are,' McCarthy said.

'I'm no more than a simple builder,' Walsh said. 'There was demolition to be done then, and so I did it, and now there's recon- struction and I'll do that too.'

'It's really as simple as that?' Jude said wryly, and Walsh looked up at her and grinned.

'Maybe not quite,' he said, and she noticed his eyes travel down her now, as though for the first time he'd noticed she was a woman.

'So how did you get to be the boss?' Jude said. 'Were you top of the school, or captain of the hurley team?'

McCarthy laughed. 'He was as hard a nut as the Brothers had ever had to crack,' he said proudly.

Walsh picked up his cup and sipped.

'Strong enough for a mouse to trot on. I miss that from the Brigade. Stewed tea takes away hunger, Miss Hursten, did you know that?'

Jude was about to say that as a matter of fact she did, when she realised it had been a rhetorical question.

'The Christian Brothers taught me discipline, and endurance. And I needed both during those times,' and he gave a short bark of a laugh. Pulling a cigarette case from his breast pocket, he flicked it open. He offered it to Jude and, as if it were an afterthought, to McCarthy. Though she would have loved a cigarette right then, Jude shook her head. She wanted her nerves just where they were. She watched him cup the match and draw on the cigarette, suck- ing the glow deep into the tobacco, and because she had known so many herself, she recognised the soldier's draw. Too many cigarettes lit in the thrust of the weather.

She had thought it would be better to be circumspect, but watching Walsh, she saw that he was as eager to tell his story as she was to hear it.

'The Brothers put steel into you,' he said. 'Had me down for a vocation, and they weren't wrong. As celibate as a priest those years, and as single-minded. You had to be. Not like this little fellow, Miss Hursten,' he said, stabbing his cigarette towards McCarthy.

'Please, boss . . .' McCarthy said, but Walsh interrupted him, leaning over to Jude, as if offering her a confidence.

'I think that's where Mack went wrong. He was a married man. Only one in the Brigade. I warned him, but he wouldn't listen. Because it softened him. He had too much to lose. You can't serve two masters.'

McCarthy was looking down at his hands. 'Please,' he said again, but Jude could tell from his voice he didn't expect Walsh to stop now.

'You tested me as much as any of my enemies,' said Walsh, relentlessly. 'Isn't that right, Mack? Very keen fellow, but squeamish. And there's no room for that in a war. You've got to be able to stomach things. Take your orders and get on with it.'

'But Miss Hursten wants to hear . . .'

'What does she want to hear?' Walsh said, interrupting. 'Not about you, anyway, Mack, with your soft heart. We'd still be under the yoke if it had been left to the likes of you.'

Jude was repulsed by Walsh, and now she pitied McCarthy, but since arriving in this room, Daniel had become strong in her mind. She saw Daniel setting fire to homes, his right hand not knowing what his left hand did, telling himself it was all legitimate, it was a fair war. And then, in that reversal, she saw him lying wounded, left for dead in the ditch, and the figure above him with his cigarette and his hard laugh. And she saw him on Horse Island standing in the roofless tower looking out beyond the current lines, and she knew she must keep her purpose in mind, not allow herself to be diverted.

'So tell me about the ambush at Clonnacook,' she said.

'What do you want to know?'

'I want to know what happened.'

'You've read about it?'

Jude shook her head. 'No. All I've done is check where it is on the map. In case of a photograph. But I was told to get it straight from the horse's mouth. No homework.'

'Maybe that's just as well,' Walsh said. 'You won't have read the English lies, then.' He pulled open a drawer in the table and drew out two worn newspaper clippings. 'The *Southern Star*, that's our local, and the *Examiner*.' He pushed them towards Jude.

She looked at the nearest one, columns of text surrounding a blurred photograph of an empty stretch of road.

'I'd prefer to hear about it from you,' she said. Yesterday she'd heard Daniel's story, seen his horror. Today, she hoped, she would hear the official Irish version, the one that didn't know there was still a survivor.

Walsh smiled. 'All right then. So the war,' he said.

'Which war?' Jude said, somewhat disingenuously.

'Our war. Of independence. Not the European one. Do you know much about it?'

Jude nodded. 'I do usually read the papers. And I have done a bit of homework,' she said.

'The Easter Rising?'

'I know about that, of course.'

'And the Black and Tans? And the Auxiliaries? Do you know what the British were getting up to by 1920?'

'I know a certain amount,' Jude said, and she saw herself again at the table in that restaurant in Cork, her fingers still sticky with lobster, reading Daniel's diary, the reprisals, the burnings. That had been the first of it, and then Dr Kelleher's story, and then Daniel yesterday, so that it was only half the truth to say she knew a certain amount, because she was brimful with those horrors.

Walsh waved his arm, sprinkling ash like favours.

'The Tans, the Auxies, they were all over the country by the time we did Clonnacook,' he said, spitting out his words. 'The country was run riot with them. They were terrorists. Thought they could get away with anything.'

'Describe them to me,' Jude said.

'They were strong, fit men, experienced soldiers. Had to have fought in the European war, that was a rule. Used to carrying all

283

the gear: rifle, revolvers, ammo, grenades. They had that swagger soldiers get. And they were paid very well. The Auxies were on a pound a day. That's a lot of money to be given to go and beat the living daylights out of a people. They said we were barbarians, but it was them.'

'What did they do round here?'

'Drove around the countryside in their Crossleys, blind drunk often as not, firing off their guns at people. I knew men killed in the fields by stray bullets. They tore villages apart. Sometimes because they'd heard there was an IRA man there, sometimes for the hell of it. They'd drive in, two lorry loads, singing their filthy songs and do whatever they felt like. Smash up the houses, steal what they could, ornaments, livestock. Sometimes they'd burn some of the houses down. Official reprisals, they called them. They'd round up the inhabitants, women, children, and search them. Beat up the men if they felt like it.'

McCarthy was shifting a little in his seat, and Walsh turned to him now.

'What is it, Paddy? You're twitching like a man on the end of a rope. Do you not agree with me?'

'No, I do,' McCarthy said. 'It's only . . .'

'Spit it out then,' Walsh said.

'If you make them all out villains, then it lets them off more. And they weren't. Some of them did those things, but they didn't start out with black hearts.'

Walsh snorted. 'And that makes it better?'

'No. It makes it worse.'

Walsh shook his head like a man perplexed. 'You're saying they began decent men. But tell Miss Hursten what they did to you, Paddy.'

McCarthy looked down at the table. Jude thought he looked abashed, shy even.

'Will you tell me?' she said, and after a moment, he did.

'It was before I joined the Brigade. I was out visiting my sister, she's in a village three miles from here or so, and they came there and did like Matt just said. Can you imagine, Miss Hursten? The

284

Auxies screaming obscenities, whipping me with their belts, beating me with their rifle butts, me standing there bollock-naked, excuse me, and my little nieces and nephews and my own sister watching on. That's what took me into the Brigade,' and Jude waited, pencil poised, to hear more, but Walsh was twitching his cigarette, impatient, and McCarthy bowed out. 'That's all.'

'Something had to be done,' Walsh said, his voice calm, and Jude reminded herself that he had probably told this story hundreds of times. 'They'd been terrorising our land for some seven months and there had been barely a shot fired against them in reply.'

'So who decided what it should be, and where and how?'

'I did,' Walsh said.

'Was that usual?'

He shrugged. 'We needed to stage something big. GHQ was up in Dublin, a long way away from Liscool, from these parts. It was very different in the city. They didn't know what it was like here, day in day out, and they didn't know what the boys were capable of. We couldn't wait any longer for their say-so.'

'So you were solely responsible,' Jude said. 'Is that the kind of man you are, would you say? Prepared to take those kinds of risk?'

Walsh stubbed out his cigarette. 'Sometimes you just have to get on and do it, step over the line, tread on a few toes. Somebody's got to be prepared to do it.'

'How did you know they would come that way, on that day?'

'We didn't know the time, but they always took that road. We'd been there ten hours before they came.'

'He didn't tell a soul beforehand,' McCarthy interrupted. 'Did all the reconnoitring himself. Only told us on the day.'

'I had the priest down to you all the night before, though. You must have known something big was up,' Walsh said with a laugh, but McCarthy shook his head.

'We just thought you'd got a touch of religion. Men do sometimes in a war. It was only that morning when we got the rifles and ammunition, before dawn and the birds still quiet, that we knew we were on for something.'

'And then?' Jude said.

'We waited most of the day for them.'

'D'you remember the cramps we got?' McCarthy said. 'They were wicked. I was wet through with the rain, and I had cramps in places I didn't know were possible. But the miracle of it was, how they disappeared when we were on. Just time for a quick prayer.'

'The lorries came around the bend,' Walsh said, 'and I flagged the front one down. They slowed, taking me for one of theirs, and before they knew any better, I lobbed the first bomb . . .'

A sudden bang on the door made him stop. Jude looked round to see the door handle turning this way and that and the door finally open to admit a diminutive figure holding a piece of paper before him in his fist.

'What is it, Jack?' Walsh said, his voice severe.

The boy took a step into the room.

'Sand, sir. There's a ton more needed up at the new house or the fellas can't be on with anything.'

'And what do you have there?'

The boy looked up at his hand, still carried high.

'A message,' he said.

'Give it to me then,' Walsh said, putting his hand out for it, flat on the table, and Jude saw a scar, a thin red line, that curved across his palm like a worm from his wrist to his little finger.

The boy stepped forward, gave it to Walsh, and stepped back again. Now that his task was done, he looked at Jude, a strong scrutinising glance.

'Thank you, Jack,' Walsh said, his voice gentler now. 'Tell O'Leary I'll be up in a half hour to see how things are doing. But we'll have to wait till tomorrow for the sand,' and he gave a short smile. A grin lit the boy's face, and snapping his heels like some small soldier, he turned and left.

'So I lobbed the first bomb, bang into the middle of the cab, and then it was a battle. But we had the advantage and it was clear pretty quickly we'd win this one.'

'Was it over quickly?' Jude said.

He shook his head. 'No. They were brave fighters, I'll give them that, and several of us were injured, but in the end we had them blistered with it, their men dead and dying all over the valley.'

'How did it stop? When the last man of theirs was killed?'

'They began shouting out their surrender and a couple of them threw away their rifles, so we stopped firing. It was hard to see clearly with the mist coming in, but they had their hands raised, the half dozen or so still on their feet. So I gave the ceasefire and four of our boys stood up and went to take their arms.

'It was so quiet for a minute, not even a bird cry, the Auxies with their hands above their heads, our boys walking towards them, the rest of us with our guns still raised ready. Then suddenly, no warning, they started firing again. Nearly point blank range. That's when Dom Murphy was hit.'

'God rest his soul,' McCarthy murmured, crossing himself.

'God rest his soul,' Walsh said. 'He was cheated by those bloody Auxies, and we let them know it. No more surrenders after that.'

'You killed them all,' Jude said.

'That's about the size of it. Took on the British Empire and won, and not a man of ours captured afterwards, though they had the country turned upside-down for us.'

'It was only the Colonel survived,' McCarthy said. 'He got away.'

'How did he manage that?' Jude said.

'We thought they were all killed,' Walsh said, 'so he must have been playing dead. That's all we could think of afterwards, when we heard he was alive. I checked them myself, and I know a dead man when I see one. But I got him wrong.'

Smooth as can be, Jude thought. He's like a politician. There's so much varnish, you have to scratch deep to get to the wood.

'Poked around amongst the dead men,' she said.

'That was my job.'

'And if you'd known he was alive?'

'We'd have taken him prisoner,' Walsh said, and Jude felt his eyes on her, glaring, as she took down her careful notes.

'Was he injured?' she said.

'Shoulder wound, we heard that too, later.'

'So nothing life-threatening. Couldn't he have identified some of you?'

Walsh shook his head. 'I heard he was a broken man. They took him straight off to England for his own safety.'

'You'd have hunted him down, would you?'

'All's fair in love and war, Miss Hursten.'

'But still, that many of their men killed, it was a disaster for them. Wouldn't the British have tried to have him identify you? Get a description from him at the very least?' Jude persisted.

McCarthy reached for the teapot, gave it a shake, and poured in some hot water from the jug.

'If you don't mind it poached?' he said to Jude. She nodded her thanks and he filled her cup, the tea as dark as blood.

'Well, they didn't,' Walsh said. 'Or he couldn't remember. I don't know, do I? He didn't come back to Ireland, and we had other battles to fight. Our victory certainly didn't make the British any gentler.'

'Must have been good for your career, though,' Jude said.

'It was good for the cause of Irish freedom,' Walsh said severely. 'It's become like a shrine. Did you know that? People go there on their wedding days, first communion. It's a place we can be proud of.'

'But I'm interested in you, Mr Walsh,' Jude said. 'And I'm interested in this ambush, because it made your name.'

'Made him as famous as Dan Breen,' McCarthy said proudly, and Walsh scowled.

'It's not to do with fame, Paddy,' he said, and McCarthy's blush, his humiliation, made Jude's anger rise. She looked at her watch.

'What do you think then, about us getting a photograph of you?'

Walsh tapped out a cigarette. 'All right,' and sticking the cigarette between his lips, he shook the box of matches. 'Last match,' he said, striking. It flared, and before he could light the cigarette, died. 'Ah, for God's,' he said. McCarthy's hand was already in his pocket, rummaging to find his boss a light, but Walsh turned to Jude. 'Would you have one?' he said.

She pulled the lighter from her pocket and struck the flint, held it across to him. He bent his head to the flame and drew the fire. She watched him suck, the shrug of his moustache, eyes closed a moment, then blow out that first, best lungful of smoke and she waited to see if he would comment.

'You given that?' he said.

'Yes.'

'By a boyfriend? Brother?'

'By a friend I nursed with.' She put the lighter on the table.

'You were a nurse,' Walsh said, staring at the lighter.

Jude wondered how much he would ask.

'Something of a change of direction then, what you're doing now.'

'Yes, thank God,' she said, 'though I loved it.'

'Where were you?'

'Belgium. Like many others,' Jude said, keeping her voice very level, unemotional.

Walsh looked up. He stared at her, and she held his gaze.

'Whereabouts?'

This was it, Jude thought. After this, something would happen no matter what, and she wouldn't be able to prevent it. She smiled to herself. Or control it.

'A village, near the front line. Bombed out. Just about only the church tower left standing, and its bell. We were nursing in a cellar.'

Walsh drew slowly on his cigarette, then tipped his head back and made smoke rings at the ceiling. Jude waited.

'In a cellar,' he said at last. 'It was number twenty-six, I think. The enamel plate was still beside the door.'

'Yes.'

Jude noticed that McCarthy was sitting very still, only his eyes moving, from her face to Walsh's and back again. And Walsh was staring now at somewhere beyond her left shoulder, but somewhere she imagined was not in this room. After what seemed an age, he spoke again.

'It was just you and another girl, wasn't it,' he said at last. 'Slight, with dark eyes. Two pretty girls and a young soldier playing mother at the stove.'

'Yes.'

'And I . . .' Walsh said, his voice uncertain. He stopped, and when he spoke again, it was as though he had decided something. 'We'll do that photograph, Miss Hursten, if you're quick about it. I'll see you and your photographer in O'Connor's Hotel in fifteen minutes. And then you can be off, on your way back home where you belong,' and he stood and put out his hand.

CHAPTER TWENTY-ONE

It was more than two hours since Jude had left Daniel at the Protestant church, but he wasn't worried by her being late. It meant that something must have happened. Far worse, in their strange scheme, if she'd returned after fifteen minutes and empty-handed.

At first he wandered in the churchyard, counting the names on the gravestones, the bird songs. He walked with a hand in his pocket, turning and turning the smooth piece of china he'd gleaned from the tide, and tried not to check his watch. But he couldn't bear to be seen by anyone, all these people he might have had to do with back then, and people kept nodding him greetings as they walked past, so then he retreated inside.

The church was dim, the stained glass throwing out a gaudy gloom. Daniel looked at the saints, their face-forward virtue. They looked so English. And they held their swords and lances so easily. He wondered what else they might have done. Whether they fought only with dragons and the infidel, or whether they had sometimes fought the wrong man, or woman, or, God help them, child.

But he mustn't think too much because he needed to stay calm till Jude returned, so he decided to set himself small tasks. The heavy stone of the floor and walls stilled him. He would eat Mrs Murray's sandwiches very slowly, and then he'd count the number of glass pieces in St Michael and the snake, he thought, that coiled beneath. If she had still not returned, he would deadhead the flowers in their vases on either side of the altar, and look up the hymn numbers, 47 and 216, still listed on the hymn board, and after that he would count more glass. St Christopher's maybe, with his great burden. And only when each whole task was done, would he allow himself to look at his watch.

So when finally Jude pushed the heavy church door open and strode over the cold stone, all her urgency and pent excitement like a wind around her, she found Daniel standing at the far side of the aisle, his hands out, palms flat against the church wall, his head craned back, counting. And when she began to speak, he put his hand up to stop her.

'Just a moment.'

'Daniel, we're meeting him. In ten minutes' time.'

And it was only when he turned from the wall a minute later and faced her, that she saw in his eyes, in the nervous movements he made with his mouth, in his hands which twisted and turned, how much he was trying to keep at bay.

Jude found a bench in one corner of the graveyard and she sat Daniel down and talked to him, quietly, carefully, about what had happened. She even made him laugh, describing Paddy McCarthy and his bomb-making.

'He might have made the ones that got thrown at us,' Daniel said, and Jude nodded.

'And he's the gentlest-seeming fellow I ever met,' she said.

'I'll be all right now,' Daniel said, 'to go and meet Walsh.'

They walked up the steps of O'Connor's Hotel and pushed open the double doors. The air, full of cooked cabbage and old beer, assailed Daniel.

'Smells like the barracks,' he said.

The hall was gloomy, lit by a single electric light. A mahogany reception desk stretched along the wall on one side, the keys to the rooms on their pegs behind like a line of shiny soldiers, and on the other side were two doorways. A low bench ran between them and a hat stand stood at one end. The walls were a dull yellow interrupted every now and then by dusty prints of weary foxes and furious hounds. Hanging her jacket with the hats, Jude walked through a doorway. A moment later she returned and beckoned to Daniel.

'He's here,' she said. 'Don't forget who you are.'

Coming close to him, she put a hand on his shoulder, her touch so light he only knew of it when she had already stepped away again. He shouldered the camera bag and followed her in.

Daniel saw that the dining room was empty except for one table in the bay window where a man in shirtsleeves sat with a coffee and a glass of whiskey. Foxes' heads and goggle-eyed fish in glass boxes watched on. Jude walked towards him, but Daniel waited further back, leaning against an empty table, pressing his fingers into the damask, taking the weight off his leg. Things seemed to be happening very slowly, all of a sudden, like a gramophone record turning at the wrong speed.

The man was big, with ginger hair and a squat moustache, and as Jude approached, he gripped the table edge and rose, pushing his chair through the carpet pile as if it were through treacle, back till it hit the wall with a soft thunk. His mouth opened in a smile and he stretched out his hand to Jude in greeting, confident and calm. Daniel saw that the man thought Jude attractive, and he saw that Jude knew this.

Outside the window swallows were practising their tricks, and inside, two flies pressed their noses against the glass and cried. The sun came through, flashing itself about the cups and teaspoons.

Daniel stared. His body was lead, cold, the weight of the bag, the pull of his leg dragging him down. It was his man there, smiling, genial. It had to be his man. But Daniel didn't recognise him. He didn't know him. And if he didn't know him?

'Judith Hursten, I presume,' the man said with an odd smile and a glance at his watch. 'At last.'

And hearing the voice, Daniel knew and his fingers on the velvet damask burned. He saw Jude's shoulder turn to him, and, for now, he remembered his part.

The man was pulling out a chair for her, and she sat, smiling, nodding. Daniel looked down. There were crumbs under his fingers, and a brown stain.

'Apologies for the delay,' she said. 'Mr Walsh, this is Daniel Brown, my photographer,' and she was looking at him, waiting, and so was Walsh. So he nodded, and sat in a chair at the table, then bent and grappled with the camera bag, as if to be busy about his job.

A waitress came in, a nervous girl in a tired pinny and a tight black bun like a respectable curse.

'Bring us some more coffee,' Walsh said, and she bobbed and said, 'Yes, sir.'

'So this is your photographer,' Walsh said, taking out a cigarette. 'He's looking a little peaky. I hope he'll have a steady hand with my face.'

'He'll get what he needs to,' Jude said. She passed him her lighter. 'He's good.'

'You look very different without the bandanna and cauldron of soup.'

He lit the cigarette, put it down in the ashtray and crossed his arms.

'So why are you here, Miss Hursten?'

'Do you remember all the photographs I took?' she said. Walsh looked blank. 'Or maybe you didn't notice. I was always snapping. The men liked it. It buoyed their spirits.'

'And?'

Daniel tapped gently at the ashtray. 'Don't forget your cigarette,' he said quietly, and his voice took the others by surprise, as if they'd half-forgotten he was there.

'Who is he?' Walsh said, his voice lower, darker than before.

Daniel thought he might be floating. He couldn't feel the chair beneath him. His mind was very clear. He smiled at Walsh.

'I'm not at all what you think,' he said. 'Am I, Jude? And you hold your cigarette just as I remember.'

Walsh frowned and jabbed the cigarette back in the ashtray.

'Let's get on with the job, then. I've a business to run.'

'I need to know something, Mr Walsh,' Daniel said.

'Daniel, please.'

But Daniel wouldn't catch her eye. 'Show him, Jude.'

'Daniel.'

Walsh ran a finger along his moustache. 'Show me what?'

'If you don't tell him, then I will,' Daniel said, his voice still very calm.

Jude looked back, her lips tight, resolute. 'I took a photograph of you in the war,' she said.

'Where?' Walsh was fidgeting, restless, adjusting his collar, pulling down his shirtsleeves, looking around as if something else must be more important than this.

'In Belgium.'

'So?'

'The man beside you in the photograph is clearly your friend. He's wounded and you have an arm around his shoulder. You're sharing a cigarette.'

'Why is that important? That's what happens in a war. Men stick together. You'll know that, after your time in one.'

Walsh pushed out his chair, as if getting ready to leave.

'But you met him later too,' Jude said. 'In Ireland.'

Daniel watched her with pride. She'd stopped Walsh dead in his tracks, and he wanted to applaud.

Walsh shook his head. 'You have it wrong there.'

Jude took out the photograph. 'It's a copy,' she said. She passed it across the table to Walsh. He picked it up and looked quickly, before pushing it away.

'What of it?' he said. 'They know over here that I was in the British army then. It's no great secret. And a man can't decide who his comrades are in the trenches. It's what I did afterwards that counts.'

But Daniel had watched him closely. From the other side of the table he'd felt the jump of his heart.

'The other man,' he said. 'Your friend with the cigarette. In the photograph he's a lieutenant, like you. But he was a colonel by the time I knew him.'

'And where did you know him?'

Daniel spoke as though it were nothing, this thing he was saying. 'I knew him over here. In Ireland,' he said.

'Not really a photographer, then,' Walsh said, his mouth tightening.

'No.'

'And you come asking me to give account of myself,' Walsh said. He shook his head. 'I know what you were, and I don't know how you can even look me in the eye.'

The waitress came with the coffee, her eyes on the carpet, and the three at the table were silent. When she'd gone, Walsh seemed to gather himself, as if he were about to make a bid for something.

'I'm going to tell you a story,' he said. 'If you can spare the time.'

'We've got all the time we need,' Jude said.

'All right. I was born in this place, brought up here. And when the European war broke out I was still in apprenticeship to my father. Bricklaying. I joined up in 1915 because my father told me not to. I might have been rushing to defend Belgium and the right of small nations, being as I came from one. Or I could have joined up because Redmond told us we'd get Home Rule if we did. I know all about that now, but I didn't know a thing then. Then, I could have named you the Kings and Queens of England, but I knew nothing of the history of my own country. Didn't know and didn't care. I wanted to go to a war so I could shoot my gun at something more than rabbits. And so I could get away from my father. I was seventeen and I was going to show him that I was a man.

'I was a clever boy, and after a year I got a commission. Somehow I stayed alive in that hell. And Lieutenant Whittam, he stayed alive too. That was enough to make you firm friends over there. Then he got injured, unconscious in the middle of no man's land. So I went over the top to pull him in, else he'd have been dead for sure by the morning. He'd have done the same for me.

'I was on furlough, months overdue, when we got news of the Easter Rising. I didn't know who any of them were, Connolly and Pearse and the rest, but now my head was full of questions. And when the British executed them in Kilmainham Gaol, then my blood rose and my heart turned. Now I really was in no man's land,

296

an Irishman fighting in the British army, fighting for the country that was killing my countrymen.

'So when I got back to Ireland, I set to and schooled myself, caught up on my history. Robert Emmet and Wolfe Tone, the Potato Famine, Parnell, the Land League, and the rest. I learned what the British had done to our people. And then I joined the IRA.'

Daniel could hear Walsh, his speech, but he was seeing things again. He couldn't help it. He tried to grab hold of the room, tried to stop himself slipping. His fingers clutched at the table and the chair, at each other, he threw his glance hard at the coffee cups and the milk jug, at the wide-eyed fish, at the netted curtains. Gripping hold with all his strength, he made himself notice. The sound of the swallows outside, a small cloud high in the window, the dust ball hanging by a hair from the skirting, the paper wad beneath his table leg keeping it steady, the mole on Jude's neck, just above the collar of her blouse, a broken nail on her left hand, which she rubbed at absently with her thumb as she listened, a tendon in Walsh's neck standing proud.

Jude put up her hand, like a child in a lesson.

'But they didn't mind, that you'd fought in the British army?' she said.

Walsh laughed. 'They did mind. I had to prove myself, prove I could be trusted.'

Daniel watched Jude's face. He knew what was happening. Walsh was enchanting her. He was that kind of man, that kind of leader. Daniel could hear him that day in the rain, his voice above the ditch.

'Poor sods,' Daniel said, the words tugging themselves out of him.

Walsh looked at him. Daniel could see other tendons now. He could see his colour rise.

'What did you say?' Jude said.

Daniel wouldn't look at her. He couldn't stop himself.

'The ones you proved yourself on,' he said. 'They must have been poor sods. You know, two men from my barracks, they

297

were buried alive. That wouldn't have been you? Proving your-self?'

'Don't,' Jude said.

'You were an Auxiliary here, weren't you?' Walsh said slowly. 'You wore that beret, you bloody mercenary. And you have the nerve to come back and accuse me of horrors. My God!'

Daniel watched him shut his eyes and shake his head.

'What did you get up to then, Mr Brown? Shall I tell your lady friend here some of the things you did?'

'It was a war,' Daniel said.

'A war. You think that excuses you, that it was a war. They were all armed, were they, the women, the old men, the children you beat and burned and killed?'

Daniel turned his head, as though to parry the blows. He couldn't think about Walsh's words or he'd have no strength for his fury. All these years he'd nursed his own injury for defence, held onto it as the truth of that time. And the question that had hung at the back of his mind had a body now and he must find out the truth. But since crossing the water he couldn't get away from the other terrible truth of what had happened over here. Which was what he had done to people. He himself, and far beyond even the awful bounds of war. And still he twisted and turned, because here was the man, and he needed to know, he needed not to break into pieces, not yet, he needed to keep his guilt at bay a little longer.

'We were under orders,' he said. 'It wasn't me. It was my leg was blasted. I tried not to.' He shook his head. He mustn't let the words in now. Not in and not out. But Walsh's voice cut into him like shrapnel, sliced between his ribs, twisted in his flesh. He could feel it sour and curdle and gather his own thoughts with it into a mess of guilt.

'I know,' Jude said, her voice breaking in. 'I know what he did. And other things were done too and that's why we're here.'

'Oh, you know. Really?' said Walsh, his voice sarcastic. 'You think it was all reported? Your newspapers didn't even want to scratch at the surface of it. Too shameful.'

'I don't know it from the newspapers,' Jude said quietly, and though Walsh didn't seem to hear her, Daniel did, and from deep inside his maze, he wondered for the first time what it was that she knew, and where from.

'What do you think you're doing anyway, coming here?' Walsh said. 'This isn't your country.'

'I'm looking for you,' Daniel said.

And when Walsh laughed, Daniel could hold himself there, in that hotel room with its coffee stains and desperate flies, no longer, and he threw off Walsh's words, blocked his ears to Jude and struck out with his own wound.

'You thought I was gone,' Daniel said. 'The mark is still on my ribs,' and his hand went to his chest as though he would show Walsh the scar. 'Where you kicked me with your muddy boot. I'd forgotten that till now, how muddy your boot was.'

'What are you talking about?' Walsh said quietly.

'But it was everybody else that was gone. You were right about them. Will and Freddie Charters and all the others. Only me and the Colonel were left, except you didn't know about me. And the raven, after you'd marched away. The raven with his horrid voice.'

'I don't know what you're talking about,' said Walsh.

'Tell me,' Daniel said, almost conversationally, 'what happened to the poor scared fellow?'

'Who?'

'He was shooting in the air and you told him not to be a coward, to get on and kill the man.'

'What are you doing, Daniel?' Jude said.

Daniel shook his head. 'Poor man,' he said, 'poor man.'

Walsh turned and looked away out of the window. 'McCarthy,' he said to himself.

'He did it, though, didn't he? He shot him in the end. "Yerra, boy", you cried. But he did it for you, not for Ireland. Or not any more than I did it for England. Bloody hands, all of us.'

'Where did you get this from?' Walsh said. 'Because you are talking of Clonnacook, and there's nobody left alive.'

Daniel leaned across the table, his face cracked in a wide smile. 'But there is, and he wants to know something.'

Walsh shook his head. 'No.'

'You knew about one of us. You knew Colonel Whittam was alive, didn't you. And you didn't know about me. You caught me in the ribs with your boot and you flicked your cigarette on to my face, ashes to ashes. But you didn't know I was breathing.'

'I don't believe you,' Walsh said, shaking his head. 'And you better watch what you say around here, because there's a lot of men would talk of tearing you limb from limb if they knew what you were.'

'I lay doggo in that ditch and you stood above me telling your men to finish us off. We were unarmed, for Christ's sake. No weapons, and you shot us all. You shot us all dead.'

'It was that kind of war,' Walsh said. 'You know that.'

'It was that kind of war. But not for the Colonel. You left him alive. "Play dead," you told him. I can hear you say it, whispering, then more whispering I couldn't hear. You shot him carefully in the shoulder. And after you'd all gone and the raven had woken him, he walked away from us.'

Daniel saw how pale Walsh had gone.

'Is that why you've come back?' Walsh said. 'Because he walked away?'

Daniel stood up. He rolled his head round on his shoulders and flexed his fingers. Taking his stick, he walked over to the far wall and stroked the fox's head stuck proud there, its coarse fur and long nose.

'So the Kilmurphy hounds had you in 1913,' he said, reading the plaque. 'That's even before the rest of us were had.' He ran his finger down to its open mouth.

'My, what sharp teeth you have, Grandmother,' he said. 'And what beady eyes.'

He looked back towards the table in the window, towards the woman he thought, he hoped, might love him, and the man he needed to hate.

'I want to know if he betrayed us to our deaths. That's why I've come to find you. Because I don't know how to live this life until I find out, because I . . .'

He stopped, not knowing what to say.

'And why should I tell you?'

Daniel shrugged. 'Out of conscience. Or because I can make you. I don't care which.'

'There had been no surrender, they weren't our prisoners,' Walsh said, looking at Jude.

Daniel lifted his hand. 'I'm leaving now. He's going to play games and I've got too old for them.'

And before Jude could reply, he had left the room.

Walsh filled Jude's cup with more coffee. He passed her the cream and the sugar. Neither of them spoke. The waitress came in, and was waved away. Jude wondered what Daniel was doing, but feeling her chest tighten with panic at the thought, she pushed it away. She sipped the lukewarm coffee. The cream was viscous, coating her mouth, smoothing her palate. This was all more frightening than she could have imagined. She didn't know where anything was going. She tried for a placatory tone.

'I'm very sorry, Mr Walsh,' she said at last. 'Maybe this was a bad idea. It's not working out as I hoped.'

Walsh shrugged, waiting.

'I thought his meeting you would exorcise something. That's why the tomfoolery about the magazine and the photograph. It was the only way I could think of to arrange it.'

'Why did you come to me first, then, if it was him all the time that needed to see me?'

'I didn't know whether he could manage it.'

'And he hasn't, has he.'

'I don't know what kind of neurasthenia he's suffering from,' she said. 'Maybe we don't have a word for it.'

'It isn't shell-shock,' Walsh said. 'Or not the kind I ever saw.'

'But he is ill. We've been hoping to find a way out of it for him.' Jude could hear herself pleading, acting the part.

'We?'

'His parents. Friends.'

'Even brutal men get sick,' Walsh said. 'This was a different war from yours, and what his lot did was indefensible. We had to meet like with like, and it was a dirty fight to free our country. Nobody has clean hands, especially not Mr Brown and his Tans. It's what he deserves, if his conscience sends him mad. You've done a dangerous thing, Miss Hursten.'

Jude nodded. 'If you play with fire, you burn your fingers. I should have listened to my mother.'

'Doesn't sound as though you've ever listened to your mother. She wouldn't have wanted you a hundred yards from the front line in Belgium either.' Walsh ran his finger over the lighter, its carved clasped hands, and looked up at Jude with a different expression.

'How is your friend? The small, pretty one.'

'Kate,' Jude said.

'Was that her name?'

Jude smiled sadly. Walsh waited.

'She got her fingers burnt,' Jude said.

'She wasn't killed?'

'She was gassed.'

'Did she die?'

'Yes.'

'I'm sorry. She's dead, and you're still acting the heroine. What's your sweetheart going to do now, then?'

'He's not my sweetheart,' Jude said, though her heart had jumped to hear him say it. 'And I don't know. But he will do something to find out what he needs to know. He's got very little to lose. Unlike you.'

'And what will I do, Miss Hursten?'

Jude heard the steel, and she waited a moment to answer.

'I don't know that either. It depends on what you're prepared to give up.' She stood. 'I'm going to go now. I have to find him.'

Jude walked round the table and picked up the camera bag. Rising too, Walsh escorted her to the door like a proper host.

'I will very likely see you again,' he said, putting out his hand. They shook, and then, before she could prevent it, he lifted her hand to his lips and kissed it.

He watched her as she walked through the hall. She picked her jacket off the hat stand and pushed open the doors to the outside.

'Miss Hursten,' Walsh called, 'he has too much to be sorry for. He will go mad, that man. Remember it.'

'He is gone there already,' Jude said, but quietly, so he could not hear.

CHAPTER TWENTY-TWO

She found him beyond the church, by the river. It wasn't hard. The tall figure over its stick watching the swallows dip by the weir. They stood in silence together, and then Daniel looked at his watch.

'We should go back.'

It was only when they had reached the motorbike that he told Jude what he wanted to do, and though she was fearful of the consequences, she agreed.

'It is very nearly on our way,' Daniel said, and Jude nodded, her skin cold-pricked with apprehension. Daniel showed her the place on the map and the route was easy to plot.

Once they were clear of the town, the road was empty. Jude checked often, but there was nobody behind them. It had been dry in Liscool, but out here the ground was wet, and the air smelt of wild flowers and rain. There was nothing much to see. Just bog and hills, small twisted trees and the shine of ground water. Jude was glad of the bike beneath her, something that travelled where she wanted it to.

Too soon she felt Daniel's hand tapping on her leg. Slowing the bike into the bend, once they were round she came to a stop. She turned towards him and he nodded. He looked old suddenly, and very tired. Opening the sidecar door, she gave him her arm and, leaning heavily, he climbed out.

The clouds had cleared, leaving the sky a clear blue, and the afternoon sun was warm on their backs. Jude looked around her. This was where it had happened, in these ditches, below these rock outcrops. She turned towards Daniel.

He had walked down the road a little way and stood, hands flat to his sides, stick trailing, eyes to the ground, like one of the street-corner figures she'd grown accustomed to since the Great War.

'This is what you wanted,' she called, but he didn't reply. He was intent upon something, and as she watched she saw him look up, towards the brow of the hill, and down to the ditch, then up, then down again.

Shouldering her camera bag, Jude walked beyond him down the road. She wondered what Tom and Elsa were doing right now. She imagined them playing outside, being called in for tea, imagined their squabbling and their eagerness. She shut her eyes, homesick for the ordinary cadences. The light was milky, gentle. It was hard to imagine an ambush here. Opening them, something caught at her sight, a hard, precise line in this unruly place. Reflexively, she took out her camera and walked up closer. On one side of the road the ditch had been levelled over and against the rise of the hill, behind a flat altar of lichened rock, stood a column of dark stone. Words were carved on it in a language she didn't understand, though she recognised the name 'Dominic Murphy', and the date, 1921. Jude crouched low to take the photograph, and the column loomed tall, monumental. She stumbled as she stood and her bag lurched out from her body, tugging at her balance so that she put her hand out for balance. There was something soft beneath it and looking down, she found a small posy of white flowers tied with a white ribbon, the petals crimped and browning at the edges, the ribbon dusty. Something about it all, about the harsh dark monument and the delicate forgotten posy, made Jude wince and she turned away and back towards Daniel. He was no longer on the road but was climbing, unsteady even with his stick, up the hillside, tripped by brambles, struggling his way through the gorse.

'Like some bloody pilgrim,' Jude said, and she laughed out loud at herself, because she understood so little of what had happened here, so little of what had happened in what was, after all, a foreign country. Then she laughed again to hear her own echo.

At the brow of the hill Daniel turned back towards Jude. She couldn't read his expression, but he called something out and pointed down the other side. Then he stepped down the far side of the hill. So she set off up the road and followed him.

By the time she reached the same point ten minutes later, Daniel was gone, but she knew where, because below her was a small cottage, one end of the roof thatched and the other sheeted in red corrugated iron. It sat snug into the hill, two small rectangles of window staring blankly up at her. She could see a track leading away from it towards the road and noted it down as an easier route back.

'There's nowhere else for him to go now,' she told herself as she scrambled down.

When she reached it, she took a photograph: a bicycle leaning beneath one window, some hens scurfing up the dust at the threshold, the turf stack piled and thatched at one end, a cart leaning on its pins at the other, and she smiled at herself, taking a picture that seemed worthy of a chocolate box, when in truth she was in the midst of something so bitter.

The door was open. Jude knocked at it, but nobody came. She called inside.

'Hello? Anybody home?'

It felt incongruous, calling out like this, but she didn't know what else to do. Still no sign of anybody. Wondering what had become of Daniel, she ducked her head through the low doorway and stepped inside. She found herself in a broad, low-ceilinged room with flitches of bacon hanging from above, a spinning-wheel on the wall above the door and a pot on the fire, banked all around with crusted, white turf embers, from which came the smell of something fresh-baked. A closed door to the left of the fire she assumed must lead through to a bedroom. The walls were whitewashed and the floor was earthen. One end of the table was laid ready for tea with plates and cups and a jug of milk brim-full. A copy of the *Irish Farmer* was spread at the other covered with dirty potatoes and a pile of peelings, and beside it a wooden doll and a bowl of peeled potatoes, shining and white in the dim light.

Jude shivered. This was eerie. Where was the woman? The child? Where was Daniel?

'Daniel?' she called.

Still there was silence, but as she listened, she thought she heard sounds from the other side of the closed door.

'Daniel?' she called again.

Dropping her bag, she walked over to the door and pushed. It was latched shut. Undecided, she put her ear against the wood and listened. There were odd noises coming from the other side, she couldn't make them out. Then, unmistakably, she heard Daniel's voice. He was speaking in a tone she'd never heard before and it made her skin go cold. She tugged down the latch and pulled open the door.

It looked as if something violent had happened in the room, a chair upturned, a rug in the middle heaped into a pile, but the figures in the corner were very still. Daniel was crouched down facing towards the far wall, like some predatory animal ready to leap, and backed up into the corner was a young woman, her eyes wide with fear or fury, turning her head this way and that as though trying to get free of his glance. The air seemed tight with static, as though any movement might provoke a fury in the gods.

She took a step closer then, wincing at the creak of the boards, and between them she saw a small child, two, perhaps three years old, sitting on the floor and playing with a pile of wooden blocks. She was chattering unconcernedly to both the adults, turning her head first to one, then to the other, a light, infant babble of sound that rose into the bright friction of the air above.

Jude watched as the child raised up a tower, each block more precarious than the last, till there were five standing proud. The child turned towards her mother, but the mother, her face bleached and tense, didn't see. So she turned back to the strange man, and Jude watched as Daniel reached out his hand and casually, as though it made no odds, swatted at the lowest block. The tower tumbled. The child looked at the blocks, then at Daniel, then at the blocks again, and her face crumpled into tears, and she let out a wail that cut like ice across Jude's skin.

The cry broke the woman's spell. She lunged forward, her pale arms flashing, and drew the little girl in close. And where before she'd been silent, motionless, now she rocked her child and spoke softly, and the child forgot her tears and smiled again and chattered.

Jude could see the woman's wedding ring, and that one of her nails was split. She could see the dirt on her fingers, no time to wipe her hands from the potatoes. She could see the thick wool of her stockings, the shape of her toes on one foot, a shoe lost on the floor, her dark skirts, her blouse, her hair somehow dragged free of its pins, falling and tumbling over her shoulders. The woman rocked her child, but still Jude saw how rigid her limbs were, as if she could make herself into something unyielding, like a hard metal, a carapace within which to keep her child safe.

When Daniel spoke, his voice was calm and cold and slow.

'Just tell me,' he said. 'Did you know he was coming? One word, and then no harm done. She can build her towers.'

'Daniel, stop,' Jude said, scared.

'Go away, Jude,' he said, his voice quiet, uninflected.

Jude felt her heart race and the sweat break down her back.

'I need the answer,' he said and he shifted slightly, moving himself closer to the woman.

Jude couldn't see what he was doing, but she saw the fear that spread itself now over the woman's face. And she saw how she hunched over her child.

'This is what you learned,' she said quietly. 'How to terrorise women and children. But it's over. You don't have to do this now.'

Daniel cuffed at his head, as though a fly were irritating him.

'For God's sake, the war's over,' Jude said. 'You're frightening her.'

'Just yes or no,' he said.

And although he had done nothing yet but knock down the tower, the violence was almost palpable, like the pressure of a storm before it breaks, and Jude was frightened that something much worse would explode through. The terrified woman would not, could not move while Daniel was crouched there. Jude looked about her for some way of distracting him, but there was nothing obvious to hand. A bed, the child's crib, a chest, a chair. So she tugged the quilt from the bed and gathered it up in her arms as best she could. It was heavy and for a moment she floundered and the floorboards groaned beneath her. But Daniel paid her no attention. He still stared at the woman. And the woman, eyes on the ground, still rocked her child. Then Jude spread her arms wide and flung the quilt over him, pushing him down onto the floorboards and gathering her arms tight around him.

Daniel struggled like a wild thing, maddened, flailing, but she held on, the muscles in her arms, her stomach, her shoulders shaking with the effort. She could feel his shoulders, bunched tight, and the force of his arms. His breath was coming in ragged bursts and he made small, fierce sounds as he fought her. She could feel the length of him, how his legs stretched just beyond hers, and how the crown of her head pressed against his cheek bone. She pushed her head harder into his face and he gave a yelp of pain. Through the clear, cotton smell of the quilt, she could smell him, a smell she didn't know she knew, and despite herself, despite her anger, her heart lurched.

She felt Daniel brace his body against hers, felt him use every ounce of his strength as he began to force her off, gaining an arm's freedom, and a shoulder's, bending his good leg beneath him for support. And then he stopped, so that for an extraordinary moment they seemed to her suspended, beyond that time and that place, for minutes, or seconds, braced each against each, till something gave way, like a wave through him. She felt his body relent and his breathing ease, as though she had brought him to quiet, and he seemed to fall across her, so that they lay with the length of each other like some strange *pietà* there on the floor.

Jude pulled herself free and as she stood up, her calm was replaced with fury, knotting her stomach.

'For Christ's sake, Daniel Brown, who the hell do you think you are?'

She was shouting, out of control. She wanted to hit him, pound her fists into him. She hadn't noticed the woman stand until she felt a hand on her arm.

'Come out of here,' the woman said, and Jude was quietened and followed her, only turning in the doorway to look back, but the bundle of quilt lay motionless, dead to the world.

In the kitchen the pot was still cooking and the potatoes were still half-peeled. The woman filled the kettle from a bucket beside the hearth, the child hoisted on one hip, and Jude sat down at the table. The child's doll looked up at her. It was a crude, wooden creature, stiff armed and legged, a smile painted on to its flat face, wool hair tied up into a bun. It wore a skirt in the same cloth as the mother's and a roughly sewn chemise. One side of the chemise was darker than the other, and damp.

Jude looked across to the woman. She was staring at the door, as if it might burst open at any moment, her eyes still wide. She was shivering.

'We could wedge it shut,' Jude said.

The woman nodded, so Jude took a chair and propped it below the latch. There was no sound from within. Still the woman stared at the door.

'I'll sit against it too,' Jude said, and she sat beside the wedged chair on the hard ground.

Setting the child down, the woman took the pot from the fire and hung the kettle to boil. She lifted the pot lid. The smell of sweet bread was overwhelming and Jude longed above anything to be home, in her own kitchen, with the children she loved. The little girl clung to her mother's skirts. The woman set the bread on a rack at the potato end of the table and pulled out a chair, lifting the child to her lap. There was no sound from the other room.

'What's her name?' Jude asked gently.

'Nora,' the woman said.

'And you?'

'Peg Riley.'

'My name's Jude. Jude Hursten.'

The woman nodded, keeping her eyes from Jude, from the closed door. Nora buried her face in her mother's lap.

'You came here with him,' Peg said.

'Yes.'

'I thought he would kill me,' she said.

'I know,' Jude said.

'I've never met him.' She was shaking. The kettle was boiling. Lifting Nora to her hip, she got up and made a pot of tea, brought it to the table. She ran her fists across her face.

'He was a Tan?'

'Yes, he was.'

Peg looked at her. 'But Ireland is its own country now,' she said. 'They can't come and . . .' She shook her head.

'I'm very sorry,' Jude said. 'If I'd known, I'd never have brought him here.'

'It's the ambush brought you.'

'He was one of the only two survivors.'

Peg shook her head. 'No,' she said.

'What do you mean?'

'There was only one survivor.'

'How do you know?'

Peg rubbed the teapot as if to conjure something. 'Because he came here afterwards, bloody as a clipped rabbit.'

'But not the man in there?' Jude pointed at the bedroom door. 'Not Daniel?'

'No. I never saw him before today.'

'He came to your cottage? The survivor?'

'He knocked at the door. After all the racket, the guns and grenades going off. Asked could he please trouble me for a glass of water.' She laughed grimly. 'Blood pouring from his shoulder and the rest of him filthy with mud and him troubling me for a glass of water.'

'How did he know the house was here?' Jude said. 'You can't see it from the road.'

'No.'

'It must have been Colonel Whittam,' Jude said.

'I don't know,' Peg said, shying her head away, pouring the tea into cups. 'He had a posh voice though.'

'What did you do?'

311

Peg shrugged. 'Took him in. Bleeding like a stuck pig. I don't know how he got up the hill. He said they were all dead behind him, and that's what I heard afterwards. That's what was printed in the papers, too. I hated them, the Tans. But I couldn't let him die.' She brought Jude over a cup, set it down on the ground.

Jude nodded. She understood this. She remembered German soldiers being brought in. She'd nursed them as carefully as any others, held their hands when they cried.

She felt it before she heard it, the sound from the next room, Daniel's voice, quiet, calm-sounding, felt his voice as a chord through the wood of the door and into her skin. She looked over at Peg. Her arms were stiff, rigid like a wall around her child. Daniel was quiet again and Jude pressed on, not knowing how long they had till he came out.

'Did you tell him this?' Jude said, 'about the bleeding man and the glass of water?'

Peg shook her head. 'Soon as he came in here, he was yelling, demanding. Shouting and mumbling. I couldn't speak to him.'

'I think he hears other voices, from that day, that time.'

Peg shivered, and crossed her arms around herself. 'I asked him to leave, and he wouldn't. He came right up to me, here, by this table, and he picked up Nora's doll, hung it from his fingers. I was so scared, I ran into the bedroom, to get her, and he followed me. She was playing, you saw, and I didn't want to alarm her, so I just crouched against the wall, and then you came.'

'So, do you know Matt Walsh?' Jude said.

Peg barely hesitated, but Jude saw it.

'You do,' she said.

'Everybody knows Matt Walsh,' Peg said finally.

'I think he will come here again,' Jude said. 'And Daniel, the man in there, was in the ambush. It's his own Colonel he's pursuing. Who's a dead man, but that doesn't stop him.'

Daniel was tangled in something soft, heavy. It was completely dark around him, and very warm, and he could smell all kinds of things: animals, turf smoke, soap, sweat. He lay still, didn't try to

312

move. The struggle with Jude had left him exhausted, his limbs aching and tight.

It was quiet inside here, only the sound of his own breathing. There was something vast outside, and he'd have to look at it soon. But just for now, for these next minutes, he'd keep it at bay.

The woman had surprised him. Her fear had bothered him. He shouldn't have minded it, he knew that. He hadn't known he was speaking out loud, had thought it was just inside his head. But if she had only answered, just the one word, he would have left her be.

The air was close. He could feel the heat of it as he breathed in and out, burning his nostrils, drawing the sweat. He was angry with Jude, angry that she'd come between him and what he needed, but lying here in his dark cocoon he admitted that he'd enjoyed it when she'd held him. That despite the pain it gave to his leg, he'd resisted her for longer just to feel her body pressed so hard up against his, her arms around him. He didn't know if he was blushing at the thought, or whether it was the heat. He pulled at the heavy fabric. Now it was smothering him and there seemed no way out of it. He felt that panic he knew from his childhood when he'd got lost under the bedclothes, making his heart pound in his chest.

'Can't breathe!' he shouted, because Johnnie would help him, lifting the blankets clear, his face at the top of the well, breaking the dark, calling down comfort. Then Daniel remembered where he was and he closed his mouth and fought his way out in silence.

Free of the quilt, he curled on his side. Jude and the woman were talking in the other room, their voices adrift in the air, but he couldn't hear the words. The blocks were still where they'd fallen. He picked one up. A rough piece of painted wood, red as the red of the iron roof. With a shaky hand he placed it on the ground, perspective thrown to the winds from where he lay, and stacked the others on top, one upon one upon one, as the child had done.

His tower was lovely. Johnnie should see it. Lying with his head on the ground, he thought it might have reached to the sky. He nudged the bottom block with a finger, set it at an angle. The tower stayed true. He nudged it again, and again, till the whole height depended on a slight incidence of wood on wood. Again his finger pressed the red, and the whole tumbled around his ears, around his eyes, so that he put his hands up in defence.

The air was loud, and then it was still. A bee nuzzled and the dust motes danced their late afternoon dance at the window. Daniel lay still and grew calm. He shut his eyes and slept for a while, and when he woke, the air smelt sweet and fragrant, and the sun lay differently. He looked at the blocks all around him. There was one just near his forehead that he could see if he rolled his eyes upwards and another beside his fingers. Another lay at the edge of the quilt, and one had rolled half under the bed, beyond his reach. He sat up, his mind quite clear. He knew something at last and he needed to be out of here. Reaching for his stick, he got to his feet. The voices still murmured, but there was another one, a man's voice, added now.

Looking about him, he was shocked. It seemed as if some violence had been done in the room. So he set the chair on its feet again and straightened the rug. He put the wooden blocks in a pile together, then went to the door. One hand on the latch, he hesitated, and then he knocked.

CHAPTER TWENTY-THREE

The women had gone outside by the time they heard the motor car. Jude had told Peg she was a photographer and promised to take Nora's photograph and the little girl stood on the threshold, her doll still held tight to her middle, her face serious.

'There's a motor car on the road,' Peg said.

Jude lowered her camera. She heard nothing. 'Are you sure?'

'Listen,' and this time Jude could hear a low roar, a vibration almost more than a sound.

'Depends if it slows,' Peg said. 'If it's him, he'll most likely stop on the road and walk the rest. You'd damage the axle, bringing it here along the track.'

They listened as the car approached, then went quiet. A door slammed.

'Just one,' Jude said. 'So he's alone.'

'I'll fill the kettle again,' Peg said.

Jude nodded. 'Make believe, like I said.'

And in the same way Jude continued taking photographs of Nora, as though she had no idea, no thought of the man walking up the track, or of the other man still silent in the bedroom behind.

Nora had got bored of the camera and they had gone around the end of the house by the time Walsh walked up. The child's timidity was gone and she tugged Jude's hand, eager to show her some treasure. So Jude, crouched by the turf stack, gazing unseeing at some withered flowers, saw Walsh before he saw her. His face was determined, but not vengeful, and she couldn't tell for certain, but she didn't think he was armed. She watched him look through the kitchen window and raise his hand to knock, then she called out.

'Hello again, Mr Walsh.'

Holding tight to Nora's hand, she walked towards him.

He turned.

'Miss Hursten,' he said, his face unsurprised. But Jude watched it light up at the sight of Nora. Crouching down, he addressed himself in a soft tone to the little girl.

'Hello there. So you're Liam's pride and joy. Such a dote, it's no wonder.'

'I thought you'd know where to find us,' Jude said.

'Where else would he go,' Walsh said with a shrug.

'It's an elegant shrine down there at the roadside. Though I don't think Daniel saw it.'

Walsh stood up again. 'You know they've had a fair on this road each year since. The priest comes and gives his blessing, and there are songs sung, there's rejoicing.'

He took Nora's hand, and swung it as he sang.

Then here's to the boys of Clonnacook
Who feared not the might of the foe,
The day they marched into battle
And laid all the Black and Tans low.

'So you've come after us Mr Walsh.'

'As you told me earlier, I'm the only one with anything to lose. Amn't I, little princess?'

He lifted Nora up and grinned at her, eye-to-eye.

Nora stared back, then putting her hands up to his face, she pushed him away with the full force of her small arms.

The little girl's hands thrust against Walsh's eyes and nose, making him gasp and his eyes water. But he said nothing, only set her down carefully and gave a chuckle.

'Maybe I asked for that.'

'We don't always ask for what we get,' Jude said as she opened the door to the house.

Peg stood by the fire, not pretending to do anything other than wait. She gave a slight shake of the head when Jude came in, so that Jude knew Daniel was still quiet. She noticed that Peg had taken the chair from against the bedroom door and set it back at the table. Nora ran into her mother's skirts with a cry, and Peg picked her up and set her on her hip.

'Mrs Riley,' Walsh said, nodding his greeting.

'Will you have some tea?' Peg said.

'That'd be great, thank you.' Walsh glanced around the room.

'He's not in here,' Jude said.

'I can see.'

'You'll meet him soon enough.'

Walsh flashed a look at her. 'What do you mean by that?'

'No more than I said.'

Peg put the teapot on the table. 'There's fresh brack. I must have known you'd all be arriving,' she said, and her words broke the tension and the three of them sat down.

'How much does Mrs Riley know?' Walsh said.

'She knows enough. Daniel threatened her this afternoon.'

'He did what?'

'You said he would go mad.'

'Where is he?'

Peg cut slices of the brack. It was still warm.

'This is delicious,' Jude said.

She watched Walsh pluck at his piece with his fingertips. Such delicate eating. It seemed incongruous in such a large man.

'Have you spoken with him, Mrs Riley?' he said.

Peg shook her head. 'It wasn't that kind of meeting.'

'But did he say anything about the ambush?'

'He did, but I didn't understand.'

Nora had finished her bit of brack and was becoming restive on her mother's lap. Fishing in her apron pocket, Peg brought out some beads. She gave them to the child, and Jude watched as Nora fingered through them, her small murmurs a parody of her mother's devotions.

Walsh sipped his tea and took another mouthful. He took his

317

time, and Jude saw him regain his composure, take stock, take control. He was a powerful man. He wouldn't give his hand away easily, and certainly not to someone as lowly as Peg Riley.

'He must have been very badly wounded, or unconscious, for us to have believed him dead that day,' he said. 'And then the shell-shock afterwards.' He shook his head. 'I wonder how much he can really remember.'

Jude rolled a small piece of brack between her fingers, forming it into a tight, hard ball. 'What do you mean?'

'He's an ill man, Miss Hursten. You'd agree about that. And he's making up all sorts in that sick head. And while I am equal to it, he cannot be allowed to threaten a young woman and her small child.'

'What exactly do you think he's making up?' Jude said.

'I was here that day. I directed the ambush. If it is my word against his, who is going to listen to him for a minute? An ex-Black and Tan against me?'

'But you've got something to lose, Mr Walsh,' Jude said. 'Or you wouldn't have come looking now.'

Jude took out cigarettes and lighter. She offered one to Walsh. He shook his head and took out his own, lit up and drew deeply, nodding slowly, as if he'd agreed with himself about something.

'I have a good business and a standing in the community,' he said. 'I've a part to play in building a new Ireland and I won't let it be jeopardised by a sick young Englishman pursuing some kind of crazy vendetta.'

'That's quite a speech,' Jude said.

Walsh leaned forward across the table. 'And you'd do well to remember that it was them were the enemy that day, not us. The Tans did things nobody should do, things they'd never dare confess to their mothers or their sweethearts, not even to you, Miss Hursten, and they deserved what they got that day. This is our country now, not yours, isn't that right, Mrs Riley?'

But Peg didn't reply. Cradling her daughter, making her arm strong across the little girl's chest, she was listening to the sounds from the other room. Small taps of wood on wood, the creak of floorboards, and finally something that everyone could hear, a knock on the door.

Nobody answered, so Daniel tugged down the latch and pushed the door with his stick. It swung open and he stepped into the kitchen as gently as a lamb.

The woman held her child tight to her, he could see that, and Jude sat beside her, one arm, protective, stretched across to the back of the woman's chair. Daniel thought Jude looked tense. Her eyes flicked about the room, and she was kneading what must have been a piece of bread on her plate with her free hand, pressing and turning it with her fingertips.

Walsh sat at the table too. His face was fierce. He wasn't doing anything, but Daniel had the feeling he would move very fast if he had to.

'Something smelt so good,' Daniel said. 'I couldn't stay out any longer.'

He walked further into the room and looked at Peg. 'I don't even know your name, I'm sorry.'

'Daniel,' Jude said, her voice rough, a warning.

'Mrs Riley,' Peg said.

'I must apologise, Mrs Riley,' he said, leaning over his stick. 'For my behaviour earlier. It was horrible, terrible. I don't know what came over me, and I'm very sorry.'

'An apology, from the British. That'll be a first.' Walsh's voice was sarcastic, but Daniel only nodded. He carried on speaking to Peg as if she would understand everything he was saying.

'I wish I'd never come to your country. I should have thrown my coin in the well earlier. I'm a man who doesn't suffer guilt gladly, but underneath the brick tower I saw that I was a guilty man. It's been building up over me for a long while and I've kept it off, which is a terrible thing to do, . . . I've no guilt towards him,' he said, pointing to Walsh, 'but towards all of you. It's like a fever that comes over you, of righteousness and power, terrible vile, that makes you big and everyone else so small, so ugly. If I stop now, I'll never get what I came for. So I can't, I won't stop, and when I do,

God knows. But at least I understand the dream, with the children and the horses.'

'What do you understand?' said Jude.

'I saw it just now, in there,' pointing to the bedroom, 'when I was putting the blocks to rights.'

'Saw what?' Jude said.

'One time we brought the wrong man in from a raid. We didn't know it of course, that he was the wrong one, and by the time we found it out, he'd been beaten up a bit, lost a tooth, some bruising. So we had a problem. We couldn't just say sorry, let him go, because it would make us look very bad and there'd be all kinds of trouble from it. So we beat him up some more, made no apology and then let him go. Because people would think he had to have done something to get that badly hurt. And besides, we knew that every Irish man was a Shinner at heart.'

'What are you telling us?' Walsh said.

'So you're lying on the floor and you build the blocks higher and higher, and nudge them further and further, till they're so high above your head and depending on so little that you know the crash is going to be very loud, and there's nothing you can do to prevent it.'

Daniel stepped forward, and the room gathered itself.

'Would you mind if I sat down?' he said to Peg. 'Being the only one standing.'

Peg nodded slightly, and he sat down at the end of the table. Cocking his head at Nora, he made a funny face, but she was still playing with the rosary and didn't see him.

'Pretty little girl,' he said, then turned to Jude. 'You see, you shouldn't have followed me out to this land.' He put his hand to his pocket. The knife was still there. He slipped his hand in his pocket and loosened the covering round the blade. 'Look what a sticky mess we've got into. And I don't have a very reliable history, when it comes to this little bit of valley.' He turned to Peg. 'Has she told you why we're here? About the picture she took? I don't think I explained myself very well.'

'Daniel, stop there,' Jude said.

'Has she told you about the photograph, and Mr Walsh's early misdemeanours?'

The threat was naked. And his voice, which had begun in such a light tone, was now almost a growl.

Walsh was up and round the table faster than Jude would have thought possible.

'You're very eloquent all of a sudden,' he said, taking hold of Daniel's arm, 'but this conversation would be better held outside.'

And before Daniel had time to resist, Walsh had levered him up and out of his chair. Jude was on her feet too. She could feel the blood pulsing in her neck, her wrists, her forehead and she was scared. This was what they had come for, this moment, and now it was here it was terrifying. Walsh pulled on Daniel's arm, swung him round towards the door like some jointed doll, then turned back to face the room. He touched the peak of his cap to Peg.

'We've taken up more than enough of your time, and eaten more than enough of your delicious brack.' Walsh's voice was so smooth.

Peg looked down at her child. She stroked her soft hair.

'So,' Walsh went on, 'give my regards to Liam, and tell him I'll be in touch. As it happens, I have a bit of work for him.'

Daniel had opened the door and stepped outside, and Walsh followed. Jude knelt beside Peg.

'Will you be all right?' she said in a low tone. 'This is a strange business.'

Peg nodded. 'It's you should be worried,' she said.

'I can always make a getaway on my bike,' Jude said, forcing a smile. She picked up her camera bag. 'I'll send you the photographs.'

'Do that. Then I'll know you've survived.'

CHAPTER TWENTY-FOUR

Daniel and Walsh had already walked down the track a short way by the time Jude got outside. They didn't turn or wait for her and it crossed her mind that it would be easy to let them go. She couldn't think why she'd gone this far. She'd had enough of Daniel's bloody war and of the ambush that had made this rough piece of nowhere into a famous site, and into a memory for Daniel that wouldn't leave him any peace. She'd taken the photograph that had brought them here, but it wasn't her battle. She could return to Cork and take the next boat home. Daniel was a grown man, this was his story, his past. She could leave him to it.

The sun had dropped so low that it kissed the far hill, and the men's shadows made long, unruly shapes, bucking and swinging over the gorse. She watched the swifts, high and noisy, playing to the crowd, the few sheep, and the rabbits below the house, heads up, ears pricked, till their appetite got the better of their caution. And she watched these two men who had already done each other such violence. They might be friends from where she stood, talking easily near the end of a long day.

They had stopped twenty yards away and were standing facing one another, and she didn't know exactly what it was she saw, but something in the bearing of both men had changed. They stood as if this was the place they had agreed and the time and now there was nothing for it but the combat. As if they might turn and count off the paces, except there was only bog and rock to pace into. Daniel had laid his stick against the wall and both men seemed very upright, poised, their arms held loosely by their sides. Neither moved, neither spoke.

Jude held her breath. She stood watching, rocking on the balls of her feet. The air was charged and the earth seemed too still. She thought she would scream with it. In France sometimes they would have to wait like this in the nursing station, knowing, because they had had a message, that an assault was about to take place and that soon men would be coming in dying and horribly wounded. The bandages would have been rolled, medical supplies checked, the stretchers and truckle beds laid out, the fires prepared and wood got in ready, water collected, so that all there was left to do was to wait. They could have read, or written letters, played cards, slept even, but they were able to do none of these. Instead they would strike up absurd arguments with one another, or pick the lice from one another's hair. So that it was a relief when eventually the first bodies arrived, and the pain and mess of them broke in on the strange trance of waiting.

She never knew what it was that snapped in the air finally. It might have been the small, alopecic dog that arrived from somewhere and stood between the two men barking; or the cloud that capped the slipping sun; or Walsh's reaching for a cigarette; or the flick of Daniel's eyes at a bird flying low. But suddenly both men were shouting, yelling, hurling words, English and Irish cadences crashing and feuding so fiercely in the sky that she couldn't pull them apart, and the words splintered out across the hillside. And before she knew she had moved, Jude was running down the hill, her eyes picking her way ahead of her between the loose stones and the pot-holes, over the streams and gullies of the landscape, her ears ringing with violence.

'You shot my friends . . . in cold blood . . . you killed . . . you killed . . . tortured my boys . . . children . . . innocent . . . unarmed . . . betrayed me . . . the women . . . all murderers . . . invaders . . . criminals . . . Shinners . . . British brutes . . . psychopaths . . .'

Looking back later, Jude didn't know who had said what. Now the men had moved in closer to one another, their hands making fists by their sides, their mouths wide with abuse shouted over and over, lips pulled back, shoulders lifted and tight with fury, and nothing was behind them and all was raw and bloody. A few yards from them, breathless, Jude slowed her pace. They didn't see her, they didn't see anything except each other. But she saw Daniel turn his shoulder and feel for his pocket. Draw his hand out slowly, his fingers wrapped tight around something. And then another inch and there was the dull gleam of metal.

She yelled. 'No! Daniel!'

And as he took the step towards Walsh and lifted the knife, pulling his arm back, she lunged at him. Walsh jerked away, stepping back, stumbling, and Daniel's hand twisted. Jude felt a keen, cold line draw itself down her side and then her legs gave way and she sank and fell between the two men. She wondered what it was that had made her drop, till she put her hand to the line and felt the warm blood between her fingers. She lay, legs, arms, hands flat to the ground with weariness, and the grass was damp against her back, and her blood-sticky fingers were rough with the grit from the track, but she couldn't move, couldn't even raise an eyebrow in surprise.

Daniel was crouched beside her, his hands desperate, smoothing and touching her, his face wide with distress.

'Jude, oh God! I'm sorry, Jude, please. Jude.'

'Bit of a mess,' Jude said.

She saw Walsh kneel down, saw the shock in his face and she wondered, from inside her great weariness, why he or Daniel should be so surprised. They had seen bodies torn open enough before. The two men were still on each side of her, paralysed. She could hear their breathing. Walsh got to his feet and shook his head, rubbed his face with his hands, as if to free himself of some miasma.

'Keep her warm,' he said, his voice cheery and too sharp, spreading his jacket over Jude's chest. He leaned over her. 'We'll rig up a stretcher and get you back up to the house.' He patted her gently on the shoulder and winked. 'A turnaround, eh?' Then he was off at a half-jog up the hill.

Daniel stayed close, half-murmuring, shaking his head. The numbness was giving way to pain like a hot lance.

'Talk to me,' she said.

'Talk to you?'

'Tell me something.'

'What?'

'Anything. Something you remember. But not about this.'

He thought a moment. 'My brother, Johnnie. He had a collection of birds' eggs. Started it when he was small. Somebody gave him a clutch to get going, the commonest ones. Robin, blackbird, wren, blue tit. And after a while he had a good number. Some rare ones too.'

He paused. Jude had her eyes shut.

'And?' she said.

'My favourite is the heron's egg.'

'Must have been hard. They nest very high up.'

'There were herons on an island not a mile from our house. Towards Kew. We'd watched them often, standing in the shallows waiting. I'd seen one pounce a couple of times, bash a fish with its beak, then take it off to the bank and pick it clean. And the nests were high up in the trees, huge platforms of sticks. But this one year, I must have been about eight, and Johnnie ten, he swore there was a pair had built a nest in the reeds near the bank, where it was marshy. They'd do that occasionally. And he wanted an egg. So, one evening, dusk, we borrowed a rowing boat. It was tied up to the bank only a short way down from the island and they'd left the oars inside, foolish things. I say "we", but it was Johnnie really. I don't remember what he bribed me with that time.'

Jude chuckled, then winced. 'What about your parents?' she said.

'We said we were off for a walk and Mother gave us sixpence for ices.'

Jude winced again. Daniel stared at her. He hadn't known how much he had come to want this woman to be part of things.

'Come on,' Jude said, her voice impatient.

325

'So we acted like it was our boat and, God knows how, managed to row across.'

'You hadn't rowed before?'

Daniel shook his head. 'First time. I waited, holding the boat, and Johnnie went for the egg. I stood there in the muddy water, trousers rolled up, and I knew we shouldn't be doing it. Even decided I'd tell him to put it back, if he got one.'

Daniel looked up the hillside towards the house. The door opened and Walsh and Peg appeared, carrying what looked like a door between them.

'Anyway,' he said, 'to cut a long story short, he came back with the egg and it was so beautiful, the shell like satin under your fingers, smooth, warm, I couldn't bear to say anything. Only we had to pretend to our mother that we'd had our ices.'

'That's it?' Jude said. 'That's the story?'

Daniel reached over and tucked a stray strand of hair away from Jude's face.

'We'll have you back to the house soon,' he said. 'And another day, some day, I'll show it to you. It's beautiful. About two and a half inches long and a pale blue that is almost a green.'

'Like your eyes then?' Jude said.

'I can't see my own eyes,' he said.

When they carried her up to the house, Walsh took one end of the door, and Daniel and Peg the other, and they stumbled sometimes. Daniel watched Jude bite her lip to stop from crying out, the tug of her skin with her teeth.

They put her on the bed in the room with the building blocks and Peg told the men to build up the fire and to boil water. In the corner Nora was tucked asleep in a crib, and the women spoke in whispers.

'You're not squeamish?' Jude said.

'I managed it for the English man,' Peg said.

'I can tell you what to do,' Jude said. 'And I think it'll be a clean cut. Not like the things we saw in the trenches.'

'You were there?'

Jude nodded, her eyes shut.

'So tell me then.'

As Peg picked up the scissors and began, very gently, to cut away Jude's clothes, the two men next door stoked the fire and heated the water. They busied themselves as long as they could, bringing in turf, making tea, moving about in silence, alert to any sound from the bedroom. But once all was done, there was no more avoiding, and so, as if they had agreed this, they sat at the table and waited to begin.

Finally Walsh spoke.

'That would make us quits now,' he said.

Daniel looked puzzled, and Walsh went on.

'I've tried to kill you, and you've tried to kill me. Impressive for two military men, that we've both failed, and from such close quarters.'

'You got nearer to it than I did,' Daniel said.

'I didn't have an impassioned woman to contend with,' Walsh said. 'Only a few bullets.'

Daniel gave a small, serious smile.

'How do you think she is?' Walsh said.

'She's the one will know that best,' Daniel said. 'If she can stay conscious.'

They fell silent again. Daniel dropped his head to the table, his forehead against the wood. He couldn't bear what he'd done. Things were crowding in, but he needed to be lucid. A sound from the bedroom broke in the air between them. Walsh took out a packet of cigarettes and drummed them on the table top. Daniel pulled his head up, sat straight again. Walsh offered him the packet.

'No, thank you,' he said.

'You'd find one useful, a time like this,' Walsh said, tapping one out. 'Good for the nerves.' He lit up and drew, then leaned back in his chair.

'You'll break the legs, doing that.' Daniel's voice sounded sunken, as though he had dredged it up through the murkiest waters.

'Don't believe everything your mother told you,' Walsh said with a private smile.

He took a deep draw on the cigarette and blew the smoke high between them, a thin blue pall.

'Now listen to me and I'll tell you my part. I'm not going to start in on the history. Enough to say that the Irish had the right to their own country, and the right not to be occupied or ruled by England. And that we were never going to get you out except by force.

'Now, I'd been in the British army during the European war. There were thousands here joined up like I did. And I'd fought alongside Whittam. Lieutenant Whittam then. But you know that. What you don't know is how we came to meet up afterwards.'

'The ambush,' Daniel said.

'No. It was six months earlier. You might remember it. Three men brought in after a raid, caught with maps, explosives. And Whittam checked his papers and found one of them a wanted man already, up in Dublin.'

Daniel shook his head. 'I don't recall every bloody Shinner brought in,' he said. 'There were too many of you.'

Walsh drummed his feet against the floor, sucked hard on his cigarette and held his temper.

'All right. But this lot, one of them escaped. The wanted man. And so the other two . . .'

Daniel tapped a finger on the table.

'I do remember that,' he said. 'The other two got sent up to Dublin Castle in his place and one of them suffered heart failure during the interrogation. There was a bit of bother outside the barracks when they brought his body back to bury.'

Walsh snorted. 'I should bloody think so. Did you see what they'd done to him? Cigarette burns, bruising, broken fingers?'

'But you would say that,' Daniel said. 'It was your job, you insurgents, to make us seem as bad as possible, so the ordinary people would side with you.'

Daniel could see them before him, the crowd of heads, the noise, stones being thrown, the women's hatred. He tapped the table again, hard, to make himself feel it. He must stay here, in the room, in the conversation. Not let himself drift, take flight.

Walsh stabbed out his cigarette. 'We didn't have to try very hard, did we?'

'Why are you telling me this?' Daniel said.

'Because I was the man who escaped. And before you ask how, I'll tell you. I was taken into an interrogation room, hands bound tight, legs hobbled, and there at the table was Whittam. I recognised him immediately. Imagine it. Imagine what that was like. For him as well as for me. The last time we'd seen each other, we'd been waving our discharge papers, arms round each other's shoulders, drunk as lords, swearing everlasting friendship. I had to bite my tongue hard, draw blood, to stop from saying anything.

'He had his head down writing, so he didn't see me at first. And when he looked up, his mouth dropped like a fish.'

'That's where his nickname came from,' Daniel said.

'What?' Walsh said frowning.

'His nickname. The Trout. Because of his face, and the fishing.'

'Not in the trenches,' Walsh said. 'But then there wasn't a lot of fishing in the trenches.'

'So what did he do then?'

'He came around the table, walked right up close and called me a bastard. Spat in my face. Shouted at me, punched me, made my nose bleed. Said he wanted to be left alone with this one, and sent the others out.'

Daniel nodded.

'So he let you escape. It makes sense now.'

He remembered this. Whittam said he'd loosened the man's bonds because he thought he was unconscious and was worried they'd have another death in custody. He said he'd only left the room for a minute, but that somehow the prisoner had revived and jumped through the window while he was out. Whittam must have feigned fury, and he sent out patrols. Dublin Castle had demanded they have the other men in his stead, and one of them had come back dead.

'Whittam knew I'd be a dead man if he sent me to Dublin

Castle, and he couldn't do it. Not after the trenches. We went through hell together and lived.'

'And so you told him about the ambush, didn't you? Said you'd make sure he'd survive.' Daniel said it casually, slipped it in.

'No!' Walsh was up from his chair, towering, raging.

Daniel spoke very calmly. 'We were unarmed. God, I can still see it so well. The lad who took my rifle, he smelt of sheep, and his hands were scratched. We'd surrendered, and then you shot us.'

'You're wrong, Mr Brown,' Walsh said.

Daniel went on, implacable. 'Whittam gave you our lives in exchange for saving his. All those men, my friends, my pals. That day you were captured, you told him about the ambush. Where it would be, what day. And he led us into this valley and let you shoot us dead.'

Walsh's face was blazing. 'It was a battle, foggy, nothing was clear. No time to consider, you have to decide instantly. And I did what I thought necessary to protect my men. Whittam and I made no compact. He was an honourable man. He was fighting a dishonourable war, a repulsive war, but he would never have betrayed his men.'

'You thought I was dead, but lying in that ditch I heard you leave Whittam his life. "Play dead," you said, and you flicked your ash on my face.'

'I couldn't kill him,' Walsh said, his voice breathy and urgent. He was pacing the floor now, turning and turning like a dog on a chain.

'The others might have been honourable men too.' Daniel's voice was assertive, hectoring. 'Will Savage, Freddie Charters, George Spring.'

'What you did here was not honourable.'

'And Whittam?'

'I couldn't kill the man I had fought with. I'd saved his life.'

'So you shot him safely.'

'In the shoulder.'

'And this house? How did he find this house?'

'I told him . . .' Walsh began, still pacing, and then he stopped.

From the other room came the sound of cries, half-uttered and then held in. 'I sent him to it, told him to walk between the rocks. He'd have very likely died otherwise.'

Walsh sat down again, his movements leaden, exhausted. 'That's the first time,' he said. 'And the last. The hardest part I ever had to play.'

The two men sat slumped and it seemed as if neither had the energy even to look at the other. The bedroom door opened and Peg came out with a bowl.

'I need some more water,' she said. 'Is it boiled?'

Walsh got to his feet and went over to pour it for her. 'How is she?'

'It's not bleeding so much now, and she tells me she's sure the blade didn't go into anything vital. But she's in a lot of pain.'

'Is there nothing we could give her?' Daniel said. 'Brandy? Whiskey?'

Peg shook her head. 'Not those. But I have some poteen.'

'Is it a smooth one?' Walsh said.

Peg nodded. 'It's very good. Father Michael liked it.'

'Give her some of that, then,' Walsh said. 'It'll take the edge off. I wouldn't mind a drop, either, if you've some spare. And he could do with a bit,' he said, nodding towards Daniel.

Peg found the bottle and poured some of the clear liquid into three small glasses. She took one back into the bedroom.

Daniel took a sip. It had a delicate flavour, not like anything he'd ever tasted, though it reminded him of the eau de vie he'd tried during his brief, abortive trip to war in France. The alcohol flooded his head and warmed his senses.

'That day won't let me be,' Daniel said.

'And now it has its final quarry,' Walsh said. 'So make your peace with it, and go back to your own country. Leave us to live in ours.'

'What would happen if I talked to people about you and Whittam? In your town? In the next town? Showed them the photograph?'

'You'd ruin me.'

'But you trust me not to?'

331

Walsh looked at Daniel. 'We've done worse in this country since then, than make friends with the wrong man. And we've done it to each other in the name of our own freedom. The blood's barely dry from the Civil War and people can bear no more wounds, old or new. They might ruin me for it, but they'd hate you more. Go home.' He looked over at the bedroom door. 'But don't lose her.'

CHAPTER TWENTY-FIVE

Taken to the Murrays' house by a shocked McCarthy, Jude recovered quickly from her injury. She wouldn't say how she had come by it, and she asked the Murrays not to question Daniel, and she refused to see their doctor.

She had spoken to Dr Kelleher, and all being well, she and Daniel would travel to Cork as soon as she was strong enough. She told Dr Kelleher what had happened in the barest terms and faced a barrage of questions, at the end of which he said he would meet her only if he could also check her wound.

'I can't believe you're not seeing a doctor down there,' he said.

'I have your photograph, of the stones,' she said.

'I said, I can't believe you're not seeing a doctor,' he repeated.

'I don't want to give any explanations. And I saw hundreds of wounds worse than this one. I know what to do.'

'I still demand to see it when we meet,' he said, and Jude found herself smiling at the telephone, pleased by this man's fierce solicitude.

Daniel barely left her side, fetching trays of food up and down for her, adjusting the curtains if she needed to sleep, reading out details he thought would interest her from a book on Irish folklore he'd found in the bookshelf.

Mr Murray took Jude's silence over what had happened in his stride. He brought her up the *Irish Times* or a bowl of early brambles he'd found, and he told her about his fishing expeditions, or showed her the piece of wood he had salvaged from the tide.

Mrs Murray took nothing in her stride, but she made no

headway against Jude's implacable refusal to explain, and so she was, by turns, solicitous and cross.

'So we have nothing to fear from Mr Walsh?' Mrs Murray said. 'You're asking me to trust you about this?'

'No,' Jude said. 'Nothing to fear from him, nor he from Daniel.'

'And Daniel's new spirit is to do with him?' Mrs Murray said, and Jude nodded. 'You know he hasn't had a nightmare since you both came back? So far as I know. And he speaks to me directly. He even thanked me the other day, for not quizzing him. He's got no shakes, no haunted looks. I'm afraid he's acting like a sane man.' And Jude laughed at this, which hurt.

When Daniel told her he was thinking of taking the day at Horse Island, before they had to return to Cork, Jude asked him a favour.

'Find me three stones,' she said. 'One like a bird, one like a fish and another,' and he smiled and brought her back exactly those.

In a reversal Jude could just about tolerate but which amused the others, Daniel rode the motorbike and she travelled in the sidecar on the return to Cork. She didn't ask how they'd retrieved the motorbike from the ambush road, but she was grateful to Mr Murray for the time he'd spent cleaning and tuning it, and most of all, teaching Daniel to ride it.

'I'll tell you one day,' Jude said to Mrs Murray, 'I promise.' And the older woman shook her head and hugged her hard, which hurt, and Jude returned it.

Jude walked up to the Whelans' house through the ordinary bustle of the weekday city, and it felt strange and hectic to her, who had seen so few people in the last two weeks, and those people with such force. She insisted she would walk in the face of Daniel's disapproval.

'Don't mollycoddle me,' she said, 'or I'll bite.'

And he stepped back, hands up in surrender.

But she felt self-protective and slow as people brushed past her, one hand on her side, sheltering her still-healing wound, and she was relieved when she had to climb uphill, because although the hill taxed her invalid strength to the limit, at least the streets emptied out. She stopped halfway up and looked back across the river. She could see the quay beside the Opera House where Dr Kelleher had faced her down. So much was changed since then.

She had Mrs Whelan sit for her photograph in the sitting room, dappled with the high thin sunlight that filtered through the trees, and between them, they worked hard to keep the conversation safe. Dr Kelleher had already delivered her excuse – a wound made while out sailing – but she knew Mrs Whelan was undeceived. Jude asked about the boys and their games, about Mary's piano-playing, about Catherine's ambition to nurse. They talked of Dr Kelleher. Jude asked why he'd never married and there was a sad tale years ago of broken promises and heartbreak. Mrs Whelan asked how Jude had found West Cork. Did she think it beautiful? And Jude told of finding the stone circle, and of the sea and the sailing. She didn't mention Horse Island.

Jude came out from behind her tripod. 'I'm going to try a few against the window, now.'

Mrs Whelan groaned. 'I didn't think it would be such a performance,' she said, 'just having my picture taken.'

'If it's to make the front pages of the *Illustrated News*, then it has to be the best,' Jude said and Mrs Whelan laughed.

'But what will we say to Martha?' she said. 'She's her heart set on that motorbike trip, and you won't be getting on a bike for some time, I'd say.'

Jude had been thinking about this, and she had a suggestion.

'I have a friend I met again in Castletowne,' she said. 'He drove me up from there. I've already asked him, and he'd be happy to take her for her ride.'

'Someone you knew already? And you happened to meet him in West Cork?'

Jude knew that Mrs Whelan didn't believe her, but that she didn't know what not to believe.

'From England, is he?'

Jude nodded.

'That's a bit of good fortune,' Mrs Whelan said in a droll voice.

'It's a long story,' Jude said. 'For another time.' She had the camera ready and her friend in the frame again.

'And English?' Mrs Whelan said, as if wanting to be sure.

'Yes.'

'Does the doctor know about him?'

'Yes.'

Mrs Whelan looked down at the floor, thinking. It was a beautiful shot, her face in profile, eyes lowered, she looked so like Kate, and Jude took it before she moved.

'That's taking advantage,' Mrs Whelan said. 'All right, she can ride out with this man. What's his name? So I know when he comes to the door?'

'Daniel. Daniel Brown.' Jude took another shot.

'And you're fond of him.'

Jude fiddled with her lens. 'I don't know,' she said. She unscrewed the lens and took her time, changing it for another, checking on the light, and the clouds outside the window. 'Tell me,' she said then, 'with your husband, were you ever anxious about what he did, in his job? Being a policeman?'

'Yes. There were times. Especially just before he died when it was becoming very ugly here. I was anxious for his safety first of all, but sometimes too I'd hear tell of things and I'd hope to God he wasn't part of them.'

'I loved a man who died in the Great War,' Jude said. 'We were barely grown up and we never had a chance. And now, I don't know, but I think perhaps I will love someone, and what about the things he's done.'

'In war?'

'Yes, I suppose. But they're not things you should ever do. Not even in a war, when you're allowed to kill.'

'I don't know, Jude. It can be hard not to forgive the people we love.'

The door-bell rang at this point, and Jude was relieved. She had said as much as she could bear to. When Dr Kelleher was shown in, both women greeted him as though he were the comic turn needed in the middle of some much graver piece of theatre.

336

'She has your stones, she tells me,' Mrs Whelan said.

'So I gather. But I am here first and foremost to view a wound, and will look at nothing else first.'

'I'm nothing to you except an interesting wound,' Jude said laughing. 'Not very gratifying.'

'Will you allow any liquid past your lips before you've viewed the wound, then? Will I bring in some tea, or are you set on your path?'

'I am set,' he said, and so Jude gave way and while Mrs Whelan went to see about the tea, she lay down on the sofa as ordered and Dr Kelleher examined the injury.

'You're a lucky young woman,' he said.

'I know.'

'Have you done what you came for?'

'I think so,' Jude said. 'And more.'

'And Matt Walsh?'

'He is a strong man, and a brave one, and he has my respect,' she said.

'There are some things that will not be laid to rest, not in this generation, but if they can be lived with and not died for, then perhaps we have done something,' Dr Kelleher said.

He had redressed Jude's wound and gently he eased her blouse back over her skin. Then he kissed her on the cheek and helped her sit again, before Mrs Whelan brought in the tea.

It was acknowledged by various people that they made a touching couple. And that they had suffered some grief, though people disagreed on what. Father Mulcahy's sister was sure that they were childhood sweethearts and, watching from the shore, Mr Murdoch said the exact same to his wife. Father Mulcahy thought it likely she had a child lost, though she wore no ring, or a parent. Mrs Murdoch, waving a handkerchief to her son, on his way to a good job in England, had observed the couple walking on to the ferry and said she thought that one or the other of them was not well, though she couldn't be sure who was supporting who.

'Perhaps it is a trip to rouse the spirits,' she said, 'or a last farewell.'

The water was skimmed silver and the sky was overcast, the atmosphere dense with moisture, as though, if you tipped back your head and opened your mouth, you might drink the air. And although it was chilly, Jude would not go in.

She had noticed all the others on the deck, of course. The priest and a woman with him, a man with a child, the child tugging all the time to be free of his father's hand, a group of four young men, friends, perhaps brothers, who Jude guessed were going to England to find work. It was something about their bearing, their bravado and their clothes, which were heavy for the time of year, as though they were being worn in anticipation of other kinds of weather.

But none of these others was as frail as Jude, and so, while she looked at all of them, she stood out, in a way that was new to her, that she didn't know.

Jude and Daniel sat and stared at the great expanse of Cork Harbour until the ferry slipped between the grey stone of Camden and Carlisle and the land took its leave, closing behind them, leaving them to the kindness of the sea.

Daniel went and leaned against the rail. After all that had gone on, it was strange to him that conversation between them should be so hard now. A pair of herons hunched waiting in the shallows on the far bank. He traced the current lines till they disappeared. When he turned back to Jude, he saw that she had lit a cigarette and shut her eyes, and that her mouth was set tight against something.

'Does it hurt?' he said. She gave no answer. 'It's cold out here. We should go in.' He had suggested this before and met with a refusal. But the air had become colder as they came closer to the open sea and except for two spots in her cheeks, she had gone very pale.

'Shall we go in?' he said again. 'Find a cup of coffee?'

'I'd like to live here,' Jude said.

'In Ireland?'

'I feel at home here. But then you couldn't, of course.'

'No. I couldn't.'

'Will you ever come back?'

Daniel shrugged. 'I'll miss the Murrays. And Horse Island. But it wouldn't be easy. I wouldn't be very welcome.' He looked over at Jude again, but she still had her eyes shut.

'I keep trying to fit two things together in my head,' she said at last, 'only the edges don't meet properly.'

'What?'

'It's like the bird table Tom brought home from school and the joints didn't fit quite, so the struts were at odd angles, but braced rigid.' Now she looked at Daniel. 'Do you know what I mean?'

He shook his head, smiling.

'Things grinding together that should sit smooth, snug. That are part of the same. When I returned from the war, I was out of kilter. I couldn't get the hang of what I came back to, and I couldn't bear very much of anything. Least of all people.'

Jude got to her feet. Daniel went to help her, but she shrugged him off and walked slowly towards the edge.

'It's odd, that it should have taken all this to change it for me finally.'

'This?' Daniel said.

Gripping the rail with one hand, Jude waved the other with a gesture that seemed to include not only the deck, but the whole boat, and the sea, and the lip of land they were steaming away from, and Daniel himself.

'That's not why I followed you over here, but that's what has happened. But you. After these last days, I don't know how to understand it. I don't know how to bear it.'

Daniel stared down at the churned water, the deep green-blue of it turned white and milky in the ferry's wake. Gulls rode the waves, lifting and dropping, lifting and dropping in search of flingings from the ship.

'They've been good, these few days, haven't they?' he said. 'I mean, aside from your wound.'

'I had a dream two nights ago,' Jude said. 'We were walking

along a quiet road, like the valley, only more wooded. Just you and I. And we came across two dead figures, a man and a woman, who had been squashed, pressed into the patina of the road so that all that remained was the polished surface of them. We stopped and tried to clear them, remove the sight of them, but we couldn't. So we had to leave them there, visible, imprinted, to be walked on and driven over. Neither of us was happy, but we couldn't help it.'

'Do you think a place, a valley, a house, has all that written onto it?' he said. 'If something has happened? Do you think you can tell if you go there?'

He looked across at Jude, but she didn't meet his gaze.

'I didn't think you'd be the sort for dreams,' he said.

Still she didn't turn her head.

'Anyway, something's been laid to rest,' he said. 'I came here to know something. Colonel Whittam didn't take us to our deaths. And now,' he gestured back towards the land, 'now I can leave it behind.'

'If Britain hadn't invented you,' Jude said, 'the Black and Tans, the Auxiliaries, and set you down in Ireland, there would have been no ambush. No need. Whittam was your leader and he did lead you to your deaths that day. And I don't know how many Irish.'

'He was obeying orders. It was a war.'

Jude turned her face and met Daniel's gaze now.

'So he was,' she said, and her voice was like a cord of steel. 'And so were you, and your friends, Will and the others. Obeying orders to burn people out of their homes, kill their livestock, torture their sons. Obeying orders, so therefore it wasn't your fault that you did those things? Your fishing trips?' She paused. 'It's far, far too easy.'

'But I can't change it now, any more than I can make my leg strong again, and I have to go on living.'

'Your bloody leg,' Jude said. 'You live as though your scar tissue carried the pain of an entire army.'

'Whittam chose to die,' Daniel said, and now his voice matched hers, hard and cold. 'And I don't know whether it was because of that day in the valley, or because he couldn't bear what he'd been a part of. But if you're not killed and you don't choose to die, then you have to go on living. I couldn't say it before, but now I can: I'm a guilty man, guilty of doing what I was told when I knew it went against humanity. I'd kept it at bay till coming over here, but I know it now. What I did was terrible and I have to live with it, walk on it, visible, imprinted, like the figures in your dream.'

Daniel stopped, exhausted. The deck was almost empty, only the father and child still there, the child snuggled now on his father's lap. Daniel turned back to the sea.

'How do you know about the fishing trips?' he said quietly. 'I never told you.'

Jude looked down at the bleached boards.

'I read your diary,' she said. 'Found it by mistake the day I went to your house. I was looking at your books.'

Daniel shook his head slowly. 'You thought you had the right to read a private diary?'

'You'd disappeared. Your parents were beside themselves. I was very worried. You'd been so strange when we'd met in Kew Gardens.'

'You've really made this your mission, haven't you?' he said. 'Who did you think you were rescuing? Me, or you?'

'That's how I found the Murrays.' Jude's voice was pleading. 'From the diary.'

'I should have guessed at something like that. I started to, when we were first with Walsh. If I hadn't been so lost, I'd have guessed. And so you think it makes it all right? Because you found me, and because what happened happened, it makes it all right to read somebody else's private words?'

'No,' Jude said. 'It doesn't, and I'm sorry.'

'Did you read it all? Every page, first to last?'

She nodded. 'That's how I know it all. What you did over here before.'

'And you still came to find me. Christ! After reading all that. Where?' he said.

She looked at him, puzzled.

'Where did you read it?'

341

'Over here. Sitting in a café in Cork. Enough to be sure you'd crossed the water.'

'And?'

'And it wasn't war, what you were doing.'

Daniel turned around and stared at her, his face slumped, his eyes puffy, his fingers twitching on the wooden rail, searching for something small to hold on to.

'I didn't want to hurt people, but I did, and I hated them for it all.'

'And Peg Riley? Was she your enemy too?'

Daniel shook his head, heavy and slow.

'Please, Jude, don't. I was mad with it,' he said. 'Poor woman, with her child. I don't know . . .'

'And then the knife? You would have killed Walsh.'

'It was to end it all. Put a stop to it. Make good finally.'

'Make good?'

Daniel raised his shoulders. 'A clean break. Colonel Whittam killed himself, and now Walsh would be dead. I'd know who my enemies were.'

'But your enemies aren't out there,' Jude said. 'And you're not innocent, any more than Whittam is, or Walsh.'

'You must despise me,' he said.

'No. Nothing as simple,' she said. She walked away from the rail, sat down on a bench and put her hands to her face as though she were taking a photograph. Daniel waited.

'A man I loved died in the Great War,' she said at last. 'I didn't know how much I loved him till he was gone. He was a friend of my brother's. He told me I should reach out, up, beyond the limit, and yet his death took away my head for heights.

'Leo used to laugh about it, but Richard always told me I should make it my business, taking pictures. It's nearly been the death of me, so now I'm going to follow his advice and go beyond the known ground and try to make it my life.'

'He was Mr Icarus wasn't he?' Daniel said. 'I'll never leap anywhere. I burned my wings badly.'

'But you're still here. Perhaps that's enough to be going on with.'

342

Jude reached inside her jacket and took out the worn envelope. Opening it, she pulled out the photograph, not of the leaping boy, but something much more ordinary. She stared at it.

'It was an innocent thing. Two friends sharing a cigarette, one wounded, the other still strong. One English, one Irish, fighting together in the same war.'

She thought how small the gestures were that led to so much else – a cigarette, a snapshot, a change of mind – and shut her eyes against it all, and felt the wind and the fine salt spray on her face. If she'd hung fire, she could be pulling on her gauntlets now in that high office room, uncovering her typewriter. She could be suspended still, just wishing.

She thought how small they were, the two of them on this boat crossing the water. And how small each had been in the scheme of their different wars. Out here the sky met the sea. There was no need for the boat, or any tiny people, to fill the view.

The sun cracked through a break in the cloud lighting the water, and a few gulls crossed and re-crossed as though seeking the spotlight. Jude envied the arc of their wings, their flight, dipping and rising effortlessly in the air. She watched the bright shaft move across the sea. In a moment it would strike the boat.

Jude held out her hand, palm to the sky, and slowly Daniel put his own to it. Then, taking her hand away, Jude stood and walked back to the edge of the boat. She held the photograph over the sea and let it go. For a moment it lifted in the wind, flirting and dipping, the snapshot figures grinning and gone by turns, and then it fell to the water, caught in a scurry of foam. And she thought perhaps it was too easy an end, or beginning. But then that was how they often were.

AUTHOR'S NOTE

Although *The Picture She Took* is entirely a work of fiction, the following books have been indispensable in the writing of it: *On Another Man's Wound* by Ernie O'Malley, *Guerilla Days* by Tom Barry, *My Fight for Freedom* by Dan Breen, *Flanders and other fields: Memoirs* by the Baroness de T'Serclaes, *The Cellar-House of Pervyse* by the Baroness de T'Serclaes and Mairi Chisolm, *Women Photographers* by Val Williams, *The Black and Tans* by Richard Bennett, *The I.R.A. and Its Enemies* by Peter Hart and *An Intimate History of Killing* by Joanna Bourke.

I would also particularly like to thank the staff in the Liddell Hart Centre for Military Archives, and in the Imperial War Museum Reading Room and the Imperial War Museum Photographic Archive for all their assistance.

Thanks to Clare Alexander, Karen Charlesworth, John Edington, Judy Giles, Lennie Goodings, Pat Palmer, Lionel Pilkington, Lawrence Rainey, Martin Riley, Fiona Shaw and Deb Taylor.